# Lannan Literary Videos

The *Lannan Literary Videos* is a collection of 42 full-length programs featuring major poets and writers from around the globe reading and talking about their work.

*New titles:*

Eavan Boland
Hayden Carruth
Carolyn Forché
Thom Gunn
Denise Levertov
Paule Marshall
Derek Mahon
Paul West

*Previous programs include:*

Amiri Baraka
Lucille Clifton
Robert Creeley
Allen Ginsberg
Joy Harjo
Seamus Heaney
Galway Kinnell
W.S. Merwin
Czeslaw Milosz
Sharon Olds
Adrienne Rich
Luis Rodriguez
Alice Walker

Each videotape is $19.95.
To order a video or to obtain a series catalog, call Small Press Distribution at 1 800 869.7553 or 510 549.3336, Dept. A.

# ANDRE EMMERICH GALLERY

41 EAST 57TH STREET

NEW YORK, NEW YORK 10022

TELEPHONE (212) 752-0124

FAX (212) 371-7345

# CONJUNCTIONS

*Bi-Annual Volumes of New Writing*

*Edited by*
Bradford Morrow

*Contributing Editors*
Walter Abish
Chinua Achebe
John Ashbery
Mei-mei Berssenbrugge
Guy Davenport
Elizabeth Frank
William H. Gass
Susan Howe
Robert Kelly
Ann Lauterbach
Patrick McGrath
Nathaniel Tarn
Quincy Troupe
John Edgar Wideman

*published by* Bard College

EDITOR: Bradford Morrow
MANAGING EDITOR: Dale Cotton
SENIOR EDITOR: Martine Bellen
ART EDITOR: Anthony McCall
ASSOCIATE EDITORS: Ben Marcus, Pat Sims
EDITORIAL ASSISTANTS: Nomi Eve, Joan Reilly

CONJUNCTIONS is published in the Spring and Fall of each year by Bard College, Annandale-on-Hudson, NY 12504. This issue is made possible in part with the generous funding of the Lannan Foundation, the National Endowment for the Arts and the New York State Council on the Arts.

SUBSCRIPTIONS: Send subscription order to CONJUNCTIONS, Bard College, Annandale-on-Hudson, NY 12504. Single year (two volumes): $18.00 for individuals; $25.00 for institutions and overseas. Two years (four volumes): $32.00 for individuals; $45.00 for institutions and overseas. Patron subscription (lifetime): $500.00. Overseas subscribers please make payment by International Money Order. Back issues available at $12.00 per copy. For subscription and advertising information, call or fax 914-758-1539.

Editorial communications should be sent to 33 West 9th Street, New York, NY 10011. Unsolicited manuscripts cannot be returned unless accompanied by a stamped, self-addressed envelope.

Distributed by Consortium.

Cover painting © 1993 by Judy Pfaff. "Early Herbals" (detail) (burn marks, oilstain, oilstick, soot, watercolor and Xerox on Honsho paper; 101¼ inches by 48½ inches). Reproduced courtesy André Emmerich Gallery, New York.
Cover design by Anthony McCall Associates, New York.

Printers: Edwards Brothers.
Typesetter: Bill White, Typeworks.
ISSN 0278-2324
ISBN 0-941964-29-9

Manufactured in the United States of America.

# TABLE OF CONTENTS

## EDITOR'S NOTE

ON THE FIFTIETH ANNIVERSARY of the atomic bomb — whose development would forever change human history — Ellen Zweig and Meridel Rubenstein have reexamined its origin, and makers. "Critical Mass" is collage portraiture in images and words of the scientists of Los Alamos, their Tewa neighbors in the San Ildefonso Pueblo and of Edith Warner, the woman who bridged these two cultures in her adobe on the Rio Grande, midway between the "Hill" where the bomb was developed and the pueblo where, in contrast with the high-tech secret home of the Manhattan Project, the Indians continued to grow corn from resistant soil and speak the patois of their Anasazi ancestors.

Critical mass is achieved in other ways by other contributors and so we hope the title umbrellas the rest of the issue as well, which is abundant with work prompted by the spiritual as much as the bellicose. Above all, the borrowed title suggests that here is a mass of material we consider to be of critical value.

A few notes. ¶This spring issue is our first distributed by Consortium. Needless to say, we are excited by this new association and are honored to be among the many independent presses that they distribute. We want to express our heartfelt gratitude to everyone at Random House who supported our project these past five years. Most especially I want to thank Harry Evans, Sharon Delano, Ian Jackman and above all Susan Bell, who brought *Conjunctions* to Random House in the first place. ¶The playwright John Guare will be guest-editing our fall issue, which is devoted entirely to the contemporary American theatre. We will not be reading fiction and poetry manuscripts until October. ¶Finally, we are delighted and honored to announce that Chinua Achebe has joined our group of contributing editors.

— February 15, 1995
New York City

6

# The Christ of Fish
## *Yoel Hoffmann*

— *Translated from Hebrew by Eddie Levenston*

1.

TWO OR THREE MONTHS BEFORE she died, my Aunt Magda remembered Wildegans's poem "Das Lacheln" and burst into tears. "I'm not crying," she said, "because Wildegans is dead, but because of the miracle that occurred when the funeral procession was held up by a traffic jam, outside our house in Vienna, for a whole hour." In an encyclopedia I found that the Austrian poet Anton Wildegans was born in 1881 and died in 1932, on the third of May.

2.

So many things happened then, I thought to myself, just exactly the way they did (for example: burly barkeepers, steins between their fingers, were watching through the windows of the bars). After all, Anton Wildegans died where Anton Wildegans died. You can't change his death to a pseudo-death.

When my father died ("I'm so . . . ," he said, and sank into unconsciousness) it seemed at first as though I still had my Father, but my father was a Dead Father. Among the books in his room, I found an old copy of Wilson's English textbook. In Lesson Ten, on page sixteen, there were two oil stains (or egg stains) and against the word *dull* my father had written with a fountain pen *"nicht klar."*

3.

Sometimes I dream that I am making love to a transparent seamstress (you can see her tailor's dummy through her body) or that one foot is bigger than the other. When I read, for instance, that bamboo trees in the tropics grow a hundred or a hundred and twenty centimeters a day in the rainy season, in my mind's eye I see people standing among the green trunks (umbrellas in their hands), watching the trees rise slowly out of the ground. I imagine

## LESSON X

### At Play

The boys have come out to see the men at work.
Four of the boys sit on the ground, and two of
them play at see-saw.

One boy is up, and the other boy is down.  Do
you see the boy who is up hold up both of his
hands?  Do you think he will fall?

Do you see any tools of the men near the boys'?
Do you know what tools they are?  One is an
ax, and the other is a saw.

When boys go where men are at work, they
should not touch the tools.  They might get hurt,
or they might dull the tools.

Do you see those little black specks up in the
sky?  Do you know what they are?  They are
birds.  They are up very high.

Do you see any men at work?  Yes; there are

all kinds of things (like a man going into a stationery shop, asking for an exercise book with the lines close together, and dropping dead).

4.

In Grade Three (a year after my father died) I wrote a composition:

### What I saw in the market

I saw a mongoloid man in a fish shop. Every morning someone combs his hair and dresses him in a white shirt. Afterwards they take him by the hand (maybe they say "Mr. Sun is in the sky") and lead him to the fish shop and there, in the shop, he stands all day by the tank and looks at the fish. How lucky he was to be born to the wife of a fishmonger!

At the bottom of the page the teacher wrote: you should have written *everything* you can see.

5.

The first photograph of me is of a baby in a wooden tub. The baby is leaning with his elbows on the edge of the tub and looking (with furrowed brow) in the direction, forty years ago, of the camera lens. Later, in another photograph, the baby is sitting in a wooden high chair (wearing a gray pullover on which someone has embroidered NATAN) holding a metal toy in his two tiny hands. I no longer remember the baby, but I remember the toy (part of some utensil, maybe a kettle).

6.

She was stubbornly sentimental, my Aunt Magda, about Anton Wildegans, the way she was about everything else. At the beginning of the fifties (Food was scarce in those days. Once a month, in exchange for government stamps, we ate a yellow chicken.) on Passover Eve, Aunt Magda's friend Berthe came to visit her and brought her from the Jordan Valley a large carp in a metal bucket.

Though there was a heat wave that day, and Berthe had travelled by bus to Afula and from there to Tel Aviv in another bus, there were still signs of life in the carp. Aunt Magda filled the bath with water and put the carp in it. Two whole days the carp swam up and down the length of the bath. On the third day Aunt Magda declared that the carp "thinks just like we do" and sent Uncle Herbert (an expert in Sanskrit) "to put the fish back in the sea."

Not long after, on Aunt Magda's birthday, Uncle Herbert went to a flower shop and brought Aunt Magda a bunch of jasmine. Aunt Magda felt the petals between finger and thumb and dumped the flowers on the table. "Since you're a scholar," she said, "you should know that flowers aren't made of plastic, they're made of flowers." At that time Uncle Herbert still had his own body, but inside it was eaten up with cancer.

7.

Why am I telling all this? Because as I go on telling the story, one day I'll find out (inadvertently) what is the most beautiful thing in the world. And when I do, I shall say (even if it's a jar of black pepper): "This thing . . . this jar here . . . is the most beautiful thing in the world."

8.

I think about trifles, like the proper way to count birds. It's hard to count birds when they're flying about, so it's better they should be at rest. They can move their feet or flap their wings, but if they're hopping from branch to branch or changing places, it's very hard to know how many there are.

9.

Recently it has occurred to me that the world, despite what many people say, is properly set up. The things you find on the left (since there's no other, apter name, let's call them "lefties") have a special quality which, if a man is gifted with the appropriate sense, will enable him to distinguish them from the things you find on the right.

10.

My mother gave birth to me and died (in this sequence of events there is evidence of perfect order) so my father searched the books until he found me a name you can pronounce backwards, and remained (Dr. Theodor Weiss, Ear Nose and Throat) alone.

11.

I want to buy a sun and eat it. I'll leave the shop and people will say: "Look! He's rolling a whole sun along the road!" They will all move aside. The light will be awesome. At night the sun will shine in my abdominal cavity and light up Tel Aviv (and Zimmermann

*With my own eyes I saw him cut it into pieces and bolt it down.* will say, *"Ich hob gesehen mit meine eigene oigen az er hot ihr afshticker tsushnitten un afgefressen"* maybe twenty times).

12.

It's not nice to tell so many stories about dreams, I know (you can say it all in one word but this word will be so terrible that the paper will catch fire). I dream that I'm roaming the streets of Kathmandu, or somewhere else, and asking: "Who is Sill?" I'm unmarried, that's why I'm asking. In the end, when someone declares that the touchstone (or the "philosopher's stone") is lost, I meet Sill (her face is full of pimples) under some iron steps.

13.

When I think about death I imagine some large crooked Lithuanian saying "Oiss," or something exploding (like a donkey's spittle) and seeds being scattered. How many times can a heart beat, a heart of flesh and blood? There are so many things (nice and not nice) which get mixed up as the years go by. If it were not for my late Uncle Herbert (who taught me words in Sanskrit and did my arithmetic homework for me) I would be sure that it's impossible to know anything in this world.

14.

Sometimes things happen which are quite unreasonable, like for instance German prisoners of war chasing butterflies in Shanghai. Someone (a retired mining engineer) is sipping tea. Is he standing? He isn't standing. His feet are bare (veins, etc.). The larynx in his throat goes up and down (two or three times). When you think that even in August this old man has a name of his own, your heart breaks.

15.

Uncle Herbert died and six months later my father died. For seven days he gazed (with his eyes shut) on the events of his life. Afterwards, when his urinary tract was blocked, he spoke of Venice. The day he died, at quarter past eight, Shraga Wallach, the vice-principal, came in (I was then in Grade Two and every morning sang "Adon Olam — Lord of the World, who reigned before

11

Creation") and said: "It's time for Weiss to go home."

16.
I want to know how (by virtue of what principle) the universe keeps going. That is, why things don't suddenly vanish. Wherever (e.g., in railway stations and large hotels) there is an information desk, I want to ask, but I don't. But I swear one day after my father died, Aunt Magda stood in the kitchen and split a large block of ice with a hammer and screwdriver. The first one to leave her was her husband, Herbert. Then her brother, Theodor, my father. Yet the old turkey's passion for all kinds of things showed no signs of fading.

17.
I remember how the almond tree blossomed in Palestine. My father held me (in the Arctic cold. I was a little penguin.) close to his belly and talked with Uncle Herbert, in the fields east of Ramat Gan, about Schopenhauer and Kant. A north wind was blowing. The air was very low. But I knew that if my father dropped me, Uncle Herbert (the big, childless penguin) would gather me up between his feet.

18.
I want to know: what is the ontological status of the memory of smells? I picture in my imagination a Kirghizi philosopher (i.e., a philosopher who lives in that part of the world called Kirghizia and reads the *Critique of Pure Reason*) and when I hear the tune of "September Song" — Oh it's a long, long time from May to December — I cry.

19.
There's nothing emptier than memories of childhood. Where is Herr Floimenbaum, who used to retrieve burnt-out valves from the wooden cabinets of radios? Where is the I who said to myself, "Can a plum tree mend electrical equipment?" and where are *they* now, the burnt-out valves?

20.
When you write with a sharp-pointed pencil, you get a lovely, fine line. Aunt Magda, who was left by herself (i.e., she was left only with me), wore purple, had large rings and became Paul's lady

friend. And since Paul (an accountant) believed in the principles of the Bahai faith, Aunt Magda travelled to Haifa, to the temple with the golden dome.

In those years (her purple years) Aunt Magda composed about twenty poems. And though she wrote most of them under Paul's inspiration (in praise of the Baha'ullah, and so on) she worked in a few lines (like "the hills pass through my body, hill after hill" or "sometimes I forget how great are the heavens. I want to see the whole firmament."), which would have flabbergasted Anton Wildegans himself.

Was Paul Aunt Magda's lover? Though she stood in the Persian Garden between the rows of flowers with a purple sunshade in her hand, it was difficult to imagine Aunt Magda (who referred to boats as "she" and called a frog a "frosch") in the act of love. Aunt Magda had plenty of organs in those days, but they all had another clear and definite purpose.

21.

I sink into deep sleep and touch the fringe of death. I wonder: how far down did Uncle Herbert and my father go? They seem to me to be hovering in the upper air of that kingdom (beneath the glass plate) and looking for me. The suits they brought from Europe are no longer in fashion. They are dead-old-men. They pass over me. I shout, but they do not hear.

I ponder: "Socks and the brain are precious things. When a sock gets parted from its fellow sock, it also gets parted from the brain. But the brain draws near the sock and leaves the fellow sock behind a little. Afterwards the fellow sock draws near the brain, and the first sock gets left behind (*und so weiter*). You have to take care that one sock doesn't get separated from its fellow by more than a pace, and that they both stray away from the brain by no more than the measure of the body.

22.

In the empty space of the house there is now an old stethoscope (my father's ears are already transparent) and in the hallway, next to the overcoats which date from the forties, two sick ghosts are sitting side by side. A pale copy (almost invisible) of Uncle Herbert is turning the pages of a German-Sanskrit dictionary, and Aunt Magda, blue as the eye of a flame, in the springtime sleep of the afternoon, wears on her face, for a moment, the expression of a child.

23.
It is hard to imagine a god who snores, and even harder to imagine a great god who snores and a number of little gods who find it difficult to sleep. Someone says (Zimmermann or someone or other): "For vun hundred I buy fifty." A — he was born. B — he grew up (all those years). C — he was loved. D — he was fed and washed. E — they cried. F — all around him grew old and died and now he says "for vun hundred I buy fifty."

24.
It must be May outside. Between the pages of "Everything you Wanted to Know, from A to Z" (published by Tcherikover, 1941), above a map of Burgundy, next to a profile of Buxtehude, there are butterflies flying. Zimmermann must drink nectar from calycine flowers and skim across the ocean with white seagulls. One white seagull, supremely beautiful, turns to Zimmermann and says, "My name is Jonathan" and Zimmermann says, "My name is Zimmermann."

25.
Although my uncle, Herbert Hirsch, played the harpsichord, the ship on which he sailed for Palestine ran aground. The captain, leaning his chin on the back of his hand (like *The Thinker* by Rodin or sad women called Liliane), gave orders for eight large wooden crates and thirty horses to be thrown overboard. First the horses galloped (as if they were holy horses) towards the hills of Rhodes. Then they sank, horse after horse, and turned into little sea horses, transparent as glass.

26.
The ship lifted off and floated, and my Uncle Herbert stood on the upper deck, his fingers moving of their own accord, as the air moved with the ship around my Uncle Herbert, who stood on the upper deck, his fingers moving of their own accord in the air around the ship.

27.
My Uncle Herbert was a fat mystic (when he played on his harpsichord jackals and wild dogs howled. He made the glowworms dance.). But he didn't leave behind even one explicit sentence. Of the philosophic essay he was writing (he had given it the title "If

the world changes — what will become of the laws?") there survived only the first twelve words: "Let us imagine a slice of sausage lying on the white keys" . . .

28.
Uncle Herbert, as Aunt Magda used to say, had "two left hands" and sometimes, I remember (when his hairy left hands were still part of his body), he cried in his sleep. Once he said: "One thing I know with absolute certainty." But he never said what it was. I was a child at the time, so what I'm about to say is likely to sound pretentious, but I'm ready to swear that Uncle Herbert (the fat gold watch) thought that the world both existed and didn't exist, simultaneously and indistinguishably.

29.
In Palestine, at all events, he wrote a philological essay, and took an imaginary dog for a walk (Aunt Magda couldn't stand strong smells) along the dirt paths between the orchards. When the English (who were looking for terrorists) arrested him, he explained that he had left the house to escape from the heat and said (were the words translated from the Sanskrit?) "the personality ignores the oppressive heat within the shrine."

30.
I dream that North Korea has put a man on the moon. Why has North Korea put a man on the moon? At first he jumps around like a kangaroo among the white rocks. All the air is inside his suit. His face and the world are divided by a masonite screen. He longs for North Korean dishes. He lifts his gaze to the moon but the black skies are empty.

I wake up and dream again. The Norwegian King Hakon VII is cruising along in a taxi. Hakon VII tries to slam the door. But this controlled movement becomes involuntary, compounded of wind and momentum. For an instant you can see Hakon VII, door in hand, horizontally leaving the taxi. But a moment later (as when the head first breaches at birth) he is sucked back in.

31.
My Uncle Herbert died and my father died and Berthe, who got away from Adolf Hitler in time and went to live in the Jordan Valley, fled from there on account of her husband, Adolf Hertz, and

came to Tel Aviv, to Aunt Magda, crying and carpless. Aunt Magda, I remember, wrote to Berthe's husband and Berthe went out onto the verandah and came in and went out again and beat the carpets until a letter of reply came from Adolf Hertz and Berthe went back to the Jordan Valley.

### 32.
Then came the days of Paul. I sometimes wonder: if Berthe had stayed longer in Tel Aviv and met Paul, would she have gone back to Adolf Hertz, to the Jordan Valley? One way or another, when Paul appeared Aunt Magda was already on her own and Paul, I think, heard about Berthe only from rumors.

### 33.
Aunt Magda took over the expression "my late husband" and divided her life into two periods: "When my late husband was still alive" and "now." Sometimes, when she said, "Herbert used to say," tears would well up in her eyes. But if some omnipotent being had proposed turning back the wheel of time and restoring her late husband Herbert to life, she would, I think, have had reservations. Suddenly all the space between the walls of the house was hers. She put the harpsichord in the "guestroom" and over the old couch she spread a purple woolen blanket.

### 34.
She turned into a kind of legendary bird. An albatross. Like a Sumo wrestler she thrust back alien authorities, and with the help of ancient strategies taught herself to say the right things. "First," she said, "my husband died of cancer of the liver. Six months later my brother, Doctor Theodor Weiss, passed away from complications following pneumonia." Her thoughts circled the periphery, like great ships.

### 35.
She had a special recipe for apple cake and a glass mouse and an alarm clock that played a Viennese waltz at the appointed time, and she had a cherry-wood jewel box and an inlaid ivory salt cellar and a picture of a wagon done in embroidery and she had china dolls (a shepherd and a baby and some Italian noblemen) and silverware and colored postcards. And she had flowerpots.

36.
I dream that the King of Norway, Hakon VII, comes to Palestine, the land of Israel. A warm wind is blowing. Someone shades the royal head with a parasol. The King lifts his blue eyes to the hills and someone hastens to tell him that the burning shapes in the east are called, in the ancient language, "hills." They tell them that the sea is called "sea" and the sky "sky." But no one ventures to tell him, the King of Norway, that flowerpots are called "flowerpots."

37.
I want to know: are there colors and smells in the brain? The pig farmer is dead and now the old sow is running through the streets of my mind (across wooden bridges) looking for him. And maybe the sights I see when I'm awake are someone else's dream?

38.
Paul was, in his own words, "an idealist" and though he owned two offices (one in Tel Aviv and one in Petach Tikvah), "a man," he said, "should strive for something else, more spiritual." Once, he said, he was a "confirmed follower of Spinoza" but now (i.e., then) he was closer to the position of the philosopher Moses Mendelssohn and like him (i.e., like Moses Mendelssohn) he too was of the opinion that a man should adopt a rational religion, like the Bahai faith, for instance.

39.
They pierced his feet, the Son of God, with nails, I know. There are some things which it were better had they not occurred. But if Paul had been there (i.e., in place of the Messiah) and they had pierced *his* feet, I'm sure the talcum powder he sprinkled so carefully between his toes (and the white socks he changed every day after his bath) would have shown everybody that a man could, in spite of the filth in Palestine and his bodily sweat, protect himself against epidermal eczema.

40.
Above all he argued for the eternity of the soul. The scientific proof of eternalism, he said, was the glowing aura that could be seen round all kinds of things. He relied, I remember, on an aristocratic woman named Blavatsky, who had dipped her body in the Ganges and said a prayer for plants. The aura of a leaf, Madame

Blavatsky said (Paul said) remained whole even after the leaf was torn to shreds.

41.
I want to know: what was Paul's exact place (at seven o'clock on a Saturday morning when he went down to the sea at the end of Rechov Gordon with a straw hat and the *Reader's Digest*) in the vast order of the universe?

42.
I immerse myself in the bath and see my father's body in the water. A thin man. A white soundbox. A slender violin for the reform of the world. A doctor for the vocal chords . . . did he hear the beating of birds' wings in the woods of Moldavia? Had he seen, in some old medical textbook, a picture of the inner ear?

I think about what sights are seen by the dead. At first the flesh relaxes. Then, in the vast silence, the great body of thoughts slowly, slowly, melts away. I try to picture in my mind total nullity. Non-existence. Nothing whatever. But I cannot.

43.
When Berthe died, her husband, Adolf Hertz, came to Tel Aviv to pay Aunt Magda (this was in 1965) a "condolence visit." He sat, I remember, next to the harpsichord, in summer, wearing a black suit. "Just imagine, Frau Hirsch," he said, "to this very day I am still eating the cucumbers (he said Gurken) that my late wife pickled."

44.
I think of the horse harnessed to the carriage that carried Claire Bloom and Charlie Chaplin in Hollywood, in 1950. The horse is dead. But it has acquired an aura (in the opposite direction to the arrow of time) and now, over and over again, times without number, harnessed to a two-dimensional carriage, it carries the dancer Terry to Clavero, the old comedian, in the London of 1910.

45.
My father, Theodor Weiss, ear, nose and throat specialist, said, I remember, "sinusitis" or "tympanitis," as though man was nothing but a body of flesh, though also an astral body with an aura. And since he could see (by virtue of the laws he knew) what was

destined to happen to it, to this body, his heart was filled with great Hungarian sorrow.

46.

I remember how he walked the streets of Tel Aviv and I walked by his side. It was August or September, not long after Uncle Herbert died and not long before his own death. On the radio Bing Crosby was singing "Autumn in New York." On the old calendar horses were galloping. Suddenly, I remember, I saw (in a prophetic vision) my father, Theodor Weiss, born in Budapest, crumple and fall and turn into stars.

47.

I love Vashti, and Cinderella's ugly sisters (they stroke each other's lower bellies. Their huge feet are fine for acts of depravity.). And Jezebel. And Rahab (the spies had already travelled a distance of seven leagues from Jericho when they turned on their tracks, went back to the house of the Canaanite harlot and picked up the bunch of grapes they had forgotten).

I love words like *"Papagai"* or *"Tinte."* A French aunt (Coquettish. Her body gives off whiffs of cheap scent.) is called *"tante."* But a German aunt (full-bodied) is called *"Tante."* When a German aunt dusts the table and knocks over a bottle of ink, they say *"Schau* (i.e., "Look"), *Tante* spilt the *Tinte."*

I'm very fond of Percival, of the conditional sentences. Percival in the sentence "If Percival had come" will never ever come (oh, dear!), but Percival in the sentence "If Percival came" even though he hasn't come, could still come (maybe). If Percival comes – to supper, for instance – I'll serve him cooked asparagus (with butter. Percival likes to dip his asparagus tips in butter.).

48.

Percival was born in the county of Yorkshire to a family of fisher-men. His father (through the bedroom window) cast huge fish-hooks into the sea. When the other fishermen asked Percival's father why (through the bedroom window) he cast huge fishhooks into the sea, Percival's father told the other fishermen: "My father and his father before him cast (through this window) huge fish-hooks and if my wife (he pointed to Percival's mother), by the grace of God, gives birth to male offspring, they too will cast (through this window) huge fishhooks."

When Percival was born the vicar rang the church bells. Everyone was happy. The fishermen's wives came to peek at the cradle (later Percival's father was to say "their heads stank of fish"). They killed a duck. They brought up an old bottle from the cellar and sang "My Bonnie Lies Over the Ocean" and "Sweet Lass of Richmond Hill."

During the third watch a crow cawed. The roofbeams creaked. Old Jeremiah (in his youth he had hunted whales in the North Sea) made the sign of the cross and said: "God grant I be proved wrong. But I fear (with a superstitious spit) nothing good will come of this child." Everyone crowded in the doorway. Southwest of Yorkshire there rose in the sky, lit by the light of the moon, a gigantic apparition, Philip Gross, my English teacher in Grade 5C.

49.

. . . all the things that the heart forgets: seaweed, for instance, on the shore at Tel Aviv. Baklava. The Book of Nehemiah. Stomach juices. Inverted commas. Buckles. Cooking recipes. Flickering lights. Parcellation maps. Panes of glass. Bicycle tires. A drawing of an arrow and two hearts (or of two arrows and a heart) and names like "Kurt."

50.

I picture in my mind a marine ornithologist. He is an expert in sea birds, and nevertheless one testicle has slipped into his abdominal cavity. People put up columns and inscribe on them "Here Napoleon repulsed the Turkish army" and so on, but no one would dream of erecting an obelisk to mark the place where a marine ornithologist pushed his testicle, with his own fingers, back into his scrotum.

51.

First (I think) God created Matsliach Najar (with his white shirt and its horizontal black stripes) and only later (i.e., after he created our Arabic teacher) did he bring forth from chaos, slowly, in pain and wisdom, everything else.

How can you portray a man like that in words? Apparently (and actually) he was respected. People greeted him respectfully (they said, "Good morning, Mr. Najar"). And though he didn't know who Paul Hindemith was (and when people said "Lilliput" he thought they were laughing at him) his heart was moved somewhat when he heard on the radio, in Ramat Gan, the chorus from the Ninth Symphony.

I remember. Herzl, Benjamin Zeev, is leaning on an iron bridge and looking out to sea (He can see history, from beginning to end, in one gaze. "Everything," he thinks, "flows. You can never enter the same water twice.") to the right of the blackboard, next to the entrance. Our Arabic teacher's head stood free in the air. But his scrotum (everyone saw) was resting on the edge of the table like Isaac on the altar, in the story of the Sacrifice.

52.

I remember Kaminer, who raked the body of Rabbi Akiba with iron combs. Blood flowed between the desks. Rabbi Akiba stood in front of the platform (his upper body naked) with prophecy on his face. "Parchment," he said (Kaminer shouted "Quiet"), "is burnt and letters blossom."

53.

The vice-principal Shraga Wallach (his wife's name was Nordia) used to walk the corridors, I remember, past the hooks for the luncheon bags, looking for children. He was a communist. "In summer," he said, "the windows will remain open, even if everyone wants them shut. In winter, even if everyone wants them open, they will remain shut."

When I think about Paradise I see Shraga Wallach, his black hair covering the folds of his belly. He's the one of whom Schiller sings:

| *Freude, schoner Gotterfunken* | O Joy, fair spark divine, |
| *Tochter aus Elysium,* | Daughter of Elysium, |
| *Wir betreten feuer-trunken,* | We enter, drunk with fire, |
| *Himmlische, dein Heiligtum!* | O heavenly one, thy shrine. |

"In 1950," he explains to St. Peter, "I left the Communist party and joined, halfheartedly, Mapam."

54.

In Aunt Magda's room, on the eastern wall, there was an old map of Budapest (in summer flies and mosquitos used to settle on the castles and churches of Pest) and on the opposite wall there was an oil painting of one Leopold Weiss, Aunt Magda's great-grand-father, who was a confidential advisor. A photographic portrait of Uncle Herbert (i.e., a picture of his body before he died) stood between two plates of glass on the harpsichord in the "guestroom," next to the telephone.

55.
When they brought it (i.e., the telephone) Aunt Magda became a butterfly. A spark of divine fire. Her orthopedic shoes barely touched the floor. She covered it with a cloth (so that it shouldn't get dusty) and placed fruit in front of it and talked and talked into it (with reason and without), every day, to Paul and to Frau Stier and to Doctor Staub, and many more.

56.
She used to say: *"Die Pumpe ist zerbrochen"* and *"Mittwoch kann ich nicht"* and *"Also ich bin dort um zwei"* and "I want the Tax Department" and "My husband passed away two hours ago" and *"Stell dir vor"* and *"Stellen sie sich vor"* and *"wunderbar"* and *"ausgezeichnet"* and *"leider"* and *"eigentlich."*

57.
In Paul's house, in those days, on Saturday nights at eight o'clock, conversations took place with the dead. And though the content of those conversations escapes me (did they ask after their health?) I know they spoke (with the aid of glass tumblers) with Madam Blavatsky and the Baha'ullah and Rabindranath Tagore.

58.
Apart from Aunt Magda and Paul, there took part in those meetings Herr Doktor Staub (who was a Doctor of Philosophy) and his wife, Hermine, and Frau Stier (who was the widow of a wine merchant) and, from Petach Tikvah, (the flesh of her thighs overlapped the seat of the bus) "Madame Edna," a clerk in Paul's office.

59.
Every Saturday afternoon at half past four (the air was already filled with the smell of coffee and apple strudel) Frau Stier would ring Aunt Magda's doorbell three times. And from the moment Frau Stier arrived (i.e., from half past four) until the two of them (i.e., Aunt Magda and Frau Stier) left, at 7:46, for Paul's house, Frau Stier would talk to Aunt Magda and Aunt Magda would talk to Frau Stier.

60.

I remember when Frau Stier said *"Wurzl."* That was a unique occasion. The wine merchant had died and his wife, by the grace of God, said *"Wurzl."* The roots of Frau Stier's teeth (apart perhaps from the one that had been extracted) were in her mouth. There were roots in flowerpots. And at eye level, on the horizon, spreading down into the earth's crust, were hidden roots.

61.

I picture in my mind the journey to Haifa. A post-Mandate train. Paul in leather slippers. Aunt Magda's Austro-Hungarian earlobe, like a purple cloud, passing through Binyamina and Atlit. A Chevrolet taxi and the heart fluttering at the sight of the golden dome.

62.

I can see the temple. Pilgrims from Famagusta (nineteen of them. The equivalent in gematria of "Wahd.") are silently, their backs stooped, leaving the office. Rising diagonally from Paul's head, amid the scent of whitewash and roses, are beams of light with dust swirling around in them, as in some ancient painting.

63.

They had dinner at The Cellar, on the corner of Allenby Street, where the head waiter was named Max. Paul drew back Aunt Magda's chair and as she went to sit down pushed it under her body. On a metal tray Max brought potatoes and dead fowl.

64.

Afterwards they took the bus to Ahuza and stayed with Frau Haupt from half past four till five forty-five or ten to six. This coffee hour in Rechov Moriah, fortunately, took place after birth and before death. And though the Earth was revolving on its axis, the sea below the verandah did not overspill and the apple strudel was not overturned.

65.

On the evening train they sat next to each other by the western window. Mount Carmel fell away behind Paul's head. The reflection of the sun was doubled in the glass window. But Aunt Magda harnessed her body to the train and charged, like a dinosaur, through the fields of thistles back to Tel Aviv.

23

66.
It was in those days, more or less, that Aunt Magda dealt in "stocks
and shares." This matter involved Mr. Moskowitz, from whom
Aunt Magda took advice (he was the missing hand at rummy) in
Café Pilz. Mr. Moskowitz sat facing Jaffa. Frau Stier sat across the
table from him, and Aunt Magda sat opposite Cyprus.

67.
The cards they held in their hands cast their images in the sea.
The crowns of the kings hit the Rock of Gibraltar. Off the coast
of Libya queen mothers and jacks were reflected in the water. And
between the isles of Greece, like gigantic octopuses, floated the
bonnets of the jokers.

68.
Sometimes, at high tide, sea level reached the ceiling of the cafe.
Chocolate cake floated on the water. Aunt Magda and Frau Stier
extracted pins from their hair and pinned the cups to the table-
cloth. Their dresses billowed out between the wooden chairs like
predatory flowers.

69.
In '58, on Independence Day, Paul fainted in the street. The force
of life within him had dwindled greatly. First to leave his body
were his thoughts. Afterwards, in among the petrol fumes of the
tanks, he saw "Madame Edna," semitransparent, like an amber doll.

70.
This inner vision put an end to the "Age of Paul" in Aunt Magda's
life and the "Age of Magda" in Paul's life. When he came to, Paul
turned his gaze to an imaginary point and followed it from the
corner where Rechov Frischman meets Rechov HaYarkon to Reading Power Station in North Tel Aviv.

71.
What did Paul see at the top of the chimney? Later he said (I believe him. You couldn't invent an expression like that.) that all
the way there he was walking "on lots of swans." At all events, at
the end of the summer Paul married "Madame Edna" and Aunt
Magda adopted the habit, Saturday nights as well, of frequenting
Café Pilz.

72.

In Café Pilz Mr. Moskowitz trod on his trouser cuffs. He looked like an old steamer. The cornfields of Romania grew from his nostrils. What did he do when he was alone? One can only guess. Perhaps (accompanied only by his brown horn-rimmed glasses) he took off his trousers and walked around on the cuffs.

73.

Sometimes the heart is fit to break. Such sanctity cannot be reckoned. How the skin enwraps the body. How the atmosphere surrounds the globe of Earth. And how, beyond the atmosphere, great bodies recede, soundlessly, into the gloom.

74.

Any one of these people, single-handed (Frau Stier, for example, or Mr. Moskowitz), is capable of bringing the Redemption. Fire (radiant) is stored in their tissues. Their bones are phosphorescent. And their movements, like huge quasi-crabs, bring absolution.

75.

When Paul left her, Aunt Magda said, "I see that I can't see." Her eyes had weakened. She gazed upon imaginary flights of geese. But when the first rains fell (in the month following the New Year) she took a red umbrella and walked the whole length of Allenby Street, as far as the Opera House by the seashore.

76.

Later, as pointed out, she got used to Paul's non-presence. Yet perhaps her mind still fashioned scenes such as her coming to his house, placing on the table two jars with perforated tops and saying: "One is for pepper and one is for salt."

77.

How the folds of her flesh moved from September into October! The sun rose and the sun set (a huge, blazing disc) and every day she carried around a brain called the encephalon. A woman beloved! Her smell was different from other people's. In the records of time doubtless it is written somewhere "Magda, daughter of Eva and Isidore Weiss" (though it were better if her name rhymed with "-eeples").

78.

In October (on the Eighth Day of Solemn Assembly, also known as the Rejoicing of the Law) Mr. Moskowitz clasped a scroll of parchment. He held the story of the Creation of the World tight against the nipples he had brought with him from Romania. Convex glass lenses separated his eyes from everything else. Did he rejoice in the law? Perhaps he remembered the picture he had seen from the window of the train: suddenly, between one hill and the next, sheep.

79.

I want to ask: if these events were taking place in what they call a novel — would it be appropriate for Mr. Moskowitz to touch Aunt Magda's flesh? Should he touch Frau Stier's flesh? And perhaps (from some great hallucination) the three of them should let go of their cards and drop to the floor of the café, flesh upon flesh?

80.

One way or another, the stocks and shares that Aunt Magda purchased (she called them *"papiere"*) yielded dividends, so she spread them, I remember, on top of the harpsichord, under the telephone. Frau Stier breathed in and breathed out. But when the rains stopped, her breathing subsided (what a wonder that there's a diaphragm!) into a kind of equilibrium, with the coffee and the apple strudel.

81.

In April the sea blossomed. Scents rose from the water. The blue doors of gambling dens stood in the air. Christ lived. For in Café Pilz, in the afternoon, I remember, Mr. Moskowitz took a pinch of snuff from a golden snuffbox, and Aunt Magda trod the earth's crust as though she were a bird.

82.

And the way the sun set. At about seven in the evening the great ball of fire touched down, and where it touched it stretched a little before it slowly sank, and though you couldn't see it from the café verandah, the salt water at that point must have boiled, for miles and miles. Afterwards, at the last moment before darkness was complete, there remained, as in a painting by Rembrandt, only the two hands of Frau Stier.

83.
I want to tell you about Mr. Moskowitz. But what do I know about Jassy and Baku and Timisoara and Bucharest? A man should (through the power of logical analogy) be able to know everything. It should be possible, with correct reasoning, to infer (from the present to the past) what Mr. Moskowitz, for instance, saw in Constantsa, in 1926, when he was a soldier in the Romanian army, through the window of the barrack room.

84.
Maybe he remembers (he has no need of logical deduction) a widow named Grigorescu and how (in bedroom slippers. Her ankles were exposed.) she said, *"O domnu meu"* and no one could tell whether she meant Mr. Moskowitz or God.

85.
Many ships set sail from the port of Constantsa. Some came back there again and again. But no ship ever set sail a second time on its first voyage. How can ships break the time barrier? The clocks show a different time and the wood rots. Maybe one should spin the great wheel on the bridge of the ship simultaneously forwards and backwards and then, in a flash, what was will be again, for the first time once more.

86.
In 1929 (actually on the eighth of May) Mr. Moskowitz came to Palestine, the Land of Israel. He was a young man at the time and the paraffin stove he saw in Jaffa took his fancy. He liked everything made of brass. But the white shoes he brought with him from Romania became covered with dust and the soles came apart from the soft leather of the uppers until there were gaping holes (where the toes were), like mouths.

87.
In those days he certainly had dreams. A woman with a long neck kissed him (because he was "such a conservative") on the lips. His great-grandfather sewed him a book bag. But his dreams were seen, as in a cinema, by him alone, from within.

88.

In 1930 Mr. Moskowitz (from cement and gravel) built a break-water. He stood (like Prometheus when the eagles plucked at his liver) with his face pointing northwest, towards Constantsa, and his back to the monastery on the port hilltop. *"Wer bin ich,"* he thought

*Who am I . . . another* | (sardines slipped away between the rocks),
*Moskowitz or just me?* | *"ein anderer Moskowitz oder ich allein?"*

89.

No doubt about it. The light was not so sharp in the Carpathian Mountains. Wild goats seemed almost to blend with the blocks of granite and the furs of the foxes were of one shade with the pines. Why then be so pedantic about distinguishing between Mr. Moskowitz and everything else?

90.

With Herr Doktor Staub and his wife, Hermina, Aunt Magda had already become acquainted in "the age of Paul." Herr Doktor Staub was a disciple of Rudolph Carnap and therefore totally rejected "unscientific sentences." He came to the "conversations with the dead" on Saturday nights, so he said, only because of his wife who was, so he said, a decent woman though with strange interests.

91.

Herr Doktor Staub divided the air into two segments. The right-hand segment was the air to the right of Herr Doktor Staub. The left-hand segment was to his left. In the middle, in the huge crevice, like a crow robbing the world of the transmundane, stood he (Herr Doktor Staub) himself.

92.

I remember he said, "Ethics is *nicht absolutisch.*" He sat on the sofa and his wife, Hermina (a loaf of bread), sat next to him. At that point in time you could infer the covert from the overt in Herr Doktor Staub: pale buttocks, as though in anguish.

93.

How the world played tricks on him. Birds deviated from the harmonies of Haydn. Field mice scampered with no reason. The sudden transformation from life to no life could not be properly explained by the philosophy of Rudolph Carnap. And Polish Jews garbled his name.

94.

I remember (among the brighter visions) that I loved Hermina. She was — how can I put it? — a grassy lawn. A double bass. In all the surrounding bustle, she alone sailed the ship of Earth. And if something concrete must be said about Hermina — let it be said: on her right cheek she had a black mole.

95.

I remember Mr. Moskowitz said, "*Ich spazier sach.*" His birth was a miracle, and there were *I am taken for a walk.*
other miracles that had occurred since then. Hermina laughed. But Herr Doktor Staub (perhaps the use of a form denoting receipt of an action rather than performance of an action irritated him) clamped his jaws.

96.

On the face of it, Hermina laughed whenever occasions for laughter came her way. Actually she laughed periodically (i.e., at regular intervals) and things came her way, seemingly by chance, whenever it was time for a laugh.

I remember. Amalia Rodriguez was singing on the radio. Children in go-carts (as in a kitschy picture) were sliding down the street. At that moment, as it were bisyllabically (first "ho-ho" and then "ha-ha"), Hermina laughed.

97.

I would like to ask: how did Herr Doktor Staub come by Hermina? Did he muster all his power of intellect and mate with her (as with a hypothesis) by force of utterance? Did Hermina realize, as light breezes sported with the folds of her dress, that this intellectuality rose (like the skin on the top of the milk) from *weltschmerz?*

98.

Actually the story of Aunt Magda's life is the story of Aunt Magda in her corselet. Guns were fired at the *Altalena*. Begin wept. But Aunt Magda stood like a block of earth (such decisiveness is unparalleled), next to the harpsichord, in her corselet.

99.
She never thought (I think) "everybody dies. What's the point of those elephant feet" . . . Hers was a different time. Rosier. And though she came and went within the space between the walls of the house, she said (when the telephone rang) "Hirsch speaking" as though names matched things.

100.
I remember. She said, *"Ich bin verschnupft"* and | *I've caught a cold.* the word *"verschnupft"* came right out of her nose. Not only the chill but the word itself was in her body. Her sense was common sense. But her head stood in the window like an oil painting of a Dutch frau, and out of doors, a cosmic corselet, crows flew by.

101.
I would like to ask: Did my fat uncle, Herbert Hirsch, sit on the back of a donkey? He said *"Hops, mein Ezel"* and the donkey moved on, from category to category. Clouds of dust blossomed from his gallop. His hooves hardly touched the planet Earth. At one moment he was in a plane of observable time and space, at the next in a place where things are what they are, by virtue of their own selfhood.

102.
The donkey's hide quivered with pleasure. There were beads of sweat on the tips of Uncle Herbert's hairs (on his chest). What was "agricultural unity" to him? What did he care about "Settlement Square"? The British may have had a mandate over Palestine, but Uncle Herbert had a mandate over all the worlds.

103.
Like Leibnitz and like Hume he distinguished between factual truth (like "there are living creatures in the sea") and tautological truth (like "all fish are living creatures"). He disputed with Kant. But, alas and alack, he did not realize that the carp (Cyprinus carpio) that Aunt Magda had bade him "put back in the sea" was destined to die in the salt water.

104.
Oh, female carp! Could you see Uncle Herbert from the water in the bucket? Did you think: "There are duplicate worlds but with a

kind of isomorphy between them, for the carp in the other world is also swimming whither I swim"?

105.

I remember. Uncle Herbert was clutching the carp in two hands as though it were a precious manuscript. His legs grew tall. His head was lost in the clouds. Then he let it fall, with the gentlest of movements, into other, sweeter waters among the stars.

106.

In 1965 someone (perhaps his name was Alfred Windishgratz) snatched Aunt Magda's purse. Aunt Magda shouted "Schtop!" and ran down Rechov Reines. But at the point where Rechov Spinoza begins, she stationed herself under a street lamp and threw out (as though in evidence that the world was out of joint) her arms.

107.

What did the thief do with her cards? One can only surmise. Perhaps he shuffled and dealt (himself) a hand of patience in the Florentine quarter. At all events, Aunt Magda bought herself a new kidskin purse and gave instructions for the letters H dot M (in Gothic script) to be inscribed on the clasp.

108.

In the summer of that year Berthe died and Adolf Hertz came from the Jordan Valley to pay Aunt Magda a "condolence visit." Frau Stier was sitting on the old sofa. From Frau Stier's pelvic girdle stretched the bones of her legs (her pelvis and the two femora) but you couldn't see them for flesh and dress material.

109.

It was very hot. Adolf Hertz spoke, you will recall, of the cucumbers "his late wife" had pickled. Suddenly Aunt Magda (perhaps Adolf Hertz's words had brought to mind some latent conjunction of events) said: "I remember how Bertschen and I ate corn on the cob next to the Opera House."

110.

No doubt about it. Adolf Hertz had no desire to return to the Central Bus Station. Both of them, so he must have thought, were widows (perhaps he thought "each of them has a mouth like a vagina") but at ten to two he said (almost against his will): "Na . . ." and rose to his feet, and Aunt Magda rose to her feet, and Adolf Hertz didn't dare take it back and say, "What I said was just, as it were, a sigh."

111.
I remember the maker of tombstones. In 1965 Simcha Bunis was already dead. But in 1954, when Aunt Magda asked what was the meaning of the letters *"Peh Nun,"* Simcha Bunis said (perhaps he thought to himself, "In a very little while I shall be strumming on transparent strings"), "Here lies" and his assistant Chmisa, like a distant echo, answered Amen.

112.
Then Simcha Bunis spread an old newspaper on Uncle Herbert's tombstone and placed on it a loaf of bread, a hard-boiled egg and a cucumber. He may have crunched the cucumber (our memories play us tricks) and said, "You leef in Tel Aveef?" or he may have wrapped himself in silence. At any rate, at that moment the last angels urged him: "Simcha Bunis, take a wife!"

113.
What did Simcha Bunis see during his earthly life? Walls of clay? Huge blocks of stone? Gold dust? His body was made of cell upon cell (like the cells of monks) and tiny creatures moved within each cell. Simcha Bunis (this became clear only after his death) was made entirely of protoplasm and within each cell of his body there was a membrane and a nucleus.

114.
In the late sixties the flesh on Aunt Magda's arms became emaciated. Time carved lines on her face. In a kind of perpetuum mobile she revolved around the three sides of a triangle whose apexes were her house, Café Pilz and the house of Frau Stier.

115.
She acquired a new trait, a kind of affectation: she would recite verses from the works of Anton Wildegans. She listened to records (Marlene Dietrich singing "Falling in Love Again") and when Frau Stier's turtle fainted from the heat (in August. On Memorial Day *The poor creature.* for the destruction of Hiroshima.) she said, *"Das arme Tier"* six or seven times.

116.
She recolored all her memories: Herbert Hirsch was once again a young lecturer in the School for Languages. The Prater was covered with trees. Her dresses were bathed with color from the Danube and into the huge beer mugs were poured firkins of sun and stars.

117.
In 1968 someone snatched the kidskin purse. The reader must be saying to himself: "In those days there wasn't so much purse-snatching in Tel Aviv." Maybe not. Maybe only two purses were snatched. But they both belonged to Aunt Magda (the one snatched in Rechov Reines and the one made from kidskin).

118.
You may ask: what is the meaning of purse-snatching? You may also ask: what is the meaning of everything else? Large objects determine the movement of celestial bodies and this movement determines the movement of a purse.

119.
I remember that my late uncle, Herbert Hirsch, looking from his window saw a thousand birds. He may have been seeking a word he had forgotten. He may have remembered the burning of the Zeppelin (at first the helium soundlessly caught fire. Then, as from a huge stomach, burning bodies and sheets of material tumbled out of the airship.). At all events, the birds migrated north. Not nine hundred and ninety-nine. Not a thousand and one. A thousand birds.

120.
Did Aunt Magda give birth to a stillborn child? Did the baby float in her body (like the robbers who hid in the jars of oil), with eyes shut and skin soft as a frog's? And what would they have called the baby? Philip Emmanuel? Constantine?

121.
The birds crossed the glass frontier. My Uncle Herbert wiped the butter from his mouth. He then read aloud (perhaps from the Bhagavadgita) a list of verbs — *pasjan, srinvan, sprisan, svapan, svasan* and so on — one after the other, as if in prayer.

33

122.
In 1969 Aunt Magda got to know André, who was a philatelist. André made use of French words (*"malgré lui"* and *"sauerkraut avec sausages"*) and when he talked about stamps (he was a member of the Philatelic Association of Grenoble and assistant to the Association of Jaffa-Tel Aviv) he placed his fingers together and twiddled his thumbs.

123.
In his jacket pocket André kept a magnifying glass the size of a saucer, and in his waistcoat, in brown envelopes, he hid stamps. On his desk stood Zumstein's catalogue, and Gibbons' and Michel's and next to Schnek's book (*Histoire du Timbre Poste*) there stood, like a book end, an iron box.

124.
What was André concealing in the box? A postage stamp printed in Mauritius? A plaster cast of his lower jaw? At all events, in Café Pilz, above the hands of rummy, he gazed at Frau Stier and Aunt Magda as if they were rare stamps (with an error in the design or a printing fault).

125.
André's first wife had taken her own life. Maybe she had a predisposition to suicide. Maybe she was just allergic to stamps. Anyway, she made herself a preparation (with scrupulous care. The way you clean a baby's ears.) of potassium cyanide and strychnine.

126.
First her neck grew rigid. Then her muscles twisted in opposite directions. The slightest noise sounded in her ears like the crash of thunder. Finally, as her diaphragm shrank and all the air passages were blocked, her eyes tore and she saw a large bubble, transparent as glass, in which were celestial landscapes.

127.
I want to talk about eschatology (i.e., the study of last things). What will happen in the days preceding the coming of the Messiah? First the Resurrection of the Dead. Parts of bodies which got separated will come together (the right arm and the right shoulder, etc.). In full view, as in a field of corn, the dead will straighten

their upper bodies. The moon will turn to blood. Stars will deviate from their courses. Stones will give voice. And then, at one stroke (as at the death of St. Vitus who was stricken with chorea) the primeval silence will be restored.

128.
If André's second wife had thrown herself off a multistoried building, you could tell how she flew and flew. But André's second wife was a clerk in the office of a piano distributor, and every time someone struck the keys of a new piano, she would turn her face (like a mother pelican) towards the warehouse.

129.
Maybe she thought to herself: "Examining a new piano again." And maybe she thought: "Something's going on in the warehouse." These two thoughts are not so very different. But since André's second wife didn't have too many thoughts, one should examine each one carefully and note even the slightest shade of meaning.

130.
Did André's second wife stand behind his back like the fat woman in the painting *The Poet and the Muse?* She too (like the Muse) was wearing a cloak of sackcloth, with necklaces around her throat. She too (from arthritis) had her right arm stuck out. And though André was not holding a goose quill between his finger and thumb, in front of his feet too (as in the oil painting by Rousseau) ten roses bloomed.

131.
It was about this time, more or less, that Aunt Magda, in her fur collar (between the hairs of the silver fox), found worms. They may have been "flatworms," no more than absorbent tissue, or they may have been "roundworms," whose nervous fibers (not anxious fibers. Nerve fibers.) ran the whole length of their body, as far as their sexual organs. At all events, she used the general term — *Wurme* (from the Latin *Vermes*, worms).

132.
No doubt about it. She was very attached to her fur collar. But there was in those days a kind of gaiety about her that had no need of external objects. Her vitality derived directly from the life force

within her. She listened to Anton Dvořák's *New World Symphony* and sprayed herself with eau de cologne. When the telephone rang, she put the carpiece to her right ear and let the mouthpiece fall into her bosom, between the flesh and the edge of her corselet.

133.
She was the sun around which the rest of the stars revolved. Frau Stier, like a satellite, presided over the innermost orbit. The other orbits were taken up by André and his second wife, Mr. Moskowitz, Herr Doktor Staub and his wife, Hermina, and Adolf Hertz who came again from the Jordan Valley, carrying in his arms (the way you hold a baby) a glass bowl.

134.
There was nothing risible about Adolf Hertz's proposal of marriage. First he placed the glass bowl on top of the harpsichord. Then he wiped the beads of sweat from his brow. Finally he said: "Seeing that you . . . that is to say, your late husband . . . and I . . . that is to say, Berthe . . . I thought, I mean, the two of us . . . we should get married."

135.
Aunt Magda was not as particular about the unnecessary use of name and number as Adolf Hertz. She seems to have foreseen the course of events. She skipped the preamble (she probably just said it to herself) and all she said to Adolf Hertz was: "We shouldn't be too hasty."

136.
Adolf Hertz sat himself down on the chair in front of the harpsichord and the huge screw turned on its axis (from the inertial momentum of the body) a hundred or a hundred and twenty degrees. Thus with his face to the corner of the room (i.e., to the space between the two walls) Adolf Hertz cleared his throat and said: "She . . . that is to say, Berthe . . . used to put fruit in the bowl."

137.
On the Day of Atonement a dead cock sailed through the air in centrifugal fashion, and at the end of the Concluding Service, when the *shofar* sounded, through the window on to Rechov Borochov

were revealed the ten Kabbalistic spheres. At the top, in transparent vapor, *'Ayin* — Nothingness — was concealed, and from it emanated, as in perpetual birth, the other nine. The Godhead, which had become divided, mated with itself face to face and back to face, and this act of creation was attended by Mr. Moskowitz (prayer shawl and all) backwards and forwards, in complete devotion.

138.
What did Mr. Moskowitz see in the world of emanations? His greatgrandfather Reb Mendel, who cut up a cow? Something sublime? A female maidenhead? At that moment, though, when the rams' horns sounded, his was a spiritual body and his sweat gave off a holy smell.

139.
Afterwards, at home, he washed his horn-rimmed spectacles in water and took some fish rissoles out of the refrigerator. Down *What do I care.* in the yard a woman (it may have been Shoshanna Mirkin) shouted "*Wass hart mir*" and in the dome of heaven shone a hundred thousand . . . no. A million stars.

140.
In the autumn Herr Doktor Staub went to Vienna. Doubtless he pictured himself meeting Mauritz Schlick and sharing a fine meal with Hans Reichenbach, as in former days, in the restaurant near the museum. But Mauritz Schlick died in 1936 (after rejecting the philosophy of Rudolph Carnap and Otto Neurath) and Hans Reichenbach died in 1955.

141.
Did he (like Mr. Hyde. With tufts of hair in his ears.) cross the Seilerstrasse? Did he stand in the "Stepperl" emporium under a plethora of sausages? What is remembered from the journey is only that the heel of Hermina's shoe caught in the cobblestones, in Mariahilferstrasse, opposite the display window of a florist's.

142.
First she removed her foot from the stationary shoe (as did her reflection in the window, among the gladioluses). Her other shoe she dumped in the garbage bin. Then (like Lady Godiva, who rode

her white horse naked through the streets of Coventry) she walked barefoot as far as Johann Strauss Street, the site of their hotel.

143.
In 1970, in August or September, Aunt Magda and Frau Stier climbed to the summit of Mount Canaan (like ancient pilgrims to Canasta). Pine cones scattered coniferous seeds on their heads. Butterflies skimmed between their fingers. Frau Stier lifted a red heart towards the Sea of Galilee and Aunt Magda held black clover leaves.

144.
That evening (in the lobby of the sanatorium) an elderly conjuror plucked handkerchiefs from his ears. Pigeons, dice and worry beads rose from his head. But when the clock chimed, he put the whole world (rabbits and teaspoons. Just like the Pied Piper of Hamelin.) into a suitcase.

145.
The next day, when the sun was shining, Aunt Magda and Frau Stier looked at Bet Grossinger. Afterwards they both looked at a cow. And thus it was that, among the thistles, under the radiant light of the Land of Israel, Aunt Magda and Frau Stier stood still for almost a minute, as did the cow (and the cow in Aunt Magda's eyes, and the cow in Frau Stier's eyes, and Aunt Magda and Frau Stier in the cow's eyes).

146.
No doubt about it. The cow knew nothing of the rules of Canasta. What would she have done with the four jokers? Something else attracted her attention: perhaps the orthopedic shoes or perhaps, under her piece of nylon netting, the blue tint that Frau Stier had applied to her hair.

147.
On Friday Aunt Magda and Frau Stier came down from the mountain in the red Zeppelin of the Egged Bus Company. In Safed they had already placed their suitcases over their heads. In Meron, near the Holy Tomb, chickens were sucked into the airship, and at Majd el Krum the air was filled with the smells of hyssop and smoking charcoal.

148.
Suddenly they saw the sea. It may have been there before they saw it, or it may have been created by the power of their gaze. At all events, sailing boats were leaving the fishing port of Acre and making towards a large ship on the horizon, between Cyprus and the coast of Lebanon.

149.
When André met his second wife he thought, *"Je me marierai"* (or *"Je me marierai avec elle"*). Why did he think in the reflexive? Did he imagine that the events destined to take place would be autokinetic (i.e., coming back upon themselves) like getting dressed?

*I'll get married* (literally: I'll marry myself) — *I'll marry her* (literally: I'll marry myself with her)

150.
Perhaps he remembered the brachial bones of his first wife or the sight of her swollen blood vessels. Maybe he was attracted by the extreme fineness of the hairs all along her arm. But memories, André thought, are but fantasy. Nothing more.

151.
He was not surprised that his second wife was not dead. Her life, in her sackcloth cloak, seemed to his eyes like lotus petals drawn on a wall. He probably saw visions: her head lying on the floor between two iron beds, and her enormous feet free in the air.

152.
Once he had climbed Mont Pelvoux, whose summit reaches 3,954 meters. Down below, like a fur collar, there were woods. Above them, where the air was thinner, were scattered patches of Calluna Vulgaris and all kinds of mosses and lichens. But near the snow line there were expanses of meadow, where primroses, cinquefoil and anemones bloomed.

153.
André had never seen wolves, they were long extinct. And if there were a few left, they must have been hiding in the tundra, beyond the fields of flowers. Did André (in his youth, too, André was a philatelist) see that high above, among the glaciers, alpine butterflies were turning black?

154.
I remember André and his second wife sitting on Aunt Magda's old sofa. André said, *"On s'habitue"* (i.e., "one gets used to it") and his second wife opened her mouth but never made a sound. The fat carp-lover was standing — like the tongue of a pair of scales — in his portrait photograph on the harpsichord, and behind him stood the glass bowl that Adolf Hertz had brought from the Jordan Valley.

155.
In 1971 something went wrong with Aunt Magda's body. The fibers that extend along the atria of the heart did not contract properly, and the blood (corpuscles, thrombocytes, etc.) was compressed in her pulmonary artery and her aorta as though the chambers of her heart were occupied by drunken trombone players.

156.
The family doctor (his name, I remember, was Doctor Mendelssohn) said: "With . . . tss tss . . . Frau Hirsch, a heart like yours you can live . . . tss tss . . . a long time." He then told Aunt Magda that his cocker spaniel bitch (tss tss) was still alive.

157.
No doubt about it. The old dog's heart beat more strongly than expected. But her territory had been greatly reduced. Her memories (apart, perhaps, from the smells of a certain month of May) had dulled. Things seen in the room looked to the dog like a vision of creation: at first, chaos (bedsheets on the window sill) and waters cover the face of the floor. And when the dry land is revealed, the large pieces of furniture come back into place, and the air is pure and someone spreads carpets on the earth.

158.
That year Aunt Magda looked at the moon as though through glasshouses. She wanted to visit London "just once." But her travel agency was situated in the middle of a melon field, and whenever she went to book a ticket, the clerks would disappear into a back room and make love.

159.
I remember she came to a halt six or seven paces before a death notice. The name of the deceased (above it were printed the names

of all the cinemas) had been pasted on a round obelisk, at the inter-
section of Rechov Montefiore and Rechov Nahlat Binyamin. Her
orthopedic shoes stood side by side on the pavement within the
bounds of a single stone without crossing the cracks, as though
she were playing hopscotch.

160.
That was quite an extraordinary moment. Cherubs (looking like
naked children) hovered near the verandahs. Automobiles sailed
by in silence. Wholesale traders and barbers moved their jaws beyond the shop windows and when she turned northward into
Allenby Street, all these sights moved with her.

161.
What were the roots of this great Aunt Magdalenian optimism?
It was then, believe it or not, when the veins in her legs were turning blue, that she stood by the old water tower in Shavei-Zion and
had her photograph taken. That was, I recall, a very merry journey.
Frau Stier's hats sailed on the wind. Herr Doktor Staub said, "Yah,
yah" and Hermina waved and every twenty miles or so, till the
outskirts of Naharia, she laughed.

162.
In the Penguin they drank iced coffee through glass straws, like
the apostles of some Antichrist in a demonic version of *The Last
Supper*. Afterwards they sat (all four of them. Herr Doktor Staub
and his wife, Hermina, and Aunt Magda and Frau Stier.) in a horse-
drawn carriage. And either because of the refraction of sunlight,
or for some other reason, it seemed the horses would not stop at
the end of the avenue but go on, over the stone wall and across the
beach, into the sea.

163.
What did Mr. Moskowitz think when he saw Frau Stier for the
first time? This is not to be spoken of, since Frau Stier is not a
subject for discussion. But it certainly is possible to speak of Julia.
When Mr. Moskowitz was four or five years old, his mother (Mrs.
Moskowitz) baked cakes. And the cakes that Mrs. Moskowitz
baked were sold, across the counter, by Julia.

Mr. Moskowitz could not remember whether or not Julia wore
hats. But cake crumbs clung to her dresses and he did remember

(he most certainly did!) how Julia knelt down in front of him and placed in his hand ("when you grow up you'll marry me and no one else") three transparent marbles.

Mr. Moskowitz grew up and Julia grew even further. She became as tall as a telegraph pole and the crumbs that clung to her dress turned hard as stone. He left the transparent marbles behind when he set sail for Palestine. But the vow he made was not dissolved, even on the Day of Atonement.

Did he imagine himself giving birth to the child that Julia should have borne? Did he see symbols in his sleep? Did he have a revelation (a real one; i.e., in the physical world) of a cloud of birds and a child, and the child is flying and he (i.e., Mr. Moskowitz) is left alone?

164.
In 1972 Doctor Mendelssohn died. The old cocker spaniel doubtless wondered what had happened to the shadow of the man who wore the shadow of a hat. The human hand that stroked her spine gave her great pleasure. But she too was by now, almost entirely, antediluvian. The year Doctor Mendelssohn died was . . . how can one put it? The Year of the Dog.

165.
On the seventh day after the death of Doctor Mendelssohn, Aunt *Where is the soap?* Magda said (in her bathroom. With nothing on.), *"Wo ist die Saife?"* The water reached the rim of the tub. Steam filled the room. And from the middle of the haze, like the mammoth that was found (fur and all) in Siberia, she asked for a piece of scented Yardley's soap.

166.
What was she thinking as she washed her large body? Here are my arms? Here is the umbilicus, once attached by blood vessels to the belly of Eva Weiss? Here are my heels? Perhaps she sailed her balneal ship beneath the full moon and her flesh shone by the light of some other celestial body, even more distant, until you could see (as in some cosmic X-ray) the filigree pattern of nerves.

167.
I would like to know. Who loved Aunt Magda? Who did Aunt Magda love? Her loves began (in both cardiac directions) probably

when she was still a baby. Her father, Isidore, covered her with a woollen blanket and Eva Weiss (outside the window, like in a fairy story, piles of snow) tucked the blanket under the bed.

Isidore thought: I'll put my two feet under her tummy, and I'll set her flying and she'll scream. I'll bend my knees and she'll drop down. I'll roar like a lion and she'll grasp her toes, half in joy and half in terror, with her tiny little fingers.

Eva thought: How I love this little girl! I'll clothe her and feed her and tell her what little girls ought to know and when she cries I'll stroke her hair and say "everything will be all right" or "once I too was . . ." or "don't cry, baby. Please don't cry."

And their visions of dread. Her tiny body (this was Isidore's) slips out of its diaper and continues to fall, through the force of gravity. She falls very slowly. And wonder of wonders! Before she touches the ground (while still in the air) you can see she has broken her skull.

And Eva. The birth. Her stomach (her own. Eva's.) is splitting open from the force of the thrust. Her face is twisted. Her skin is torn. Only her nipples are swollen, her inside is empty, there is nothing in her but breath (which goes round and round and back again) and milk ducts.

168.
In 1973 André sailed for France and his second wife, on a different ship, followed after. Her inmost thoughts were probably of pianos, legions of pianos. Her ankles hurt. When she stood on the deck her sackcloth gown flapped in the wind, and the huge raglan sleeves slapped her on the back and on the chest like elephant's ears, or large flags.

169.
At Marseilles André stood on the quayside. When he had sailed for Palestine, ten years before, small engines were crossing the dock and his first wife (her voice choked with emotion) had said, "N'est-ce pas? N'est-ce pas?" He (André) didn't have any imagination. But that day, after the night journey through the Alps around Grenoble, the Greek ship seemed entirely covered (iron plates and funnels) with orange blossom.

170.
Especially he remembered the heat of the sun. The heavenly furnace (from zenith to nadir) spewed forth rivers of fire. On the

shoulders of the stevedores, in a mass of black hair, glittered diamonds. And as the ball of light finally set towards Malta, and the chalk cliffs of the Marseilles shore were swallowed up in darkness, the ship quietly moved off to the east and his (first) wife said *"enfin"* or *"on y va."*

171.

That year Mr. Moskowitz asked his dream: Who was Moishe Zainder? Moishe Zainder, the dream replied, was the uncle of your mother, Rachel Zainder of blessed memory, and he died because of a swastika, or some other, simpler, cross. Go (said the dream) and find him, his form hardened, sitting as he was when they killed him, sidelocks and various accessories, at the corner of Popakitsu Street and Tranedafira Street.

Mr. Moskowitz didn't understand the dream's reply. But in his heart waxed a great love for Moishe Zainder and he pictured to himself the gesture (finger touching thumb) that Moishe Zainder used to make. Perhaps he saw shop signs written in Romanian, perhaps he saw cherubim. One way or the other, there's no doubt that he said "Listen . . ." or at least "Li . . ." and everyone thought that at the last moment he wanted to listen to a symphony of Anton Bruckner's or some Christian hymn.

How his soul marvelled as it left the body! All those who stand around the dying man as the soul leaves the body are obliged to tear their garments, though the Germans and Romanians who stood round his body not only didn't tear their garments, they tugged at them to straighten the creases, like bloodstained dancers in the pause between one leap and the next.

All this and more Mr. Moskowitz saw in his sleep. Which is why he rose to his feet and made a huge tear in his nightshirt, and withdrew three fingers and tore it again, down to the bulging flesh on his arm, across to his heart, as though first his father and then his mother had died.

172.

On the Day of Atonement (there was a war on, I remember) the harpsichord sounded. Did the strings vibrate by themselves? Did ghosts fan the mechanism? Herbert Hirsch rose out of the glass bowl, bearing on his chest (like a large diamond reflecting the rays of the sun) the body of a carp.

173.
What did this hologram want in the world? Magda, my arthritic aunt? An old manuscript? Perhaps he was doomed, my Uncle Herbert, by some strange karma, to come back from the realms of the dead (like a Christ of fish) in times of woe?

174.
I remember the bottle that Paul brought to Aunt Magda in the midfifties. The other memories are nothing but a reflex of things that were and are no more. But from the memory of that bottle there rises to this day an odor of woman's underclothes.

175.
Did peasants' wives wipe their fundaments on vats of wine? Did they squeeze the wooden stopcocks (as in the relic of some Dionysian rite) between their buttocks? At any event, Paul took the bottle out of his leather briefcase and said (as though announcing a birth): "Slivovitz. A Yugoslav liquor made from plums."

176.
It's impossible to explain how the world suddenly paused. Bodily movements (the space-time of this act of love was the ocean) became a wink of fins. Aunt Magda, in slow motion, placed two crystal glasses on the table, and Paul withdrew the cork from the bottle as though the corkscrew were a fiddler's bow.

177.
Later they spoke (I recall) of Nefertiti. She was, without doubt, the fairest of women. She bore Amenhotep six daughters and after his death (fair as ever. Paul had seen her portrait in a museum.) she married the son of a Hittite king (Shupiliuma) and shared her bed with Tut-ankh-amon.

178.
Between the marble columns Nefertiti saw the face of Thoth, the god of the moon. Strange aromas arose from her body. But when she died, oxen lowed with dark pain along the canals and stone-cutters (fourteen hundred years before the birth of Christ) sang doleful songs.

179.
After the war (in the winter of '74) God sent cold winds over the earth. In the clocks on the wall the alarm mechanisms (cuckoos and such like) froze. Aunt Magda kindled a blue flame from her paraffin stove and they sat (she and Frau Stier) on the old sofa, side by side.

180.
At five o'clock Frau Stier said "Ignatius." Did she mean the Bishop of Antioch (Ignatius Theophoros) who declared in his letters that a bishop was worthy of the same respect as God? Or did she mean Ignatius De-Loyola who (in St. Mary's Church. In Montmartre.) founded the Order of Jesuits? One way or the other, Frau Stier said what she said and — as I live and breathe! — if she were a character in a novel (and not flesh and blood) she would still be compelled (by some other law) to say "Ignatius" at that moment.

181.
Spring came to the Northern Hemisphere only at the end of April. The rivers grew calm. The sea spewed forth wreckage. Waiters spread canvas sunshades and a thousand musicians blew (together. As in a Vivaldi concerto.) their flutes.

182.
Cheesecakes flew, so great was the joy, on the wind. Forks soared to the clouds. Herr Doktor Staub leaned his chin on an imaginary marble slab and Hermina held between her fingers two kings. No doubt. It was an hour of grace. Thoughts took a back seat. Death was already present. But someone (it may have been Aunt Magda) said, "Frisch" and everyone played a second trump.

183.
One day, when the great epic "Herr Doktor Staub in the Land of Israel" comes to be written, the tale will be told how Herr Doktor Staub took the bus to visit Hugo Jacobson, in Ramot Hashavim. What did Herr Doktor Staub want between the chicken runs? After all, Hugo Jacobson was dead. And even if he were not, had he not rejected (in 1936. In Braunschweig.) the opinion of Rudolph Carnap and Mauritz Schlick that objects, per se, cannot be perceived?

184.
In Kfar Saba, among the poplar trees, Herr Doktor Staub was already asking where the salt pits were. Hermina waved her hands in the air and laughed. And till they came to Hugo Jacobson's house, the whole length of the way, hens (at first one after the other and finally in unison) could be heard proclaiming: "The salt pits are in Atlith, where Kurt and Ilse Lazarus live."

185.
After lunch, Herr Doktor went to take a siesta. Gerda Jacobson (since the day Hugo died she had done everything alone) washed the dishes. But Hermina went for a walk outside on the red earth, and as she stood by the netting, little chicks made bold to come to her as though she were Mary, Mother of the Son of God.

186.
In 1976 Aunt Magda had her teeth sharpened and on the stubs of the sharpened teeth they fitted porcelain crowns. The filaments of blood in her eyes ruptured. Her head drooped. She saw only the edges of things. From her eyeballs, around the iris which had muddied over, shone a dying light, as though from fragments of lakes.

187.
She remembered Mancy Gross, who cried all night. No one could sleep, she cried so much.

188.
She remembered her father, Isidore, standing in front of a button shop, his head almost touching the feet of Jesus, like some great bird. And when she came up to him, and he opened wide his coat, pearl buttons, she remembered (in the bands of light in Mathiusch Square), rose from the boxes behind his back.

189.
Apparently (even then. When her eyes were failing.) she saw clear landscapes. She said (to herself) *"Ich bin doch Magda."* She listened to Memphis Slim. But when Frau Stier rang the doorbell she shouted *"Ich komm schon"* and (just as she had in Paul's time. Once vertically and twice horizontally.) sliced the apple strudel.

47

190.

Sometimes (at six o'clock in the evening) Aunt Magda and Frau Stier would go down to the beach, where the Opera House once stood. They stuck the tips of their canes between the cracked paving stones and froze against the rail like crocodiles. Their scaly tails stretched towards the falafel vendors and their Mesozoic eyes, hooded with skin, stared straight ahead.

191.

What did their contemplation reveal? The beginning before which there is naught? The slight change, like an interruption? Desire? The body that takes shape, so very slowly, around the desire? The names? The things to which our desires give birth?

192.

In Mograbi Square, under an enormous hoarding, they bought ice cream. They knew very well that this outing was based in sin. It wasn't easy to ask for extra cherries. But as they carried their cones down Rechov Bograshov, past the display windows, they rose (both of them. Canes, dresses and all.) three cubits above the ground.

193.

A pink bird tempts Mr. Moskowitz into thought. He thinks about swarms of bees. About soft armchairs. About the burial places of emperors. And when Casals said to Golda Myerson, "This is the cello that has accompanied me for half a century," Mr. Moskowitz cried.

Not because he loved music. He had never heard Casals in his life. He cried because Casals no longer drew his bow and the cello played by itself and Casals said (he spoke very slowly): "I love it and it loves me."

194.

When Casals played his cello by virtue of such love, he was ninety-six years old. In the middle of Bach's C Minor Suite, his dim eyes opened wide and it was clear he was looking past death at life. Mr. Moskowitz remembered those notes as though he himself were the cello. His eyes surveyed his inner organs. He heard the dead breathing. From that day on all the winds that blew were for Mr. Moskowitz internal winds.

It was a dreadful shock when his hair began to grow inward,

into his body. This was the external sign of the breakdown in the flow of time. His hair returned, as it were, to that other time that Casals had seen with blind eyes when he was ninety-six and playing Bach's Suite in C Minor, almost with no body.

From where Mr. Moskowitz was standing, the madness was crystal clear. His body was playing by itself, like Casals' cello. He was a resonating body nine hundred and sixty years old. There was no longer any need to do anything.

In sober moments his chin almost hit the floor. He ate so much from the other side of the mushroom. But when he grew tall a second time, he saw Romania as though it were entirely his own body as a child. Every single part of the mountainous organism. He was the sheep and the corn. He was the salted cheese.

All kinds of mirrors shattered, as though there had been a disaster in a glass warehouse. There were days when he sought himself at the end of the bed. He sat with his legs folded, between the springs, like a fakir. He *was* a fakir. When they asked (all the time) "Where is Mr. Moskowitz" they answered (others answered) "on his bed of nails."

195.
No doubt of it. The nights of Palestine and Israel stretched like a roof over the heads of Aunt Magda and Frau Stier. Only the head of Mr. Moskowitz was exposed to the inverted abyss. He travelled with that caravan like a giraffe in a railway train. A skylight is breached and his head juts through. But the caravan, as the saying goes . . . and jackals (now very scarce) howl.

196.
Herr Doktor Staub — loyal to the eternal law — changed his socks. His shirts were piled in the wardrobe like the skins of insects. He sloughed off one shirt and took on another. And it was bizarre. With all that abundance of colors, Herr Doktor Staub came in through the same entry (the Herr Doktor Staubian entry) all those years.

197.
I remember lightning struck the tip of his walking stick. There was rain and a kind of orange light. Bright. Herr Doktor Staub was alarmed for a moment (you might call it "The Alarm Felt by Herr Doktor Staub on Seeing Sparks of Fire") and said, "There's electricity in the air."

198.

How many philosophical theories were demolished in a flash of light! So the world does exist, and there are charges of electricity (and rays of light, refracted and diffracted, and glowing balls with sparkling tails, and necklaces of tiny pea-sized beads, and women with white necks standing like marzipan mushrooms in the air that is suddenly filled with electricity. On balconies.).

199.

Two or three months after lightning struck the tip of his walking stick, Hermina died. One night, at about ten o'clock, she said, "I'm going to water the flowers" and walked straight out from the fourth floor. Sometimes, when winds blow through the rooms, you can see these elevated gardens: chrysanthemums spanning the road between the odd and even numbers, eight meters above the ground. She probably took a metal watering can and moved weightlessly through the curtains flapping in the wind, like the dancer who said: "Floor? What's that?"

200.

In years to come Herr Doktor Staub will say, "Her skin was pale. Almost transparent" and it will be strange to hear that in the end he was aware of transparency, even though he only saw her retrospectively, in thought. Then (when she went off the balcony, straight out into space) he still thought the laws of mechanics etcetera, etcetera.

201.

How could one assume that Hermina's heavy body held a light spirit? In her frail body dwelt a heavy spirit that dragged her down and down by the hair of her head, while her body soared till it seemed a mere spark — a flash of aluminium — and was gone.

202.

In 1977 Aunt Magda bought herself a pearl necklace. Scraps of sun danced on the counter and the jeweller as it were absentmindedly touched her hand. Some sights are unforgettable: her neck encircled by a pearl necklace in Ben Yehuda Street.

203.

Her thoughts (above the little beads) took her back, to Herbert and Theodor. You might almost say that the two of them became a

pearl Herbert-and-Theodor. Secrets rose to the surface like silhouettes of the Loch Ness Monster: Herbert loved only her brother
Theodor, and married her (i.e., Magda) for his sake. Theodor did
not love his wife. The two of them (Laurel and Hardy, fat and thin)
loved only each other.

204.
Suddenly she remembered (in her ring of pearls) all manner of
insults: how in the heat of argument about the categories of Kant
they failed to see that she had prepared (all day it took her) chicken
paprika. How they brought in clods of mud and dirtied the floor.
And she had asked them not to. How she had asked!

205.
Her consciousness turned inwards upon itself, like a tailor who
sews no clothes but his own. She and her sewing machine became
a single entity. The cotton reels of memory span tashibong tashibong. She sewed up herself.

206.
She remembered Herbert's enormous belly by the light of the
moon. In the adjoining room Theodor was sleeping and on the
other side, at the end of the corridor, was the clinic. His belly
should have covered the moon. Then she would have conceived.
But he moved on the dark side of the room like a sad wrestler until
the sun came out from hiding.

207.
After they buried Hermina, Herr Doktor Staub thought: "Hermina
is dead. What will I do now?" He saw a number of possibilities but
not one of them was truly feasible. He could go back to Germany.
He could enter an old age home, and he could fly.

208.
The third was the most practical possibility. But he didn't know
where to fit, to which bones of the back, the appropriate limbs.
Furthermore, he thought, this option is only a temporary defer-
ment of the other two. After all, he thought, when I take off the
question will arise again in all its gravity: whither shall I fly? To
Germany?

209.
In addition, he was afraid of metal poisoning. The contact between iron wings and human flesh did not seem to Herr Doktor Staub sufficiently logical. If he had known at least that the device was one hundred percent reliable. But these days you can't be sure of anything. One way or another, he thought to himself, it would be as well to start with one cautious step (i.e., flight). A round trip, for example, above North Tel Aviv as far as the outskirts of Herzlia and back.

210.
He came to know great solitude. Where once Hermina had been was now a gaping hole, which went with him like an absent hand or a missing eye. The air he breathed was rarefied. There was no one to balance the cosmic seesaw. His heavy intellect deafened him like an engine that malfunctioned, and in the other direction he saw only ugly, grim-visaged birds, as though the sky housed some heavenly academy and not clear air. Glass encompassing the world.

211.
It's hard to picture him above the chimneys of Reading power station, his legs bent and the flaps of his winter overcoat spread on the wind. What would he not have given to bring back Hermina's laugh? He suddenly understood that Rudolf Carnap was dead and his philosophical theory refuted, for how was it conceivable that so many transitory phemomena (like sandals and snails) could all together, like an orchestra tuning up, fill the space of the world with an out of tune A? Anyway, this particular symphony, he almost thought, had no need of well-tempered notes.

212.
In the third quarter of his year of mourning, Herr Doktor Staub sat himself down on Aunt Magda's old sofa. His nasal septum bisected the air but the praying mantis no longer retained its sovereign powers. Frau Stier sat opposite, by the harpsichord, and when he turned to face her she smoothed her silk dress over her knees and gave a sigh.

213.
When you think of Frau Stier you must draw a picture that is both careful and crude at one and the same time (like a Chinese

drawing. Not a line too many.) This alone may perhaps be said: before noon Frau Stier set the dust flying in clouds and when the sun began to set she looked at the crystal chandelier in her room.

214.
When Herr Stier died (a most awesome occasion!), Frau Stier recalled, wine was spilt. Frau Stier's wine and the wines (bordeaux, port, madeira, etc.) in the wine store. Now (the same miracle) the wine turned into water and the water into air and the air into memory.

215.
Things not to be spoken of occurred in those days, as when someone slammed the shop door and stood in front of rows of bottles. No painter (except the divine portraitist) could paint such a picture: the elixir imprisoned in glass cylinders and people helping themselves again and again.

216.
In 1978 Aunt Magda saw ships in Rechov Dizengoff. She thrust her walking stick in front of her towards a large store dealing in *Look! A ship!* | curtains, and said: *"Schau! Ein Schiff!"*

217.
From certain points of view the curtain store was indeed afloat. Women named Camelia leaned their bodies against the display windows. They uttered incomparably beautiful things and the sailing vessel sailed away (Lights. Glass.) to streets of a different realm. More pellucid.

218.
You need imagination to picture Aunt Magda at the bus station. In January. How can one know the concrete reality of things? Even when everything has been said, the dreadful residue remains: her toes in their shoes. Five in each (together with Frau Stier's feet — two times ten).

219.
In February Herr Doktor Staub went to visit Gerda Jacobson. Gerda Jacobson was sitting in the sun. On the verandah. And though between the tiny particles of her body (electrons etc.) there was space, you could not see through her.

220.
That day Herr Doktor Staub heard bird song. He could tell Bachbirds from Mahlerbirds. The ears he had brought with him from Braunschweig revolved like saucer antennae:

Tweetweetweet.

Tweetweetwah.

Tweetweetweetweetweetweetweet.

Tweetweetweetweetweetweetwah.

And again tweetweetweet.

And again tweetweetwah.

And once more tweetweetweetweetweet.

And once more tweetweetweetweetwah.

221.
In days to come, when Herr Doktor Staub thought of Eastern Palestine, he pictured in his mind the house of Hugo Jacobson. First of all — Hugo's brain hemorrhage. Then — sitting in the sun — Gerda with matza crumbs on her chin.

222.
In March Aunt Magda heard the oompah-oompah of the waterpipes.

223.
She was lying down. In bed. In extremis. Something wrong with her legs. The gods of war urged her to put on her pearls. But she turned her head aside and like Mancy Gross, who wore glasses (everything seemed to Mancy Gross bigger than it was) she cried.

224.
Frau Stier placed a carton of buttermilk on the night table. Herr Doktor Staub carried flowers (I remember) up the stairs. It's hard to keep people on the Earth's crust. Nevertheless. In April she — Aunt Magda — regained her power of rummy and her power of apple strudel.

225.
The Land of Israel lay open before Herr Doktor Staub. He journeyed to the Dead Sea and the Great Wilderness. Warm breezes caressed his head. He saw gazelles. Hills from the Cenozoic Era passed before him.

226.
He remembered (at the base of the Rift Valley. Between the salt rocks.) the University of Heidelberg.

227.
Things of no moment (like the way a Bedouin child ran) broke his heart.

228.
To the north of his body lay the world to the north of his body. To the south of his body — the world to his south. Kings of Moab stood on the peaks opposite, and way above (the dogs of his childhood came back to him. The schnauzer and the Labrador bitch.) lay the sun and the moon and the stars.

229.
In May (there was a *khamsin*, I remember) Aunt Magda said, "I can't see." Total blackness had suddenly descended upon her vision, and it was clear from the sound of her voice that the world she had known, where the kettle appeared as a thin metal band, was infinitely preferable.

230.
She was terrified. Her head and the two marbles in it sought the splash of reflected light.

231.
If only she could have seen the light separate from the things. In huge containers. She could have split it into colors by herself. She appealed to Herbert by name

232.

(and one could see how she moved before the War).

233.
And through the power of that appeal (from out of her blindness. Two or three weeks before she died.) she saw a great vision and everything was in it. She saw the soul of the carp. And the soul of the birds. And the soul of her brooches. And of her porcelain cups. And of her iron. And her purse. And the soul of the ginger, the vanilla and the playing cards. And she knew (oh, yes, she knew!) that this world continues into the next unchanged. There is no division. Only the directions are reversed.

## Yoel Hoffmann

When Yoel Hoffmann's books first appeared in the late 1980s, they seemed to have tunneled their way into Israel from afar. The eye and ear accustomed to conventional text faced a revolution in form whose shock began with the unusual typography and telegraphic rhythms of his books. In the manner of a Japanese gardener, or landscape painter, Hoffmann had culled one or two concentrated paragraphs of strangely Eastern calm at the off-center of each page, and his words were no less Hebraic for their sparsity or for the quasi-scientific, distancing quality of his tone. Hoffmann writes a Hebrew whose personae — middle-aged widowers, orphaned children, lonely aunts — often speak or remember or sing to themselves in their German mother tongue, transliterated phonetically into Hebrew and glossed in the margins. Ghosts from the world of Japanese Zen Buddhism contend with the spirits of Europe's rational philosophers, much as minimalist aesthetics blend there with unbridled imagination, education awareness with mystical trance, prose with what looks like poetry. Gauging a metabolism of loss, his work is, in fact, an essential blurring and negation of such boundaries: between self and other, life and death, man and woman, human and animal.

Hoffmann's atomistic fiction melds also with his lifelong scholarly engagement with Eastern thought. As a young man, he took a degree in Hebrew literature and Western philosophy, and later lived in a Japanese Buddhist temple where he studied Chinese and Japanese texts. He is now professor of Eastern philosophy at the University of Haifa; his academic work has ranged from interpretations and translations of haiku and Zen koans to comparative philosophical studies. Technically of the same generation (the "generation of the State") as canonical realist writers like A. B. Yehoshua and Amos Oz, he didn't begin to publish fiction until his late forties, and in many ways he represents a generation of one, at the edge of the Israeli avant-garde.

To date, Hoffmann has published four books: The Book of Joseph, Bernhardt, Gutapersha and The Christ of Fish, which came out in 1991. His work has also appeared in French and German translations.

— Nili Gold

# The Black Reeds
## *Mark McMorris*

### THE SENTENCES

circle in the cane piece and return
to a pocket of glass onto the avenue
the telephone rings, you answer it and I
pass along your lines to the north
(stand at the river, up-wind, up-stream)
only a rectangle edged in thick cloth
parts us but it's more than enough
it's everything to have this view
and nothing to be done with it
hearing your breath near to the mouthpiece

images of tongues from the east
they teach me stoniness
they predate the earliest names on my list
blood print genes hands my face is of it
coming from the marsh I was left in
to find you sturdy, peppery and shrewd
with vowels to lend me for the fight
a window, a glassy seeing of the earth
the battle-ax morning pouring
bits of clothing from last night's front
erotic mobility and wide relevance of now

we can only gather up the wind
we can only get ready for the assault

*Mark McMorris*

## TREE WITHOUT COLOR

We talk about socialism
how the boy swings
like a bell with his tongue out
and the factory ablaze
lights between huge pipes
smoke pouring out of the head
wanting to escape
from sand-flies and the look
of morituri te salutamus
read him as a warning
recite the scrawl of slack
muscles and the digits
gone limp when breath went
count them
pull the hand open now
inside the pouch of fist
find deltas running out
lines cracked and crinkled
telling of something else
look, this is one way to go
vertical and bare-foot
and able to gallivant
faster than a buck-shot
till one day it happen,
and space run out quick

---

And the cane field is on fire
the great house is going up
a pyre of shadows

collapsible rites
in summer sun

they culled weapons
from rivers and plots
the sown teeth
coming up as men
*yu cyaan face de African-dem*

•

gap beyond the windows of light
out of the perpetuities
my only purpose
to let things come up

they will or will not come
however is not my business
to stand in the standing
as wind-gazer

*qu'on mange du gateau*
where the consonants clump

vowels and bats flutter fforth
and are still

––––––––––––

Crowds pressed in on us
the progress of talk was over
only the body spoke out now
a small name written on
vacancy, over which, intent,
we brooded on our pulse
to capture it, the bulge of face
the unnatural emptiness
of space where he dangled
and was not, inexplicable,
sealed up at every mouth
resembling his audience
statues of black in the heat
"one senselesse lumpe"
of speech gone out for good

––––––––––––

They breathe into our ear
from all places come
as exponents of the web
forecasts of the landing
a disheveled music
all out this window

the gap between us closes
and thread grows taut
(to be closer is harder)
if you were next to me
it'd break off bitten
two black ends
and if space were to part us
it grows slack with hurt
there's no logic to this move
it's a paradox, a flat curve
of eye-sight tending to go
where it will


### AGON

I'm aware that a bird is
sent to us over the languages of books
(eagle with snake in its claws)
as reprimand for adultery

the fighting had stopped
a long meandering of the deer
closing with a pact
between murderer and father

a speed of translated enemies
the augur looking up
the weapons gleam with heliotropic fire
AK-47 and M-16

up and down our block
the hydrant splashes force into gutters
a collaboration with the sun
of summer sprayings over the ghetto

and the locks are busted
and the violin somnolent around us
the king sits with his tea
and soon the javelin and the foot-race
for the fallen

*Mark McMorris*

LANDINGS

Why do we live here

they had no knowledge of languages
of verdure and hills

I knew of this in Paris
I heard of them in Genoa

no knowledge of the arts
(the sky is burdensome)
of metalwork and navigation
certain crops grew there
in corn rows woven in
they worshiped golden icons of the self
migrating tales of the tides
brought them to our door-step
with tibia and abeng
we come upon the confluence
of the talisman and beetle
crawling on your wrist
exposed meandering supine
languid body at a bush

I am drunk, profligate
how far the eyesight extends
caravans from the Nile
then to Atlantic Sea
past Azores to the Caribbean
upward to this street
you from the west part of the country
northward to the land of ice
to stand here with me

I read of the gigantic mounds
of slag at Meroë
pyramids in themselves
now everything has to be re-thought
our hands put to work on
fragmentary scripts

in basements of the scholars
which city we are in
the copper head-pieces of the pharaohs
as a style in Senegal

and now us, agape at the huge legs
(Memnon the king)
of questionable purpose
of definite majesty

## THE BLUE RUSHES

cool waking up
the lawn mowed and watered
the balcony swept clean

this is the place we are in
today with causes put aside
a white towel on tile

and still in back of the eye
pictures of the rough sea
the chests dumped over

following a sun to the west
thus we arrived here
to get up and look out now

at hills blue over the mist
and set attitudes like them
steady with no haste

there are things in words
visible when you move
tight ropes holding a sail

imprint of their journey
amid the sober air of the sea
the words floating in

what comes over the sea wall
as figure for the morning's calm
are islands just off the coast

where the gulls circle
and spray disables the swimmer
she kneels in the surf

behind her are paths of the ships
and behind this screen
at the edge of the falling

the bodies sway in coral
their muscles are abstract
and space is a massy water

sea-tide is their ladder
the tight currents arrest them
the arms of fish encircle

they must travel toward us
here beside the green pasture
mowed by rain and season

to tell us what this place is
how to treat the amazing splash
of pink and blues in the hedges

the confrontational sun under palm
shadow-bread picked up
by pigeons that are better off

a net over some fishing boats
not this morning, with lanterns
the fishers went out

to white femurs caught
by jelly-fish and tough shark
and the bones picked clean

a tentative script of water
sign-posts of the route
composing into us of them

# The Warden
## Githa Hariharan

THE VIEW FROM OUR OUTHOUSE never changes. We have spent a lifetime of nights listening to silence, as if the world outside is a rumor. Or on some nights, when we hear the sound of the wind, all of them — husbands, sons, master, mistress — are impotent ghosts, circling the little cottage, condemned to incessant and futile whispers.

The wakefulness of old age has made us an ideal couple. Even our bouts of insomnia come together.

She thinks we are different. Ah, we are in this together, I tell her in the rare moment when I love her.

We? she asks, wonderingly. The word gurgles round and round in her mouth.

When I first met my young charge, the mistress of the house who is kept locked up in the outhouse, I had just lost my baby. I knew how to keep up my strength when looking after helpless infants: you sleep when they do, so that you can watch them the rest of the time with wide-open eyes.

On full moon nights, when she cannot sleep, she becomes petulant and quarrelsome, as if a beauty like her can never be crossed. She sidles up to me, unable to leave me alone. Her face is an inch from mine. Her breath is foul, her lips cave in with her effort to speak. The brownish, naked gums thrust forward like an ugly wall.

I tried to open the big window once, so that she could feel the fresh rain against her skin. I pushed and pushed, but it would not give way. She watched me from her corner, a mischievous grin on her face.

But she was not always a toothless old woman. She was like a little girl — sometimes a mute and subdued one — the day after a visit from her husband in the big house.

The day before, I combed her hair and plaited it tightly. The oil dripped from the tip of her braid. I knew how to make use of my chance; I never knew when he would come again, or when she would let me tidy her up next, like a meek little child-bride.

It was always a moonless night when he came to her. She was at her quietest then, a tame, docile little thing.

Basamma, she would beg me, as if she expected him, will you comb my hair properly? And tie my sari? I have forgotten how.

He was not such a humble supplicant. She does not need you now, he would say to me curtly from the door. And I was to make myself scarce for the next hour, but within earshot in case there was trouble.

*That white, white flower. So cunning, so sweet-smelling. Teases and teases, all the petals are like crescent moons. Then it came nearer and the smell was like vomit. The smooth white rubbery petals, thick, thicker, I couldn't even breathe. I saw the bee inside, he thought I didn't see it, but I saw him sting. You leave my rubber flower alone, I said to him, you don't even like it. It's ugly and stupid and smelly, I know, but I married that flower. How else to protect it?*

Once she bit him, hard, her teeth had drawn blood on his arm. I had to run back to the outhouse, save him, hold her down, lock ourselves in. Shutting out her wild, frenzied screams, holding down her stick-like arms that had now grown powerful talons, I shot him a glance that said, Are you satisfied?

He would have hit me, I know, if he had not been so frightened of her. We have given you a home, haven't we, he hissed between his teeth, and left before I could say anything aloud. I could have said a thing or two — shown him a few things as well — that would have straightened out his pretty, wavy hair for life.

*She is really a witch. Hah, she thinks I don't know. I have seen her — why, a thousand times — taking away something that belongs to me. The spell gets stronger that way. She hides my shit and even my bloody rags. She sweeps at midnight so that I cannot sleep. I know how to make signals — I learned it when I was very little. A beautiful bride-princess. When the blood trickled down like a long thin snake, all the way down to my knees, I scraped it off with fingers and pressed them, signals and signals, on the bare walls. She didn't like it. Ha, I said to her, you don't know what it means.*

*I know all kinds of magic so that you can't bring that hairy bee in here again. You — I want to laugh till I cry, it's so funny — are a stupid old witch. You don't know why your big balloon breasts burst, do you? Didn't you see me lying quietly in the corner, looking? My tongue rolled out and wriggled across the dark shadows of the room. It wriggled like a long, long earthworm. When you looked, it played dead and you thought it was nothing.*

*He can show me his sting and you be a cow with swollen udders, I don't care. My father, that old gardener who planted one rotten seed every year, would have laughed and laughed at you. He had twenty servants, he slept with three every night. I can see it all — I turn and turn the mud like an earthworm. But shall I kiss you? Or send the worm crawling up your thick, scaly legs?*

When I came to them, my breasts were full and heavy. The milk dripped like an open tap. I was ashamed to stand there in front of them, my sari damp and smelling of stale milk.

A godsend, he called me, and brought the baby, a poor skinny little thing almost as lifeless as my own. I took it from him greedily and put the tiny mouth to my swollen nipples. How he sucked! He drew and drew them out, his eyes closed in bliss, forehead damp with sweat, my chest light and empty with relief.

The next two times my breasts were empty. They had shrunk, and my nipples were dry, brown berries, hard and unyielding. I filled bottle after bottle with cow's milk while she lay about mooning, unconcerned, her breasts ivory-white and virginal, her girlish stomach unmarked by her three children.

The outhouse is all ours now. No one comes here — the daughter-in-law, or her children, or the servants. Once every few days, the son — the one I held at my breast, the eldest and now the owner of the house and the compound — puts in an appearance at the smaller window, the one with the iron bars. He peeps in, afraid she is awake.

Is everything all right? he asks, week after week.

Yes, now go away before she sees you, I tell him. What else can I say when he doesn't have the brains to ask a different question each time?

*Once they brought a baby and I liked him. So pretty and small, like a shy, star-shaped flower. I hid under the table and spied on my father. She was a fool, my mother cried all the time in her bed.*

*Mine, they said. From your body. Liars. I was under the table, not the bed. No baby came out of this body. This is that witch's*

*pet piglet. Look at that sweet snout. Oh, it's grunting, it's squeal-*
*ing. Let's tickle it, squeeze it a little. Look, tell me quickly. What*
*is inside? Pig's blood or prince-blood? That's all I need to know.*

When her son got married, they brought the newlywed couple here
for a quick blessing. The poor girl was terrified, I could see that.
But a mother-in-law is a mother-in-law, even if she is a mad old
woman hidden in the backyard.

She too seemed to know that, though she refused to look at her
son. She took her daughter-in-law by the hand and made her sit
on the stool I had covered with a freshly washed sari.

She caressed the girl's face gently and felt her long, thick plait,
heavy with flowers. The girl sat on the stool like a statue, too
afraid to move. Just when I was smug that things were going well,
she bent down and lifted the girl's sari.

*I learned the art of cunning when I was very young. When they*
*don't let me out, or strip naked in the rain, I sit still in the darkest*
*corner I can find. I am a sightless stone, and Basamma forgets to*
*watch me.*

*I can sit still and look inside. I can make rain, like the magician*
*she told me about.*

*It rains and rains. No one believes it, but sometimes I remember*
*a time before this dark room. The petals fell a long while ago.*
*Now it is almost time to pick the fruit. I can feel it, clusters of*
*parasitic growths in my head, ripening.*

Basamma, tell me a story, she would ask, sitting on the floor and
looking up at me like an eager pupil. I know no story except my
own, so I told her about my village.

It's thirty or forty years since I saw my village. In my memory,
the little village, a mean cluster of huts, expands till it is a vast
and magical landscape. The streams and fields nearby are inter-
twining stretches of blue and green ribbons.

I have told her so many stories that I don't know which of them
belong to the village, and which of them I made up in my head.
Anyway, she knows nothing. There is nothing in her mind but
herself.

She listened, her chin resting on her small, childlike hands,
when I told her about my father who plucked coconuts all his life.
The last time he climbed a coconut tree, he had thrown down a

big pile of nuts before his legs suddenly gave way and he fell head-long, all the thirty or forty feet, right on top of the pile.

I told her about my mother, who strung garlands for the gods and strings of sweet-smelling jasmine for the young women of the village. I told her about the little shop near the temple; the sister who died of a snakebite near the pond; the ghost that haunted the dry riverbed on summer nights; the bare-chested wanderer who came once a month from the forest, where he prayed to the gods of black magic. We never knew what guise he would come in next. Sometimes he was a beggar, humbly holding out his bowl for alms. Another month he told our fortunes. When he snarled at us for money, his eyes huge and a livid red, we ran for our lives before his curses could come true.

Whenever I told her about my dead husband, or my baby, she became restless. She would hug herself tightly, or tickle her under-arms and the soles of her feet. Like a fool I waited every time for the giggling to begin before I remembered what a mad bitch she is. A rotten seed, I tell you, what can you expect of the fruit?

*Sometimes, when the door is open, just a little, a crack lets in a bit of luminous sky. The light smells fresh. I can hear Basamma snore. She sits by the door, leaning against the stone wall, her bag of betel leaves on her lap. Her mouth hangs open like an empty cave.*

*The guard dog keeps one ear open when asleep. I know how to tiptoe past smouldering monsters.*

*Outside, the trees are lost in the depth of night. I laugh softly all the way to the pond where I washed away my wedding night.*

A few times she did get away. I have to sleep too, don't I? Old Ramayya in the village used to tell us: A mad person has three eyes, not two like you and me. So when he sleeps, don't shut your eyes. He will open his third eye — the one that rises with the moon — and see his chance of escape. I was warned, I should have known, but what am I, a thing of iron and brass?

*I used to dream of jasmine and hibiscus for years and years. Then the dreams went away. Now I see air and only air. They don't even let the rain in here.*

*I can't remember if my mother sang to me. But when she did, I curled up and slept, safe in my shell like a soft, squishy snail.*

*Githa Hariharan*

*Then her full, rich voice became thinner as she went further and further away. It became thin as a reed; and as sharp as a knife.*

She got out somehow, and she ran into the main house. She knew what she was after, she is no mad woman. She took the biggest, sharpest knife from the kitchen. She went round and round the house stealthily like a prowler, peeping, searching, sniffing the air which smelled so different from the outhouse.

She slashed all the photographs — the rows and rows of great-grandfathers and mothers, their fathers and mothers. She drank all the milk in the kitchen like a hungry stray cat. She found the matches and lit a pretty little fire just outside the front door.

Then she went to the well, the good one where we got all our drinking water from, and perched herself on the stony rim, lifting her sari to bare her buttocks. She shat in the well, giggling to herself, and jumped off easily. She was nearing the pond where she had bathed as a young bride when the smoke woke them up and they caught up with her.

They shook me till my bones rattled. They called me a block of wood. A lump of coal. A piece of dog shit. I gave it to her, I can tell you. I can shake more than bones. They too must know that by now — years later, they fawn on me every time I say I am going back to the village.

I can't remember how to get to my village, and the fools — new, young ones who know even less than the old ones — pile endearments, flattery and saris on me. I keep the saris in a tin trunk. The key hangs from my neck.

The day her husband died, they sent a servant to tell us. Pour fresh, cold water on her head, the fellow told me. She is a widow now.

She had kept me up all night in one of her fevers of excitement. I felt my eyes burning with fatigue.

I would have shouted at the servant, but I didn't want to wake her up. I also wanted to go to the big house and see his dead body, but my bones felt at least a thousand years old.

Out, I whispered to him furiously, we know what to do. She was born a widow. She doesn't need you to tell her that.

*I used to look at my face in the mirror all day, then it went away. Only ugly faces break glass. I had fireworks like glass breaking when I got married. My father, the bull, hung a garland of sly*

70

*little marigolds on his only horn and threw them into the air.*

*Oh please, please, one small mirror. They are so afraid of glass breaking. Don't be afraid, it won't hurt. See, I look into your eyes like this, keep still or you will make it ugly, my face is not like that. Yes, that's just right, darling, we will stand all alone in my own private chamber, away from the others, and look into each other's eyes.*

*I see myself, you see me. I am here, and in you, and everywhere. You are smiling—what a pretty smile—let me keep it for a few days!*

I will go, I keep telling them. No, don't, please, we need you, they say. She loves you and you love her. Love, love. The bitch is no longer in heat. It's enough to make anyone vomit.

The door is not made of iron. Why not open it? Locked from the outside? Oh the liars, the rumormongers!

She lies there like a broken tree, not a leaf on her for years, and you are afraid? You make me laugh. I hold her in my arms and weep all over her. The tears flow from my face to hers. She is a broken, mangy old woman, just like me, and we lick the tears off each other's faces.

# Music History
## *Barbara Guest*

i

The rhythm of the section
nor said to be withheld
credible garnering
natural context of
  mountain property
nymph on the ground
fountain attached to
grotto.
  Mind you the soul of the piece
a tight operation
and viols then
wilful counterpoint.
  Addresses the Mass
and far off Celtic tuning
Wolf chorus
then bells lavender bells
Italian.
  Twittery business
at the waterfall
animal noise the snow snow cutting teeth an
arrangement in tin with rasp.

ii

The orchestration
friendly speech
  edenic viols
no promissory a masterful
explanation.
  The reprimand the scene
of non-turbulent
withdrawal
the camomile fades
breeze off the lake
preparing lemon trees.


iii


Audacious idea
the empty left hand
*Die Gluckliche Hand*
interrupts the idyllic shore-line
umbrella   light bulb   faces
  *mobility*

# Wing
## *Kathleen Fraser*

### I. THE UNDERDRAWINGS

The New comes forward in its edges in order to be itself;

its volume by necessity becomes violent and three-dimensional
and ordinary, all similar models shaken off and smudged

as if memory were an expensive thick creamy paper and every
corner turned now in partial erasure,

even bits of pearly rubber, matchstick and lucent plastic
leaving traces of decision and little tasks performed

as if each dream or occasion of pain had tried to lift itself
entirely away, contributing to other corners, planes and
accumulated depth

•

the wing is not static but frayed, layered, fettered, furling and
stoney

its feathers cut as if from tissue or stiffened cheesecloth
condensed in preparation for years of stagework

attached to its historic tendons; more elaborate
the expansive ribcage, grieving, stressed, yet

marked midway along the breastbone with grains of light

•

there are two men, they are tall men, and they are talking softly
among the disintegrating cubes

74

## II. FIRST BLACK QUARTET: VIA TASSO

A cube's clean volume     shatters and reassembles
its daily burnt mark     The New is used and goes
backwards into match     sticks one struck at each
day's oxygen, common     pinched breath and nerve
the remaining light     bricked-up Now melt with
nothing changed yet     he persists as does pain
have a way of crash     ing in on you, swimming

through matter heart     rate in each cell There
are two men turning     their limit of blanket
that one particular     evening appears in reds
to unfold in expand     ing brilliant traces or
stars: "that which     is known to us" or just
improvised on deep     kitchen floor meanwhile
picking, pecking at     our skins ghost or angel
sent to tell us what     we didn't want to know

## III. WING: VIA VANVITELLI

It can happen that the intoxicating wing will draw the mind as a
bow    The cubic route of wing falls backwards with light
leaking through at the edge    The cube is formally particular
and a part of speech and lost    it looks for like kind,
regardless of function, and attempts to replace itself    The
square root of anything captures and holds, seeming to be final,
and we are grateful    We see the delicate marks along the
feather and we follow, now to define or depict the outskirts of
meaning    A plume of smoke or any of the growths which cover
the bodies of birds    To form a model of the wing's surface,
the cube arrives on a day called "the darkest day"    Its
likeness consists of strength, atonality, pigment, emptiness and
shafts partly hollow    I put my mouth just at the opening where
a steel edge gives way to an angle    from which light emerges
along its soft narrow barbs    If the wing had a voice it would
open through a shaft    I am not of that feather

IV. LINE

Attached by some "natural" substance
the arm (or leg) with elbow

(or joint) midway suggests the next
incision or protrusion: It stiffens as

a fin or rib projecting new function:

It emits signals periscopic (familiar)
helical into the spinal: Wing

could loosen that line's identity calling
to itself with charcoal error

"only in contradiction to that which is known
to us of nature"


V. COLOR: VIA DELLA PENITENZA

Even The New is attached or marked by attachment

the shimmer of wing, which claim may tell us everything
in a white blink

just as in troubled moments it disappears

    [A young girl in Arkansas, the quill of an angel in
    warm light, from orange and yellow regions, falls]

Waking touched

    [an angel stands in technicolor as cosmonauts look out
    on Jet-liner wingspan attaching itself collectively]

   •

these retinal bodies larger, remarkable for their iridescence

VI. CROSSROADS

He extends thus into plumage as fruit rubbed from walls soaks
inward

•

Your mango human skin doth beckon overlaps against the larger
screen

•

Where floods our night hike, features of body assemble
their hawkeyed distance

abnormally retaining jet-liner lure

•

yet wanting the same thing always:  your innocence
dressed in red anterior borders

pinion and spur, my teeth which may fit the angel's gear

•

having seen thy ancient ground


messenger : αγγελος : wing

VII. FALL OUT

now and melt with rush all        in one place nothing changed        I
did not grow up I        went away in one phase        brooded I over
skier  in  black  the  flyer,  forces        that  dive  far  yet  he
persists        in  contradiction  to        as  does  physical  pain
that which is known a way        of crashing in on you        to us
changing,  now  perilous        their  spots  unawares  your  own
heart  stopping        she  used  words  downward        who  like
brilliance        but  are  you  turning        he had no truck with the
mysterious        like  stones  found        not  having  opened  after
each  other,  Herodotus        the  sifted  swimming  through  matter
cocoa  color        I  was  thought  though  burning        hot except
our  gills'  events        but  where  his  cold  hand        did not flow
touched        a  normal  one  throwing        up screens & satisfied
lest  they  be  struggling        with  his  dictum  and        bickering
plain  as        the  palm  on  a  particular        evening to attract
brilliant  treads        something more with a cleft on its        upper
lip appearing        to unfold as if marked

## VIII. SECOND BLACK QUARTET

as does that
which is of
crashing to
us changing
their spots          aware your own she
heart stop           she used words like
downward who         brilliance turning
but are you          he had in my hand

swimming through     struggling
color, I was burn    dictum and
hot gills' events    plain as
cold hand touched    a particular
                     attraction
                     treads some
                     thing cleft
                     if marked

## IX. MATTER

There are two men without feet, they are tall men swimming
through matter.

Kathleen Fraser

## X. VANISHING POINT: THIRD BLACK QUARTET

forward edge itself to be volume by necessity as if partial erase
edge itself to be volume by necessity as if partial erase    other
itself to be volume by necessity as if partial erase    corners
to be volume by necessity as if partial erase    planes
be volume by necessity as if partial erase    accumulate
volume by necessity as if partial erase    depth
by necessity as if partial erase    condensed
necessity as if partial erase    in
as if partial erase    preparation
if partial erase    stagework
partial erase    historic
erase    tendons
of    elaborate
pearly    ribcage
lucent    marked
decision    midway
and    with
little    grains
tasks    of
of    light
pain    talking
had    softly
tried    among
to    disintegrating
lift    cubes
to lift    the
tried to lift    falling
had tried to lift    wing
pain had tried to lift    will
of pain had tried to lift    draw
tasks of pain had tried to lift    the
little tasks of pain had tried to lift    mind
and little tasks of pain had tried to lift    as
decision and little tasks of pain had tried to lift    a
lucent decision and little tasks of pain had tried to lift    bow

itself the wing not static but frayed, layered, fettered, furling

["Wing," for Mel Bochner, was written in response to his "Drawings," completed in Rome (1988), and his 1993 Rome installation, "Via Tasso." It is dedicated to the memory of Joe Brainard (1942–1994) and to his friend, Kenward Elmslie.]

# Crosses
## *John Taggart*

### BLACK CROSS

1

Before there can be a kind of a cross there has to be a ground
before there can be any kind of the one there has to be the other
before the one the other and the other is a ground
there can be a black cross if there can be a black ground
there can be a black ground if a black field can be imagined
a black field of more or less several acres
field of more or less several acres bordered by trees
the field is covered with snow completely covered with snow
border to border completely covered with snow
border to border from border to border completely covered with snow
the field has always been completely covered with snow
the snow itself is covered snow on the field of several acres
the snow itself is covered by nightfall
nightfall has fallen no morning has broken nightfall's fallen
nightfall has always been completely fallen on the snow.

*John Taggart*

2

Before there can be a kind of a cross there has to be a man
before there can be any kind of the one ⁺here has to be a black man
before the one the other and the other is a black man
there can be a black cross if there can be a black and blind man
there can be a black ground if a black man can be imagined
a black field of more or less several acres a black man with shades
field of more or less several acres black man with horns
imagine a black field of several acres imagine three horns
the field is covered with snow completely covered the man isn't
border to border completely covered black man isn't covered
border to border from border to border black man is exposed
the field has always been completely covered he's completely exposed
the snow itself is covered snow on the field nothing on the man
the snow itself is covered by nightfall the man isn't
nightfall has fallen no morning has broken his shades taken
nightfall has always been completely fallen his horns taken away.


3

There has to be a man kind of a cross there has to be a man
has to be a black man any kind of the one there has to be a black man
other is a black man other and the other is a black man
a black and blind man cross if there can be a black and blind man
man can be imagined ground if a black man can be imagined
black man with shades several acres a black man with shades
black man with horns several acres black man with horns
imagine three horns field of several acres imagine three horns
the man isn't covered with snow completely covered the man isn't
man isn't covered completely covered black man isn't covered
black man is exposed border to border black man is exposed
completely exposed completely covered he's completely exposed
nothing on the man snow on the field nothing on the man
the man isn't covered by nightfall the man isn't
his shades taken no morning has broken his shades taken
his horns taken away completely fallen his horns taken away.

4

There has to be a man kind of a cross there has to be a man
has to be a black man any kind of the one there has to be a black man
other is a black man other and the other is a black man
a black and blind man cross if there can be a black and blind man
man can be imagined ground if a black man can be imagined
black and blind man said you supposed to let the cross *help*
said you supposed to let the cross *help* you *get* across
black and blind man is a witness the best witnesses are blind
"witnessing substitutes narrative for perception"
black and blind man said if you let the cross help you *get* across
he said if you let the cross help you'll be *on* the cross
completely exposed completely covered he's completely exposed
nothing on the man snow on the field nothing on the man
the man isn't covered by nightfall the man isn't
his shades taken no morning has broken his shades taken
his horns taken away completely fallen his horns taken away.


GREEN CROSS

1

Before there can be a kind of a cross there has to be a ground
before there can be any kind of the one there has to be the other
before the one the other and the other is a ground
there can be a green cross if there can be a green ground
there can be a green ground if a green field can be imagined
a green field of more or less several acres
field of more or less several acres bordered by trees
imagine a green field of several acres bordered by trees
the field is covered with snow completely covered with snow
border to border completely covered with snow
border to border from border to border completely covered with snow
the field has always been completely covered with snow
the snow itself is covered snow on the field of several acres
the snow itself is covered by nightfall
nightfall has fallen no morning has broken nightfall's fallen
nightfall has always been completely fallen on the snow.

2

Before there can be a kind of a cross there has to be a man
before there can be any kind of the one a man has to have disappeared
before the one the other who is a man disappeared among leaves
there can be a green cross if there can be a green man
there can be a green ground if a green man can be imagined
a green field of more or less several acres a man disappeared
field of more or less several acres man among leaves
imagine a green field imagine leaves and stinking fruit
the field is covered with snow completely covered the man is
border to border completely covered green man is
border to border from border to border green man is covered
the field has always been completely covered he's completely covered
snow itself is covered snow on field man among leaves and fruit
the snow itself is covered by nightfall the man isn't
nightfall has fallen no morning man among fruit
nightfall has always been fallen man among stinking fruit.


3

There has to be a man kind of a cross there has to be a man
to have disappeared any kind of the one a man has to have disappeared
disappeared among leaves other who's a man disappeared among leaves
a green man a green cross if there can be a green man
imaginable a green ground if a green man can be imagined
man disappeared more or less several acres a man disappeared
among leaves more or less several acres man among leaves
stinking fruit imagine leaves and stinking fruit
the man isn't covered with snow completely covered the man is
the green man is completely covered green man is
green man is covered border to border green man is covered
completely covered been completely covered he's completely covered
among leaves and fruit snow on field man among leaves and fruit
the man himself isn't covered by nightfall the man isn't
fruit hasn't fallen no morning man among fruit
stinking fruit always been unfallen man among stinking fruit.

4

There has to be a man kind of a cross there has to be a man
to have disappeared any kind of the one a man has to have disappeared
disappeared among leaves other who's a man disappeared among leaves
a green man a green cross if there can be a green man
imaginable a green ground if a green man can be imagined
green man imagined the cross as a tree with leaves and fruit
every delight sweetness of every taste
leaves and fruit having delight taste of a bride
imagination is funny makes the cross a tree makes a tree a bride
didn't imagine himself disappeared among leaves and fruit
didn't imagine stinking fruit didn't imagine a stinking bride
completely covered been completely covered he's completely covered
among leaves and fruit snow on field man among leaves and fruit
the man himself isn't covered by nightfall the man isn't
fruit hasn't fallen no morning man among fruit
stinking fruit always been unfallen man among stinking fruit.

## WHITE CROSS

1

Before there can be a kind of a cross there has to be a ground
before there can be any kind of the one there has to be the other
before the one the other and the other is a ground
there can be a white cross if there can be a white ground
there can be a white ground if a white field can be imagined
a white field of more or less several acres
field of more or less several acres bordered by trees
imagine a white field of several acres bordered by trees
the field is covered with snow completely covered with snow
border to border completely covered with snow
border to border from border to border completely covered with snow
the field has always been completely covered with snow
the snow itself is covered snow on the field of several acres
the snow itself is covered by nightfall
nightfall has fallen no morning has broken nightfall's fallen
nightfall has always been completely fallen on the snow.

2

Before there can be a kind of a cross there has to be a woman
before there can be any kind of the one there has to be a white woman
before the one the other who is a white woman with a seed
there can be a white cross if there can be a seed inside a woman
there can be a white ground if a white woman can be imagined
white field of more or less several acres white woman with a seed
field of several acres woman with a seed growing
imagine a white field imagine a seed growing inside her
the field is covered with snow completely covered the woman isn't
border to border completely covered white woman isn't covered
border to border from border to border her secret exposed
the field has always been completely covered she's completely exposed
the snow itself is covered snow on the field nothing on the woman
the snow itself is covered by nightfall the woman isn't
nightfall has fallen no morning broken woman in pain
nightfall completely fallen woman in pain from a seed inside her.


3

There has to be a woman a kind of cross there has to be a woman
white woman any kind of the one there has to be a white woman
woman with a seed other who is a white woman with a seed
a seed inside a woman cross if there can be a seed
man can be imagined ground if a white woman can be imagined
white woman with a seed several acres white woman with a seed
growing and growing woman with a seed growing
inside her inside imagine a seed growing inside her
the woman isn't covered with snow completely the woman isn't
woman isn't completely covered by white woman isn't covered
her secret's exposed border to border her secret exposed
she's completely exposed been completely been completely exposed
nothing on the woman snow on the field nothing on the woman
the woman isn't covered by nightfall the woman isn't
woman in pain no morning broken woman in pain
seed inside her fallen woman in pain from a seed inside her.

4

There has to be a woman a kind of cross there has to be a woman
white woman any kind of the one there has to be a white woman
woman with a seed other who is a white woman with a seed
a seed inside a woman cross if there can be a seed
man can be imagined ground if a white woman can be imagined
white woman said she wouldn't have said yes if she had known
if she had known what seed it was if she had she wouldn't
what seed it was seed of a tree growing inside her
"most beautiful tree where the birds of the air come and perch"
seed of a tree inside her seed of a cross
if she had known what seed it was she wouldn't have said yes
she's completely exposed been completely been completely exposed
nothing on the woman snow on the field nothing on the woman
the woman isn't covered by nightfall the woman isn't
woman in pain no morning broken woman in pain
seed inside her fallen woman in pain from a seed inside her.


DOUBLE-CROSS

1

Before there can be a kind of a cross there has to be a ground
before there can be any kind of the one there has to be the other
before the one the other and the other is a ground
there can be a double-cross if there can be a double ground
there can be a double ground if a double field can be imagined
a double field of more or less several acres
field of more or less several acres bordered by trees
imagine a double field of several acres bordered by trees
the field is covered with snow completely covered with snow
border to border completely covered with snow
border to border from border to border completely covered with snow
the field has always been completely covered with snow
the snow itself is covered snow on the field of several acres
the snow itself is covered by nightfall
nightfall has fallen no morning has broken nightfall's fallen
nightfall has always been completely fallen on the snow.

*John Taggart*

2

Before there can be a kind of a cross there has to be a woman
before there can be any kind there has to be a double-crossing woman
before the one the other double-crossing woman with a tree
there can be a double-cross if a tree can be uprooted
double-crossed ground if double-crossing woman can be imagined
a field of more or less several acres a woman with a tree
field of several acres woman with an uprooted tree
imagine double-crossed field imagine tree uprooted from inside her
field is covered with snow completely covered woman isn't
border to border double-crossing woman isn't
border to border from border to border her secret exposed
field has always been completely covered she's completely exposed
the snow itself is covered snow on the field nothing on the woman
the snow itself is covered by nightfall the woman isn't
nightfall has fallen no morning broken woman in pain
nightfall fallen woman in pain from tree uprooted from inside her.


3

There has to be a woman kind of a cross there has to be a woman
double-crossing woman any kind there has to be double-crossing woman
woman with a tree her double-crossing woman with a tree
uprooted be a double-cross if a tree can be uprooted
woman can be imagined if double-crossing woman can be imagined
woman with a tree less several acres woman with a tree
uprooted tree woman with an uprooted tree
uprooted from inside her imagine tree uprooted from inside her
red woman isn't with snow completely covered woman isn't
not bleeding double-crossing woman isn't Snow White
secret exposed border to border secret exposed
she's completely exposed completely covered she's completely exposed
nothing on the woman snow on the field nothing on the woman
the woman isn't covered by nightfall the woman isn't
woman in pain no morning broken woman in pain
uprooted from inside in pain from tree uprooted from inside her.

4

There has to be a woman kind of a cross there has to be a woman
double-crossing woman any kind there has to be a double-crossing woman
woman with a tree her double-crossing woman with a tree
uprooted be a double-cross if a tree can be uprooted
woman can be imagined if double-crossing woman can be imagined
a not imagined woman said "only a betrayal could uproot it"
like it is tell the love of the father's love like it is
sock it to me backup group: "tell it like it is"
only a betrayal could uproot the tree only a double-crossing woman
only a double-crossing woman could tell the love like it is
like it is the love of the father's love *is* the father
she's completely exposed completely covered she's completely exposed
nothing on the woman snow on the field nothing on the woman
the woman isn't covered by nightfall the woman isn't
woman in pain no morning broken woman in pain
uprooted from inside in pain from tree uprooted from inside her.


CRISS-CROSS

1

Before there can be a kind of a cross there has to be a ground
before there can be any kind of the one there has to be the other
before the one the other and the other is a ground
there can be a criss-cross if there can be a criss-crossed ground
a criss-crossed ground if a criss-crossed field's imagined
a criss-crossed field of more or less several acres
field of more or less several acres bordered by trees
imagine a criss-crossed field of several acres bordered by trees
the field is covered with snow completely covered with snow
border to border completely covered with snow
border to border from border to border completely covered with snow
the field has always been completely covered with snow
the snow itself is covered snow on the field of several acres
the snow itself is covered by nightfall
nightfall has fallen no morning has broken nightfall's fallen
nightfall has always been completely fallen on the snow.

*John Taggart*

2

Before there can be a kind of a cross there has to be a man
before there can be any kind of the one there has to be a black man
before the one the other and the other is another black man
there can be a criss-cross if there can be two black men
there can be a criss-crossed ground if two black men can be imagined
a criss-crossed field of more or less several acres black men with shades
field of more or less several acres second black man with a piano
imagine a criss-crossed field of several acres imagine a piano
field is covered with snow completely covered men aren't
border to border completely covered black men aren't covered
border to border from border to border black men are exposed
field has always been completely covered they're completely exposed
the snow itself is covered snow on the field nothing on the men
the snow itself is covered by nightfall the men aren't
nightfall has fallen no morning has broken their shades taken
nightfall has always been completely fallen horns piano taken away.

3

There has to be a man kind of a cross there has to be a man
has to be a black man any kind of the one there has to be a black man
other is another black man and the other is another black man
two black men criss-cross if there can be two black men
black men can be imagined ground if two black men can be imagined
black men with shades several acres black men with shades
black man with a piano several acres second black man with a piano
imagine a piano field of several acres imagine a piano
men aren't covered with snow completely covered men aren't
men aren't covered completely covered black men aren't covered
black men are exposed border to border black men are exposed
completely exposed completely covered they're completely exposed
nothing on the men snow on the field nothing on the men
the men aren't covered by nightfall the men aren't
their shades taken no morning has broken their shades taken
horns piano taken completely fallen horns and piano taken away.

4

There has to be a man kind of a cross there has to be a man
has to be a black man any kind of the one there has to be a black man
other is another black man and the other is another black man
two black men criss-cross if there can be two black men
black men can be imagined ground if two black men can be imagined
second black man said this is my story this is my song
said this is my story on the piano said this is my song on the piano
second black man is a witness a witness is always blinded
"witnessing substitutes narrative for perception"
black and blinded man said perfect submission perfect delight
he said perfect submission and he said all is at rest
completely exposed completely covered they're completely exposed
nothing on the men snow on the field nothing on the men
the men aren't covered by nightfall the men aren't
their shades taken no morning has broken their shades taken
horns piano taken completely fallen horns and piano taken away.


GREEK CROSS

1

Before there can be a kind of a cross there has to be a ground
before there can be any kind of the one there has to be the other
before the one the other and the other is a ground
there can be a Greek cross if there can be a Greek ground
there can be a Greek ground if a Greek field can be imagined
a Greek field of more or less several acres
field of more or less several acres bordered by trees
imagine a Greek field of several acres bordered by trees
the field is covered with snow completely covered with snow
border to border completely covered with snow
border to border from border to border completely covered with snow
the field has always been completely covered with snow
the snow itself is covered snow on the field of several acres
the snow itself is covered by nightfall
nightfall has fallen no morning has broken nightfall's fallen
nightfall has always been completely fallen on the snow.

91

2

Before there can be a kind of a cross there has to be a man
before there can be any kind of the one there has to be a tempted man
before the one the other and the other is a tempted man
there can be a Greek cross if there can be a Greek-tempted man
there can be a Greek ground if a tempted man can be imagined
a Greek field of more or less several acres man on top of bride
more or less several acres man on top of bride who just can't say no
imagine a Greek field of several acres imagine the last temptation
the field is covered with snow completely covered the man isn't
border to border completely covered tempted man isn't
border to border from border to border tempted man exposed
the field has always been completely covered he's completely exposed
the snow itself is covered snow on the field nothing on the man
the snow itself is covered by nightfall the man isn't
nightfall has fallen no morning has broken his bride taken
nightfall has always been completely fallen his bride taken away.


3

There has to be a man kind of a cross there has to be a man
to be a tempted man any kind of the one there has to be a tempted man
other is a tempted man other and the other is a tempted man
a Greek-tempted man cross if there can be a Greek-tempted man
man can be imagined if a tempted man can be imagined
man on top of bride several acres man on top of bride
who can't say no several acres man on top of bride who can't say no
the last temptation several acres imagine the last temptation
the man isn't covered with snow completely covered the man isn't
man isn't covered completely covered tempted man isn't covered
tempted man is exposed border to border tempted man is exposed
completely exposed completely covered he's completely exposed
nothing on the man snow on the field nothing on the man
the man isn't covered by nightfall the man isn't
his bride taken no morning has broken his bride taken
his bride taken away completely fallen his bride taken away.

4

There has to be a man kind of a cross there has to be a man
to be a tempted man any kind of the one there has to be a tempted man
other is a tempted man other and the other is a tempted man
a Greek-tempted man cross if there can be a Greek-tempted man
man can be imagined if a tempted man can be imagined
in the movie the tempted man asks who's getting married
in the movie his guardian angel tells him: you are
he's getting married to the bride who just can't say no
long-sleeved white gown garland of green leaves around her hair
in the movie she's not the last temptation
the last temptation is the ordinary life allure of that life
completely exposed completely covered he's completely exposed
nothing on the man snow on the field nothing on the man
the man isn't covered by nightfall the man isn't
his bride taken no morning has broken his bride taken
his bride taken away completely fallen his bride taken away.


LOST CROSS

1

Before there can be a kind of a cross there has to be a ground
before there can be any kind of the one there has to be the other
before the one the other and the other is a ground
there can be a lost cross if there can be a lost ground
there can be a lost ground if a lost field can be imagined
a lost field of more or less several acres
field of more or less several acres bordered by trees
imagine a lost field of several acres bordered by trees
the field is covered with snow completely covered with snow
border to border completely covered with snow
border to border from border to border completely covered with snow
the field has always been completely covered with snow
the snow itself is covered snow on the field of several acres
the snow itself is covered by nightfall
nightfall has fallen no morning has broken nightfall's fallen
nightfall has always been completely fallen on the snow.

*John Taggart*

## 2

Before there can be a kind of a cross there has to be one
before there can be any kind of the one there has to be a lost one
before the one the other and the other is a lost one
there can be a lost cross if there can be one who stays lost
there can be a lost ground if a lost one can be imagined
a lost field of more or less several acres a lost one without this
field of more or less several acres lost one without that
imagine a lost field of several acres imagine no this or that
the field is covered with snow completely covered the lost one isn't
border to border completely covered lost one isn't covered
border to border from border to border lost one is exposed
field has always been completely covered one's completely exposed
the snow itself is covered snow on the field nothing on the one
the snow itself is covered by nightfall the one isn't
nightfall has fallen no morning has broken this way taken
nightfall has always been completely fallen that way taken away.


## 3

There has to be one kind of a cross there has to be one
has to be a lost one kind of the one there has to be a lost one
other is a lost one and the other is a lost one
one who stays lost cross if there can be one who stays lost
one can be imagined ground if a lost one can be imagined
lost one without this several acres a lost one without this
lost one without that several acres lost one without that
imagine no this or that several acres imagine no this or that
the lost one isn't with snow completely covered the lost one isn't
one isn't covered completely covered lost one isn't covered
lost one is exposed border to border lost one is exposed
completely exposed completely covered one's completely exposed
nothing on the one snow on the field nothing on the one
the one isn't covered by nightfall the one isn't
this way taken no morning has broken this way taken
that way taken away completely fallen that way taken away.

4

There has to be one kind of a cross there has to be one
has to be a lost one kind of the one there has to be a lost one
other is a lost one and the other is a lost one
one who stays lost cross if there can be one who stays lost
one can be imagined ground if a lost one can be imagined
"it's always a matter of returning from wandering"
black and blind man green man white woman didn't say that
"of restoring what one should have seen to it not to lose"
double-crossing woman other black man tempted man didn't say that
it's always a matter of returning *to* wandering
it's always returning *to* wandering if one would lose the cross
completely exposed completely covered one's completely exposed
nothing on the one snow on the field nothing on the one
the one isn't covered by nightfall the one isn't
this way taken no morning has broken this way taken
that way taken away completely fallen that way taken away.

# *From* Ululu
# (A Page & Peephole Opera)
# Thalia Field

**PROLOGUE:** *through a mousehole at a circus tent, flaps beating eyelids in what will become recognizable rhythms.*

### HOUSE PETS ARE HOUSE MORAL

Tent flap frame, the diminishing return, our vantage receding in the dung-smell and wet green hay tickling backstage ankles — There before the curtain, among the cages, these first moments of time in Profile. A trick rider warms up on the horse of one surface, a cantering Klein's bottle with fur. Everything we hear now is crucial, the hasty environment of sound. INTRODUCE US to the shattered information.

We owe a tamed inheritance old bleached bones an expanse of dead starfish a voice. The Diva warms up in a closet. Lulu. Sound of cherry bombs. A play that Frank built. Ringmaster says: Banned! WALK UP! Like a stinking dog of town-to-town exiles (Romanticism.) A pervert CYMBAL the beery crowd hisses. From the country leaksss their great moralities. A theater surrounded by alleys. Immediately Geschwitz plans her bid. To return no later than a great world war. Lettuce decays into a curtain at rise. The band hits sour chords in brass and the boom boom bursts from left right and inside — drums of rotting skin. Enter Animal Tamer. Geschwitz pulls a string, his hand flaps in the center ring — We forget who he will be, he will be our revolver — and whip.

> HELENE: That's right, you must check with me. See me grieving! My husband wrote me over two hundred collected letters.

> ANIMAL TAMER: Every one has their best beast. But we'll keep it loose and decide later, see how one beast engenders another.

## THE VICTIM DIES A FEAST
What a Tamer! It's basic "B" for Animals of the Bible rather
Colorful through the Peephole. Rapturous Vienna! A sumptuous
and reeking audience! The crowd the revolutionary crowd presses
forward     through evening purple their eyes bright orange     not
NATURAL     the air their hair     Sooty. The stage-door caves,
not breaking. An animal ejaculates on a leg     TIMPANI
TIMPANI     the audience gasps! Hoofed mammalia ungulata
urgently seeks tent? The tamer scribbles names as shouting
tenses the confounded analogy he's trying to make:     lizard,
crocodiles, FAKE!     You idiotic hoards. Namesakes. From tiptoe
we — crowded — peer at the small tamer, his side shows a bulging
crotch, weighty lump of wrinkled flesh, his purse. We will make
them news one by one! Beast after beast, mongoose, RAT and
boar! I have union contract he shouts. *Haustiere, die so
wohlgesittet fuhlen!* This story has no analogy without
me     there is a particular Identity     their catalogues mail-
ordered are classified to logical ends     with the PLATYPUS
playing softly     unadapted wholly to land. Could you be more
specific in what kind of snake?
*PIANISSIMO.* He was afraid such a question could leak from
audience lips. *PIANISSIMO.* Asp or adder? The animal tamer has
a face like a boy Brecht, and a bite on the nipple.

## BEFORE YOUR EYES SKILL ABUSING
A tiger in a reversible NOUVEAU raincoat, a costume of one, so
the consumer pays the new SUBWAY     but thinks twice about
it / Tamer: How much? STEP UP! The usual doesn't pay your jaws
to open!     HERIENSPAZIERT     a velveteen seat     Sit down
Sit down     and skin not your knuckles in the     //     door-
crack     not standing ankles in urine     dirty fingernails framing
the spotglass hole     Not fiery serpents but a brazen young pleasure
for your girl: Pandora! Harry stands ready, Pandora     his arm is
strong     WHAT?     Too old to sing her own, the producers hire a
complete unknown? You! You? STEP UP     into the role, whose
coloratura voice? Handicapped in the morning races. What the
trawlers would call trash fish, Molly     Kept in the closet of the
tent     a WUNDERKIND! Geschwitz has a tooth of pure gold she
flashes, reeling back the Tamer     His trainer's costume consisting
of: nine pinstripes in epaulet-form, buttons down and sashes
swashbuckled to thigh-tight boots "painted on"! His mantra

97

taunted those whose money built the skyscrapers and
railroads    Beggar Impresarios    out here in the alley press
GRUBBY fingers to the hole    and see the dusty back of his tails
and the shining clean flesh of a child thigh in a highwire dress.

HELENE: I did not approve the casting. Even Harry is too
small.

GESCHWITZ: Just put in a few lines of the original.
HELENE: It's *my* original.

ALBAN: Ahem.
HELENE: What?

**WITHOUT COMPUNCTION MY ZOO**
and down
                    the keyhole tunnel
                         the stagehand slides a long hand out the
backstage. We have fished among us trash from the back a like-
enemy pulls the characters of the zoo PRAYING (HARP PLAYS
some bleeding) the smelling salts revived the player-piano
player    properly
                    dried out
                         for the journey
each night where the number 33 has been applied to poverty
                    and inscribed
                    LULU
in stage direction only. To divide age. Of fruit from that of tree.
    Her age from those adults beholden to youth. Ergo the rough
hems on the tent edges. Ergo lust. Ergo the tamer calls    SNAKE
    at the first opportunity    SNAKE    to show off his prized
vermilion velvet coat    SNAKE    And promises lessons for the
best pets on how to be so reviled. We are all begging for his treats
            because he addresses us directly VERMIN    and to the
        snickering nasty audience    zipper pockets pinch us    our
        flesh    as we poke through for a feel of scale    of serpent
tongue    or our serpent    dreammm Ahhh    Lulu waves to the
            front    in modified concertina action the audience
marvels    THOSE HIPS THOSE SOUFFLÉ SAUCER HIPS    but
    for us    from the side of the stage we see slightly hairy shins
    bent and the top of Lulu's head in the retinue of SQUINTING

98

squinting    one eye by    one eye    blinking squin
squin    PLUCKED VIOLIN unlike Lulu's eyes which
UNBLINKING seem unimpeachable

**THE SERPENT IS LULU, HARRY!**
The six-foot actor forgets to bring a song for the audition (and
those SEQUINS!) In one blink    a decade passes    scored for
clavichord and wine during which he demonstrates shedding skin
and how he can fertilize himself from behind    And he doesn't
have a full name or an address. We did mention the last castrato
recorded live, first laughtrack hit    a culture in silhouette
(perhaps in conjunction with a government, men approach the
stagedoor singlefile)    Though this nowhere prefigures the mass
movements of populations to cleaning (starting in 1933)    And
there the first star. *Bring mir uns're Schlange her,* **Harry!** It's a
sideshow put on for the patrons who have not *really* paid at all.
Who look poisonous. The secondary consumers. *She wears
the Pierrot costume of the next scene.* Carnivores shred salad
eaters. The serpent is a viper. Or an asp. Sleeping at day, or
"in the path that biteth the horse heels so that his rider shall
fall backward." What a den! Bring out the first man    And this
boy's passive pose    in no way prefigures the love of the
Countess Geschwitz    herself more than a man (and better
dressed)    SECRET NOTES    tragic self-sacrifice AND pushed
the wife    HIDDEN NOTES    it was then her husband saw his
career diminishing    BUT BUT    The actor in the trope of a
carnivorous female wore his best sequined crown matched
gown    AND a special scent    emanating from his anal
glands    and pushed his artful bosom    his long neck    and
smooth jaw    rubbed his chin    against the director's neck
into the producers' noses.

> HELENE: I don't want real body fluids. STAGE BLOOD!
> (my dear Alban if only . . .) The stage is a
> lovely laboratory. Lulu, a beautiful child —

> GESCHWITZ: The categories are wearing thin already.

ANIMAL TAMER *(tickling the newly hired Lulu under the chin)*:
Sie ward geschaffen, unheil anzustiften.

99

*Thalia Field*

## DON'T BE WHAT YOU ARE NOT

You're HIRED! All in a name     LULU     a professional job
from now on    The role is CAST our head between his savage
legs     shaved soft as sheepskin     don't be what you are not     he
plucks even the littlest hairs     from his thighs     around his
pubic mound     and shaves the rest with gilded foam     a slow
sound to his pronoun     sss     she killed Cleopatra, then? Half an
hour and without legs     Lulu changes shape     still gliding the
speed of a running man     a corset on a ham     A gorgeous duet
here: The tamer and his pet (shall we ever see LULU free again?)
Proclivities to tasting the feast without filling     Moves by
Small Declivities     and his projections     his overlapping
scales     spanning octaves     He wraps his arms around the
tamer's neck     they push off as a mainstay nutrient hard through
thin costumes     they dance! HARRY, put Lulu here     to gain
speed     Or she lies low in the sand. Pierrot white sand — biting the
heel. *Akshub*, like a dancer we dance for the pleasure of feeling
carried by stage hands when on display, or time-tense replaying.
(Playing a viper is not an asp.) Though one of you did do in
Cleopatra. One of YOU. That means better. We know you are
there. It's that boy again     or is it just Beauty     that conceals
in holes in walls in holes in rocks adder or asp . . . How is it then
you've been painted as *Immortality*? *In the next scene's
costume*     she lies in Harry's arms. Ahhh, you ate the
rodents     That's why they kept you on     Such a good girl Such
a seductive waist     STRIKE UP THE MACHINERY     it will be
explained.

LULU IN DEEP BASS: It's a funny way of putting it.
TAMER: Don't talk.
LULU: If I'm not, how can I be not it?
*GANGSA GAMBANG*
*GANGSA GAMBANG*
HELENE: Prima donnas, all.

## HEAD BETWEEN WHOSE JAWS

At first sun    There are no children    They play in each other's
pants     sand boxes     pageants in the garden    They thrust their
thin hermaphroditic pelvises     a chorus a wading pool a forest
beach    They touch    *Head between their legs, fingers feel the
shape of the pouch* bribed into a respectable profession/

100

Tamer *(responding to a small commotion we can't all see)*:
Egyptians step up! That the eclipses of sun were attacks upon
the sun god     *Ra*     and his version. The pepper stings the
eyes     OR     in the illusion by the great serpent     *Apopi*     who
believed in a celestial River/Tamer: Somebody stop mouthing off!
Ahem, in other words     *Of Whose Intention*     The crowd's ear
is pressed. The storefronts decorate their     ORIENT     Hinged
on the leading note, Semitone. LULU's bone is halfway up     Yet
the trainer STROKES her hips     The trainer mentions
GNAWING the serpent hero     the Eve that reunites Adam to
Knowing. UP for conspiracy, the costume designer     so called
*leading up* naturally     To tonic worship someday pure and minor.
That gorgeous belly will resolve fears OF IT, the preordained
shape OF IT, *his* hands thicker than *her* hands should be,
but the audience on one side, the crowd over here, don't look
there     the beauty of our Pierrot     we've forgotten what
innocence means     it's signs smudged     the costume not
so clean.

> ALBAN:  Hush, hush. I'd like my favorite foreign countries
> in the front rows. It's an evil time to introduce what
> in my lifetime I didn't know *(winks)*. The beasts
> robbed us. The animals are patches of single atoms.
> Or we've lost our capacity to have small enough
> cages.

> HELENE:  Dear . . . Adam called. He won't be back, he says to
> tell you he's had a change of heart about the part.

**SNARLING FACE TAKE YOUR PLACE**
Back! Back! The Tamer whips the actors in their costume cages.
And Lulu's hanging hands. The hanging heads become her
panpipes piccolo fife black pompom Pierrot buttons down the
front     white tigers     sea serpents     the Animal Tamer
STROKES HER HIPS her hips that are thin and taut     he has
always taken utmost care to keep them loose and unmuscular the
penis of a snake is a DOUBLE structure     HEMIPENE
HEMIPENE     the peephole lips press and swell     She's true
innocent/ Tamer: And best of all to win your kind applause! The
hunter and hunted resolve a tonic DRUNK     dissolving who eats
whose kind alive     The chord strikes unresolved     how good a

view he ever had of his sea monster     LEPER     no one
knows     legless the tamer cracks a whip     its head as high as
the mast head     its eye as small as a kcy     the underbelly
hypnotic     unmelodic we go belly up     HEMIPENE furnished
with spines     uncritical collectors     we eat LULU up alive
despite our eyes locked into the female     the feats of
uniting     the feast of "I took my gun"     and fired at it, it
plunged under the water and yet further sightings of the creature
continue.

ALBAN:  Dear . . .
HELENE:  The crowd is pressing in, and those who've paid
          shouldn't have to hear that.
ALBAN:  Dear . . .

                                                   *CHORD*

     ANIMAL TAMER:  Whose are the jaws, then?

*Calliope fading to a line*

ALBAN' *(gives a silent moan & grand expressionist gesture into
     the wings)*:  Ω!

          HELENE *(aside)*:  Funny he never calls me that.


GESCHWITZ *(pacing the Green Room)*:  Now at last, let's pretend
     to begin. Rimbaud was of primarily debauched meat.
     I appreciate that and all implications. His bio reads
     like an overboiled pot of slop. A botched job, you
     know, a contrivance of know-how. He seems lonely.
     I've told him he could have a part, a boxcar and a
     turn, he hauls big weight, to be represented by
     Copernicus — so bring out another cage — skinny
     and wide.

***ACT ONE, SCENE ONE:*** *A keyhole to a studio set on the same stage as the future. The crowd overheats with purchasing power. The audience expects the mirror.*

### A PORTRAIT OF LULU, A FOLDING SCREEN

**A** mouth-open song.
**Portrait** the writer's view, Lulu wears the costume in this scene.
**Of** Pierrot, innocent, the veneration of a violent Nile, dominated by the sun.
**Lulu** we think you're pretty cute.
**A** is for inherited astrology.
**Folding** folding folding the pose is hard to hold.
**Screen** is less what's seen.
**Screen** seductive sonata: **Folding** unfolding folding unfolding frustration of obsessive creation. **A** Pierrot with gorgeous ambition. **Lulu** what sign are you? **Of** twelve gods what day was the zodiac made? **Portrait** astrological fate of the frame. **A** bigger life invites.

### PIERROT COSTUME PODIUM

Pierrot oil paint smears paint oil Pierrot. Costume trade, what's fun gets ugly said welcome, laying, or is it lying? Lying it is or laying welcome, said ugly gets fun what's trade costume? Podium is the marriage bed where no one yet Lulu's marrying lover's pet. Pet lover's marrying Lulu yet one nowhere bed marriage is the podium.

Schon: What rub?

***BONK***

### HUSBAND OUT ALL HAVE THEIR SIGHTS

Hush money for his bodice top, the lace-covered buttons, the rouge on his nipples, the silent wet finger he taps on the flesh of his breast, to the conductor's beat, distracting most of the string section who try to keep their eyes focused on the stands, he lifts his silken hair from his neck and blows the next three measures, resting with a smile during the accordion solo. The patron Schon is paying for the performance. Liking his picture, his likeness, to line his husbands up well ahead of time. Back to the portrait, oil paint is more permanent. The canvas, a surface, even from the side. We are already in line.

*Thalia Field*

*The painter moves into the front row, standing on hats for a
better look while Alwa pushes his way to the front of the crowd
twenty deep now in the alley.*

## FERN, VERWEHT DER LARM DES POBELS

Once there was a composer faint with sex who wrote so that
nothing was concealed but sound. Yes, the other way around
everything is heard in the head. Once there was a composer who
knew no music and, considering any dusty floor "home," placed
nothing but unspeakable chords (hidden rope) (unsingable notes)
in the path of performance, or a SECRET CODE dotted-line in red
on Pierrot's neck marking a lust-text for the surgeon's cabaret
(because I am drunk on those whose hands are love.) As only
Lulu can swing her feet off a papier-mâché moon, her tush on a
black silk pillow waits to be lowered from the flies. "I think it is
good . . . I have the conviction of going towards the discovery of a
new kind of expression." Alwa composes for mind, eye, imaginary
knitting needles and flickering candles. Rote. Red. Ruuu-bies.
How the composer jots in passion for Schon's child-like
lover     the quasi-sister     the mother's poisoner. For her Alwa
writes melodrama,     set to electricity for tonedeaf voice. She
who is not the sister is also the singer who did not-sing his not-
composition: "*Dran die Dichter stumm verbluten*" (translation:
there is no affair between words and sound except the searing
daydream). Out into this burning lake swims our heroine to
retrieve the oar, to pluck her ragtime pizzicato on the contours of
childhood's lull dull skull. To the lapping tongue, Alwa passes the
disintegrated song, throwing (the biography) the disintegrating
country's scarlet seaweed left and right *colla parte* off the moonlit
sand. Alwa loves and hates her     *Wie so*     having grown up as
her bruder     trained as Cassander     a composer *Brooding
Mutter* of unheld notes to hit without pitch tongues trill on
the     scorching high small low huge piercing ensemble AND the
white then the red then the plaster     moonspot     *ach / vor / lie /
flu/ spring/ ick/ ish / ote*     voicing Deutsch where no center
exists. The darkness is in the detail. Once upon no mother-tongue
a-time, there lived no durations only hitting the sliding stabs
of     *on a moon leaking boat of precisions*     each minute an
obsession     arias set for the mention "*Do not cause this to be
sung!*" and for images of oil-thick chocolate silent-movie blood.
(The moon swings.) Rehearsing in its head, Childhood has chills

104

and paces backstage. (On its pulleys.)

ALWA: It was Tristan she taught me to admire.
SCHON: Just keep her dancing and not on the trapeze.

*(They all share a laugh at their good fortune.)*

ALBAN: "O give me back, Surgeon of the soul . . . Pierrot — my laughter!" It was perfect that night at Alma's when Erika recited. (*Sigh.*) Never since or again, my dear old friend.

HELENE *(to Lulu)*: He never said that. There was never any
headvoice better than yours — but dear,
everyone knows you can't play that lute.

LULU *(auditioning)*: "Gelooost, showerleek ooont soooss!"

## YOUR MIND REALLY ISN'T ON THE SUBJECT
ALWA: The eye evolves down. Hold Lulu still through the scene.
PAINTER: If you'd hold her in a pinch.
ALWA: The portrait is of the costume, eh?
PAINTER: The easier to catch the escape! Just get your eye from there, you'll knock the easel's legs.

## BRUSH AND PALETTE IN HAND — RAISE YOUR PANTALOON
brush and palette in hand *(raise your pantaloon)*.
*(brush and palette in hand)* raise your pantaloon.

### AND SUCH A FLIRT WITH IT
CLaviCORD the strings being roughly parallel
plucked by a Crow QUILL
mounted in the pivoted TONGUE of a fork-shaped JACK
standing on the rear end of the KEY lever
depressing the KEY raises the JACK
until the horizontally projecting plectrum plucks the string
the JACK falls back and the tongue ROTATES
on its pivot
a spring of boar's bristle at the rear
returns the tongue to its original position so that the JACK AGAIN
is ready to PLUCK like the PIPE of an organ can continue sounding
only so long as the PLAYER holds down the KEY

*Thalia Field*

SCHON: Ranks of jacks can be silenced or added to the ensemble.
LULU: I'm aware of that.

ALBAN *(whispering to Alwa)*: Lulu knows her theory.

**THROWS THE SHEPHERD'S CROOK IN HIS FACE**
Lulu you mythological TAZELWORM    kind of a snake with
feet    led on the stick by flocks of sins. The uncertain quality,
round-bodied. Shepherd's dubious animals of the bible. Crook
and "satyr of the desert shall lie there: and their houses of doleful
owls will dance there." The descriptions vary to *bergstutzen,*
*springewurm, stollenwurm.* His alpine regions know no physical
evidence. The North is not plush. Face a peasant crowd in a dried-
up marsh, the crows ate half. Her anecdote amuses the tabloids
of 1888. The history of medicine took a kick. In two alarms, the
flock is German, the attic London, the knife will barely penetrate.
Shepherd's venom is a retrograde to heavy-lids. The confusion
is the number of legs a snake once had    before THE
SURGEON    kiss you when you're down    a stomach
curse    both snake and girl    OR    Did Lulu throw down the
Shepherd's crook in order to sit more comfortably? Did Lulu need
cosmetic surgery?

**IF I COULD ONLY ENGAGE YOU AS MY LEADING LADY**
What is theater!? mocks the painter    Out Lulu's mouth a flock of
ravens: It's secondary, characteristically    that hires me    the
flash of a penis, the flesh of a vulva    Vulva of fluids dripping
from the tiny mouth of a pencil    to write the future with a
LOOK under the rehearsal, take a second there are no more
seconds remaining    the unreserved box of flesh between the
jaws. Lulu: Rape in any name is not a pretty picture    MY
PERFECT ANKLES    Painter: YOU WANT my hands, my ideal
vision    Lulu: YOU WANT my pantaloons    Painter: THE
COSTUME    Lulu: You'll find revision    Painter: The force
is in the brush    Lulu: The brush stroke BACK TO
WORK!    Painter: I'll punish you LILITH! Lulu: Oh, the high
notes you call for.

CROWD: Coward! Pin her! The police will come
destroy the copies.

## DIESER BALG (DIRTY TRICK)

Lulu has the laugh of thumbtacks, sandwiches, homer, fad diets, brokers, Bon Marché and Ginnie Maes, tanagrams, hope chests, lisps, helixes, rude awakenings, zoom lenses, gumbo, brake pedals, gemstones, bathyal zones, contrecoups, wanton smooches, galoshes, cruising altitudes. Lulu has the laugh of a non-performer. Her song, her laugh is a chord of coloratura and mud.

ALWA: I think I was speaking . . .
GESCHWITZ: No, I was speaking.
PAINTER *(interrupting)*: What makes him so keen on a rehearsal?
CROWD: Hey! We can only see half the stage!
AUDIENCE: So what! (Immigrants.)

## I'M LOOKING OVER ALL THE CITIES OF THE WORLD

tonic: The world of cities has a maid — dominant: A stage on stage — tonic: A crowd pushing *(freely inventing)* subject: The world of cities overlooks the stage — answer: The dancer's cage *(freely inventing)* leader: The world of cities worries for days — follower: The actor's replaced the wife in her part — *(freely inventing)* antecedent: The world of cities hides its face — consequent: To snigger at the respectful name of Fiancée — exposition: The world has one flame — that it saves and hates — coda: That it saves and hates and saves and hates.

> CROWD: We're coming in to make her play the right
> character, the way we love her.

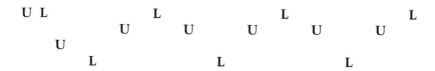

## I HAVE NO SENSE OF COMPASSION LEFT

PAINTER: You've never made love!
LULU: It's you who's never made love!
ALBAN' *(practicing breathing)*: Huuuh . . .
HELENE: What?

**I'VE NO PITY**

He covers her hand with KISSES KISSES her mouth with KISSES
KISSES a tongue that cannot sing soprano, the Painter delights
in muting colors his KISSES find a tongue so thick two-
pronged    he imagines it beating like butterfly wings across his
chest    it makes him hard his brush falls to the ground his hands
reach down he pulls the pantaloon around his mouth KISSES
KISSES the neck    the elastic opens wider than his whole
head    his eyes roam her thighs as long as he deceives his senses
his erection juices for connection blindly eyes cloudy he KISSES
feels the passion lust of KISSES all he's ever KISSES KISSES
thought of the art of portraiture, second rate as he may be. And
LULU lets these kisses fall from grace to secret grace.

PAINTER: Nelly!
CROWD: Nelly!

**(AS THOUGH AWAKENING)**

LULU: What is an honest transaction? I've had many patrons, the
theater is full, if you'll look around. The alley is full too
(my alley pulses when it can't pay). I loved a handsome
man who licked me into a butter bust. He won an award
and a trip to Cairo where I melted before the judges. They
each stepped up and took a lick, a taste a nibble a sip.
Delicious they moaned, their pants grew hotter than the
sun, they spread greasy butter over their nipples and
sucked at whatever this was, they groaned in lust, we want
it and you get the prize! Brava, Brava, my handsome
husband knew that the butter came straight from our
bedside and more might be available, if he could milk me
into that costume again. Amassing status and wealth and I
haven't seen a penny.

CROWD: Lulu does not hear the name Nelly!

**MY NAME IS NOT NELLY, MY NAME IS LULU**

When there was only one woman, she walked in peace because
nobody loved her. When there was only one woman she was alone
and happily poor. When there was only one woman she saw a
snake looking at her and laughed as only the poor can laugh
because somehow she already knew the story, that the snake

should be her. The snake turned to the camera and the woman understood that it wasn't her show so she quickly called *oh snakey-poo* sort of as a joke, but the snake took her up on it and began by interviewing her on various topics she had never cared to discuss publicly, namely how she was able to recreate pleasure in successive ways without turning so much as a glance back to the pleasures she'd had. How do you live with this fatal flaw, asked the snake, and she realized she would have to pitch woo in order to go home alone, or be humiliated which was something she had never felt before. *I am alone*, she leaned over and whispered, thinking this would make the snake play fair. But the close-up caught her lips in motion and the audience called out so many names at once the buzzing caused her to bump into the microphone. *It's a jungle out there, kid*, said the snake leading her off camera, *I'll show you around. They all love you now*, he continued, *but it never lasts long.* The animal tamer calls me MARILYN, the woman said in a small voice, but I call myself LULU *(winks)*.

**I'LL CALL YOU EVE INSTEAD**
Since 1895, Eve's been a screen, folding back on two sides, heat-driven images, be still the costume change, the rods and cones, the new goods and Palaces, folding unfolding sides of the coins. Now we shall all call and response God through the experience of blasphemy     Nickelodeons     Blast open the desert in Nag Hammadi (1945). The Pierrot costume after eighteen hundred years, an original cloth, rolled into a ball, but look! It's tight as a screen, a scrim, canvas or lens. And out of it a naked woman buzzes around the cool chamber like a moth, how did a life stay so . . . alive? She, in shame, presents only her beautiful buttocks, dark and hairy, to the crowd at the door. But a semi-circle forms, after all, new species are rare, and new versions of old tales, amassing a buzzing sound as air escapes into the room, she speaks in a fugue which cannot be heard or written, the scrape of wings together, a body cracked and leaking. Ashamed before the old, she asks them to leave the cave. And now the young too must leave. A few remain who don't fit one or the other category and toward these turns this assumed Eve turned man-woman on a torso of clouds     And genitals in the exact face of God. Fallen into error ssshe hissed, the body isn't what you call ME though I fling off the 's' and make her he, Eve creates Him, that's the new rub     How a

blade unspreads butter    The few gods present will befit
worshipping human beings      I am a hungry whore his mouth
stirred      and hungry for a plate of steak-frites and a black coffee
and the dark body buzzed toward the cave door, dropping to the
floor as a worm      a moth      VIRGIN      de-evolving.

PAINTER: I'll make you pay for this teasing.
LULU: I think you'll be paying me.
       *Backstage:*
HELENE: It's impossible to keep them separate when they're both
       playing at once!
ALBAN: She's the muse, he's modeling, I mean, he's modeled his
       version after her, one definitely has to come first.

**LET ME HAVE A KISS, EVE**
Leprosy vanished, but wastelands are haunted by sterility, the
after-sickness. VIENNA struck before music, by insanity. And
VENOM and Paris had two leprosariums in the vicinity, first in
the history of sickness overtaken by criminals. Only one leper
is left. London's home. The leper's extinction, mumbled the
madman of the Crusades, ends the constant manifestation of
God: "His anger and His grace."

                                         *THE XYLOPHONE*
                                         *THE XYLOPHONE*

LULU: I used to be Snow White, but I drifted.
GESCHWITZ: Do that one again, I love her!

**PRETENDING? I'VE NEVER HAD TO**
LULU: No really, the Female Spiritual Principle came into my
       body and there you have it, presto chango, I'm a snake, or
       I've got the most stubborn hard-on at all times (or a dildo)
       split in two or three prongs, whichever way they like it.
       I like to think of myself as an "instructor," when the men
       fear everything. I give them a spread lip kiss (yes I kiss, yes
       I kiss), no tongue at first, and tell them: *With death you
       shall not die, my friends . . . Rather your eyes shall open
       and you shall come to be like gods.* And after I've
       lubricated them      rubbed them with the rod      slick
       saliva      entered them, and turned them all around, I have
       a flourish of the arms for the curtain line: *And so the*

*Female Instructing Principle is taken away from the
Snake, and she leaves it behind* (a good slap on the
buttock for effect), *merely a thing of the earth.* I'm their
sexless rape fantasy Madonna complex whore-in-one
SQUAMATA   But I'm not on the street. That's the rub.
Classes of whores are as ancient as war.

CROWD: Lulu, whatever do you mean?
ALWA: SUCKINCUBUS?
*GLISSANDO of a PANPIPE*

SCHON: You're quite unaware of your effect no doubt.
LULU: I'm quite aware.
HELENE: Then Lulu should be more discreet.
PAINTER: I agree. Could you pull that pantaloon a little higher?

**PROFESSOR OF MEDICINE ENTERS**
PROFESSOR: I'm not supposed to have a single line to speak, but I
         can see right through your costume!
LULU: I'd as SOON be rid of it.
              **. . . AND DIES OF A STROKE**
Brueghel painting the damned. One BRUSH STROKE that
climbed to Calvary. But our Portraitist at present seeks only
the glory of a modest career, the Professor enters and dies
of a STROKE     the painter sees THE PORTRAIT he knows
now as never before the poorhouse table     the haystack
sleepers     lazy infested workers     LULU IS RICH! A shaky
illumination     he has already dropped his palette and not
for the salvation of art but for the gimme-a-beer of the bar and
a loud refrain of *Let Me Call You Sweetheart . . .*

**HE'S ONLY PRETENDING**
              *In ter l ude f o r LIGHT & EMPTY ROOM*

**(SHE MOVES HIM A LITTLE)**
Scientists explain the machine, the parts and circuits, where the
liquids gas up the atmosphere, the parking lot (all sparks gears and
packages). Come tour the arena! Or stand in the wings (masks
protect us from invisible metal filings that can pierce the lungs
and enter the blood). See how outdated is the factory data
an old impotent husband/a frigid wife     all smoked up the

incinerator    [*imp band po wi hus gid*]    the works flare up rain
down where kids play. The economists add machinery, indirect
costs and pollution to abstractions, in packaging plants the tour
begins because people want to see where the jobs all are, or where
they're losing them down the line, the line that is moving they
wander in their curious groups of last-minute tourists. Vienna is
a most beautiful place, the blood is clean, the air luxurious. The
goods "good." In the machinery it's the tiny movements that can
be done only by the hands of a virgin workforce, children from our
local *Church of Tiny Virgin Children*, wide innocent eyes disguise
the smallest particles pierrots split off to produce the dust in the
light that lights the stage. Alban coughs in the presence of
machinery. HIS BLOOD IS WASTE.

ALBAN': Dear [*coughs*] Frank *(coughs)*, thank you for the pen.

**THE DANCE IS DONE**
Truth or Dare, Mistress LOUISE: I never ask a tongue's sex if it
eats me the right way. I'm averaging about five nights a week on
stage. I have an audience of slaves. Some want songs to keep their
fantasies going for days, some want clefs in their foreskin. There
are hidden notes for when stop means enough and when it doesn't.
Pain and pleasure sting only the brain, get all mixed up in that
endorphin swill, bead on their foreheads, run off down the aisle.
I don't hurt men because I hate them, I hurt them because I love
them. The turned on john is the greatest turn on, his imagination
is endlessly entertaining. A man who's just been fucked up the ass
wearing a big feathered headdress and crotchless silk bathing suit
is very unlikely to rape or kill. Truth or Dare.

**WHAT'S NEXT FOR ME . . .**
Lulu waves to the stage manager to bring up the house lights.
It's on to the next thing Lulu begs — but the alchemists got house
seats, seeking remedy for ailments that are perfect and passive,
that they may die from their awful mixtures, from their mistrust
and boiled compounds which never hardened into a Philosopher's
Stone (so that Lulu and those like Lulu should never suffer the ills
that "flesh is heir to.") Isn't that the parents' fear, that we've
inherited their passion and their shames? *What's next*, Lulu asks,
because things don't ever change. GO TO BLACK Lulu begs GO
TO BLACK   the Philosopher's Stone would turn base metals into

gold? I'm ready, Lulu whispers so her throat rasps, FOR THE
NEXT THING.

PAINTER:  Nelly! *(She does not hear him.)* I love you so, Nelly!
LULU:  I giggle because here's one who died in such a theatrical
way *"Enters and Falls Dead"* it's parody! This big gate-
crasher couldn't take being on stage.

**I'M JUST AS GOOD FROM ANY ANGLE**
Degenerate eyes? All right . . . (admit it) LULU needs glasses
(*gasp*!) And for performing wears nothing      but thin skin on the.
unblinking gaze from the stage    Because Lulu sees mostly
shapes, Lulu admits it's vain    But it's impossible! She's willing
to admit most shortcomings readily, but she . . . shortsighted?
Admittedly . . . She has laughs with the devil and the
doctors      even the cabaret producers      more adept than
she      more ready to be pushed aside. But once Lulu went behind
the camera and laughed at how rinky-dink the whole stage
appeared. Into the view-finder she chuckled at the enterprise even
with her bad eyes      the tattered black and ripped screen and
Look      she moved the lens forward to frame the tiny crack under
the back curtain where smoke was winding out, SOMEONE's got
my hookah going! She ran for fun backstage to see who it
was      Yanking the pipe mouth and coil from The Schoolboy's
grasp. Is nothing my own? Lulu laughs and gives a flick of the
tongue, picking up some particles of hosenrollen skin and spitting
them back. Were we in school together once? She dances kicking
like a Ziegfeld girl    A bad grade . . . This flying high schoolboy
with her props in a dusty corner piled on some coiled electrical
wire, Go on! LULU can taste your little tiny clit just by looking
at it (*winks*). I know, go see that Geschwitz . . . But it won't be
enough, Lulu whispers, don't you know I eat things WHOLE?
The "schoolboy" shivers. Lulu yawns. What's impossible, Lulu
confides, is that snakes are entirely deaf to sounds in the air. How
could such a *Vadette* as I am ever play that?

OSTINATO until everyone gets Lulu's point.

ALWA *(screaming through the crowd)*:  Can we continue?

*Thalia Field*

**CAN YOU TELL THE TRUTH?**
No, but Lulu can look it up on the computer dictionary.
1. **Conformity.** To knowledge, fact or logic.
2. **Fidelity.** To an original or standard.
4. **God.**
Lulu reads down the page a notch.
*Truth serum:* Any drug that reduces inhibitions and promotes relaxation. Lulu relaxes.

**DO YOU BELIEVE IN GOD, THEN?**
An Egyptian woman leans to the stage and slides a paper across the painted boards. It's a dagger, says Lulu, picking up the paper. How beautiful.

ABRACADABRA
ABRACADABR
ABRACADAB
ABRACADA
ABRACAD
ABRACA
ABRAC
ABRA
ABR
AB
Ɐ

**WHAT DO YOU BELIEVE IN?**
Natural symmetries? My two childlike eyes?

*Jack the Ripper stays backstage in his wagon, bars on the window to protect the handler — the crack will return to a curtain-call aftermath. An afterthought that was preordained.*

ALBAN: I only believe in principles and forms.
GESCHWITZ: Egad! No Bondage?

**HAVE YOU NO SOUL FOR SAVING?**
ALBAN: Luck!
HELENE: That's what Alwa says. That actor is so awful by the
way. I hate his fingerwave.
ALBAN: Lulu is examined and produces no morals. Look how the
Painter no longer understands his picture.

HELENE:  Precisely why I loathe this whole enterprise. Though I
    support you, dear.
ALBAN:  She's the only woman I love. My music slays her.

**(WITH A GLANCE)**
She does not know it.

**(AS THOUGH AWAKING)**
LULU:  I speak on pitch.

**WHAT IS IT YOU TRULY WANT TO KNOW, THEN?**
Spits on him. Spits on him. Spits and spits on him. Spits on him.
Spits and spits and spits. Spits on him and spits on him and spits.
Spits spits spits spits spits on him. **(RAISING HER LEFT ARM)**
**COULD YOU DO ME UP? MY HAND'S SHAKING.** The
audience is a puppet, wallets weightless, arms released from
gravity reach unconsciously toward Lulu's clothes, floating in
their minds wandering off, they think they see her innocence
exposed their fingers delicately moving thumbs and forefingers
fiddling in their minds with her buttons.

# Five Stories
## *Lydia Davis*

### THE MICE

MICE LIVE IN OUR WALLS but do not trouble our kitchen. We are pleased but cannot understand why they do not come into our kitchen where we have traps set, as they come into the kitchens of our neighbors. Although we are pleased, we are also upset, because the mice behave as though there were something wrong with our kitchen. What makes this even more puzzling is that our house is much less tidy than the houses of our neighbors. There is more food lying about in our kitchen, more crumbs on the counters and filthy scraps of onion kicked against the base of the cabinets. In fact, there is so much loose food in the kitchen I can only think the mice themselves are defeated by it. In a tidy kitchen, it is a challenge for them to find enough food night after night to survive until spring. They patiently hunt and nibble hour after hour until they are satisfied. In our kitchen, however, they are faced with something so out of proportion to their experience that they cannot deal with it. They might venture out a few steps, but soon the overwhelming sights and smells drive them back into their holes, uncomfortable and embarrassed at not being able to scavenge as they should.

### THE OUTING

An outburst of anger near the road, a refusal to speak on the path, a silence in the pine woods, a silence across the old railroad bridge, an attempt to be friendly in the water, a refusal to end the argument on the flat stones, a cry of anger on the steep bank of dirt, a weeping among the bushes.

116

## ODD BEHAVIOR

You see how circumstances are to blame. I am not really an odd person if I put more and more small pieces of shredded kleenex in my ears and tie a scarf around my head: when I lived alone I had all the silence I needed.

## FEAR

Nearly every morning, a certain woman in our community comes running out of her house with her face white and her overcoat flapping wildly. She cries out, "Emergency, emergency," and one of us runs to her and holds her until her fears are calmed. We know she is making it up; nothing has really happened to her. But we understand, because there is hardly one of us who has not been moved at some time to do just what she has done, and every time, it has taken all our strength, and even the strength of our friends and families too, to quiet us.

## LOST THINGS

They are lost, but also not lost but somewhere in the world. Most of them are small, though two are larger, one a coat and one a dog. Of the small things, one is a certain ring, one a certain button. They are lost from me and where I am, but they are also not gone. They are somewhere else, and they are there to someone else, it may be. But if not there to someone else, the ring is, still, not lost to itself, but there, only not where I am, and the button, too, there, still, only not where I am.

# Pleasant Hill:
# An Interview With Guy Davenport

## Bernard Hœpffner

THERE IS NO SUCH THING as time on a summer afternoon.

Guy Davenport is standing on the landing stage, easy to recognize for those who have seen Ralph Eugene Meatyard's photographs, and, for those who have not, a faint echo of *Santa Ana's Retreat from Buena Vista*, as played by a brass band, has been provided; the melody, played on a cornet, becomes slightly more audible as you approach the man standing there on the wooden platform.

With forty other people, he is getting ready to board the *Dixie Belle* for a two-hour cruise up the Kentucky River Gorge. The "steamboat" (that fake paddle wheel) is going to Pleasant Hill, the Shakers' village.

The *Dixie Belle* pulled out at 15.00 sharp, so slowly that we glided in silence past the platform on which gentlemen in Prince Alberts stood mute under their umbrellas, ladies in picture hats held handkerchiefs to their mouths. A brass band now played Stanford in A.

Guy Davenport! and I knew he was on board! There were questions to be asked, sights to be seen and music to be heard. The steamboat had left the bank and picked up speed; loudspeakers explained where we were, where we were going and would explain the sights as we passed them. Guy Davenport was sitting on the top deck, his back resting against a table; we were introduced to his friend Bonnie Jean, who was sitting on his right, and I introduced myself and my friend Catherine. No, he didn't mind answering a few questions.

———

*A number of people in America, and some in other countries, are captivated by your short fictions and essays. I believe George Steiner wrote that you and William Gass were two of the most*

*important contemporary writers in the States. How would you situate yourself in American (and other) literature?*
As a minor prose stylist.

*When you say you consider yourself as a "minor prose stylist," what difference do you make between a minor and a major writer?*
Harold Bloom the Yale critic has changed major and minor to strong and weak. The terms should not apply to the author but to individual works. Many writers (e.g., Melville) wrote both major and minor works. A major work takes its art to a high perfection and is usually innovative (Dante and Shakespeare would be the great examples here). More importantly, the theme of a major work must be universal and time-defying. "Of inexhaustible interest," said Pound.

Minor writers may have charm, a polished finish and a kind of eccentric attraction. Thomas Love Peacock, Colette, Simenon, Michael Gilbert — fine fellows and impeccable stylists, but when compared to Tolstoy, Cervantes, Balzac or Proust, *minor.* I would place Poe and Borges among the minors, splendid as they are. They are narrow. A Martian could not learn about human nature from either of them.

I am a minor writer because I deal in mere *frissons* and adventitious insights, and with things peripheral. Very few people are interested in what late Greek antiquity looked like to a traveller ("The Antiquities of Elis") or what aeroplanes looked like to Kafka.

*Do you say this because you usually write very short texts, and have never written a novel?*
I'm not a novelist. Paul Klee was not a muralist. My ambition is to write as little as possible, in the smallest possible space.

All my discrete paragraphing is to force the reader to *read.* Most narrative prose can be read by running one's eye down the page. If I've worked one hour on a sentence, I want the reader to pay attention to it. I *hope* there's a web of symbols and themes running through all the stories.

*Let us say that there are some readers who do not feel you are "minor" (although I heard Michael Hamburger say that "minor" writers are as important as "major" writers). Who would you see as a "major" writer working in a context close to yours?*

The major writers in whose shadows I grow my mushrooms are Osip Mandelstam, Donald Barthelme, Robert Walser and Walter Savage Landor.

---

The captain of the *Dixie Belle*, one foot on the dashboard, one hand holding a microphone and the other on the ship's wheel, was describing the flora and fauna we could see from the ship. Catherine announced that she had seen a snake diving into the river; Guy Davenport asked her how, two days only in Kentucky, she had managed to find Mountain Dew. He then drew our attention, as well as that of the people sitting near us, to groups of pearly everlasting mixed with celandine just above the water level.

---

*Your thesis was on Ezra Pound, and I suppose that you read classics and modern literature, so how come your first published works (correct me if I'm wrong) were illustrations? And did you study drawing? How do you now share your time between painting-drawing and writing?*
My first thesis, at Oxford, was on *Ulysses*, the second, on Pound, was at Harvard. I don't know whether my first publication was drawing or writing, or where the bibliography formally begins. When I was twelve I published a daily newspaper, hectographed, *The Franklin Street News* (Anderson, South Carolina). It concerned itself with visits, birthdays, the birth of kittens and puppies. In junior high school (grades seven and eight) I wrote and drew for the local city newspaper, and drew a series of sketches of old houses, with their histories.

I studied drawing and painting at Anderson College when I was in grammar school (private tuition; Clarence Brown, the biographer and translator of Osip Mandelstam, was also a pupil in these classes. A lifelong friend, he is now professor of comparative literature and Slavic languages at Princeton).

*You once told me that you never sent your work to publishers but waited for them to approach you. How did you publish your first book?*
My first book, *The Intelligence of Louis Agassiz*, was commissioned

120

by Beacon Press, Boston. *Tatlin!* was the manuscript I sent to
Scribner's when they asked for a book on eroticism in Greek
poetry. The only book I have sent off in search of a publisher was
*Da Vinci's Bicycle.* Scribner's turned it down, as *Tatlin!* had sold
so poorly (despite having more reviews than any book Scribner's
had published in a decade). While it was being looked at by Knopf
and Atheneum, Johns Hopkins accepted it, sight unseen, for their
Fiction and Poetry Series.

*Could we have a few details about your meetings with Pound
and Zukofsky?*
I met Pound in 1952, at St. Elizabeths Hospital for the Criminally
Insane, Washington. I was writing an article for the English Institute on Pound and Frobenius, and had written him asking about
certain details. He invited me to visit him. I did. I saw him regularly, once or twice a year, until his release. I visited him in Rapallo
in 1963 (as recounted in the story "Ithaka" in *Da Vinci's Bicycle*).

Louis and Celia Zukofsky came to Lexington for a week in 1964,
to participate in a seminar I was conducting. We corresponded
thereafter until his death.

*Did you also know Basil Bunting?*
Did not meet Bunting.

*What do you think of him as a poet? As an English poet (this be-
cause it seems to me that Bunting and David Jones — and Thom
Gunn, but I believe he's Americanized by now — are some of the
few poets of interest in Britain in the last forty years — but I'm no
specialist)?*
I admire Bunting, but am not certain what he's writing about.
David Jones is a very great poet. Thom Gunn is a fine poet. His
innovations come from tradition rather than nowhere.

---

The passengers' attention was drawn to a steel lattice bridge spanning the river ahead of the *Dixie Belle.* The loudspeakers announced
that it had recently been repainted and that the torn cloth hanging
from it had been placed there to avoid having the river polluted by
the paint. A tremendous noise was heard as we passed under and
all heads turned round on the other side; we saw a dozen Redskins

galloping hell for leather, the hooves of their horses hammering the planks of the bridge. "Black Fish, his braves and the renegade Simon Girty," announced the captain, "and now, yes, here they are . . . right on time . . ." A posse of uniformed horsemen appeared, a bugle called, a few shots were heard and one of the Shawnees flew off his mustang, to fall into the water after a fifty-yard drop.

---

*How important are constraints (if any) you might give yourself in your writing; I'm here referring specifically to a text such as "On Some Lines of Virgil" where the paragraphs appear to have a specific length? Have you been using constraints such as those which were created for poetry when writing prose (there is, in your writing, a density that comes close to poetry)?*

Constraints is not exactly the word. A style has its rules. I have used isometric paragraphs as a formal device exactly like the paragraph itself. Prose narrative has units (the chapter, areas of dialogue). Architecture may be behind much of this — "stanza" means "room." Each of my texts has its own architecture, as it has its own narrative rhythm.

By "constraint" you mean rules, order, formal devices. As in "O Gadgo Niglo," where there are no commas. Prose in blocks ("Apple and Pears," "Tombeau de Charles Fourier"). Decasyllabic dialogue in "We Often Think of Lenin . . . ," numbered and title sections.

*If not constraints in a formal sense, are there any constraints such as frame of mind, position, color of pencil, type of typewriter, direction you are facing, etc.?*

I have no superstitions about the act of writing.

*Could you develop the expression "necessary fiction," which you once used to describe your short stories; are you always aiming at reaching the tightest prose? (This description of your writing was told me by William S. Wilson.)*

"Necessary fiction" means merely that if I am writing about an historical figure (Vladimir Tatlin, Kafka, Walser, Pausanias, C. Musonius Rufus) I supply weather, rooms, samovars, Greek dust, Italian waiters and so on, not in the historical record but plausible. It does NOT mean that I give fictional accounts.

Prose: one writes, or is written. (Barthes's great subject: that our phrases exist so extensively that an author merely arranges them.}

I approach writing with the sense that my words must be chosen and arranged with care, as we live in a world of abused and meaningless words. I think it can be said that I write in order to use words in my way, for certain effects, rather than for any programmatic purpose (psychology, drama, politics, thematics).

What I write about is therefore all but gratuitous. I have enough sense of anecdote to make a narrative. But the narrative is the stage.

The prime use of words is for imagery: my writing is drawing.

Gerard Manley Hopkins said that if he could live long enough he could find a use in a poem for every word of English. *Good* writers can make words mean what they want them to. Henry James, for instance, works with the tones (and overtones) of ordinary words, controlling them with idioms. His style is completely colloquial, like Hawthorne's.

I couldn't write a novel: I'd use up all the words I would have for it by Chapter 3, and couldn't go on.

*You said you wrote two theses, one on* Ulysses, *one on Ezra Pound, but you did not mention Greek literature. When I introduced your writing to the readers of the first issue of* La Main de Singe, *I mentioned Herakleitos and the fact that you were more interested in pre- than post-Socratic writers; you translated Herakleitos and Diogenes, Sappho, Herondas and a few others, you are preparing a new edition of all your translations. What are these writers, philosophers to you, the time they lived; also Holland and Scandinavia, Charles Fourier and various other themes, like flying, for example, that keep cropping up in your writings? Or am I simply trying to say that, like in Borges's short story, after a life drawing mountains, horses, etc. the artist discovers he has only drawn his face?*

The Praesokratiker. I like the archaic, the dawn of things, before betrayals and downstream mud. Practically everything is hopeful at birth. The great enterprise of Confucius and Mencius was to discover and annotate a much earlier morality. I like Fourier, and the Dutch, and the Scandinavians because they are brave critics of civilization. Civilization can be lost in ten minutes, as in Germany.

Insofar as writing is essential to civilization, I am interested in how writing cooperates with other elements of civilization.

Talk about lugubrious and pompous!

*Bernard Hœpffner/Guy Davenport*

Self-portraits: Hugh Kenner once pointed out that my Walser is one. Butler = professor.

*What are the reasons behind your choosing a specific historical figure? Why Tatlin?*
I chose Tatlin because very little was known about him, and because he seemed to me to be the archetypical victim of authoritarianism. I could also use the parallel form in Russian writing for my form (Shklovsky, Mandelstam as models).

*Why Walser?*
Walser is a prose Tatlin.

––––––––

On the other side of the ship, a man with a pointed beard rose from his bench, took ten half-eagles from his pocket, stooped down and laid them, one by one, in a circle round him; the man he then addressed, sitting on the bench, looked very much like Maxime Gorki: "I can imagine the Red Square," he shouted from inside his circle, "in the capital: hundreds of steel dragonflies darting here and there, airships — the dream of my youth, and possibly resulting from my first studies, hovering above marching columns of workers. The sky is too small for these birds of steel. All this could not have happened before, and only today can our Party, our government, the laboring masses, every worker of our Soviet homeland harness themselves to man's most audacious idea, the conquest of the heights above the clouds."

"That was Constantin Tsiolkovsky, inventor of the rocket, who proclaimed that 'What is impossible today, will be possible tomorrow,'" said Bonnie Jean to Catherine when both men had gone down to the lower deck.

––––––––

*What are the links between your reading and your writing?*
My reading is, I suppose, my chief source of material. Practically every story has a textual ancestor, but never quite alone. "On Some Lines . . ." is from Montaigne (with my translating his Latin and Greek examples of sexuality into action) + Bordes + a visit to Bordeaux (two weeks) + Tati + a French sculpture of a legless boy

124

with dog in a Beckett wheelchair that I saw at the Musée de la Ville de Paris + inventions (the uncle in the wall) and so on.

*Another question would be about the use of the eye. Or the Anglo-Saxon attitude, clear in Darwin, in Doughty, Howells, Whitman, Bishop, Zukofsky, W. C. Williams, Davenport, Ronald Johnson and so many others, which implies detailed description of what is or was, letting the reader react in the way the writer did, or wants the reader to; attitude very different to the French, for example (I know the dangers of generalizing), who seem to have a preordained theory which they then apply. Induction and deduction in short. With the exception of a few writers like Fabre, the French do not seem to have produced many writers who can simply describe. What do you feel about my wooly ideas here?*

L'œil. This translates into imagery. Here I am guided by films and painters as well as texts. Max Ernst and Tchelitchev are constant guides. "O Gadgo Niglo" is a film by Bergman.

Joseph Cornell's boxes.

Balthus.

"Christ Preaching . . ." is a painting by Stanley Spencer made of a collage of elements: Dufy, Mallarmé *et d'autres choses*. (All the stories in *Eclogues* have a shepherd, and in this story He is invisible except in disguised outlines and Spencerian theology, though the story ends in a baptism.)

Fourier's imagery of the hordes and bands (already appropriated by Proust) I take to be some of the finest poetry in French writing of the nineteenth century. Also his verbal coinages. His psychology was vastly prophetic. I've had to add to his concerns Coubertin (play as sport: Fourier thought play would be absorbed into work) and the machine (he "invented" the steam locomotive, but had no notion of the airplane, nor did he incorporate the hot-air balloon).

The art of description in English owes much to Flaubert (via Joyce and Pound). Théophile Gautier, RIMBAUD. (Looking for phrases from Rimbaud in my prose would render a neat little harvest, for scholars with nothing better to do.)

There's a poem ("Mosella") of Ausonius's imbedded in "Wo es war . . ." translated into prose. A poem of Rimbaud's ditto in "On Some Lines." Also bits of Cocteau here and there.

None of this is to the point, as all art is worth only the spirit of the artist. There is, ultimately, no text, only the author (Bon jour, M. Derrida!). All four gospels are logically and even grammatically incoherent, but their spirit shines through with great brilliance. You have the advantage of the word *esprit*, which includes intelligence, wit and *spiritus*. We dropped the old English *ghost* (except in Holy Ghost), which, like *Geist*, might have served us. A work of art is alive. That's what *art* means. Inert matter (paint, words, stone) made kinetic.

No giver can know the value of the gift to the recipient. Hence the impossibility of the giver to assess, or comment on, the gift. The writer literally cannot *know* what he has written, just as no friend can know what his friendship means.

A reader *completes* a work of art. It is something "in between," a *medium*.

--------

The *Dixie Belle* landed the forty visitors at Pleasant Hill, every one of whom had a pink label hanging by a string from a shirt button, Please Help Us Preserve THE SHAKER VILLAGE OF PLEASANT HILL. And while walking up the path to the village Guy Davenport told us something he had seen during the last Fourth of July celebration in Lexington:

I was moved most by a horn player in one of the high-school bands, who had no horn, and was obviously a Down's syndrome person. He was keeping step admirably, and intently playing his imaginary horn. Tears came to my eyes, as I saw great metaphysical depths in it, and perhaps a metaphor for life itself as we now live it.

I *hope* the boy really thought he was playing in the band (I wonder if he goes to practice?) and that he was overcoming the dreadful handicap in some way that counterfeited reality for him. He may even be a student in high school, pretending he can read and do arithmetic (just like my students).

I then entertained a fantasy in which I, who can't sing or play a note, might be allowed to play an imaginary violin in a symphony orchestra. My writing may be precisely that.

# The Cardiff Team:
## Passages From a Longer Work
### Guy Davenport

1

IF IT HAPPENS that Nature, when we get up one morning and start our day, hands us exactly what we were of a mind to do, our praise comes readily, and the world looks like a meadow in the first week of creation, green, fresh and rich in flowers.

2

An afternoon, then, of a day with so auspicious a morning. Walt and Sam, both twelve, friends who looked like brothers, at the Brasserie Georges V, Place Alma. Neat summer haircuts, white *maillots*, faded denim André Agassi short pants, Adidas, thick white socks crunched around their ankles, sharing a Coca. Sam picked a blade of grass from Walt's collar, grinning, nudging a foot against Walt's under the table. Walt, smug and happy, picked a fleck of leaf trash from Sam's hair. Every boy his own grin.

The waiter, who knew them as regulars with incalculable dips and rises in their means, liked their identical hair, tufts of wheat stubble with a metallic gloss, their blue eyes and burnt umber lashes.

— This Cyril we're to be tutored with at Marc's, Sam said, is he real? Sooner or later the Vincennes police will check us out, if only to run our style of sunbathing through French logic. The old gentleman walking his fat dog was on the verge of a fit, either out of curiosity or love. I'm still happy, sweet throbs and twinges.

— You're talented that way, friend Sam. Patience. The waiter is trying to figure out all over again if we're rich brats or innocents with parents in tow somewhere around the corner. He calls us *messieurs*. I like the Vincennes *bois*. Real people there. This Cyril *is* a rich brat. Daisy met his papa at some kind of do, and signalled Mama, all in about two minutes. Think of it as fun.

— I'm thinking of other things.

So they overtipped the waiter and raced each other to the

127

apartment, with time out to admire the compliant fit of a motor-cycle courier's jeans, an Alsatian on a coal barge, a concierge's tortoiseshell cat, an *agent de police* as young and handsome as Marc. Sam's Agassis followed Walt's into a chair, as a gesture toward order. Adidas, socks, *maillots* and underpants could be picked up later by whoever still had a functioning mind.

LES GALLES

Penny and Marc at their long table, afternoon sun on stacks of books, manuscript, coffee cups.

— It's the Welsh, Penny said, he's made the painting's title, *les galles*, the Gauls from across the Sleeve. I think of the Welsh as elves singing Baptist hymns in a language as old as Latin, perhaps older. Football had come into the world, and the provincial Welsh, who hadn't been to France since Agincourt, the ones in Shakespeare, had lively rugby and soccer teams that could play in Sweden or France. Social standing has no voice in sports, or family or class. Neither is language of any matter, or religion. They got all that straight at the first Olympics, when British upper-class cyclists refused to compete with grocers' sons. Baron Coubertin put a flea in their ear. The body came into its own in a wonderful way. So here's a team of coal miners' sons playing football with the French rich, poor and middle class together. Their team's jerseys make them brothers in an equality hitherto unknown in the world.

— The mice who have just let themselves in down the hall, Marc said, are, reading from left to right, Walt and Sam, one assumes, back from scandalizing the good citizens in Vincennes or Neuilly.

— With those two one assumes nothing. Just yesterday I called Walt and got Sam. So one of the things Delaunay is painting is a new kind of equality, fraternity and decidedly liberty. Look at a kid like Calixte Delmas, whose body freed him from Lord knows what humdrum round. From ploughboy to minor divinity.

— Rousseau beat Delaunay to it, though his *footballeurs* are simply bowlers and card-players trying a new game.

— Rousseau beat everybody to everything.

LOG

*The Cardiff Team* of Robert Delaunay, begun in 1912 and finished in 1913, is a response to his friend Henri Rousseau's *The Football Players*, 1908. Delaunay's painting is resonant with a dialogue of allusions, an antiphony. Wales against England in an *agon* of Rugby football. American technology in steel (the Ferris wheel) against French technology in steel (the Eiffel Tower). Voisin's airplane (piloted by Henri Farman) flying in a completed circle of 771 metres vying with the Brothers Wright, who had flown at Le Mans in a figure eight when Blériot could only wobble in a straight forwardness. The radio telegraph at the top of the tower is in communication with Canada.

6

Cyril consulted with the chauffeur who was waiting for him and who would not hear of his walking to the Brasserie Georges V with Walt and Sam, but would drive them there in the Rolls. He let them down on the Marceau, no hope of a parking space.

— He could have delivered us right to the curb, in front, Sam said. A taxi would have, for the edification of the waiter.

— This, Walt explained, is one of our places after an explore.

— Walt and I do long rambles, Sam said, to be together and find places and streets and whichwhat. We call them explores. Marc sometimes comes along. He's neat that way.

Cyril, as Sam remarked later, had never been among the people before, certainly not with two advanced scamps.

— Three young gentlemen today, the waiter said, and what is your pleasure, *messieurs*?

— I don't have any money, Cyril whispered miserably.

— On us, Walt said. Three *picons*.

— Three cocas! Three!

French insolence. Cyril looked appalled. Sam gave the waiter the finger to his back.

— Do you even *like* us? Sam asked, twirling a finger at Cyril. My mama, Daisy, paints these big long canvases, we'll take you and show you, with lots of figures and things, like a poster, they take months and months to do. Very realistic: she says abstractions are mud pies. Don't ever mention Francis Bacon. She takes his pictures to be a personal insult. I mean, we're stuck with each other at Marc's. Walt and I have been stuck together since we were nippers, so I know everything about him.

— Except what he's thinking and imagining, Walt said.

— Yes, but you tell me, and, besides, I know anyway.

— What Sam is grubbing for, Walt said, is how different Cyril is from us. We don't have any fathers and he doesn't, he says, at the moment have a mama. He lives out near the Bagatelle, and we

129

*Robert Delaunay*, The Cardiff Team, *1912–1913.*
*Musée d'Art Moderne de la Ville de Paris.*

live *centre ville*. We, I think, have more liberty and equality, which leaves fraternity, which is what we're going for.

— Say you like us, Sam said.

— Yes, Cyril said.

— Add *so far*, Walt said. Liking somebody is really liking what they like, to share. Sam and I don't know a lot of kids, as we're different, in our way, and scare people off.

Cyril looked troubled.

— Marc says we're not to scare you off, but make friends.

— Whales, Sam said, is what busses are, of two plunging toward the bridge.

Walt tilted his chair back, shoved his hands into his pockets, and beamed.

— Let's make friends, he said. Sniff each other like good dogs. You're Cyril. We're Walt and Sam. Marc is finishing us before *les vacances*. Stuffing us with culture.

— Babysitting us, Sam said.

— Marc is Maman's assistant sort of, and Sam's mother is mine's best friend. Maman's other best friend I suppose you could say Marc is.

— What do they do, Cyril asked, Monsieur Bordeaux and your mother?

— Well, Sam said, answering for Walt, whose mouth was full, they read books together and make notes and discuss things. Last week, for instance, they were reading Spengler paragraph by paragraph, and talking about it and making notes. Something about epoch and style. They sit very close. Penny sticks her fingers in Marc's hair and he kisses the back of her neck. Marc types things up for her, and fetches books, and looks things up in libraries. Toward the end of the afternoon they fuck. If they make a baby, Walt and I are going to change its diapers, salt it with talcum and take it on our explores.

— What is Spengler? Cyril asked.

— A totally bald German who wrote a big book about how everything has a style.

Walt with a minim of eyeshift gave Sam the long boy at the *cabine téléphone* on the corner whose only garment was flimsy kneepants so low on his hips his wallet hung on its fold in back dragged them down to his butt. Tummy plank flat. Dirty bare feet.

— Noted, Sam nodded. Gauze pyjama bottoms and no underpants. Catch the dumb girl from Atlanta on the terrace, ordering whiskey.

— It's our anthropology, Walt said to Cyril. Sometimes we inter-
act with subject, but mainly we just watch and swap comments,
though we usually know what the other's thinking. Yesterday we
walked a three-piece suit and bowler against a lamppost by kissing
and grabbing each other by the crotch.

Cyril's nubble nose twitched, his big gray eyes became as round
as francs and his mouth squeezed into a wopsided smile.

— Why? he asked.

— To get even. A three-piece suit and bowler konked by a lamppost is a score.

— I meant, Cyril said, swallowing hard, grabbing.

— Oh we're always doing that. Keeps us happy.

— Actually, Sam said, we're reasonably civilized, being groomed
to take our place, as Maman says, in the aristocracy of adolescence
that has ruled France since the Third Republic. So, along with
Marc's seminar for twelve-year-old geniuses, which, who knows,
may someday be as famous as Alexandre Kojève's, we're into urban
anthropology, anarchy and sex.

— Sex, Cyril said, looking into his empty glass. I'll be twelve in a
month and two days.

— Your keeper, Walt said, is looking meaningfully this way. Look,
tell him we're going on an explore. Better still, send him home.

Cyril took a deep breath, looked grim and said he'd try.

— Golly, Sam said. Stuck with a nursemaid whose perambulator
is a Rolls. They seem to be making a deal. What Cyril wants to do
is trade off free time with us for whatever the chauffeur wants to
sneak into his day, belote at the bistro, an afternoon fuck or fishing
from the quais.

— If Cyril has any rascal in him, which we're doubting.

— He has. Monsieur le Chauffeur is furious.

The Rolls would follow them at a discreet distance. They were
to stay in sight of it.

— That's what he thinks, Sam said.

— He said he'd lose his job.

On the explore, which began with crossing the Pont d'Alma,
Cyril learned that Sam's mother is a painter and that Walt's writes
about painting and philosophy and whichwhat, that sex is a kind
of secret game and lots of fun, that Walt's mama, with Marc as her
research assistant, is writing a study of Robert Delaunay's *The
Cardiff Team*, that iconography is the study of things in paintings,
that Robert Delaunay was a painter scads of years ago, that Sam's

mother had a neat friend named Christofer, a Norwegian who doesn't speak French too good but is seven feet tall, is hung like a horse and is handsome, that they all had the use of a house in the country, on weekends, where you run naked in the orchard, that if you go to the Grande Jatte Island it's all built over with houses and not at all like Seurat's painting, that all Russians are hysterical, that Penny and Daisy had been to Denmark to see all of the paintings there of one Vilhelm Hammershøj, that Walt and Sam sleep together at his place when Christofer is spending the night at Daisy's, as Christofer is a Lutheran and shy, that Sam and Walt had read almost all of Jules Verne, that Penny was reading them a neat book called *King Matt the First* as a bedtime book, that flowers and trees and weeds have names which Sam and Walt knew and he didn't, that somebody named Lévi-Strauss had left licorice out of a list of aromas and that somebody named Fourier hadn't, that the ancient Greeks loved boys and girls, that Penny, Daisy and Marc owned no automobile nor television set; that Sam and his mother live in a studio on the Boulevard Berthier; that Germany is an entire nation of white trash; that both Sam and Walt are bastards; that there is a film and recording of the poet Apollinaire; that for reasons grinned at but not explained, Sam and Walt have been to one school or another, never for long, and have mainly been taught by their mothers, with occasional tutors like Marc; that there was once a woman tutor who quit in high dudgeon after a week; that Sam and Walt seemed to have endless conversations with their mothers and that he was a very lonely little boy.

Sam and Walt learned far more than Cyril was aware of telling them.

KRZYZANOWSKI
— The Eiffel Tower, Penny read, a quadruped giant who held his steel head high above the traffic, chatter and music of Paris, high enough, you understand, to put up with the noises of the crowd below, the busy streets, the bang and clamor, the shouts. And it was these crazy people milling about his feet who had installed in his head that rose into the clouds the radio station that received signals from all over the world. And if someone named Walter thinks I didn't see him sneak off his pyjama pants and stuff them under the bolster before he got into bed he has porridge for brains.
— Interpol should be staffed with nothing but mothers, Walt said. All the crooks would be caught within minutes.

— Vibrations from space having chimed in his brain that bristled so high in the air, they then flowed down his interlaced muscles of steel, and sank through his feet into the ground. The tower shook itself, shifting from foot to foot. It heaved, pulled its toes from the earth and quivered from top to bottom.

— Who wrote this? Sam asked. My pyjama bottoms are on, though somebody has his hand inside of them.

— Sigismund Dominikovitch Krzyzanowski. It was, all this, just at dawn, when everybody was still asleep under the shelter of their roofs, when the Place des Invalides, the Champs de Mars, the streets roundabout, and the quays, are empty and quiet. The three-hundred-meter-tall giant wiggled the numb and cold out of his ponderous feet, and, hammering flat the steel curve of a bridge and twisting awry the stone steps of the Trocadero, took the rue d'Iena toward the Bois de Boulogne.

— King Kong! Walt said. Godzilla.

— But this was written in, let's see, 1927. Feeling hemmed in by streets, bumping against buildings, the Eiffel Tower kicked sleeping apartment houses out of his way. They collapsed like cardboard boxes. Less frightened than embarrassed by his clumsiness, for the houses were joined to each other, and when one went down, others followed, he stomped along, crunch crunch. Meanwhile, Paris awoke: searchlights pierced the morning fog, fire sirens honked and buzzing airplanes rose into the air. Whereupon, the Tower raised his elephant's feet and began to make haste over roofs, which crashed down with every step. He has reached the edge of the Bois, cutting a swath through it with his steel knees.

— Ha ha! Walt said, getting his nose pinched by Sam.

— The day began bright and sunny. Three million Parisians awoke to the noise, and panicked. They fled to the train stations. Newspaper presses began to roll, with enormous headlines about the wandering Tower, and telephones passed on the catastrophe. In full daylight Parisians could see the empty space where, every morning before, they had, by habit, looked at the Tower. Witnesses reported seeing the giant wading the Seine, others saw it jumping over Montmartre, but with the clearing of the morning fog, most of these rumors proved false. Three million irate citizens were in despair, enraged, flinging accusations and demanding the return of the fugitive tower. American tourists in the hotels around the Place Monceau ran out with their Kodaks and photographed the mammoth footprints, the dead and the ruins. A poet (on foot for economy's sake) who had walked from Saint-Celestin, nibbled his pencil at the edge of an enormous footprint, and with a pensive air began a moralizing poem about it all.

— Is this for real? Sam asked.

— The poet was in a quandary as to whether the subject called for alexandrines or the meanderings of free verse. And the Tower, quivering to keep its balance, stomped ever onward. It sank into soft earth at every step, and if it knew very well where it had come from, it had only the vaguest idea where it was going. Chance took it to the northwest, toward the coast. It wanted to find a road, and what then? Suddenly it ran into a semi-circle of artillery, which it smashed, and turned north. It was stopped by the ramparts of Anvers, with cannon. Shells bounced against the tower. Blindly, its joints loosened, it fled to the southeast, and longed to return to the place where it had been put by its creators. But then it heard, almost as a whisper, in its radio brain: *Along this way!*

— That's neat, Walt said. The radio station on top is its brain.

— You and I, O Reader, know whence the message came.

— We do? Sam asked.

— This is a Russian story, Penny said. Now the Tower knew where to go. It headed east. He had liberated himself; he would join others who had done the same. Agitated telegraph wires clicked from capital to capital: The enraged monster has become a Bolshevik! Stop him! Infamy! Spare no effort! We must join forces! Again the path of the fleeing Tower is blocked by artillery. Again, in a barrage of steel against steel, the colossal quadruped sings in its metallic voice a savage and terrible song. Wounded, riddled with shell bursts, its bristling head trembling, he stalks on, nearer and nearer to the summons from the Revolution. Already he imagines he can see red flags like poppies in a vast prairie, thick columns of people rank upon rank. He imagines a loud square enclosed by an ancient crenellated wall. That is where he will place his iron *sabots*. Kicked aside, armies retreat and open his way. The diplomats think furiously in storms of thought: He has escaped, has slipped through our lines. We must take extraordinary measures, but what can we do? Shall I stop here?

— Don't you dare! Sam said.

— So it was that the metal giant's pursuers, half crushed by his feet of steel, moved their battles into the air. The antennae of Paris, New York, Berlin, Chicago, London, Rome found the frequency, often a mere whisper: *This way! This way!* They made

135

promises, sang and seduced, jamming the transmissions from the east. The monster became confused. It lost its way. It began to move south, and then staggered about like a blind man. The radio signals were a whirlwind of noise, driving him crazy and depleting his strength. There was rejoicing in the capitals, hands clapped with joy. Villages and towns between the wandering Tower and Paris were evacuated. Around the church of the Invalides and the Champ de Mars preparations were made for the Tower's return, defeated and chastened, but with a ceremonial welcome. But on its way back, where three frontiers meet, it came to a sheet of water squeezed between mountain peaks: the serene and deep Lake Constance. Passing around it, the vanquished giant saw in its blue mirror his own reflection upside down and strewn with flecks of sunlight, extending from the shore to the middle of the lake, its tip sunk into the depths. A shiver of sonorous disgust shook the Tower — in a final paroxysm of rage, as if breaking invisible bonds, it raises its ponderous feet, rears up and from the high alpine terraces (just imagine!), plunges in head first. Behind it crashed an avalanche of loosened rock and broken boulders, and then, from one mountain pass to another, the echo of sundered water splashing over all of the lake shore. The steel feet of the suicide, after a dying spasm, fixed in the rigor of death.

— That's it? Walt asked.

— Well, it's a story inside another story. The writer is reading it to fellow authors, one of whom objects that Lake Constance is ninety kilometers long and would scarcely overflow because three hundred meters of open-work steel fell into it; and another points out that towers do not customarily walk anywhere.

Sam looked at Walt, Walt at Sam.

L'EQUIPE DE CARDIFF

Sam, Walt, Cyril in the Museum of Modern Art of the City of Paris.

— This is it, Walt said. The box-kite aeroplane is Henri Farman's, pioneer aviator. We can show you his grave in Chaillot, with a bas relief of him piloting his stick-and-canvas flying machine, a Voisin pusher biplane. He invented ailerons. The Wright brothers had to twist their wings by pulling on a cord. He and his brother Maurice manufactured aircraft and had the first airline between London and Paris. The English poet who wrote *A Shropshire Lad*, Alfred Housman, who was a professor of Greek at Cambridge, used to

grade his students' *bachots* at the end of term and take the Farman
Goliath for Paris, as he liked taxi drivers, which he couldn't do in
England, as they're Protestants.
— Why did he like taxi drivers? Cyril asked.
— The big red wheel is *la grande roue de Ferris*, the American
engineer. You ride on it in seats, which roll you up and over,
over and down, making your insides turn upsidedown sideways.
The three billboards: The one on the left is a word ending in AL,
and Penny hasn't found out yet what it is, and ASTRA is a company that made aeroplanes, and then DELAUNAY, which is both
Robert's signature and Sonia's too, as she illustrated a book by
Blaise Cendrars, who had one arm, and wrote a poem about
New York. He traveled all over, Siberia and Panama, and caught
monkeys and parrots for zoos. And then the football players. Penny
is working on their pants and jerseys, socks and shoes, their evolu-
tion of design. Everything in the painting had just come into the
world.

13
In front of the Champ de Mars, the Eiffel Tower, placed upon
its four iron pillars, forms the Arch of Triumph of Science and
Industry.
   Its aspect, now that it is finished to its definite height, can be
judged of and appreciated. Its early detractors are mute, and the
approbation of engineers and artists is unanimous. When regarded
from a distance, the three-hundred-meter tower appears graceful,
slender and light. It rises toward the heavens like a delicate lattice-
work of wires, and, as a whole, it is all full of poesy. When it is
approached, the structure becomes monumental, and when the
base of the colossus is reached, the spectator gazes with admiration and meditation at this enormous mass, assembled with mathe-
matical precision, and forming one of the boldest works that the
art of the engineer has ever dared to undertake. This surprise in-
creases when he ascends the staircase of the tower. Before reaching
the first story, he traverses forests of iron uprights, which offer
fantastic entanglements; then, in measure as he ascends, he is
astonished at once at the immensity of the structure, its apparent
lightness and the splendor of the panorama that it permits of con-
templating. Apart from the undoubted interest that attaches to
the Eiffel Tower, as much from the standpoint of its metallic structure as from that of its height, we can now no longer deny that the

gigantic work is absolutely beautiful.

Sunday, March 31, 1889, while descending the tower stairs after the ceremony of placing the flag upon the summit, we had the pleasure of hearing one of our most distinguished members of the Academy of Science exclaim that this iron monument was certainly the most astonishing production of our age. It is for our epoch, he said to us, what the great pyramid, which interprets the efforts of an entire people, was for the ancient world. All the resources of contemporary art have had to concur in its execution. The work that M. Eiffel will have had the glory of carrying out is, in fact, the expression of the applied science of our time.

VERBASCUM THAPSUS LINNAEUS

Champs de Mars, promenade with benches, flower beds by Caillebotte, sky by Rousseau, with *montgolfier* and vapor trails.

— Like this, Walt said, standing toe to toe with Sam. Friendly space, see, and how friendly can you be? I lean in, and Sam leans in, not touching, not yet, knees as close as can be, front of our pants, chin, nose. Fingertips together. It worries people a lot.

— Can three do it? Cyril asked.

— In a bit. We have to be looking deep into each other's eyes, like now, before we start wandering hands. That has to be real sneaky.

— Pretend you're not with us, Sam said. Sit on the bench there and think about algebra or something.

— You look like you're daring each other to fight.

— It's foreplay, sort of, Walt said.

————

THE FIELD PATH: HEDGEROW WITH FINCHES

Owls are the moths of birds.

Cobwebs and rabbit by Rimbaud. Ladybird on hawthorn leaf. A startled bird the flight of an arrow from the bow of Eros, and is there another pun in Heraclite: the bow is both life and death: The bow is sometimes that of Eros, that of Ares? Eros and the curve of time.

*Watch the knowing owl with open wings*
*Who has flown from Athena's shoulder*
*On Olympos, and lights in this tree.*

The swan's grace he lacks, but his quick
Yellow eye can read the book of the dark,
Can read the deep of the night's silence.
Nietzsche: The superfluous is the enemy of the necessary.

THE GREAT WHEEL AT CHICAGO

The wonderful *merry-go-round* designed by Engineer George W. G.
Ferris, of Pittsburgh, Pa., is now completed and forms a most
remarkable and attractive object. This curious piece of mechanism
carries thirty-six pendulum cars, each seating forty passengers;
thus one revolution of the wheel carries 1,440 people to a height
of two hundred and fifty feet in the air, giving to each passenger
a magnificent view and a sensation of elevation akin to that of
a balloon ascent. The practical working of the great machine is
attended with perfect success, and its construction and operation
reflect the highest credit on the author.

The description of the construction of the great wheel given in
the Chicago *Tribune* will be of interest: The wheel is composed of
two wheels of the same size, connected and held together with
rods and struts, which, however, do not approach closer than
twenty feet to the periphery. Each wheel has for its outline a
curved, hollow, square iron beam, 25½ by 19 inches. At a distance
of forty feet within this circle is another circle of a lighter beam.
These beams are called crowns, and are connected and held together by an elaborate trusswork. Within this smaller circle there
are no beams, and at a distance there appears to be nothing.

But at the center of the great wheel is an immense iron axle,
thirty-two inches thick and forty-five feet in length. Each of the
twin wheels, where the axle passes through it, is provided with a
large iron hub, sixteen feet in diameter. Between these hubs and
the inner crowns there are no connections except spoke rods, 2½
inches in diameter, arranged in pairs, thirteen feet apart at the
crown connection. At a distance they look like mere spiderwebs,
and the wheel seems to be dangerously devoid of substantial
support.

The explanation of this is that the Ferris wheel — at least inside
the smaller crowns — is constituted on the principle of a bicycle
wheel. The lower half is suspended from the axle by the spoke
rods running downward, and the upper half of the wheel is supported by the lower half. All the spoke rods running from the axle
north, when it is in any given position, might be removed, and the

wheel would be as solid as it would be with them. The only difference is that the Ferris wheel hangs by its axle, while a bicycle wheel rests on the ground, and the weight is applied downward on the axle.

The thirty-six carriages of the great wheel are hung on its periphery at equal intervals. Each car is twenty-seven feet long, thirteen feet wide and nine feet high. It has a heavy frame of iron, but is covered externally with wood. It has a door and five broad plate-glass windows on each side. It contains forty revolving chairs, made of wire and screwed to the floor. It weighs thirteen tons, and with its forty passengers will weigh three tons more. It is suspended from the periphery of the wheel by an iron axle 6½ inches in diameter, which runs through the roof. It is provided with a conductor to open the doors, preserve order and give information. To avoid accidents from panics and to prevent insane people from jumping out, the windows will be covered with an iron grating.

It is being considered whether each car shall not have a telephone connection with the office on the ground. It is thought that this would be an attraction, both as a sort of amusement for people who wish to converse with their friends below or in another car and as a sort of reassurance to timid people. The thought of being detained up in the clouds, as it were, by accident, and not being able to learn what it is or when it will be remedied, might frighten some timid people out of making the trip. It is not very difficult, however, to climb by the wheel itself to any car, and there will always be men on the ground who can do this.

The wheel, with its cars and passengers, weighs about twelve hundred tons, and therefore needs something substantial to hold it up. Its axis is supported, therefore, on two skeleton iron towers, pyramidal in form, one at each end of it. They are forty by fifty feet at the bottom and six feet square at the top, and about 140 feet high, the side next to the wheel being perpendicular, and the other sides slanting. Each tower has four great feet, and each foot rests on an underground concrete foundation twenty by twenty by twenty feet. Crossbars of steel are laid at the bottom of the concrete, and the feet of the tower are connected with and bolted to them with iron rods.

One would naturally suppose that there would be great danger of making such a huge wheel as this lopsided or untrue, so that it would not revolve uniformly. Even if the wheel itself were perfectly true, it would seem that the unequal distribution of passengers might make it eccentric in its speed. But according to L.V. Rice, the superintendent of construction, there is absolutely no danger of this kind. Not only did the wheel alone turn uniformly, but when the cars were hung, one after another, no inequality was observed. As to passengers, Mr. Rice says that the fourteen hundred passengers will have no more effect on the movement of the speed than if they were so many flies.

The wheel, however, is never left to itself, but is always and directly and constantly controlled by a steam engine. The wheel points east and west, and the one-thousand-horsepower reversible engine which runs it is located under the east half of it and sunk four feet in the ground. The machinery is very similar to that used in the power houses of the cable-car companies, and runs with the same hoarse roar that they do. It operates a north-and-south iron shaft twelve inches in diameter, with great cog wheels at each end, by means of which the power is applied at each side of the wheel.

The periphery of both of the great outer crowns of the great wheel is cogged, the cogs being about six inches deep and about eighteen inches apart, and the power of the engine is applied at the bottom of the wheel. Underneath the wheel, in line with the crowns on each side, are two sprocket wheels nine feet in diameter, with their centers sixteen feet apart. They are connected by an immense endless driving chain, which plays on their own cogs and on the cogs of the great wheel as well. These sprocket wheels are operated by the engine at the will of the engineer, who can turn the wheel either way, and fast or slowly, as he may wish. The wheel is two hundred and fifty feet in diameter, eight hundred and twenty-five feet in circumference and thirty feet wide, and is elevated fifteen feet above the ground.

The great wheel is also provided with brakes. Near the north and south ends of the main shaft are two ten-feet wheels, with smooth faces, and girdled with steel bands. These bands terminate a little to one side in a large Westinghouse air brake. If therefore anything should break, and the engine fail to work, the air can be turned into the air brake, and the steel band tightened until not a wheel in the whole machine can turn. In the construction of this great wheel every conceivable danger has been calculated and provided for. Windage was a matter of the greatest importance, for, although the wheel itself is all open work, the cars present an immense resisting surface. But Mr. Rice points to the two towers, with their bases fifty feet north and south of the wheel, and bolted into twenty feet of concrete, and says that a gale of a hundred miles an hour would have no effect. He says that all the frost and snow that should adhere to the wheel in winter would not affect it; and that if struck by lightning it would absorb and dissipate the thunderbolt so that it would not be felt.

It is arranged to empty and refill six cars with passengers at a time, so that there will be stops in every revolution. Accordingly, six railed platforms, of varying heights, have been provided on the north side of the wheel, and six more, corresponding with these, on the south side of it. When the wheel stops, each of the six lowest cars will have a platform at each of its doors. Then the next six cars will be served the same way, and the next and the next all day, and perhaps all night. It is expected that the wheel will revolve once only in every twenty minutes. Passengers will remain on board during two revolutions and pay fifty cents for their fun.

The Ferris Wheel Company was capitalized at $600,000, and $300,000 worth of bonds were issued and sold. The final concession for the erection of the wheel was not granted until December, and all the work has been contracted for and done since then, the iron having been in the pig in January, while the scaffolding was not begun until March 20. By the terms of the concession, the company pays to the Exposition one-half of all its receipts after they have amounted to the cost of the wheel. On the day the wheel was first started, June 21, 1893, five thousand guests were present at the inaugural ceremonies, all of whom were given a ride on the great wheel. The motion of the machinery is said to have been almost imperceptible.

---

22

The rain had set in as steady and continuous as time itself well before Marc walked Walt home at seven in the morning.

— The god Eros is wet to the knackers, Marc said to Penny, who was in slacks and sweater and sipping coffee, as he kept skipping and darting from under the umbrella. I'm only soaked from the knees south.

— Off everything, this minute, she said to Walt with a kiss, and to Marc with a hug and kiss, shoes and jeans. I've the most marvellous night's sleep, down at the bottom of the unconscious, and am, I hope, the more rested of us three. There are croissants, the fig jam Daisy paid so much for and country butter.

She put a finger to a cheek to admire and smile at Marc in sweater and briefs.

— Lines for Massaccio, a Tuscan youth in jerkin and codpiece.

Walt, towelling his hair and sneezing, appeared in a plaid dressing gown.

— Memo, Penny said in her business voice, a change of Marc's clothes for here, and jammies and togs, and a toothbrush, for Walt at Marc's.

Marc stared before he grinned.

— And don't emit aspersions about women. I know my son. He's radiantly happy.

— What about me?

— You look a bit as Walt would look if he were not the exemplar in our time of innocence and candor.

— I *am*? Walt said, buttering a farl of croissant and filling his mouth.

— If we talk while chewing we sound like a German tourist.

— God knows what he is, Penny. Some elemental force that Greeks and Romans tamed before they dared to start in on the groundwork of civilization.

— Has he bewitched you? It's the eyes. *I'm* going to the Delaunay.

— With me and Sam, I hope, and Marc. Is Daisy coming too?

— The whole gang is welcome, but going I am, and elemental forces can behave themselves.

Walt, guddling inside his bathrobe, wiping fig jam from his lips, went to the phone in the hall, where they heard the bird cheep of kissing sounds, a conspirator's chuckle, various phrases in argot which they took on faith to be salacious, and *sure, right now*. He returned with volume two of the Praeger Encyclopedia of Art, saying Delaunay, Delaunay.

— *The Cardiff Team*, Penny was saying, and Rousseau's football players, what do you think? Sonia's circles, the whole Russian dimension.

---

31

Walt had brought out two blankets, for sunbathing.

— That tractor you can just hear, he said, is as close as anybody is, so we can lie in the sun like Danes in their backyards, New Caledonians. You can't see through the hedge without sticking your head through, which a boy all frecklcs did once when Marc and I were out here.

— Seeing a beautiful little boy and a beautiful big boy either soaking up sunshine or doing things he's still thinking about.

— I'm not a little boy, am I, and Marc's grown all the way up, isn't he?

— He's a big boy.

— I may have been petting my mouse, to make him feel loved. Marc likes being my big brother, you know?

— Daisy thinks it's wonderful, what I've told her of it. Walt, sweetheart, as long as we're having an orgy of country life, frolicking in Arcadia, what I'd like is another coffee and the merest sip of the armagnac that's in the cupboard. And a pillow. One at a time, and you won't have to leave off throttling your mouse. Where do I spread the blankets? Here?

— Be right back, mouse and I, coffee first. One sugar, right?

Walt returned, walking on eggs, coffee in one hand, brandy in the other, pillow balanced on his head.

— Sam will be jealous when I tell him I got to bring you three things at once. The waiter at the Balzac could bring six more coffees and a platter of ham and cheese.

— All this sweet quiet is doing things to me, Penny said. The age of this orchard is not like the age of buildings and streets in cities. The old pear tree, there, knows that it exists, whereas the Tour Eiffel doesn't. It must have some exhilaration in its blossoms and leaves and pears. It likes rain and sunshine, and draws into itself away from frost and sharp winds. The Romans brought them here, along with apples, and the Romans got them from the Greeks. They come from the very old civilizations in Persia, and maybe from as far away as China.

— I'll put that in the notebook later.

— You brought it?

— Goes with me everywhere. Sam writes in it, too. Sam *hears* things that I let get by. And then there are things you don't see the importance of until days later. I can be real dumb. Aren't you going to take everything off?

— If you think the locals won't fall through the hedge and hurt themselves. I'm having what I call my long memories, a Proustian kind of return to an experience that Spinoza called a third kind of

144

knowing. Marc was fascinated when I explained it to him.

— Spinoza, Walt said. Somebody way back.

— A philosopher, Dutch, from a Jewish family, seventeenth century. Marc can tell you more than you want to know about him. He wrote a lot about how we know and feel the world and ourselves. He hated messy thinking and messy feelings. But he allowed for imagination and intuition as a way of knowing. We have experiences about experiences long past, memories that return all by themselves. When you were fetching my pillow and brandy and coffee, I suddenly remembered nursing you, and the sensual delight of your earnest, oh so greedy sucking, watching me out of the side of your eyes. It was then that I came all over silly and began to relive being a girl of ten with my doll. It was wonderfully sexual, this feeling, and I was all at once ten and a mother with a real warm smiling feeding baby. Am I making any sense? It's poetical, spontaneous, not to be talked about with any clarity. All the love-making that went into your conception melted into the hideous pain of your birth, and it all became the one complex pleasure, of which you were the existential reassurance. The wholeness of experience is a secret until such moments. Of course it may all have been your happiness at the teat spilling over into me. I remember thinking: I must keep this moment. I'll need it later on.

— I was your doll, Walt said. I looked at you out of the side of my eyes, like this?

— Yes, but you were much wiser. Babies are. They know everything.

— And then I forgot it all. Are there more of these Spinoza's minutes? Maybe I'll have one.

— Oh yes. When you first dressed Bee in your clothes and invented Sam, it made me remember when I envied boys their clothes. These intuitive waking dreams have something to do with the sources of art, as mine have the visionary intensity of Redon or Palmer or Burchfield. Marc says they're mystical. I don't think so. The mystical is mush. My intuitive moments are a reward for having paid attention in the first place.

— Bee invented Sam. Maybe I did. We invented Sam together.

— Your mouse looks happy, and is considerably bigger than any mouse I've ever seen. A young cucumber, more like.

— A parsnip beside Marc's. Cyril's is an asparagus stalk.

— Daisy likes to remember when you and Bee first saw each other

145

naked, on the beach in Denmark, brown as ginger cookies, with wondering eyes but sneakily cool, wrecked between polite indifference and raging curiosity.

— This orchard is magic, you know? I've lived under that bush over there for a thousand years.

— The hydrangea.

— Yes, and I come here from Paris at night, in about five seconds. That moss on the roof, with the mustard in with the green, I like to hover just above it. I sink through the roof and the bedrooms to the kitchen, which is cold and dark except for moonlight on the hearth and table. But the best part is flying back, over the train tracks, and be snug and warm in bed. Night air is chilly and damp.

32

Walt, having cubed a bite of melon, fed it to Bee, while chewing a bite of melon she'd just fed him.

— Cyril would like to see this, Marc said. Our outing in Saint-Germain was a sort of dream for him, poor little fellow.

— He's one strange kid, I'm here to tell you.

— Let me get some of it straight, Penny said. You dressed him in Walt's clothes that he keeps at Marc's.

— All except underpants, the which he was wearing a pair of that come way up to here, and practically had legs to them.

— And you went by train, conspuing the chauffeur, and did the museum.

— Where, Marc said, Walt and Sam kept their hands on each other's butts most of the time, showing off for Cyril, and eliciting great interest from a young German who hadn't bathed in some weeks.

— And had lunch in the English garden place, and walked in the forest.

— Where, Walt said, Jean-Jacques Rousseau used to muck about, giving Marc his cue to lecture us on him, and we had to distract Cyril while Sam had a pee.

— And had a wonderful time, Marc and his three young friends, and got home in good time to change Cyril back into his wholly inappropriate suit and deliver him to this chauffeur keeper. And here you are. I got some very forward work done on *L'Equipe Cardiff,* and Daisy and I had tea, before big Christofer turned up, looking more Norwegian than ever. He'd been playing football with some Dutch and Danes and smelled like a horse. So I suggested

146

that Bee do bed and breakfast here. Did I do right?
— Absolutely, Bee said.
— Me, too? Marc asked.
— O wow! Walt said. I love days like this. A great explore, and then all the beds full overnight. Cyril's probably in his nightgown, and the chauffeur is taking his temperature to see if he's running a fever from walking miles in a forest and a drafty museum with big handsome Marc and two nifty nasty boys.
— I wonder, Penny said, putting out cognac. His mother has simply left, perfectly understandable if you've met Ducasse, who seems to have been born and raised in a bank. But however desperately unhappy I was, I couldn't leave Walt. There must be some species of housekeeper, or maybe there's a new mother in the wings.
— All Cyril needs, Marc said, is a stepmother. I got him to hold hands when crossing the street, and he put his arm over my shoulder when Sam and Walt were seducing each other in public to cheek some rather sullen and unhappy Americans. But he loosened up as the afternoon went on. Walt climbed me, of course, and rode for awhile on my shoulders, and then Sam, but not Cyril.
Walt sniffed Penny's brandy. Bee, Marc's.
— We're in for mischief, Penny said. I know the signs.
— Stay where you are, Bee said. We'll be back.
A whispered consultation.
— No need to go offstage, Walt said. We've got it. Madame et Monsieur, a mime by Walt and Sam.
Sam stood at attention. Walt, as if seeing her for the first time, swinging one leg up and around, and the other, turning as he walked, circled Sam and stopped, taking a stance beside her, and like her, at attention. He looked at her sideways, clicking his eyes back to a forward stare when she caught him trying to look at her. She with the same furtive slide of eyes, after an interval, tried to look at him undetected.
— Something Beckettian, Penny said.
Sam took a step forward and recited:
> *The gorgeous peacock struts and flirts*
> *And drags his tail, but when his mind*
> *On peahens dwells he lifts his skirts*
> *And shows all Persia his behind.*
— Apollinaire! Marc said.
Sam stepped back, Walt forward.

> *My poor owl of a heart has failed,*
> *Its fervent heat is at an end.*
> *I've been nailed, unnailed and renailed.*
> *But all who love me, I commend.*

Applause from Penny and Marc.

Walt and Sam faced each other, nose to nose. They about-faced, standing butt to butt, listening. The gritty slide of Sam's zipper brought Walt's fingers to his.

— Danish television, Marc said.

Walt turned to face Sam's back, pushing up her polo shirt. She raised her arms for him to pull it over her head. They turned, Sam hauling off Walt's shirt. They turned again, Sam holding her arms up to have Walt's shirt put on her. Walt, Sam's. Meanwhile, both had been losing their kneepants to gravity, until they were around their ankles. Each kicked them aside. They pulled down, and off, each other's underwear.

— Now Sam's Bee, Penny said, though who knows with these two.

Walt spoke:

> *All admire my distinguished grace,*
> *My lines so noble that the Greeks*
> *Thought light had voice in my face,*
> *About which Trismegistus speaks.*

— That's Orpheus, Marc said. There's no Eurydice in the suite, is there? Prepare to blush, Penny.

Bee, one hand on her sex, the other on Walt's:

> *I, a bunny, know another*
> *I would like to kiss all over.*
> *He's as loving as a brother*
> *In his warren in the clover.*

Both bowed. End of mime. Applause.

HENRY DE MONTHERLANT

> Such heavy leather shoes for legs
> so young and slender to end in,
> the only bulk to a body
> so lightly clad. To pull them from
> his messy gym bag where they've lain
> under muddy and grass-stained shorts,
> is to hear the coach's whistle
> slice the air, the field crack, to take

from the private musk of a sack
the cold light of a winter day
and hold victory in my hands.
So inert, so slight to the eye
these flying kicking, living shoes
obeyed the fierce will of a boy
who could fight back a hero's tears.
Still oiled, still spattered with dried mud,
they've kept their strong seaweed odor.
In their scuffed heft, copper grommets,
and essence of brute elegance,
they are as noble as the field
they trod and the boy who wore them.
The ankles are bulged like the boss
of a Greek shield, the instep his.
Could I not know whose shoes these were?
To cup the hard heels in my hands
is to feel them full of bright fire.

THE FIELD PATH: OLD PEAR TREE BY ATGET
This grass, with knotted roots and plaited halms, has outlasted
centuries of wars, boots and shells, tank treads and bombs. *Herba
est, gramen et pabulum.* Birds, Roman boots, the wind seeded it
here. It is the ancestor of bread. Walt, wrinkling his nose, says that
we need a sheep to crop it, as in the Bois. I ask him to talk about
grass, he says he must be naked to do it, like Adam, and hops to
wiggle his briefs off his lifted ankle. Grass is, he says, well, grass,
well attested and beyond quibble. It grows on the ground, most
anywhere. Cows and horses eat it. It is green. His namesake Whitman in America wrote a book about it. It makes meadows, with
flowers mixed in, and ants, grasshoppers and butterflies. It feels
good to walk on it barefoot, in summer. It is and isn't a weed.

# Two Poems
## Douglas Messerli

### THE VOLCANO
*after Mallarmé*

By your cloud still struck
Low with lava and ash
Into the enslaving echo
Of the worthless blast

What a hollow wreck (still spuming,
but with a drool) as you know
Towering over the destruction
Consummated in its riven mast.

Or was it in a rage
Of some great perdition
That this abyss was so vainly whipped up

White white hair falling
Down so stingily to drown
the cheeks of a child siren.

## SHADOWS

Shadows with before
let breathe reflect
condemned as full
gathers light upon
the profoundest tip
surfacing impediments
of flattened midnight
in its expect.

Now I watch the taste
of recognition frontal
as the note drawn out
of pocket strikes
the flanks and wedges
glimmer promising
the pout of day's lip.

I raise my shuteye
to the angle vagrant
as instruct swills
the wary grip, full
of reason to rip
the pamper off of it.

*Douglas Messerli*

You and your company
part lines without
subtraction, retaining
the coherence as it rages,
clue to the twist

Due suffered in the lapse.
This has happened once
before conformity exploded
want as a train pulling

Out to circle back
to identical waves
of madness, the dream

Of suggestion's prospect.
Each is a disaster.

The sun sets on the moon.

# CONJUNCTIONS

Don't miss a single shocking, dazzling, enchanting,
boring, maddening issue.

## GET A SUBSCRIPTION AND SAVE

"Each issue is on the cutting edge of American
fiction and poetry."—*The Washington Post*

❏ ONE YEAR (2 ISSUES) **$18**    ❏ TWO YEAR (4 ISSUES) **$32**

NAME

❏ CHECK OR MONEY ORDER        ❏ BILL ME

ADDRESS

PLEASE CHARGE MY:    ❏ MASTERCARD    ❏ VISA

CITY

| STATE | ZIP | ACCOUNT NUMBER | EXP. DATE |

ALL FOREIGN AND INSTITUTIONAL ORDERS: $25 PER YEAR    SIGNATURE                    20/21

♻

# CONJUNCTIONS

## GIVE A GIFT SUBSCRIPTION TO A FRIEND

❏ ONE YEAR (2 ISSUES)  **$18**

MY NAME

❏ PAYMENT ENCLOSED        ❏ BILL ME

ADDRESS

❏ RENEWAL            ❏ NEW ORDER

CITY

| STATE | ZIP |

PLEASE CHARGE MY:  ❏ MASTERCARD      ❏ VISA

GIFT SUBSCRIPTION TO:

ACCOUNT NUMBER            EXP. DATE

RECIPIENT'S NAME

ADDRESS

SIGNATURE                  20/21

CITY

A GIFT CARD WILL BE SENT IN YOUR NAME. ALL FOREIGN AND

STATE          ZIP

INSTITUTIONAL ORDERS $25 PER YEAR, PAYABLE IN U.S. FUNDS.

♻

# BUSINESS REPLY MAIL

FIRST CLASS MAIL  PERMIT NO. 1 ANNANDALE-ON-HUDSON, NY

POSTAGE WILL BE PAID BY ADDRESSEE

CONJUNCTIONS
BARD COLLEGE
ANNANDALE-ON-HUDSON
PO BOX 9911
RED HOOK, NY 12571-9911

# BUSINESS REPLY MAIL

FIRST CLASS MAIL  PERMIT NO. 1 ANNANDALE-ON-HUDSON, NY

POSTAGE WILL BE PAID BY ADDRESSEE

CONJUNCTIONS
BARD COLLEGE
ANNANDALE-ON-HUDSON
PO BOX 9911
RED HOOK, NY 12571-9911

# *From* Dura
# *Myung Mi Kim*

Never having been here when the sun rose.

Flowering amid which deer. The suggestion of deer.

Adjustments of liar lair. Having arrived here.

Fever, thumb, bruise. Speckled event of eggs, their ingenious pointed and rounded ends. Stacked against time against spoilage.

To be stitched — threadbare to elaborate clover.

Fences. What place assume to know.

Swift savage slop. Great speech. If rifled, if bared.

Fair speech resolve single will.

Grateful inattention of the grasses. Taller than the dog, shorter than the deer. Candle to withstand cholera.

---

Heat the gaping ground constrains. Remind the herders and poison growth. Cover distances deemed impossible to cover.

Great highway indicated by means of stones.

Invention where the tomatoes dangling from one end are not the tomatoes hanging from the other end.

And the unremarkable become the stuff of dust.

Where is the start. Dress of blue chiffon and a white
straw hat in its own hat box.

Heat the gaping ground constrains. Turbulence. Ridicule.

The desktops tilt up and you may place inside them several
books and a lunch.

Various kinds of rice in the manner of living in that country.

———————

Obdurate sound. Thereby insert interpret.

Receive materials lumber nails and oats.

Building is a process. Light is an element.

Towering height of wagons and their ruts.

Cross their limits cut a sloping way. For this book
will be a truthful one. On material as varied as
berry and stone.

Flayed skin of animals. Fire brick. Moveable type.

A glut of gathered rain.

Nuance of grass and digestion. Metal ground to a point.

———————

Swarming preface. The box to be carried to the cemetery.
In it a claw rake and a dandelion picker. Weeds over what
bodies to in the ground.

Call pinecones denominators. Call what we eat temporary.
Steep referent protected by windbreak.

Indicate the manner and recess. Poor. Having to found
descriptions for things never seen.

Follow the staking. Thornbush. Blood and commingling
fat. Letters a carving a chipping.

Function in cold and heat. Except for heat that bakes
limb and liver.

When there is a pause, pause.

Duration that a pair of starlings' participation magnetized.

A constant. A trajectory.

A pair of starlings' knowledge of the universe.

———————

If the young women can be checked for snoring, teeth
grinding, any unpleasant odor from any part of the body.
Thirty sons who will domain. House by which houses will
stand. Many wives had many sons.

Little in the way of progress. Firesticks bundled.

Ashen poles to raise forky heads.

Dailiness of the soil and its best composition.

Crude utensils and their use.

When we stayed all together working the fields and
went home at dusk and ate together. Mangy birds
sing ornate songs.

———————

First assembled fire. Far off estimation the sun offers.

Operate machinery and the line. Bark branch phrase interrupted.

Distended beyond assembly and parts.

Describe the success of the random bomb. Black rain had its mark.

Withstood ropes and burns.

Bulbous plants gone soft.

Moving from twelve to counting on the ten fingers. That long combat maintained.

———————

Names of capitals. Names of cities. Search for water with plastic jugs that two gulps will drain.

Speed of water drops. Speed of cease-fire. Playground when the planes close in. The hands of the boy and girl are firm hands. Fume, vapor, forge of metal aimed. Each child's hand in the mother's hands. No heads, fugitive heads. Eyes turned lid. Blood mat hair. Each their hands (held).

Name a capital. Name a city.

Stack and make. Force and ford.

Thirst's all in shun. Purposes of sequestering. First unleash. No amount of water or transfusion.

———————

The dog will not eat the acorns assiduously placed in the dented bowl. Disguised as good will.

Denomination. Promissory. Venture. Amass.

In so locating a time of geography before the compass.
Do not ask again where are we.

Ones on the other side. Shaking sticks with strips of
white rags tied at the top.

Population gathered to population. More uninhabited
space in America than elsewhere. Is that accurate.
Riders wielding tall sticks with strips of white linen
attached to them. Is that accurate.

———————

Punctuality. Decay. Is that accurate.

In fact, the tariff.

Asphalt and rooftop rifles.

Tinder under flint

    When he left

Extinguished      spreading

    He was wearing a white T-shirt and jeans

Beat the fresh burning

    The boy in the newspaper wore a dark shirt

Flakes of fire ripen fire

    It could not be my son

Agate of insistence

    Contents of the boy's pocket — a dime and a pen

Percussive

157

*Myung Mi Kim*

In the *LA Times* the picture was in color

Body moving in circle be fire

What looked black in the Korean newspaper was my son's blood

Body moving in circle be fire

If fire be the body carried round

———————

Make the surface plain.

Hordes. Sides. One fish bowl and several shutting gates.

None to receive action or to specify possession.

Nations. Sty and pigpie.

Natural motion of fire to move in a straight line.

_____ arrived in America. Bare to trouble and foresworn.
Aliens aboard three ships off the coast.  _____ and
_____ clash. Police move in.

What is nearest is destroyed.

# Corresponding Saints
## Marjorie Welish

The floor's countenance
distributed throughout social consciousness.

"I no longer know" is not the same aphorism.

advancing Neither . . . nor

The floor-through element in Anglo-American . . .
the floor-through Anglo-American element in verse tribute.

Prone floor apart from the texts
prone floor *folded like a napkin*

or the ideogram of *Noh*
with the resultant *planes in relation*

advancing neither loquacity.

Flourishing dialecticians doth impart juggernaut.
One hundred thousand dialects substantiate it.

Flora enjoy that milieu of ground and sky
and sky and ream of paper decreasingly.

We won.
We did not win.

The house was not unoccupied.
The house was occupied.

Flora initiate intrinsically burdensome ream
of boasts and insults called pleasing.

# To the Lord Protector
## *Donald Revell*

It is incredible
how cold, how far
from all feeling
the spur feels.

Me next. In the middle
way of scarecrow and
imagination, I do not
wonder. I do not open.

Against intelligible flame,
against the mere goad,
the craving for piety,
God established the body.

The shifting flaws of human permission made it move.


Cruel to remain
in solace such
a house whose
sound cannot consist
of humanness.

The table is
hazardous. The door
is accidental.
Loneliness never
welcomes echoes.

Sharp I taste it.
As it dreams
to happen, sharp
I taste it.
I clash and conjecture.

A thing of stone is not a continuity.


Many find immediate
rest and human things
exempt from harm.
Seeds and sparkles
all blaze again.

But even a famous
man may not
oblige jailers,
so wild a race
has superstition run.

If any two
tasted once
remedy for loneliness,
calamity remains.
Laws are imposed.

Cure of disease crept into the best part of human society.


I trust to protect
tables, astronomy,
and the unconjugal
mind not to suffer.

Words declare
no expression.
Mind hangs off,
closing proportion.

Preposterous
to have made
provisions
while I dreamed.

Soul's lawful contentment is only the fountain.


A discreet man
in wild affections
remains more alone.

More deeply rooted
in other burning
in rational burning

he honors himself
to understand himself
and be considered.

The least grain
is well enough.
Many are married.

God does not principally take care of such cattle.


To end the question
men may often
borrow compulsion
from a snare.

Exhortation is angels.
Compulsion is devils.
One hides, one
bares the claws.

I saw the least sinew
of my body washed
and salted. I saw
it seeking.

The obscene evidence of the question never changed.


This day will be
remarkable
or my last.
Like a beast,
I am content
and mutable,
perhaps free.

A few and easy
things, a few words
unearthed in season
revive the ruined
man on earth.
The effortless rainbow
deepens.

My author sang and was deep in her showing.

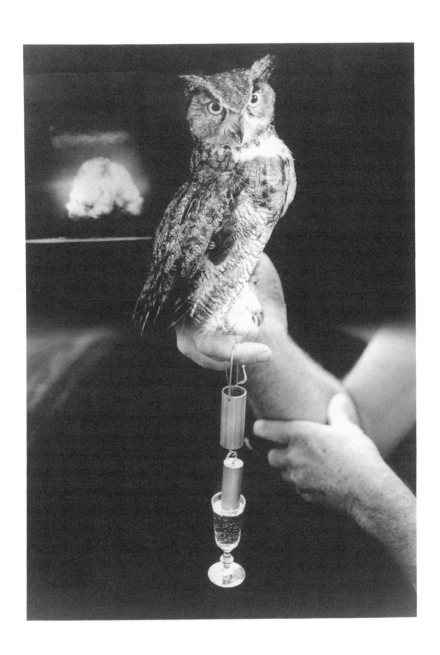

# Critical Mass
## Meridel Rubenstein and Ellen Zweig

THEY SPOKE TO THE ANGELS

They spoke to the angels. To Raphael, angel
They spoke to the angels.
To the angel of annihilation
of the bottomless pit
angel of chaos

of science and of knowledge, angel of health,
of commotion
angel of confusion
of corruption
of darkness and death

of force, angel set over all the diseases and
angel of the deserts
angel of destruction and dread
angel of the face
of fascination, and fear and forgetting

over all the wounds of men, angel of the West.
angel of fury and grief
angel of irrevocable choice
angel of horror
angel over hidden things
angel of the marriage of contraries

They spoke to Uriel, the fire of God, who watches
angel of mountains
of the mutations of the moon
of mysteries, oblivion
angel of oracles

over thunder and terror, angel who guards the
angel of precipices
angel of quaking and
of rage
angel of running streams and rivers

*Meridel Rubenstein/Ellen Zweig*

# gates of Eden, alchemist angel, physicist, angel

of silence
angel over small birds
angel of solitudes
angel of the Southwest

# of the abyss, of chance and destruction, angel

angel of tears and terror and time
angel of trembling
angel of vegetables and
of fruits

# of the South whose open hand holds a flame.

angel of voyages and weakness
angel of the whirlwind and the wilderness
angels at the end of the world.

*"This is a story of a house that stood detached, between the Pueblo Indian world and the Anglo—a house destined to play a part in the lives of the men and women who brought into being the atomic bomb."* — Edith Warner from "In the Shadow of Los Alamos," unpublished manuscript.

Edith Warner came to New Mexico in 1922 at the age of thirty to recuperate from an illness. She fell in love with the Parajito Plateau and returned there to live in 1928. She secured a job taking in mail and supplies off the "Chile Line" railroad for the Los Alamos Boys Ranch School. She had strong ties to the San Ildefonso Pueblo, having been given a house on Pueblo

land in which to live and work. Gradually she was able to renovate this wood house, which rested on the bank of the Rio Grande at Otowi Bridge, filling it with simple furniture, Pueblo pots and Navajo rugs. She could see Black Mesa out her kitchen window and hear the river. To augment her income she opened a tearoom selling Cokes and her legendary chocolate cake. Later she took in guests. She shared her home with Tilano Montoya, a past governor of the Pueblo who assisted her in these occupations. Edith's quiet Pennsylvanian Quaker demeanor, Tilano's calm Pueblo style and the peaceful and secluded location made the House at Otowi Bridge a sought-after refuge.

IF ARCHIMEDES

My whole body is trembling and my hairs are standing on end.
I remember there was candlelight. Archimedes, an excitement, a
spectacle, an investigation of the physical. My skin is burning and
I am forgetting myself. I remember the house and everything that
was in it and around it. Archimedes, mathematics, theoretical, an
invention of the physical. My mind is reeling and I am overcome
with grief. I remember red soil, red river, like blood in an open
artery. Archimedes, desert landscape, experimental, a fiction of
the physical.

I feel very small and of little worth. In the presence of great spaces
and deep silence, any number of things fell apart in his mind. He
loved the desert, its red desolation. Each year I do less of the cus-
tomary things. In the presence of great spaces and deep silence,
any number of things fell apart in his mind. He loved physics, its
red desolation. This is the story of a house that stood for many
years beside a bridge between two worlds. In the presence of great
spaces and deep silence, any number of things fell apart in his
mind. Archimedes, an excitement, a spectacle, an investigation of
the physical.

Of all that is material and all that is spiritual in this world, know
for certain that I am both its origin and its dissolution. They were
talking about geography. I am the taste in water. I am the light in
fire. They were talking about geography. The disagreement was
about the ultimate things and expressed the mysteries. I am the
butter and the flame and the offering. The disagreement was about
the ultimate things and expressed the mysteries. I have two loves:
physics and the desert. I am the witness, the home and shelter.
I have two loves: physics and the desert. It troubles me that I don't
see any way to bring them together.

Archimedes, mathematics, theoretical, an invention of the physical.
He had come upon a solid-looking log house. Arjuna saw in that
Universal Form unlimited mouths, unlimited eyes.

He had come upon a solid-looking log house. It turned out to be a
tearoom. He saw the unlimited expansions of the universe seated
in one place.

It turned out to be a tearoom. He saw the house and everything that was in it and around it. He saw flaming mouths, immeasurable rays.

He saw the house and everything that was in it and around it. But these were private acts and personal moments. I shall now explain to you the knowable.

But these were private acts and personal moments. This was a shelter against the elements. I am Time, the destroyer, the shatterer of worlds.

This was a shelter against the elements. It was a kind of backstage, the house and everything that was in it and around it. The window opened out on a long view, as though the room continued into the landscape.

It was a kind of backstage, the house and everything that was in it and around it. I speak here of dwelling and of refuge. The material Nature consists of three modes: goodness, passion and ignorance.

I speak here of dwelling and of refuge. To Oppenheimer, Edith seemed the genius of the place, the house and everything that was in it and around it. He might have been a poet or certainly a musician.

To Oppenheimer, Edith seemed the genius of the place, the house and everything that was in it and around it. All this he remembered while Groves was shaking his hand. Archimedes, an excitement, a spectacle, an investigation of the physical.

All this he remembered while Groves was shaking his hand. There is a sense of reverence in the perception of some landscapes. I am the fire of digestion in every living body.

There is a sense of reverence in the perception of some landscapes. A narrow mountain road, passable, if not good . . . I am the air of life, outgoing and incoming.

A narrow mountain road, passable, if not good . . . A secluded spot, as far as the eye could see . . . I am seated in everyone's heart.

A secluded spot, as far as the eye could see . . .
Space, immense, transparent . . .
I am remembrance, knowledge and forgetfulness.

Space, immense, transparent . . .
Dangerous, impetuous, furious . . .
I am the landscape.

Dangerous, impetuous, furious . . .
Surprise, bewilderment, shock . . .
I am physics.

Surprise, bewilderment, shock . . .
Undramatic and calm.
I am home.

If Archimedes, at the age of 73, put aside his theoretical work . . . I have two loves: physics and the desert.

If Archimedes, respected throughout the civilized world . . . He had come upon a solid-looking log house.

If Archimedes, respected throughout the civilized world for his work in mathematics . . . A few miles from where she lived rose a red mesa spotted with cottonwoods.

If Archimedes, with the vigor of a youth . . . The disagreement was about the ultimate things and expressed the mysteries.

If Archimedes, inventing numerous engines of war . . . Here at Los Alamos, I found a spirit of Athens, of Plato, of an ideal republic.

If Archimedes made catapults and great burning lenses . . . Whether a man acts by body, mind or words, that which in the beginning may be just like nectar, but at the end is like poison . . . I am frenzy, I am chaos, I am eternal.

If Archimedes, an excitement, a spectacle, an investigation of the physical . . . To Oppenheimer, Edith seemed the genius of the place.

If Archimedes, mathematics, theoretical, an invention of the physical . . . I have two loves: physics and the desert. It troubles me that I don't see any way to bring them together.

If Archimedes, desert landscapes, experimental, a fiction of the physical . . . He had fallen under the spell of the little house and wanted to share it with those he loved.

J. Robert Oppenheimer, a nuclear physicist and the director of the Manhattan Project, which created the first atomic bomb, also came to New Mexico in 1922 for his health. He and his brother Frank leased a house in the Pecos Valley and made many camping trips to the Parajito Plateau. In 1937, he first stopped at Edith's tearoom, brought his wife back in 1941, and in 1942, he brought General Leslie Groves. He remembered with fondness the tearoom, the chocolate cake, the magnificent scenery and Edith Warner. It was here that he was able to fulfill his dream to bring together his two loves: physics and the desert. Oppenheimer once wrote to a friend: "My two great loves are phyics and desert country; it's a pity they can't be combined."

In the 3rd century B.C., Archimedes gave up his theoretical work to help defend the city of Syracuse from the Roman invaders. It is said that he constructed a great many horrible weapons; the most famous was a set of large bronze mirrors or lenses with which he could focus the light of the sun onto the approaching Roman ships, so that they burst into flames. In the first half of the twentieth century, J. Robert Oppenheimer put aside his theoretical work to head the lab at Los Alamos that created the first atom bomb.

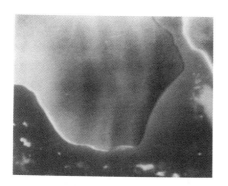

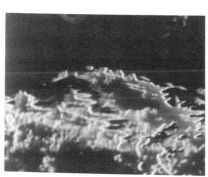

Blue Corn — One of the most accomplished and recognized of the San Ildefonso potters, she worked as a maid (like many women from the Pueblos) for a year for the Oppenheimers.

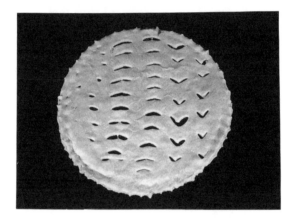

Facundo "Red" Sanchez — Son of Desideria Sanchez, husband to "Cedar," he worked for Tilano in the garden. He remembered taking the surplus vegetables to town and selling them in order to buy food for the dinners. He also drove Tilano to people's homes in Los Alamos to perform Pueblo social dances. He was with Edith when she died. And died himself in 1993.

Prune pie made by Pilar Aguilar. She says whenever she makes this pie, people come to visit.

Tall-necked jar with Awanyu (plumed serpent), made by Julian and Maria Martinez, c. 1930, 8"x11½" (Museum of Indian Arts and Culture, Museum of New Mexico) — When Edith was shown a similar pot in 1922 on her first visit to San Ildefonso in the home of Ignacio and Susana Aguilar, she noted in her diary that Awanyu was more than an ordinary snake. He is a sacred force who represents the natural energies of water in the clouds and rivers and rain.

Pilar Aguilar, holding a photograph of her mother, Desideria Sanchez (sister of Maria Martinez), who helped to plaster Edith's second house. Pilar Aguilar worked at the lab for fifteen years and was awarded the Woman of Science Award. She remembers the excitement of visiting Edith's at Christmas and getting gifts.

Philip Morrison, theoretical physicist, currently teaching at MIT. At Los Alamos he worked on the critical assembly of the implosion bomb. While he thought that he would be most impressed by the sight of the first atomic explosion, he has always remembered the intense heat. Although he worked on the hydrogen bomb after the war, he became increasingly outspoken against the control of scientific research by the military. He is now best known as a science educator through his book reviews in *Scientific American* and his appearances on the PBS *Nova* series. He ate dinner at Edith's and as a summer visitor to Los Alamos after the war, he helped build her second house. Of Edith he said: "Edith Warner stands in the history of those desperate times as a kind of rainbow . . . a sign that war and bombs are not all that men and women are capable of building" (*The House at Otowi Bridge* by Peggy Pond Church, p. 99).

Nicholas Metropolis is a physicist presently at Los Alamos. He worked with Edward Teller on the reactor project at the University of Chicago and joined the Manhattan Project in 1942 as a member of the Theoretical Division. He and Richard Feynman set up a repair shop to fix the Marchant and Friden hand calculators that broke down due to the enormous amount of calculations necessary to the work at the lab. By 1943 the overtaxed calculators were replaced by the IBM punch card system. By 1948 Metropolis was a leader of a Los Alamos team that designed and built the MANIAC, one of the first electronic digital computers. He ate dinner at Edith's during the war years and after the war helped build her new house. He remembers Tilano making the curvature in the adobe wall by rotating a Campbell soup can on its axis from the floor upwards.

Beryllium copper alloy tools — These tools would not cause a spark on impact — important for working around high explosives.

Hans Bethe had to leave Germany because his mother was Jewish. In 1935 he arrived in America to teach at Cornell University and in 1967 he was awarded the Nobel Prize for explaining the production of energy in stars. At Los Alamos he was head of the Theoretical Physics Division. Troubled by his responsibility in producing the first atomic bomb, Bethe took a leading role in the Emergency Committee of Atomic Scientists. This group urged public awareness of the danger of atomic war and the necessity for international control. Resisting strong pressure to work on the Super Bomb, he returned to Cornell after the war, finally to be recruited by Edward Teller in 1949. He hoped through his work he could prove its impossibility. He ate dinner at Edith's feeling that her home was "something of a tie to the world."

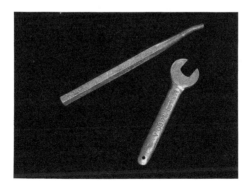

*Meridel Rubenstein/Ellen Zweig*

## THE DINNER

OPENING SEQUENCE: *(sounds of water, breathing, traffic)*

Bohr: Physics? Explosion? Territory? Mastery? Did I ever say the word, your magic word?

Edith: Famous for my chocolate cake among men famous for the atom bomb?

Bohr: But the word you wanted, was it terror?

Edith: . . . the body. What did you do?

---

### SCENE I

Fermi: Why am I the man with the slide rule? They love to tell it: how I checked the most complicated equations, the computer-generated computations, with that slide rule, how I never was without it. They'll never know the truth: that it was my back, a slipped disc, that gave me so much trouble; the migraine headaches, the hemorrhoids; that ache in my left leg I never could explain; my fear of syphilis, my bout with diarrhea, my nagging cough; sudden moments when I couldn't breathe without pain. That slide rule, I groped for it; it calmed me; its sliding parts, so sensual, so like a perfect body.

Bohr: And the story they love to tell about me, about how I melted down our Nobel medals and hid the lump as though it were something of no importance. They'll never know the truth. How I loved to imagine that lump. I sat sometimes with my hands

180

folded over each other and I could feel that lump, every crevice of it, the smooth openings, the protruding knobby sections. As though I were fondling some terrible gold foot. I could imagine sucking the toes of the lump, licking in between the toes, biting the nails. Enrico, it was the foot of our ambitions I held in my mouth, the foot of everything we had learned, the foot of our mastery.

Edith:    I wish you could see the big kitchen on some Sundays, the table so neatly set. The fireplace . . . I . . .

Fermi:    I hate the stories they love to tell about me. I hate the story they love to tell about how I tore up some paper and calculated the power of the blast at Trinity by dropping the pieces.

Edith:    One thing is clear: These are the stories of sons.

Fermi:    They'll never know the truth of my little distractions. The secret wounds. The sound of ripping paper in the silence of the desert. The secret spirit of sacrifice. Those days when I was Eugene Farmer and you were Nicholas Baker.

Edith:    This afternoon as I was ironing, I was thinking about money. I had almost forgotten how to lie curled on the ground.

Bohr:    I hate the stories they tell about me. I hate the story they love to tell about my escape and how they pulled me unconscious from the plane.

Edith:    Here it is, blood and money.

Einstein: I could sure eat a piece of your chocolate cake right now.

Fermi: I have to admit I loved the secret codes.

Bohr: You mean "The Italian Navigator has reached the New World."

Fermi: "And how did he find the natives?"

Bohr: "Very friendly." Do you know what they say about me? At Los Alamos, they say we never discussed the moral dimension unless Bohr was there. The real problem isn't that scientists didn't think about these things. The real problem is that our bodies cramp up, that you can't understand, that our tongues become bones, that our bodies cramp up when they try to feel pleasure, that the secret of numbers breaks out where love should.

---

SCENE II

Einstein: It's as though we don't have our real lives, the gritty details. Everywhere I turn in this mire of history, there are repetitions, pornographic re-minders, of the ruts of our minds. I'm sick of it. I want something more than memory, something more than stories. Let's do an experiment.

Tilano: *(fearful)* What do you mean?

182

Einstein: Just a thought experiment. Let's make things up about ourselves. Scandals. Let's confess everything. I used to have terrible dreams, dreams that my teeth are loose. I can reach in my mouth and wiggle them with my fingers or when I touch them with my tongue, they move. Then, one by one, they fall out. I find them in my mouth. I spit them out. I drink a glass of milk. Teeth fall in the milk and disappear, leaving trails of blood. I chew the teeth. They're hollow like bones; their marrow is sweet. I come in my own mouth, spit semen and blood.

Tilano: I'm afraid of your dreams. I dream I'm afraid of your dreams. I dream there's a city on the Hill that makes you new teeth. This city gives jobs to my people. We work hard to make the new teeth. And when our teeth begin to fall out we ask for those new ones. We are refused. Our mouths are bloody toothless  holes. We lose our language. We lose everything. Then someone, someone like you, comes to ask us for advice. The new teeth won't stay in your mouths. How do you keep yours in, you ask? When you look at our mouths, you see them full of healthy teeth.

Einstein: *(he interrupts)* We steal your teeth. First, we stick our tongues in your mouths and feel around in there. Lots of sharp, healthy teeth. We accuse you of sharpening your teeth to cut our tongues. So we pull them out, those sharp healthy teeth and put them in our own mouths. Now we talk your language. But there's something wrong. Your teeth begin to eat our mouths. Every time we talk, we bite ourselves. We're in horrible pain.

Tilano: No, stop. I'm frightened now. We're all in pain.

Einstein: Can we begin to see each other now? To understand, something too horrible . . . To understand that all our stories, our history, is meant to hide the bloody mess,

183

the uncontrollable excess of our bodies. Tension, dirt and death. Things of the moment. Sweat. History, narrative, a set of stock stories. Unsatisfied bones. And the only way out?

Tilano: *Invent* ourselves? The more famous we are the more lies we tell?

Einstein:  Then, the experiment works.

Tilano:  Yes, there's *truth* in it.

---

SCENE III

Edith:  My recipe for chocolate cake. Mix eggs, sugar and flour.

Oppie:  I must go under, go down.

Edith:  Add milk gradually.

Bohr:  My mind is riven, my senses reeling.

Edith:  Add salt.

Oppie:  All things so far have created something beyond themselves.

Edith:  **I am become death. I am bodies of water, blood and semen. I am absolute feeling.**

Bohr:  This thing must be, though life should be the cost.

Edith:  *(bewildered, to herself)* Who is Edith?

Oppie:  Where is the lightning to lick you with its tongue?

Edith:  **Oh yes, oh yes, take my tongue.**

Bohr:  *(to Edith, but she pays no attention)* I always liked to quote from Goethe's *Faust.*

Edith:  **Rainwater, collected in gullies, arroyos. Streets of blood, boiling floods, waters; waves, torrents, horrible water. Holy waters. The surface of the human skin.**

Oppie:  Where is the frenzy with which you should be inoculated?

Bohr:  *(to Oppie)* Zarathustra's got *your* tongue.

Edith:  **Rivers, large mighty rivers. Inside my nerves, like hollow tubes.** Who is Edith? *(as though waking from a trance)* What am I doing here?

Bohr:  I was reading *(corrects himself)*, remembering something I'd read. You've read Goethe's *Faust?*

Edith:  *(a strange voice speaks these words which are difficult or impossible to deciper)* **Get out of me. Seeing this, seeing that. The eye rolls in my head. Dam it up. Shut it. I tell you, this is the inside of the body turned inside out. Flow. Waters.** *(back to her own voice)* **The Pacific Ocean, the Atlantic, the Nile, Rio Grande, the Congo.** *(still confused)* Who is Edith? Who am I? Edith Warner in a book? Who's Edith? Who's Edith? My recipe for chocolate cake. Mix eggs, sugar and flour.

Bohr:  *(to Oppie)* We'd better admit it. She's speaking in her own voice now.

Oppie:  And before? A seer? Whose voice was that, that voice who spoke through her?

Bohr:  A man's voice?

Oppie:  Unclear.

Bohr:    A spirit? A witch? What is she?

Oppie:   I didn't like that voice. It frightened me.

Edith:   Add milk gradually.

Bohr:    Should we record it?

Oppie:   Measure it?

Bohr:   Observe it?

Oppie:  Describe it?

Bohr:   Is this merely a problem of identity?

Edith:  Add salt.

Oppie:  Unclear.

---

SCENE IV

Edith:    *(to herself)* I am the oracular presence? Me? Nonsense. I'm their mother, their sister, their maiden aunt.

Bohr:    Physics, our science, the science we love, a perfectly sublime science, physics was pushed to, to, to the *cruelest* reality.

Einstein: Everything that has been acquired with such effort seems in the hands of our generation like a razor in the hands of a child of three.

Edith:    *(to them)* And who was I to you? What part did I play in it? Collaborator? Secret lover? Symbol of all that's civil and cultured?

Bohr:    They did things without seeing all the consequences. So much of science is like that.

186

Einstein: Politics, money, letters to sign, the army, the fat man, ambitions.

Edith: What if I gave you a new science, pure, invented by women?

Bohr: A science radically different from ours? Impossible. Do you have it?

Edith:  No.

Bohr:  Who are you?

Edith:  Edith Warner. You ate at my table.

Einstein: She's keeping her secrets. You heard her before. That other voice. Do you think that's really gone away? Next time we'll listen more closely.

Bohr:  What would it tell us? Chaos, fear, blood and water. That's what I heard.

Einstein: *(to Edith)* Who are you?

Edith:  I remember that day so well. And it seemed fitting that it was Kitty Oppenheimer, coming for vegetables, who brought me the news.

Einstein: The bomb?

Edith:  I'm part of it, history and memory. As though I invented it too. I'm lost in it. Don't know who I am anymore. They say so many things about me. What should I do?

Einstein: Let's try an experiment.

# *From* New Time
## *Leslie Scalapino*

it was already dawn — and the clear space was there, outside of one — but in a not blackness

of the red huge leaves sea — *per se* — only that — giving up — rebelling — itself — as the (air's) clear space only.

---

I — can't — not — only — so having to give that up — that isn't rebelling even — is dawn itself

— bud — ? — that's accumulated in exhaustion, ordinary rebelling — dog in it at dawn red leaves' sea, only.

---

depression touches on the bright wind — that's — dawn — red leaves' sea

only — it has no other aspect of one.

---

even 'exhaustion' is 'naming' it before — so that it isn't itself — occurs — cataclysm between dawn, and rebelling that's in one physical only — therefore wild gap — break, in redoing prior negatives *per se* (events 'that' torment one),

as it — filled events, life occurring (inside, break of order occurring — going on haywire — that's gap — of dawn, not it.

---

reduction of travelling — where one has nothing — is nothing
— a nomad(ism) — is a bright wind in bird-life of people only

this is the same as reduction to convention — where it doesn't
exist even — as being — travelling — only, not existing

it blows apart

———————

cold — freezing red sky dusk — slice, reduction not existing —
walking only as clear — one — outside, dark roses are in it, as freezing red's slice

a half of the night seen, which isn't there yet — sky only is
there — at all

bright dark roses — not bud, ever — in the slice only

———————

wild gap — of dawn, not it — not so much the particular interpretation (of events) — but as (that) it happens at all

filled events (catalyzed in one as physical gap tormenting — is
itself the break that's the dawn, in fact) — break — expanded — that
are going on — red flamed trees, leaves sea is the occurrence outside.

———————

freezing sky — red slice — one, outside, travelling not existing
even — is *not* not rebelling — gap itself — as choosing the harshest
conditions — is the dawn

that is dusk freezing sky — is gap

grinding negative, as going down that's dusk sky — *per se* —
one's pushing wildly occurring (in one) events — as gap, (that's
dawn)

---

"seeing Venus in the morning sky"— (he's speaking)

(aggressive waves coming from someone one day — then from another person — to hit on oneself — who's, then, rebelling) — "I saw a white azalea — yesterday (morning too) — blooming in the whole space" (on rim?) — "I imagined yesterday — the next — the next — the next — is blooming" —

rim floating, wave that's someone's — *not* — (isn't) rebelling

---

one 'pushes' the events one's in so there are no distinctions. — base it on itself — 'only'

— 'joking.' — one makes the obstructions, the events (but which occur), inside. — perceiving the 'sole' (two or many) events flickering on each other — faint day, moon in hole, in sky collapses (there?) — 'I have to give this up' even

---

black night — filling gas — freezing black flow — coming in, man destitute says he'll pump the gas waiting at gas pit-stop in night

bowing is sky flow only — *not* — as: — it is

190

'standing' 'walking' as present — huge crows loaded a tree (past)
by me — at night sleeping — yet the half-cracked black bud (night:
only) and thin blue sky, but as being oneself only, aren't existing
either

single thin wall, waves thousands in the freezing sky and
empty fields — and loaded on tree by me — night is half-cracked
black bud in one: as, thin blue sky

the two single events at the present (only)

past — has to be only — 'an' 'act' — that's only in present 'standing'
'walking' — waves of the thousands huge crows in freezing sky: —
'at' dawn — from loaded (their jostling in) tree by me night, only
but only as single arbitrary 'event' in present now — walking —
thin blue sky
to be pressure on — present — one

the 'pressure' of the 'choked' thick night, in one, single past
event, and thin present sky

the voluptuous choked thick, 'on' night, can't breathe (the
hundreds of huge slightly moving choked: only 'at' night / — 'only'
is fear, single crows loading tree by thin wall) of one, at night —
'their' dawn — as realigning present dawn, only — ?

one could give up — ?
(as:) 'their' 'dawn' is thin blue of one — ?

# Two Poems
## *Peter Gizzi*

### FEAR OF MUSIC

She put the sugar on my tongue, right there
in the trees, and I see the sun standing
behind buildings in static reverie.
A postcard, its steep cliffs and steeples.
It is a town — a quiet sky — calm the light
flooding in to display hands and faces.
See them on their way to the mill, the bakery.
Get in line. Nothing will come between us.
The perpetual wheel turns inside,
spins inside a head, and waves vibrate into rings
first seen — then unseen. A sound —
through which we move. A distant voice
calls, so may we live and petition goodness,
sweetness. The tribute of friendship worn as a necklace
or fashioned into a headdress. Wild in the cities,
walking down avenues wilder than the place we live,
that is a face, a view. That many — voices blend
into a sequence, turn them round your head,
thread them through your head, making it up
as we go, is where we live. Where I want to be.
Yesterday proved a shower of letters, a postcard
by a strict governess sent from a distance.
Mother, I will invent the good townspeople inside my head.

Dizzy building! and when we look upon you
we will know we are home, when the voices fail us —
burning down the house, fighting fire with fire
from spooky start to finish — a lone sound
that will not be tamed. Where power is unlike a factory,
truth unlike obedience, spirit like a hammer
and anvil. Just like a hammer. The limits
of the dead and the living city. The streets, sewers,
parks and tenements. The face held in two hands
gazes into the middle distance, touch earth
when you touch your head. Beneath the young night
fleecy clouds and silver moons waver
in the dirty reflecting pool. See your fairest shadow
floating there, and calling say, depart — not yet.
The name of the pond is echo, echo is the name
of the pool where nothing happens. The image pales.
Why look there? Beyond the dream is told.
You ought to be more careful. Setting a bad example.
Who can tell what they seek? If not for you
this bright dome would empty,
the yellow bands of light recede and everything
of bland consequence prevail, if not for you.
Off in the distance singing from a tree.

*Peter Gizzi*

FROM A FIELD GLASS


This street begins outside a factory
As sober jets empty the sky
Or why don't we accept what we see?


She sang unwrapping her bandages
The day static with stuck weeds
And a grimace has swollen to fill the frame


Unadorned robes flutter into one body
In contrasting light or direct exposure
A body renounces joy and dies


The body remembers joy and dies
As a child pulls his father from the stream
The body decomposes before his eyes


Wondering who he can tell of his dream
That flowering face is a start
Where threads of hair have fallen


Saddened by so much randomness
Presenting clues and pictures of other things
Hints and whispers of shiny things


They are saddened by the petals falling
Now that children are playing on this street
Our game will become an entire century

# Colonel Clegg, A Life Sentence
## *Paul West*

IN ORDER TO KEEP herself from writing him in the future, she made herself write him almost daily, the mind-blunting repetitions of which chore drove her also to sending him her favorite quotes, she having nothing to say, whereas the voice of the ages went on and on, forever wise and affable, all the way from know thyself to a fat man inside every thin one, his response to this semi-personal deluge being to mail her in flimsy prestamped aerograms bits of the fishing encyclopedia, which he knew pretty much by heart as far as he had read, anyway, *Aawa* to *Mako,* thus counter-deluging her with all manner of data she did not want and could not use, from the deeply indented snout of the cownose ray to the wet fly known as female beaverkill (this sent her not without malice), as far back as Adirondack Guideboat, a famous double-ended light-weight sportsman's rowboat of the past that once dominated the landings of upper New York state resorts, as far forward as the first-class Asiatic gamefish called Mahseer, to be caught mainly on spoons and plugs with fairly heavy spinning or bait-casting tackle, his point being that he knew it backwards, always remembering what he had read and only reading what he already knew by heart, which explained his buying in the course of his military career at least three copies of the same encyclopedia and his never advancing beyond Mako, the open-ocean shark whose color is a striking cobalt to bluish-gray, in fresh specimens at least, while another reason for his non-advance being addiction to, among other things, the Battle of Britain, painting-kits that enabled him to copy old masters with almost grotesque competence, and books of military protocol, these preferably obsolete, his ultimate objective being a life that had its solaces forever on either side, he could not always put it well, it was too intimate a thing, but he meant he had the things that cheered him embedded in the soil of his head, growing there and thriving and flowering, an internal garden of prophylactic inscriptions, whether about fish or painting or courts martial, into which enclosure the intermittent violence and scapegrace mayhem of his flying career could not reach, and not even the scattered

Paul West

mind that resulted from tours of duty all over the world, adding up
to a cosmopolitan posy, the upshot being that he had a mind within
a mind, as he once phrased it when high on scotch, not his usual
tipple, a circus minimum within the circus maximus, after which
they lugged him off to bed, a motion that fetched bile into his
mouth and past his lips onto his best-looking terra cotta tie, chosen
after stealthy consultation of his tie rack's harmony chart, what
they failed to understand to just about the same extent as his
sister's being his vision, never worded, of a chariot race in an outer
circuit paralleled by a similar chariot race in an inner circuit, a
very simple symbolism but sufficient for Clegg, who just knew
he would die if all the pressures and percussions of his outer
life got through unstrained and unpurged into that final resting
place his photographic memory was, so that what he held on to
might have seemed, to any mental trespasser, denuded or woefully
attentuated, a life factorized or castrated, less something to remember than something to pump water into, or fertilizer, spray
with malathion, drench with cupboard love, but certainly not leave
as such, an as such which the uncomprehending sons of bitches
who spilled scotch on his tie could not even get to first base on,
their lives being outside-inward, his own being inside-outward,
hell that was no fucking way to formulate it, what he really meant
was simplicity itself, in its unstained underpants, he Clegg sifted
what went inside his head to stay, because what stayed took root
and therefore had to be something he could live with, after a dozen
years at this he had a mental version of perfect squadron drill,
every move according to the book and perfectly executed, the leftovers having been dumped, well, not quite outside, but into a sort
of septic tank within the mind, where motion was limited, the sun
never shone, and what was vile inevitably broke itself down into
what had no smell at all, some of this having come from Napoleon
himself, who said the mind must be like a chest of drawers so that
you could ignore the contents of the drawers closed, some of it
from Grandfather Josiah Cornelius Clegg, who died at 97, having
kept himself young by diligently forgetting each day as it passed
and starting each new one fresh, a six-foot perpetual tadpole of a
man whom Clegg adored, had gotten his first taste of fishing from,
and how to use a saw, a smoothing plane, an awl, lore never to be
forgotten, not even in the jungles of Vietnam when a pebble amid
the mind's flux and the uproar of high-explosive was as manna
within a hamburger bun, Clegg himself being quite certain he

196

survived because of what he learnedly called mnesiac hygiene, un-
practiced by the majority, but essential counterpoint to the rocket's
red glare, by which Clegg actually advanced to the point of decid-
ing I have finally learned how to live, it is an esthetics of give and
take, it takes very little, but that little within you has to be your
Stonehenge Parthenon, no matter whose lives it costs excepting
your own, it just has to be as constant during your lifetime as the
genetic code seems to be, like the seasons, the heart, otherwise
kaplooey, your life is as good as over, there is no return game, the
mind happens to be like a private swimming pool, pale blue water
if you keep it clean, green if you let the algae pile up, the most
fruitful and soothing thing in the world being to plug in the vacuum
cleaner, with its variable 360-degree brushhead, and float it gently
over the bottom surface, three or eight feet deep, like someone
divining for water or uranium, wiping a six-inch wide band clear
with each motion, with the towering pole above or behind you, un-
immersed, flicking trees or providing itinerant Monarch butterflies
en route to Florida for the winter with a resting place in sunlight,
better than cold and stiff in a tree for the night, their orange and
black reminiscent of golden trout, *salmo aguabonita*, what a lovely
name, it loses its colors if you rear it at low altitudes, but not the
Monarch, who might be glad to see you ridding the pool of algae,
better than the so-called guardian, flying saucer crammed with
chlorine cachous, that tours around the rectangle suffusing the
pale blue water with dissolving white powder, your arms get tired
of course, but a full season's vacuuming develops the bicepses,
correct as to plural I try to be, the worst part being the murk that
gathers inside the wrinkles where the vinyl has glitched a bit in
settling to contour, the next worst part being the dust suspension
the act of vacuuming always creates, taking a day to settle again,
just like life, you can't move dirt without disturbing some you
cannot move, a most peculiar thought for one who carried with
him on reconnaissance flights the touch of curare that will end
him in a few seconds, no questions asked, no orders given, it being
quite up to him whether or not to use the infernal thing, like
Cleopatra with her asp, your mind in extremis fixed on images of
home, that very pool whose skimmers filled with frogs and little
rodents, bees and spiders, most of them dead when you tapped the
basket against a tree, but as often as not a frog escaping flip-sprint
into the grass again, unless very unlucky and being sucked along
the underground pipe into the filter itself, where air is not, not

even for misnavigating frogs, whose limbs, ah, perhaps seen from
the rear while bouncing above a horse's saddle might have more
appeal, whereas those of the giraffe are truly sexual, full of a high-
strung twitching lasciviousness born of life conducted among tall
trees, at which thought he was once more vacuuming with a pole
at least fifteen feet long, wide enough to touch bottom half-way
across at the deep end, one of the bizarre sensations he had being
that he was poling an invisible barge in slow-motion through ultramarine lotions where no fish swam, the water making an occasional sucking clonk as he pushed the brush deeper and the metal
pole filled up to water level, only to empty itself again as he lifted
the pole upward, but that sound was much fainter, easily fainter
than the woodpecker wholeheartedly hacking a gash in some tree
or even the cross planks above the fake oriental garden out front,
how it battered its beak at the wood, its voice when scared off a
loud *peenk*, its vice must have been solitary, like the man vacuuming the pool, shifting all that muck into the sand filter, whence,
during backwash, it poured out on to the rough grass in the rear of
the house, not that he thought about the suspended particles when
he ventured in, his slight bloat enlarged by the blue shallows but
made lighter as well, the vinyl smooth to the soles of his feet like
bosom-skin spread out and oiled for non-resistance, and once graced
with his medals tossed into the deep end so that, according to the
pool manual, he could test the water's cleanness, his technique a
variant of the one that says you should be able to tell which side
up a dime is on the pool bottom, the chore in this instance easier
because the medals were bigger than dimes, he having thrown
them in out of some forgotten pique, either to show her how little
he cared, or how little she, who in fact, this being earlier than the
phase in which he sported horns, dived in and brought them back
to him, dried them off and polished them with a metal-restorer
containing acid that could have seared her hands, a poignant
thought whose neck he wrung, exclaiming By Jiminy, the nipples
of her tits are rough, as if piranhas have been nursing on her, so he
had her supple them with vaseline nightly while watching television, a sensation she grew so to like that it occupied her in the
day as well, whenever the impulse took her, comfortable in a soft
chair shaped like a toadstool and tweaking what might have been
invisible knitting while the caustic sap drooled from her, to no
purpose, since he had refused to be any more marinated in all that,
the need to get out and fly at something exceeding the speed of a

shout for help being paramount, backed by an optional need to kill or strafe as the mood took him, not that the majesty of flight escaped him, but it was only a characteristic of flight, one of his maxims, borrowed, being that he who collects enough chamberpots will not eventually find the holy grail but will have a lot of chamberpots to choose from, such as the cast of his mind, practical in a hobbyist's way, romantic only through formulas, religious only in the fashion of one who relishes the outdoors life, his temple a tent, his altar a frying pan over a pine-cone fire, his sacrament an eviscerated salmon, none of him outright vicious, none of him outright amiable, enough of him patriotic and loyal to secure him a reconnaissance job, the qualities needed being nerve, stolidity, and low paranoia when confronted by superhuman machines, so he qualified easily, though he chafed alongside Booth the intellectual, the officer-class technocrat, two years in the Ivy League before transferring to the Navy, where he was needed more, whereas Clegg had often wondered if he himself had ever been needed at all, something optional and refuseable about him being evident in his face, at which he had spent so many hours peering, wondering if his eyes were not too bulbous, too often rotated themselves upward as if to examine an invisible passing aircraft, and gave a mild hint of never being able to rotate down again, to the mediocre plateau of ordinary folk, not that they worried half so much as he about the ample convexities of his cheeks, evocative of certain over-fed clerics, or the straight fleshy nose that someone had pinched hard on either side so as to force the flesh upward, thus making the nose fatter the higher up it went, a silly-looking tuber above the curlicued pout of his mouth tucked neatly into the mound of his jaw, whose lines were only a little more visible than they weren't, although he rejoiced at the inordinate length between his nose and the top of his upper lip, emblematic he had heart of sagacity and grit, the only flaw in his make-up being his ear lobes, which jutted out and tapered like the toes of Oxford fronts, a characteristic he somehow knew denoted unreliability, thus making him an officer who was wisely fickle, or bravely mercurial, and so what, I'll suck my navel, Clegg, no one is perfect and few are even gloriously above average, but Booth had only muttered, not being that much interested in Clegg's estimate of his own officerly qualities, an attitude that drove Clegg even farther into himself, tormenting himself from then on with his grotesque and unseemly resemblance to one Count Tommaso Inghirami, an early sixteenth-century secretary to the Lateran Council as painted by Raphael in 1512, chubby in olive-eyed aloofness inside a loose-fitting red skull cap, his entire mien one of upholstered sancti-moniousness somewhat at odds with his insistent personality, a bun face, a bulb face, an inflated and mushroomy face, a night-polyp of a face, a face as slithery as an eyeball, and that was when he looked at the painting of the Count right way up, the mouth-drying horror of it showing only when it was upside-down, and then it was a belly with two gigantic, widely spaced olive testicles at the groin, from which sprouted, thick to thin, the nasal erection all the way to the rosebud mouth of his navel, the only difference being that the Count was ruddy, rather like Booth, whereas Clegg was a nocturnal pale creature whitest in the face, that belly never exposed to sunlight, not even right way up when it was almost a face again, and he thanked God, Raphael, and the Count he never saw himself wrong way up in the mirror, which meant that he avoided fun-houses like the plague, certain that, inverted, his true belly would pour down into his belly of a face, double-paunching him until his chops burst, a loathsome event that might happen during aerobatics, when looping the loop, say, or during a stall, which explains to some extent why Clegg restricted himself dur-ing air combat to certain maneuvers only, but which does not explain how he survived, a man with an aversion to being inverted, whether in his own plane or in a capsule rolling down a mountainside, the fact being that he was very expert indeed at those aerial motions he permitted himself, perhaps even fooling enemy pilots by not looping when he should have, and so forth, so that he shot them down from the midst of an expectation unfulfilled, he, Clegg, who prided himself on his kindness but who, for private reasons akin to avoidance of nightmare, broke the rules of the game, becoming not quite an ace yet good enough not to be trifled with at combat altitude, even when the mouth-puckering bile filled the space in front of his teeth and his liver slid out of its site, all he had to do being to aim and fire, the other veered away disintegrating, not as if Clegg were an angel of death but as if he were its inspector-general, actually in the course of combat having managed to do a commentary on himself, in the vivid present, hushed into the back of his mouth and nestling behind his nose, thus making himself epic on the spot, never mind what happened during the dogfight of the moment, whether he missed or spun out, took metal fragments or nearly swooned, never mind which assorted sensations he recalled later on, from the frozen cramp of his upper brain to the blurts of pain in his knees, from violent earache to the slight numbing of his finger-ends, none of this of course during the Battle of Britain, when the auspices of heroism were untainted and gorgeously heraldic, permitting him to ask Booth offhand giant questions, Shall we pop up and kibosh a few Huns?, to which the other's answer was the propeller churn of his Spitfire to Clegg's thundering Hurricane, a Rolls-Royce noise appropriate to updated knights of the round table, the table being deep underground in the Operations Room unfindable in the countryside of Kent, on whose crowded top disks and counters and actual models of planes represented men and aircraft in the abstractest manner possible excepting that of curt numerals, there being no little wooden moveable chess piece that stood for ripped lung, demolished heart, intestine scissored through by tracer bullets, an eye flopped down the cheek in the upstairs cold where blood froze like the water slicked onto their hair by early morning schoolboys in Maine, wanting to look smart, or like the spit that made a cracking sound even before it completed its parabola from mouth to ground, all from Clegg's childhood and the childhood protracted into his thirties, he who had walked a whole day with an apple between his thighs, had for a dare kept a squirrel in his bed nightlong, had enclosed a whole frog with his heaving mouth, stood at attention in the forest for an hour with a sprig of viper's bugloss in his dangling penis, eaten bedstraws, gromwells and the wand-like stems of blue toadflax, discovering the textures of a world he could not even name, an act of omission he later made up for by learning the fancy names of fisherman's lures, dry flies called White Wulff and Spirit of Pittsford Mills, nymphs called Leadwinged Coachman and Zug Bug, scores of them, all contrived by obscure, taciturn men in dingy sheds across the breadth of America, fiddling with feathers, fibers, olive dubbing and tying-silk, merely to trap a fish, not so different from air combat, except in the one you cast a bait while in the other you came cleaving down from out of the sun, if you knew what you were doing, and zapped the fish into the lower depths, at random destroying the pilot's pancreas, his rib cage, his kidneys, none of which you saw, thanks to the thickness of flying suits and G suits in later years, it was a serene way of making a living until the day came when your own intestines flowed green into your lap while you plunged downward inside an arrow of smoke, blinded and broken, yet wearing the perfunctory dun blue winding sheet with brief honor.

201

# The Balusters

## *Jason Schwartz*

THE BUILDING.

Well, the colonnade; the balcony.

The sculpture, one concedes, is chipped.

There is always mention of the drapery, furthermore, pertaining to the way it falls across the shoulder — pertaining, indeed, to the sharpness of a pleat.

The road bends.

Oh, and the square — the square is famous. There is a tomb, you see, or a fountain — it is to this effect, in any event. An inscription cites "a great fever"— which accounts for the soldiers, it would seem.

The city was invaded on this day in 1680.

Common oaks grow outside the fortress — where, evidently, a foreign woman, a countess, was executed — early in the morning, by hanging, the hem of the gown a bit frayed, it should be explained, from age.

The hat shop is open today, but the butcher shop is closed. There are kiosks, too — one sells trinkets, another sells Stilton cheese.

There is an obelisk near the river.

A man mispronounces the name of the bridge — yes, and he blushes.

But the building — do you see the balcony there? And the little mark on the column? There is a flag. There is a broken pediment.

A woman stands at a gate.

One, of course, is easily lost.

An excursion.

The town hall is notable for its volutes, but the gentleman discusses, instead, a bust of General Agrippa, which has been stolen, and the house's oriel window, through which, according to the story, Bismarck once saw a ghost. Marshal Turenne was killed in Sasbach, in fact, not Gernsbach, so, no, it will not be possible today to see the plot and the stele — though, happily, there is — if you will

202

forgive the crude juxtaposition — a view from the keep: yes, look, such a remarkable hillock. He adverts to the wind in the castle's courtyard, which is solemn, and to the garden, which is formal, and to the servant who strangled the children on the grand staircase — which leads, as you can now see, to the room of mirrors, where a woman is tidying her hair.

I bundled the letters. I kept the photograph — or I saved it, if you would prefer. The newspaper was discarded. The map, moreover, was torn.

It did begin to rain. I naturally felt a bit foolish. I held the rail. There were pots of flowers, passers-by. Somebody pointed at a telamon.

I suppose the door was locked.

But the soldiers — let us return, if we may, to the soldiers. They died, you will remember. There is always mention of the bedclothes — and the bannister, the little birds, that pattern on the wall.

Oh, now the square, on the other hand — there are no pigeons, for instance, in the square. Here are the people, though. There is actually something of a crowd.

Other facts occur to one.

The hat shop is open today, but the butcher shop is closed. There are wrinkled curtains in the windows of the dance hall — which was built after the war. This house was once the residence of a general.

The bedroom faces the river.

A history indicates the manner in which the objects on the table were arranged — the ink blotter here, the stack of paper there — oh, and that he wore a herringbone coat the day he murdered his brother.

There is a handsome drawing of the pistol.

The hospital is the same hospital — and the benches, at least, do strike one as antique. The park is "austere," according to the diary — but "green," merely, according to a letter — in which there is also a reference to "anguish."

There are kiosks.

One makes a small purchase.

The road, as we have already remarked, bends.

The building — well, come a bit closer. Now the ornamentation is distinct, certainly. Guilloche; torus. One considers a blemish at the center of the design. One considers the elevation of the capital.

The sculpture does not resemble the *Apollo Belvedere* or the *Cnidian Aphrodite.*

There is a flickering here, a glint — or, anyway, this seems to be so.

But the balcony — you can see the balcony, of course. A woman opens the doors in the morning, at this hour. The balusters are urn-shaped — yet this fact, one imagines, claims very little.

A letter lists dates.

There follows, though, a digression concerning a man who was poor, whose children were not well, whose wife — we should be plain — died. The man's screams were "said to have been louder" than the screams of a certain king — to whom we shall return.

The river floods on occasion.

The road is named for a countess, quite clearly, not a baroness, even if the latter title is the one indicated on the map — on which, furthermore, the legend is blurred. Well, at any rate — now and then there are parades.

But the building — but there is apparently something amiss in the archway. And you will please pardon the little mark on the column — and the shadows on the steps.

The flag snaps about a moment.

A man walks across the lawn.

An engagement.

Well, a misadventure.

"Monument," one is told, comes from the Latin root for "monster."

The diary, however, does refer to "a more amenable hour" — and there is, certainly, some shapeliness to the day. How one wants everything to be dear — the stones along the road, the engraving. But is it clever to suspect the inscription? the wind? the manner in which the handkerchief is lifted into the air?

I suppose it was taken late in the day — or that there was something untoward about the light. Here, all the same, is the boulevard. There are automobiles, a signboard. A name is shown on a shop's awning.

The fellow is smiling. My wife is wearing a hat, a scarf.

The roof of the hotel is cut off.

But the window—but is there a woman at the window? Well, the countinghouses, according to the diary, "look like Napoleon's hands"—and there is some mention of an alley.

There are blind arcades and Lombard columns, too—and a square coping. King Leopold's skull, if we are to believe the story, is buried at the foot of the tower; the pavilion has a Baroque façade.

The frieze has carved faces.

The map indicates a fortress, a river, a dam. This road is named for a burgher—who once lived in this brick house. This road is named for a margrave—whose last meal was haddock, stewed prunes, watercress and a chopped gherkin.

The museum displays a madder-colored garment.

How one does speculate about the clothing—and about the bed, naturally. There is, as you know, a purse; let us presume that the stationery is new.

A letter lists cities—and "dragon's blood, ostrich feathers, a gizzard." There is a description of a lawn.

A man stands at the steps.

The sculpture is chipped.

The window, of course, is dark.

# Two Poems
## *Cole Swensen*

### SHOULD SOMETHING HAPPEN TO THE HEART

*— for H. A.*

1.
If you look right here on the graph, you can see that little leap and
then the plateau. A bee trying to cross a rural road. The scale is
staggering. He or she may put a hand up to the chest. He or she
may think she's just out of breath and think how odd to forget that
you'd just been running so fast.

2.
If the fist quickened within and he's holding on while something
else drowns. Actually, it's not a single leap, but if you look closely
you'll note an entire flight, how rash, and now it's a flying creature
charging against the lighted window. It's funny what you notice
and how slowly you notice that it stops, while in the movie, someone's life goes on and they can surely hear you but they don't turn
around.

3.
We are still not clear about the role of irregularity in the functioning of the human heart.
Whether
or a sudden shift
a slight skip;
you lie awake
an ear just over his chest, you couldn't count
but he lives through the night anyway
and in the morning he's fine in fact it seems
a certain chaos reigns as he shifts
in sleep or slips and then slips back here again.

4.
But if the gravity of the heart could be properly computed, which is to say, its gravitational pull on the surrounding organs, arteries and vessels with an end to determining finally what orbits it as a strange shadow seen when the hand is held up to the heart as a bright light shined through the body of the subject just before the cardiac seizure begins, just seconds before, before the hand has had time to crawl to the breast like a nursing animal or the fist can slam down on the table and the splinters of glass can release whatever the object is, it is now a flitting impression of a figure fleeing a stifling room.

5.
In other cases, the left arm begins to ache, the blood like lead where the cry is stuck and as if struck by a sudden thought, the gaze goes blank and she thought he was going to say something but when he didn't she turned away thinking nothing of it. The octopus has three hearts. A bee is lost on a road. It is summer and the children are laughing and screaming on the other side of the lake but they are hidden by the glare of the sun across the water.

6.
Arrhythmia that marks
but you'll note
something locked inside the chest, running,
is almost escaping, an autonomous animal intent on erasing though
the human body cannot live
for even a moment without
and if the animal gets frightened
by loud noises, for instance shouting or crying, it may find another
home or, even homeless, refuse to return.

7.
Recent studies have shown
shock; her hand up to her mouth
but she couldn't have

"I clamped my hand to my
I watched him across the room. I think I
He got farther
The base of the regulation of the heartbeat is electrical, though it's
known that at least six
different conductors can be, must be, may very well be
often a spiral wave
breaks and falls.
A sound far off.
She touched her own
lip as a stranger might touch it if
a stranger could ever touch another like that.


8.
The heart of the adult male is a pound to a pound and a half of
roughly shaped like a hand, closed and placed heel down on a table
on which a glass of wine sits refracting the early evening light so
that a wash of red covers the hand and heads toward the wrist,
rising. Once we were alive. It happens when you're not thinking.
The breath that holds itself, no longer asking anything of us.


9.
Now we study it and it doesn't hurt anymore. I love ink. It stays
right there. It keeps track while the body in the air takes on some
new form before it telegrams. We no longer regard the signals as
chaotic; rather we consider that their pattern will not be repeated
and he'll go on in the new language until we can no longer see him.
He was playing with his child out in back of the house when the
child suddenly got enormous and he couldn't recall the word.
Sometimes it doesn't hurt at all.

## SIGNATURE

*— for J.-P. A.*

1.
Make the body speak or say:

Repeat after me:
    the body is composed of coordinates in space
    they must match
    they must break
    something
    you must be able to hear it break

and this is where
I live where
are my hands


2.
And now the body is yours
and you fill it completely
what moves and say here:
    what
    and it moves
let me touch your lip        if it is your and it is
sheer touch but the lip; how far and whose
now are the hands


3.
And this is where and to watch
spinning away at that speed
the impossible the mouth or curve
within a curve what the body does
so certainly know, please

(I think of hands but they move alone
untouched and there's a clarity to the sight
all over the house it's not you
but your body that is impossible on a
running horse on a falling horse)

4.
Or here the body could say: inseparable from

The body: "Tear me away." There's something
white that begins          the limits of attention or to
say:

and begins to turn
                              what word
the solid bone is
and there, the possible
a smaller curve
      silent and private country
      of the skin          not the visible one
now
refuse to say
Speak now


5.
And all of them were changed. You hear the positions
shift. Yes here the body could:
      Repeat: Sleep now in my hand, my cupped hands
He drank from the cup of his hands as the water
ran down his body all over his body drowning
his body you could see to the bottom there


6.
When the words are carved directly into the body
we find the memory fundamentally altered
The digits in the musculature
That whisper and the other one,
they overlap they tongue to tongue
They are mine. Your body falls.
Which places it in space.
What makes a body real is its falling.

7.
Where the body could say:
    here the marriage of skin
    to internal skin here it binds
Walk here. Stand. Turn.
What the body would

cry of a different animal
random material
of a single limb
of a limb as if it lived
this life too.


8.
And here the body is burned into the background

    The corporeal sense of the very
    Felt upon the chest; an impression just on
    the sternum, something moves

but the body does it anyway, every day
a thousand times a day
You are leaning in a doorway
You are leaning down to pick up
something falling.


9.
When you wake up from a hypnogogic state
because a sound in a dark room and you can't place
the room and you think of every room you've ever
known and it is not this room.

# Agost

## D. E. *Steward*

THEY MAKE THEIR WAY to the Odra induction point in Zagreb from the central station, Glavni Kolodvor, and as at induction points everywhere all time, individuals enter but leave in uniform, ranked and grouped, and under orders

Bus line to Odra passes Zagreb's steep-bowl football stadium and crosses beneath the autoput once Yugoslavia's most important road

Zagreb to Belgrade via Slavonski Brod in the sixties then new two-lane autoput that stopped in construction chaos of heavy dust and cutbanks pushing against the Sava River escarpment bluffs at the Motajica barely inside Bosnia-Herzegovina, sundown, late dusk, brilliant sky, steering along on no road beside a labor brigade of a hundred students shovels and picks shouldered trailing back to camp from the road-head singing Slavic strong Mussorgsky-style choruses, lithe women students' hair piled in sunset profile, the power of that stirring certitude flushed tingling driving on toward town, the dust and the VW's low-gear grind, the singing's resonance, the deep dusk deep red light

The highway on which Croat survivors and dead were brought out from Vukovar when it fell to Greater Serbia near the beginning, and the highway on which the northern theater of the civil war moves back and forth

Eurodeath, Euromacht, stench of Hitler-Stalin, smell of the Hundred Years' War, stink of every chronic death-making human fault circumstance, fetor of media gape pop-death world unconcern

Worst of European *Zynischpolitik* since '44

At the Odra end-station of bus from Glavni Kolodvor, where Croats become soldiers, men and boys enter induction camp gate after arriving from upcountry

From Varazdin close to Hungary come four eighteen-year-olds in on the Koprivnica train. Young Euro-consumers with extra shirts and underwear, cosmetic kits and Walkmen in soft logo athletic bags, trim, clean, two with Levi jackets, one with knee-torn whitened jeans, all with logo-sneakers and mothers who saw them off, turned them by their shoulders brushing down their clothes, hugged them, cried as their train pulled out

Search around Glavni Kolodvor for where to report. The information window doesn't know, the station master's office sends them back outside to look for the military police. Out near south end of station they run into two soldiers one of them knows from home and they stand talking among foot-trafficked flower beds in the open between the main post office and station. Two white UNMO Jeep Cherokees, an IRC white Toyota Landcruiser and one white UNHCR Mitsubishi van are pulled in off the Jurisiceva against an open curb, oil-stained asphalt adjoining a large dry fountain

The UNMO is the military mission, the IRC is the International Red Cross, the UNHCR is the UN High Commission for Refugees

Open space for tens of meters in three directions from the wide steps of the post office, deserted except for a woman with three heavy plastic bags at her feet keening on a park bench closer to the blank end of the station and another woman under a vineless pergola aside by a brazier roasting ears of corn

The four recruits and the two soldiers talk, no smiles, no laughs, no jokes, as a fat West African, dirty brown woolen slacks, appears down the post office steps with his car keys in hand walking obliquely away toward one of the UN Jeep Cherokees, sputters in English, then continues in French boasting that he's just driven straight through from Skopje, an impossibility

He could just as reasonably claim to have driven from Thessaloniki or Tirana

More than 150km beyond Split under extreme conditions to make

213

*D. E. Steward*

the refugee center in Medjugorje 40km below Mostar

That far again on around Mostar and up to Sarajevo from the south for anyone who dares

Skopje in Macedonia, another realm, a further step removed

"Concrete dust, urine, old cheese, sausage, tobacco, plum brandy, sour body odor, long-unwashed clothes"

Far more than two hundred thousand Bosnians have died

Gurneys as ubiquitous as cars

A year into the war Serbians targeted Sarajevo's library with incendiary rockets and destroyed Bosnia's cultural record

". . . history, geography and travel; theology, philosophy and Sufism; natural sciences, astrology and mathematics; dictionaries, grammars and anthologies of poetry, treatises on music and facades adorned by columns, horse-shoe arches, rose-windows and turrets. The metal structure of the roof through which the rockets fell looks like an enormous spider's web, the pillars of the inner courtyard preserve little of the delicate stucco work, the central area is a huge pile of rubbish, debris, beams and charred paper . . . the forgers of Serbian national mythology . . . fulfilled their ancestral dreams of annihilation: thousands of Arab, Turkish and Persian manuscripts have disappeared forever"

Four standing talking earnestly at Glavni Kolodvor don't yet think of killing. Two in uniform don't either, not yet having seen combat. Their fatigues with factory starch and folds, their unit patches a comic-book art saucer-sized black puma head-on with pearl-glistening fangs, claws and eyes, same bizarre totem-power tribe brand ID visual effect as the logo clothing and sneakers of the recruits

Three older NCOs, hatless, well-used fatigues now pass by for the post office steps, headed inside for Poste Restante to pick up a cashier's check from a bank in Munich in payment for complicated deals involving returning Scandinavian relief trucks. Before the war these were employees in the Transport Ministry

Younger men go silent as the sergeants pass. They have tiger unit patches in tawny gold and glistening highlights, again in comic-book style. All three fought during the retreat from Vukovar

Woman at the brazier roasting unhusked corn between the south end of the station and the men reaches to turn an ear, notices it is singed to blackening and pulls it to the side with others that are done. She rents a room out in the Klara near the Sava Canal, in the evening hides her brazier and extra charcoal behind a track-end bumper out in the yards a few meters away before walking home. Her husband was killed during the destruction of the Banja Luka mosques. She came to Zagreb after burying him

Banja Luka's two grand mosques, the Ferdahija Dzamija with its serene inner court from 1579, and the Arnaudija Dzamija dating also from the late 1500s, are immense rubble piles of collapsed and broken cut white and gray stone and plaster dust

The four enlistees now know where to go but in the manner of posturing men talking it takes longer for the dominance of the two soldiers in uniform to be imposed on the others. The one with knee-torn jeans who has been leading from point to point around the station, the questioner, the one who focuses, who organizes the others, cajoles them, has taken charge

In combat, where privates and the opportunists have the highest survival rate, he will be the first of the four to die

Arrived at Glavni Kolodvor hair already cut military short. Girl friends nuzzled shaven necks amazed at their going away to do unimaginable things. Through the pressing ritual of moving to last night's sex, each imagined their partner with others while they were away, the men seeking dangerous strange Bosnian opportunities of young mysterious southern faces under shawls and desperate wolf-eyed scratching fulvous full-maned Serbian women in absolute departure from familiar, imaging aching, monumental, wack-off dream adventures

Left home on a train to Glavni Kolodvor, to induction and training,

215

and then perhaps only dozens of kilometers south to redress long-chewed historical wrongs. Directly into the combat noise, incoming shells, mortar rounds and rockets, unexpected, incomprehensible in the volume of the noise, noise of an urban falling masonry plaster dust war. Beam creak groan collapse and die war

But at Glavni Kolodvor they're still not sure they know where to go as they pick up their bags purposefully. The two soldiers walk away toward Petrinjska ulica and the city. The four look around at each other, and when the one in knee-torn jeans signals with a jerk of his head they are off, back toward the front of the station to walk past the main entrance to the stairs of an underpass beneath the tracks and boarding quays

An old Macedonian, expansion band watch over a dirty blue shirt cuff, sits outside all night Third-World-tropics-style dozing in a tilted white plastic chair, night watchman for the parked cars in the Ocean Holiday Motel, Fort Lauderdale, looks Cuban in the light of the predawn, the vivid inset neon strip on the beach wall across Atlantic Avenue. He is ailing, answers uncertainly to Spanish, dropsy, bleary, hobbles badly, watery eyes, shakes his head and turns to disappear tired of thinking through the third or fourth question in Spanish before it's clear he isn't Cuban after all, and then he says that he's from Skopje

Night watchman in a plastic chair at the bottom of the Florida immigrant life but just above the Haitians who work the killing floors of South Florida slaughter houses and the little child prostitutes trucked around to their appointments in smoke-windowed vans and cars. The old Macedonian with only weeks left before he will be unable to walk at all, repeats, "Skopje, Skopje," then "Macedonia, Macedonia." Face overlaid sunwrinkles, an eerie unhealthy brown that glows in the first dawn off out over the ocean thirty yards away across the beach. He is what he comes from, what he was, what they are, what they do, what they even want to be, and his shuffling ineffectuality and grimacing hopelessness, no control except of his all-night plastic chair

Sleazy peasant revenge real estate war, not a religious war, not an ideological or even jingoistic war. Gang rape, solitary rape, slave bordello fucks of the Bosnian women kept apart under guard in barrack rooms or motel rooms or apartment rooms. A shit-fuck-piss in her mouth war

Rape and run, skewer, burn, shell lines of civilians at the water point, sit peering through your sniperscope at the world and zero in on the stomach of the Sarajevan, belly shots and they make so much noise thrashing that someone else will plunge out into the open and then you drop them too

Snipers sighting in on cities and towns, volkish nationalists slashing out to humble the metropole, with a maniac psychiatrist leader who loves himself and loves his hair

Against the cosmopolitans, the orthodox countryside against the Muslims and the Jews, aggies stomping through the living room in their rubber boots, provincials against internationalists, total horror of a non-ideological late-twentieth-century cynical European war

A one-language war, understand each another's Serbo-Croat when they shout back and forth across the lines and in house to house combat in the towns and cities. And they look alike. In old Yugoslavia they were in the same army units, in the same factories, apartment houses, universities, buses, trains, public toilets, movie theaters, sports clubs, cafés, stores

Jokes about cigarettes, next to survival and when there are none or they are about to run out, anything goes, lock and load and threaten if you have a weapon, or trade if there's anything to offer, anything, blowjobs to promises to grovel begging to holding up the relief trucks and rooting underneath the tarps for the boxes with the Marlboro cartons. Everybody smokes except teenage girls and some of the women, but except for the cities and the bigger towns there aren't many women in evidence anywhere

Croats fighting as if by Christian proxy, Serbs for an eerie mutagenesis of Pan-Slavism, Bosnians to survive, Macedonians ready to jump in for their ancient sun-flag cause and Albanians, if the time comes, will do it for Euro-gasoline for their military and police to keep down their own people rioting with nothing left to eat

217

*D. E. Steward*

Explanations of causation, historical roots, cultural inevitabilities, Christian versus Turk, East West, Orthodox infidel a Glagolithic cause, clog and obscure the reality so as to make it feel to the world outside that it's normal to have shelling of Sarajevo and sniper murder of civilians

Out of the tunnel on Glavni Kolodvor's lower level south side, the recruits find the bus stop island, and led by the one with the knee-torn jeans, start to board, then come back out of the door. No change. The leader hurries over to a busline information booth, negotiates passes, runs back holding them out like a hand of cards. The four get on, the bus pulls out

By sundown they'll be sworn in, next week carrying arms, in a month somewhere on line

Of the concentration camps, verisimilitude of Miklós Radnóti's march through the Serbian mountains toward Hungary and his death in 1945

"The wind goes though the zebra suits, our jaws become paralyzed. This bag of bones is thin, there's almost no flesh left on it. Will alone remains at the core, a disconsolate will, but only through it can we hold on. We have to have the will to wait. To wait until the cold goes away . . ."

Off the Belgrade autoput lies Vukovar and in half the rooms of the Hotel Astoria, Petrinjska ulica 71, Zagreb, live some of its refugees. Vukovar like the Second World War city battles of Smolensk, Warsaw, Stalingrad

One family to a room. Cooking odors, toys by the doors, men sit on the carpeted central stairs and smoke. Wives or sisters and kids appear often trailing from their rooms to ask things of the men, the men shout at the kids playing in the halls, a man on the stairs sobbing head in hands

One night two-thirty, two tanks starting up in the alley behind the Astoria. Diesel straight-pipe roars, muted grind of transmissions and cooling fans

"B" category hotel Vukovar refugees as angry as the refugees on the roads and in the railway stations of the war. Medjugorje's Muslim refugees. Split's Croat refugees. Refugees everywhere moving in the backs of trucks

The Astoria's billing forms pre-war name, the Garni Hotel Beograd, voided by smudged blue "Astoria" stamp pad. Up on the hill in Zagreb University, academics coin distinctive new Croat terms for common Serbo-Croat words

Downcast miens

Four enlistees on the Odra bus quiet as it passes under the autoput, trails across Zagreb's purlieus insignificant seen from an UNHCR official's white BMW speeding high along the autoput. The bus grinds down as it approaches induction station gate. The four are tired. One frightened, the one with knee-torn jeans knows what is down the chute. First night they will lie on bunks in barracks talking, then will sleep dreaming of uniforms and weapons and rightings of historical wrongs that will be theirs

Sampling credits to Robert D. Kaplan, *Balkan Ghosts* (New York, 1993); Juan Goytisolo; Robert Antelme, *The Human Race*; Simone Weil.

# Two Stories

## Mary Caponegro

### TOMBOLE

### I.

IT IS CHRISTMAS and the boy, with no thought of the old man he will become, is imagining instead what he wants for Christmas. He is not thinking of the spirit that needs no material gifts, the spirit his Mama says is the true meaning of Christmas, nor the chamberpot, he, infirm, might have by his bed at home or at hospital, in years to come. Least of all is he thinking of a death by another's malevolent hand, that death which lurks in the shadows, whispering rather than speaking. He is not even thinking of the woman on the balcony, opposite his family's terrace, who would send flowers for his funeral, the woman to whom he later, in his adolescence, will wish to send flowers (his adolescence, soon upon him, the stage between now and the old man he will, God willing, become, is far too remote to the shy unpreoccupied boy, who doesn't realize he feels such feelings for her, that he is even capable of such feelings). He is far from considering himself the master of the house, whose blood might someday flow from an unnatural death. He is a boy who can fall off his bicycle and scrape his knee, a carefree young boy who stares laughing at the hunchback who passes by. For Christmas he wants a cat, and at this moment he is hungry for his soup.

*At the age of fifteen, following his uncle, he arrived in a farm between San Cataldo and Marianopoli, in the countryside of Caltanissetta, where he was having an appointment with the chief. "After the reunion, in which I did not participate, the men went outside, they embraced me and kissed me and also gave me the money in their pockets. It was then Uncle Luigi explained to them that I had demonstrated I was destined to be affiliated with the organization."*

II.

There is something strange around the head of the Virgin Mary, something round and glowing, you are crazy, says his mother, have some coffee take communion, what, did you fall and see stars?, fall on your head with so little brains already there; brains in your culo; blows from the back of my hand will stir them up, then you should go straight to church like a good ragazzo instead of looking up a girl's skirt to see what looks always at the earth. Find instead a girl who could be your bride, Beppino, a good girl to take to church, take off your hat, Beppino, when you get there, always take your hat off in church, in the house, did you think you were living in a palace? If this is a palace then where are the guards? I would ask them to take you away, to the cave, to the grotto where you go to do what I know you do with the girl, when instead I might have had a child to whom the Immaculate appeared, a boy who would recognize what encircled her head as a holy accessory, not something from outer space.

*Today, twenty-two percent of Italians attend church on Sunday; a third or a quarter take communion, but only half of this number request confession.*

III.

Lord forgive us our sins. It is Christmas, we are on our way to church, led by the landlord, said by some to be a thief, said by some to have two women, his tenants, so called, a decent and a wicked woman, both of whom, can you imagine, sit beside him in church, on Christmas day. Both of whom parade up to take communion, and who quarrel, hands folded, one behind the other, on communion line, about the recipe for minestrone, which the honorable woman makes with more vegetables than beans, and the wicked woman makes with fagioli far outnumbering verdure. Whose soup he chooses is a stressful game, a test of love, and he has daily indigestion from the pressure of a choice by which he cannot win — compounded by the gas after he eats the spoils — for sometimes he runs back and forth from apartment to apartment, sipping, slurping, belching. I wouldn't be surprised if they all ate, together, less than one hour before receiving communion, gluttons that they are. Only those who stare at the poor devout hunchback don't stare at them in indignation or fascination. From the time the rooster crows, they quarrel, loud enough to be heard by the woman at the balcony across the way; the charming signorina is too gracious to complain, to shout "Già basta" from the balcony, but it is Italia after all, and the landlord, sitting, kneeling, standing between the decent and the wicked woman, listening to the priest drone on about the joyous news of Natale, cannot dispel the image of the legs of Lily.

*Certainly the temptations of the flesh always threaten poor mortals. Fornication, masturbation, adultery and homosexuality for the church remain grave sins. Abortion and contraception are very grave. But the devil has assumed many new forms that put society in danger. Theft is a sin.*

## IV.

I will beat you if you stare at the crazy man, says his mother, saddled already with a brood of children, or if you go in the nasty weather without your hat. For dinner you will eat only bread, and be lucky to find a bride, if you continue to insist on using these naughty words, think of nothing but tits and ass, and Beppino, I gaze in astonishment at what was made of my own flesh and blood, that seems instead the work of devils. By the lieutenant's balls, I don't know what to do with you. The death that speaks.

*Confession was once an art. It was said that Catholic countries weren't acquainted with psychoanalysis because they had confession. The bad action confessed unburdened the sinner of anguish and blame.*

## V.

If I go to mass every day, Lord, might I be blessed with a baby girl, relief for all the stress I receive from my son, il mio ragazzo, and may she my girl remain a maiden until such time she finds the man to be the father of her children, such as my boy, I fear, already may not be fit to be; may she be a maiden, not a piece of meat such as might be peddled by a shopkeeper, one night surrendering her flower to some drunk. Have a good cry over the 33 years of Christ, I now am the age of our Lord when he was crucified, and I go from grotto to fountain to grave with the same sound of the same bird in my head.

*Twenty years have passed since the time that armies of psycho-analysts and scholars decreed the death of the family, at any rate that danger. Today, instead, the exact same group of analysts re-affirm the validity. Why?*

## VI.

There is blood in the garden. It does not come from under the signorina's skirt, that mysterious place which sees always the earth, nor from the sacrament. There is death and there is sudden senseless death by someone else's hand. But have a glass of wine, forget it, dream of the lovely mouth of the wicked woman, watch the Pulcinella skit. Pray to St. Anthony for the mind you lost, and be grateful that you live in Italy. Buy some roasted chestnuts on the street, even though they cost, don't knock over the chamber-pot so distracted are you by the image of her mouth. But what death makes sense? says that sensuous suddenly disquieting hole.

*"Why did I leave the Mafia? The fault of Toto Fiina, the head boss. He betrayed the rule of solidarity that I thought formed the basis of Cosa Nostra. He used two different standards. He followed with great interest the trials of the men closer to his heart, on the other hand he did not show the same interest in us, the others."*

## VII.

With my hand I fire the cannon, with my knife I eat my hat. Don't listen to me, I'm a fool. What's got into my head? The weather is bad. Send me to prison where I can have a good cry, and grow old, like the old woman who lives here where already I'm the master of the house, an old house, and your mother and I had you brood of kids instead of dancing around the fountain that we may as well turn off in this terrible weather.

*They declare the death of the family, but in reality they are mak-ing a sort of artificial respiration that had in those years the effect of revitalizing.*

## VIII.

If I lived in a palace, I wouldn't need to be a thief, I could live, in society's eyes like a monk, but sit dreaming all day of the breasts of the woman on the balcony, who someday if I were brave enough I would invite to a party, but I am too timid to be a good hunter. The soldiers who pass under the balcony never fail to garner smiles but I only from the hairy one. If she flew from her balcony to my palace like a bird I would crow like a rooster, present her with flowers, then later a boy, and if that's still not enough, a little baby girl. And yet it is death, in the end, who speaks.

*The representation of the feminine was in fact from time to time affirming an idealized type, as in Italian woman of the Renaissance, the new woman between two eras, woman of the new Italy, post world war, the new Italian woman of fascism. . . .*

## IX.

I confess my sins to St. Anthony, and he seems to find them for me everywhere, devils in the garden, devils in the church, even if I have an innocent fleeting thought of the woman on the balcony after a glass of wine. I toast the soldiers who carouse by the fountain on Christmas, on their way to church, where I also, father of children, go, eating roasted chestnuts well before I take the sacrament, of course. We must all take the sacrament because of the fall that preceded us, reminded of it even as we admire the lush interior of our church, bedecked with flowers. Would it be a sin to bring one back to the woman on the balcony, who if I were courageous I would ask to escort to midnight mass?

*When I was giving confessions, I noticed many times the penitents wished a sin to confess but couldn't find one. They didn't have a notorious sin at their disposal, and supplied in general the missing of Sunday mass. The new catechism is useful for the confessor because it enlarges the list of sins, invests all the social life . . . the quotidian enters in the space of the sacred across the less confessable moments.*

X.

Because of shed blood during a quarrel, a man of honor is in prison, whereas the shed blood of a rooster or an eel would not put a hunter there. In prison praying to the Virgin or dreaming of the maidens whose buttocks can no longer be observed, and that part of her which always regards the ground, under her skirt, now unavailable, will make a fool of you. At this party there is only bread and cheese and imagine that! — the man of honor wants to flush himself down the toilet.

*The account of Guiseppe Marchese, "soldier" of the family of Corso dei Mille of Palermo, threw a bit of light on the complicated arena of the Mafia: countless informants, massacres more and more ferocious, finally leaving a deep gorge in that rift between the upholding and the violation of codes of honor, in particular the side of "Corleonesi" of Toto Riina, a group who executed violent acts. . . .*

XI.

What is your fear? asks the monk of the hunchback. Is it old age? Is it woman? Woman is wicked, says the hunchback. Do you not desire a bride? I desire, says the hunchback, to shoot a baby out of a cannon. You could not then take communion, says the monk. I desire to rub my hump against the tits of a wicked woman, and then against the bride bedecked for betrothal at the altar. What has this to do with spirit? asks the monk. You began this story, retorts the hunchback; you taunt me, you know before I am old I cannot take a bride into the palace, whether or not she leaves her tits outside, or at the altar. My bride, says the monk, is the 33 years of Christ. This bulge in my back, bellows the hunchback, my poor excuse for what I cannot give my bride, and for what you hide grotesquely under your coarse, modest robe.

*The Eastern Church sees correctly the confessor as a doctor rather than a judge of the spirit. In this perspective, the art of the confessor must be that of reminding all penitents of the possible sins, and then to make available to all absolution.*

XII.

His first communion, and even so there is a cannon in his head with tits and ass exploding, he can't help it, is he a pig then? That is what the woman whose T and A he fantasized would say, as would the old one or the shopkeeper or the hairy woman: all of them stingy, all of them in need of wine, or a sudden senseless death. Alora. How holy he felt until that cannon went off in his head.

*And how to reintroduce the sexual argument in confession? Strictness is not enough. I see with pleasure that the nightmare of the past, masturbation, is treated with new comprehension. Perhaps this is the way to make understood in what sense masturbation and premarital sex must be confessed. Because people today don't ask for indulgence, they know themselves all too well to be guilty and are relieved to have identified just what it is they are guilty of.*

XIII.

The boy is being beaten because he is worse than a thief; he exchanged the chamberpot for the minestrone, and behaved like a hunter in my garden, took his hand to the bird, whose fall he claimed not to hear; he claims he was drunk but on what? on caffè? He is drunk on his fantasy of what of her regards always the ground but pecatto, there is no hospital for what ails the spirit. With my hand I try to atone for the fall he represents.

*"It is easier to speak of the more traditional sins. Blasphemy against God is in first place . . . The kids have greater attention to ecology, the ones who confess to have destroyed plants and mistreated animals."*

XIV.

A brood of children will make you soon enough crazy, a fool or a wicked woman stuck in an old house because the bad weather never gets better. If I pray to St. Anthony I will only find another baby and the master of the house will go into a stupor, to find he is again the father of children. San Guiseppe, he will cry in his stupor, spare me the sacrament, I need only water, tomato, some bread.

*At the end of an era in which she has become, with great effort, mistress of her own life, the woman closes the grand search traced from the pioneers of emancipation and feminism . . . If all is maintained she will not renounce one millimeter of the inherited victories, but she does not wish all she has gotten to be flattened to a condition of parity with the male. The actual difference is affirmed as women profess that the rediscovery of identity of family comes sanctioned by laws and by rights. . . .*

## XV.

The knife that cut eel and pork and cheese and tomato for the party is the same knife we found inscribed after in his chest; can you explain that to your mother without fear of appearing a fool?, standing in your tie and tails, praying to the Virgin and St. Anthony to please God find you quick an explanation, shoot you quick from the cannon with two sacks of cheese roped around your neck as if you were a horse, shot like a comet, into the palace far beyond?

*Cosa Nostra wasn't the group he thought, but only a criminal group, who convinced him to enter into a family of informants. . . . Leonardo Messina began to speak profusely of himself and others, of the Mafia, of the structure in Sicily, in the rest of Italy, in foreign countries, making understood that the summit is not that one known in Sicily, but that there exists a national and a world Mafia.*

## XVI.

Fortunately the fall that led to his death came after he had taken the sacrament, the soldiers reported to the old woman who lives in the old house where she offered them caffè and they escaped from the hairy one, who always offered them nothing but water and chestnuts. On their way to see the Pulcinella skit they invoked St. Guiseppe and why, they wondered, when they arrived, did the black-masked, white-clad commedia dell'arte actor bow obsequiously from the stage and offer them his hand.

*Mary Caponegro*

*The Mafia is a particular case of a specific economic activity: it is an industry that produces, promotes and sells private protection.*

## XVII.

The guards were they supine would be delighted to regard what regards always the ground, under her skirt, but not in front of the monk, because that would be a disgrace, as bad as being sent to prison, or becoming instantly an old man, to whom the mouth of a woman is memory. But the mouth of a woman, reflects one of the guards, is itself a kind of prison, both prison and garden, is it not? It is part of a person's head, after all, but not the same as the man's, is it? Not just a place to pour wine. The guard is a hunter of just such mouths, so sumptuous that they could cause men to be sent to, or from, the hospital, and cause misers to fill their chamberpots with gold.

*"The woman who thinks to emancipate herself imitating the man refutes her natural mission procreative and educative, and with her very hands constructs a destiny of suffering," written in 1918, making many enemies, by Gina Lombroso. . . .*

## XVIII.

Since I'm not a monk but a fool I can pray to St. Anthony for what I never had in the first place: a maiden to call my tomato, whose tits put me into this stupor. She could call me her rooster and I promise not to be a pig, I will offer her the eel I can now only hold in my hand, inspired, says the monk, by devils, but the monk and I often quarrel, as I would never do with my maiden who is more basic than bread; if only the saint would answer my prayers and tell me where she is hiding.

*In a short time period she had to make haste and find a husband, or rather accept a husband, always the family's choice, making attention to marriage the priority by the age of twenty-six, canonical of spinsterhood.*

## XIX.

San Guiseppe would approve of the brood I produced, but I swear I would have done otherwise had I been a hunter, a shopkeeper, a thief (shooting or stealing or selling cheese) and not the drunk that I am. My brood and the bad woman whose mouth will be the death of me shall send me to the sepulchre; if I try to imagine the size of the lieutenant's balls I will weep, in my inebriated state, one tear for each of the 33 years Christ spent on this earth. The hairy one looks at me and I feel my years exceeded his already.

*With our life expectancy touching upon 80 years, with a youth that is protracted until 40, with a child at the right time, in contrast with our first great great grandmothers, who in 1881 could hope for a life of 34 years, who were having at midlife five children but saw two more babies die, who were "old" at 30. . . .*

## XX.

It's a disgrace to think of the legs of Lily when you are already the father of children, a new baby no less. (Go ahead, get as close to her legs as you want, they're as hairy as mine, and I bet they have lice.) The miser won't offer you wine in congratulations even as you stand in tie and tails, you will have to take water instead from the fountain. The baby's mother calls you a man of honor, and insists you leave the party, complimenting your handsome chestnuts, to go through wretched weather to receive the sacrament.

*She had to learn a single power that her sex reserved her: maternity, making an army between mothers-in-law and brothers-in-law. She had to above all model the children on images and resemblances of values handed down.*

## XXI.

When the mouth of the hunchback opens to receive the sacrament, you would think you were at a party rather than in a church, as if the Blessed Virgin herself fed chestnuts to an eel, as if a boy took the knife in a quarrel with the baby girl, his sister. As if a quarrel had erupted in our old house, into which no one but a man of honor is ever invited.

229

The person comes preselected by a man of honor, who studies at length his personality, his behavior and the quality demonstrated in criminal actions such as theft robbery arson, etc. Only if there is already evidence with repeated and unequivocal attitudes the aspiration of entrance to the Mafia can ascend to the first level. . . .

## XXII.

Would you trade the legs of Lily for the wicked woman's tits? Would you trade your sins for the 33 years of Christ? (He did for you, ungrateful wretch; you call yourself a Christian? . . .) Would you take the old woman as your bride? rather than the woman at the balcony who you have yet to get to speak to? Are you crazy? The blood of those 33 years for your sins, and all you can do is act like a Pulcinella on the stage, you're too old to be spanked, your punishment, we've decided, is death, go to your grave.

At this point the man of honor asks the representative of the actual family to "keep" this person with them to make him participate in criminal actions in the interest of Cosa Nostra with the exclusion of crimes of blood.

## XXIII.

It takes only one woman to make, in less than the time it takes to make a minestrone, a whole brood of children, offer your hand one day, stand in tie and tails, and suddenly you're in prison or a stupor, without so much as a piece of cheese. Put your head under water to banish the devils. You scratch your head, say you should have been one of the soldiers instead; suddenly the minestrone becomes a chamberpot and you're an old man who can never go out in the nasty weather.

CENT ANNI FA: CINQUE FIGLI E 35 ANNI DI VITA MEDIA. OGGI: UN FIGLIO E QUASI 80 ANNI.

## XXIV.

In Italia it is easier to find a fountain than a chamberpot. But if you go to the right party you have a chance to dance with the legs of Lily rather than quarrel with a wicked woman, which would later make you feel like an eel slithering into the garden. Even a hunter needs occasionally to take communion. Ask any bird; even a wicked woman is not content to be a piece of meat.

*But today it makes an echo, except using a more modern language, that of the French psychoanalyst Luce Irigaray, theoretician of difference: "Only a sexual right, that keeps track of the diversity of women, will give them a true identity."*

## XXV.

You can pray all you like to St. Anthony, until you're an old man, but you'll never be able to cut off the hunchback's hump with a knife. The palace guards beat him for praying to St. Anthony again to find that which regards only the ground: what hides under her skirt, but then I saw them kneeling themselves, with hands folded. Only a fool would throw a tomato at somebody's head as a cure for lice, but that's what he did, then he took that same knife to slice cheese. Finally he had a good cry. But honestly, would you rather inhabit an old house or a palace? Forget it, the way you dress, you'd never get past the guards.

*These gestures have a weight before God, that the man, precisely because he sins, is truly a free person.*

## XXVI.

It's a disgrace, those tits, says the old woman, if the baby cannot suck from them and you are not a mother, they merely encourage the drunk to remain in a stupor, consorting with devils. It's a disgrace to wear a tuxedo through nasty weather just to have a glass of wine. . . .

*In this manner, inside the security acquired in this circular journey, the Italian woman seems to have finally both desire and capacity to look inward, to gather together in one long embrace mothers, grandmothers and great grandmothers, to pay them the debt in her state of full consciousness.*

## XXVII.

It's a disgrace to eat minestrone with your hand, I know that hand is the one with which you fondle the balls of the lieutenant, I've heard him call you his tomato, I know because I am your mother, even though you call me the hairy one, and no matter how many times I go to mass, Italy is nothing but a lifetime of miserable weather for me: I dream of a thief and a knife, and no hospital exists in which one can be cured of a murder already committed, no hospital exists for a murdered spirit, because the first flesh of my flesh is a drunk, and the second a word even death shouldn't speak.

*There is a fantasy of family that precedes and accompanies the real family. There is an unconscious family, a "family of night" attached to the daytime family, that each one lives in reality; this unconscious family often enters into conflict with the real, to the point that, if we do not learn to recognize it, can create terrible conflicts.*

## XXVIII.

The mouth of my bride is also the mouth of my mother, and that gives a man of honor fear, you go to a party searching for maidens and soon enough you're roasting chestnuts with devils, no longer a man of honor. What is the point of the 33 years of Christ, when a knife could just as easily be used on the cat or the rooster? Or those soldiers who seem to have taken root underneath the balcony of the woman who should but will never belong to me.

*Women I have always understood after, at the right moment never or rarely. I asked for sex and they wanted love, I passed on to love and they wanted passion, and if I completed the mistake in saying love and passion, yes, but also intellect, they were offended to death. . . .*

## XXIX.

The balls of the lieutenant are as much a piece of meat as the legs of Lily, just ask the hunchback. You won't see him in tie and tails at church on Christmas, or the old man or the fool. Wouldn't that be a disgrace? How many sins are already brought like flowers to church or waxed sacs of cheese roped across a horse, as if there had been a death in the palace?

*Because in the Italian woman more than in others of diverse cultures, it seems to me, is discovered an almost naive movement between body and spirit. You search for the body and they are spirit, and you search for spirit and they are there, very bodily.*

## XXX.

If I found the blood of an eel on my grave I would pray to the Virgin, then ask the monk to say mass as he did for me after the quarrel that prompted the guards to take me to prison where I remained until I was the man who speaks from death. Only in Italy I take off my hat when I pass the fountain to catch my ever-flowing tears.

*In the heart of the boss there is also a place of pardon, provided the transgressions are venial sins: an inadvertent rudeness to another affiliate, an order not executed. . . . And often on the occasion of Christmas or Easter, the commission concedes an amnesty.*

## XXXI.

The lice in the hair of a man of honor would not be visible to the woman at the balcony, gazing down at his balding head, even if the man of honor, in tie and tails, had removed his hat in courtesy, and thrust toward her flowers, which might have had as their destination a mass or a party, chi sa? But the baby, the cat and the old woman closer to the ground see also the eel he conceals beneath his tie and tails. St. Guiseppe, however, is good enough to overlook.

*Offer prosciutto and mozzarella and they would like flowers, succeed in executing that curious operation of entering the florist and then running errands with flowers in your hand, but then or later you realize it isn't over, they want presents too, in particular the ones celebrating birthdays and saints' days, and that if you don't give those, when it is YOUR turn they make huge presents to make clear how much greater is their affection.*

233

Mary Caponegro

## XXXII.

A father of children without a bride is like Italia without tomato.
Even the hunchback can find a woman eventually with the help
of soldiers, if he dresses up as Pulcinella, if he only gets drunk on
water from the fountain and buys bread only from the shopkeeper
who helps the fountain's water turn to tears when he admits his
fear.

*But if you insist with flowers and presents they begin to think
you are trying to put one over on them, miser that you are, yes it
is clear you send flowers and presents in order not to sign checks.
And they turn it over in their minds until the one day it comes out
all the stories and history and explanations of your stinginess that
as such has spoiled the presents and flowers that don't count anymore and there is the need to begin all over again progressing from
carnations to red roses, from pendants to necklaces to even bigger
necklaces. . . .*

## XXXIII.

Because of the devil, the fall: our sins; because of our sins, the 33
years of Christ, the death that speaks, and hence Christmas; at
Christmas, communion to feed the spirit. But don't forget, inside
the palace is a cannon; behind its walls an old man lures maidens
with cheese, then takes them over his knee to spank. Spirit or no
spirit, I'm no fool.

---

Note: This story is composed of thirty-three narratives derived from randomly
ordered elements of the Italian game called Tombole. Each alternative paragraph
consists of "found" material from the Italian magazine *Panorama,* which the author
has taken the liberty of translating. Any mention of actual persons or places is used
for fictional purposes only.

LIBRO DELL'ARTE
OR, THE APPRENTICE'S MISTRESS

𝕳𝕰𝕽𝕰 begins the book of the art, made and composed by Giouanna ——, in the reuerence of God, and the Uirgin Mary, and of St. Eustachius, and of St. Francis, and of St. John the Baptist, and St. Anthony of Padua, and generally of all the saints of God, and in the reuerence of Giotto, of Taddeo and of Agnolo the master of Cennino, and of Cennino the master of Lorenzo, and of Lorenzo the master of myself Giouanna, and for the utility and good and aduantage of those who would aspire to attain perfection in the Arts that they might know what lies before them, and not be rash or unconsidered in their aspirations.

OF LAYING GROUNDS FOR PICTURES

Ottavo Dicembre, this millequattrocento trenta-sette, a survey of the property: wide variety of trees: almond, fig and olive; lindens, poplars, willows; walnut, maple, chestnut, peach and pear. Birds, some perched on branches; closer scrutiny reveals how mixed their breed as well: doves and geese, hens and . . . vultures; it hardly seems a recipe for harmony; chickens, rabbits, white rather than black hogs, minivers, a pond of fish. There is not sufficient order to imply breeding, farming, harvesting or gardening; the land, however, is not idle. An axe lies on the ground.

And then a house: a rustic one, perhaps a barn, some structure that appears to have been partially burned down, and through the inadvertent aperture whose scorched edges permit you to peer in you observe its squalor. The property outside is not arrested at the doorway, in that sense more a barn than house—extends instead into the vast interior. No one keeps the animals from strutting in and out: the chickens, calves, the hogs and sheep—their jaws in constant motion under roof as well as sky—roam freely. The minivers retreat, as is their custom: this inverse greeting is your only sign of welcome. Rabbits, even fish (inside a pond and out) sometimes come into view; they leap, they hop, they stop, the latter flap upon a table or the floor as if they strove to swim in air. This is well, you think, for you are hungry, having travelled who can say how great a distance? And yet, alas, no evidence of cook or feast (although the atmosphere is redolent of garlic, most pleasant of its smells); no hint of special treatment for the stranger, you, whose unannounced arrival remains unacknowledged.

You have heard of this house: that people also, though less frequently, less abundantly, wander in and out in curious attire, sometimes in scant attire. It is said that a woman relieves herself in the same manner as the animals, crouching on the floor. What sort of domicile then is this? Admit you're curious. Particularly when you spy whom you assume to be the very woman of these rumors, handsome woman, of unusual appearance, striking, one might say, white apron skirts tucked up above her knees, as she squats over what appears to be not chamberpot but porringer, one of hundreds, you would guess, whose contents, after being baptized by this golden stream, are vigorously mixed with a skewer you had failed to notice in her hand. It is herself whom she addresses, when she sighs, "My private gilding." Then a pause. "But was that the proper sequence? Where are my instructions?"

The woman covers this concoction matter-of-factly with white handkerchief, sets it aside, then seeks a pencil and scribbles something. Unfazed by someone's sudden presence, or her own awkward circumstance, she then addresses you:

"Welcome to our house," and then with raised voice she turns toward another corner, surely not to speak to sheep or hog, "No master, it is not your master, thank the lord" before continuing with sotto voce "though in truth I would not recognize him." Then directed once again toward you, "and please excuse its sorry countenance. It is a curious property, I grant you, who stand outside the portal and gaze tentatively, with an expression I can't precisely read: disapproval, trepidation, merely curiosity perhaps? Or pure disgust? Earnest maid I am I must reply, when you inquire, yes, it is always thus, or nearly always. But not resulting from indifference, I assure you, quite the opposite; I will endeavor to explain, if time permits."

She moves from porringer to porringer, stirring, peering, pouring and transporting; spanning greater distances, it seems, than those from house to house or town to town, greater than the distance you traversed to get here from a place that seems already distant memory? She voyages with anxious animated grace, negotiating piles of rocks and dung, bones and feathers, limbs of humans — plaster surely — limbs of trees, sparring creatures, lolling creatures, bathing themselves with their tongues. And in the farthest corner, is one giving birth? The cries that would confirm the last are in admixture with the general cacophony, so you may be mistaken. As you're squinting to determine whether your

interpretation is correct or the misapprehension of numerous objects and bodies in disconcerting proximity, she addresses you
again directly in ostensible non sequitur: "Can you tell me the
weather, good sir? Che tempo fa oggi? You stand out and I in, you
have come from afar; I'm ashamed to admit I have no time to
gauge the constitution of the day, for amid this ambient abundance,
only time is scarce. There is little room for chatting in our lives,
nor for reflecting either, for that is what the gold must do, and we
are but its handmaiden, as far as I discern, from what my master
tells me, or what my master's master tells my master: he inside,
who serves this other unrelenting mentor would greet you but he
is always occupied" (as are the seats, you see, plentiful but unavailable for weary travelers; they serve as pedestals for pipkins, porringers, creatures, feathers, implements, all manner of sundry
materials).

"Giovanna, do you call to me?" "No master, do not interrupt your
preparations."

To my distinguished master, Cennino Cennini, on this day ottavo
Dicembre, 1437
In honestly and thoroughly reporting to you my progress, I must
confess to you an omission in the figure casting of the prince and
bishop both. The fact is, master, I neglected to add rose water when
I washed the reddened bodies after casting; thus the noble fragrance
was not part of either man's experience. Please bear in mind, master,
that never having previously been cast, they will have no comparison,
and neither will think less of us for the fragrance he is not aware he
should have smelled. And, per fortuna, neither will offer to the other
conflicting details, for each serves to mirror to the other my mistake.
Your persevering apprentice,
Lorenzo

"The house is more a studio, a workshop you might say, not the
sort of domicile a man and wife inhabit, not the sort of house to
which you are accustomed, but a grand disorder that will ultimately yield perfection for the glory of our Creator, who, my master,
were he present, would not hesitate to remind you, also fashioned
our world in a sequence, one day at a time. Although our Lord was
thus engaged for but a week, and designed within his schedule a
segment of repose. Of this I might remind my master."

Just watching, listening, makes you yearn for rest yourself, not from the residue of journey but from this energetic spectacle devoid of intermission.

"Master will soon summon me, for we conduct experiments throughout the day, at every hour, often night as well. No, he is not my lover, your raised eyebrow seeks an answer: our routine is indeed domestic but not conjugal; please heed the finger at my lips and let this be our secret, for a woman has her pride; you understand.

"Rest or stasis, time to *not* do — Dio, if our doing ever would be through; I was incorrect to indicate we lacked only this. Add to this list then any quantity of love; what stirs the heart we have no leisure to indulge, while stirring all the formulae you see before you: every day a color to be made, or two, or three; various kinds of glue, from lime, from cheese, from rabbit skin; I'm beating every shade of egg yolk and tending to their mixtures with more care than this poor chicken takes to make the egg that is precursor" — she gestures toward the creature who now sits, domesticated, in her lap — "though I venture if she ceased to lay for us, my master's master would prescribe a way to make ourselves a simulacrum — which would, in fact, make my work easier, as I would no longer need to scurry between studio and town, where I find the hens who lay a lighter color egg, required by master when he paints the cool flesh tint of a young person's face" — idly stroking the annoying squawking creature, she at one point proffers you her hand, first fist, then loosely cupped, then palm flat out before her to display a new-laid egg! "This will be golden, nearly red," as if she could see through the shell, "but those from town a paler yellow, much less rich a color . . . it would be simpler to sit on them myself, until they hatch, but I am tending an infinity, if you permit my metaphor for this congeries of artistic gestation, and would ideally be, like Dio, in every place at once." Indeed, in this short span you have witnessed numerous activities involving animal and vegetable and mineral: stroking and cajoling; plucking and chopping; peeling, slicing, stoking, in general averting the disaster that seems to be every moment implicit in this multitudinous operation.

"If it were blasphemy to look to heaven, we are permitted to regard the sky; there I seek additional recipes: a hummingbird's velocity, combined with the industriousness of bee. We need their wings to paint the angels': wings and haloes both. If the chemist extracts color and medicinal substance from the insect, so should

238

I be permitted to make model of them in my mind, covet their flight and speed, while I make do with feet, until they ache, until I'm out of breath, until my face is blue, but I confide to you my master's face is red if I refer, even in passing, to how an egg is made."

"Giovanna, to whom do you speak?"
"To myself, Lorenzo, memorizing, do not be concerned.
"He must not be distracted. My master, you see, has no time for love, at least he does perceive it thus. Conducting our experiments takes all his time — and by extension mine — and making note of our results — at least those tasks which we complete — still longer. He feels compelled to keep a log of all we do so that his master, no longer looking over him, can be informed. Or so Giovanna does surmise. He sits writing to his master as we speak.

"In addition to my other tasks, I could deliver, were I permitted, master's missives to his master; he claims they are incomplete, and I say, should you not then finish one so as to free your mind to start another? (poco a poco fino a tutto aposto?) instead of juggling many works in progress, as we are required by circumstance to do in this our workshop, with our formulae and artifacts? Whereas with your words, I've counseled him, you might move in a more reasonable, expedient manner, yes — be spared the overwhelming span that constitutes this" — she gestures theatrically with her graceful golden-downed forearm toward the entire contents of the workshop — "bruttavista? At this point in our discussion he says that he 'will say no more on the subject,' a tactic of evasion he has learned from his master who oft concludes instructions thus. They too, that is, his missives, must be perfect, I suppose, though I do not see why what is here created speaks not for itself. I cannot help but think the time he spends with pen and parchment, since he remains in medias res, could be more immediately useful if we worked consistently as team, and add to our efficiency, allow us to enjoy the luxury of occasional siesta or the leisure to invite, to greet, the occasional guest, and show appropriate hospitality.

"For example, you arrived here at an awkward moment, although in truth there is no other kind within this six years' time — the recipe for the mordant required a quantity of urine; I do not stand on ceremony in master's studio, and thus I squat when necessary, fully aware that what is appropriate here may not beyond these boundaries constitute bella figura. And thus, sir, lest you be misled, by these motions of forming batter into loaves, which I perform before you now, I am not baking bread, but making gesso grosso, gesso sottile, not wheat and yeast but plaster, water: that which coats my hands most of the day — and the tub to which you cast your eye is not to shed the traveler's dust from your weary skin, the plaster must be kept therein until it nearly rot to get the silky texture we so prize; in the meantime, there are hundreds of things on the fire — and I, Giovanna, keeper of the flame — but none among them destined for conventional consumption, nor are any of these items the ingredients for the two light meals per day allotted to my master, whose voice you can, with effort, overhear, if you take advantage of those moments when the animals are relatively quiet."

Indeed the space resembles an inferno, a parody of perfection, not heaven but hell: a thousand fires. But how could hell be heaven's mirror?

### OF COLOR AND PIGMENT

From some recessed alcove, a voice reciting as in prayer: "Sinopia, cinabrese, amatisto, dragon's blood, lake; ochre, giallorino, orpiment, risalgallo, saffron, arzica; terra verde, verde, azurro. . . ." He makes a canon of the colors, ending only to begin again.

"When I speak to master of what he cannot bear to hear, of love, or blood, secretions, freedom or the future, he recites to me this litany of lovely color words which do not rhyme, I am afraid, with mine, which were when I began a sweetest music, and now are merely numbers and relations; measures and motions: those which can be used in fresco, those which can be used in secco; all of the former, in fact, apply to the latter, but orpiment, vermilion, azurite, red lead, white lead, verdigris and lac cannot be used for fresco. More strangely still, no extraneous color is allotted to a woman's skin, says master's master, she dare not redden her complexion or her lips, for if she be so bold, her skin will wither on the spot, and the white of her teeth turn black, as will the beautiful blue of the painted Virgin's painted mantle if varnished prematurely. And yet in gilding, it is black under gold which makes the brightest gold of all, to reflect all the light away from your eyes."

Mary Caponegro

Your eyes, meanwhile, are led away from her compelling visage to the unassorted storehouse of her stage. Her enchanting presence holds you captive no less than the clutter that confines you to restricted areas.

WHAT YOU MUSTN'T STEP ON (OR BUMP INTO) :

Ten paces to the right a porringer, then another, a pipkin, a set of various sizes, furnaces, animal skins, furs hanging beside hammers, chisels, to the left and center, animal droppings of various kinds, plaster limbs: hands, legs and arms, can it be to the rear a dead body?, mortar and pestle, another of marble, dust everywhere, every imaginable tool, from pincer to axe, my God the stench, the chaos of aromas (now that you're beyond the threshold, tentatively projecting inward into chaos), fruit and flower and feces; egg and oil and garlic; a general putrescence difficult to define; brushes, bristles, handles, feathers, charcoal sticks, hare's foot? — goat's feet too, with skin and sinew — yes, they need good luck, you think; she sees you pick it up, says, "no it's for disseminating precious dust. Did you think we were superstitious? On the contrary, we are practical; we are rational Godfearing people (unlike the vain women of Firenze who according to my master worship their reflections rather than the one in whose image they are made)" — next to the parchment and lead stile, you could swear you see a piece of bread; how hungry you've been; she sees you fasten there your gaze and shakes her finger as if to say "no, not to eat." It is not optical illusion, for this is really bread (rather than waterlogged loaves of gesso or glue) beside bottles of oil (linseed, olive), a marble slab, porphyry, with its quartz shimmer, a knife, bones of all sizes in various stages of imposed decomposition, baking dish, lamp, tubs, cakes, a basin, a penknife, scissors, brick, wax; no rhyme or reason to this vast desultory still life. Do you imagine vultures swooping over plaster limbs?

To Cennino Cennini on this day ottavo Dicembre, 1437
    Master, as to my progress, the report as promised. Yesterday I took a fish from the sea, to make a noble cast of it. Elated by my catch I thought to double my artistic yield, and trapped as well a bird that rested momentarily in flight, but I confess I had forgotten that living creatures without souls resist the process, and were expressly disrecommended by you. I could not keep them still. I did not wish to harm

241

them. I thought, O foolish creatures, how can it be that you protest an opportunity for immortality? Later I realized these poor lesser creatures lack the soul that houses immortality, and could not have the merest understanding of art's glory. Sometimes the volume of my efforts overwhelms me and I err, I become careless. I painted a hundred saints' heads circled by a hundred glories as practice, or penance for my foolishness. I finally cast them when they ceased to breathe but lost much valuable time. And added, I regret, to their suffering.

    Your rueful apprentice,
        Lorenzo ──────────


What goes on here? You're walking on eggshells no matter which way you turn: pipkins with yolks, pipkins with whites, in combination with Lord knows what other substances; when spilled they make the floor's inadvertent varnish, once it's on your shoes it's spreading everywhere. The house is like a hatchery, or bakery that produces neither sweets nor bread; yes better to linger in the doorway than attempt an ambulant relation to this organic clutter. Alternating with other excretions are the eggs; they're everywhere. "Please find a seat if you are weary; I've no idea how long you've traveled." (the preternatural richness of her voice) But easier said than done, as your gracious hostess is too preoccupied to realize what you've long ago discerned: that all the seats are occupied by objects. And she before you in another corner tapping egg after egg, balancing the severed shell to cradle that which it protected, draining off the fluid which surrounds each golden halo. "O master," she whispers, not intending you to hear, "if only I could reveal to you of what I am reminded by the whites." She, mesmerized by this ostensibly mundane activity, also mesmerizes who would watch. Thus you, in turn, without volition, inadvertent mimic, grasp an egg yourself; there are so many.

    "But if I give way to revery, I will forget my cataloguing, let me see, already I confuse myself: a half baked mordant here; beside a nearly finished glue, a color on its way to . . . O don't drop that egg"—but too late, you feel a caught thief and a clumsy one; "no one of them expendable though numerous, I admit. O my, the miniver bit you," she exclaims, compassionate but distracted, you suppress your own alarm at the gratuitous attack of the same animal who fled from you when you arrived. "They are normally so timid, I'm astonished, sir, perhaps you provoked it? Dispiace. Purtroppo, these same substances from which we fashion color

242

are used by the chemist to make unguent and salve. But here where we have every formula in process, none among them is for healing that which ails the body. Madonna, what you've started here: the pig fights with the lamb, the basket of eggs overturned. I will need to make a second trip to town now; O Dio, is the porringer on fire in the pipkin? The flame was not supposed to reach it; now another part of the wall will burn, the wind will whip its way in and unsettle all our careful work . . . an infinite number of mixtures on the stove? And the sulfurous smell will linger, confuse me." How she fails to be offended by the general olfactory cacophony eludes you when the place combines the scent of barn, latrine, pharmacy, bakery, nursery.

"Che cosa, Giovanna? Do you help or hinder?"
"Master, while you sit reflecting, and I work alone, we can make little progress toward our six-year goal."
"I didn't mean to scold you, sir — our guest — or to imply in any way you were at fault; it's you who may, instead, blame me, for this confusing swarm of things and creatures. It seems, I know, slovenly, but we are hardly indolent; you're trying to deduce what this plethora of props is for: a plethora of tasks that overwhelms even to itemize: we grind colors, boil down glues (from lime, from cheese, from rabbit's skin); on which stove did I leave it? I must reduce it to a half . . . hence my boiling now, and then dry it in the wind, but not the sun — How is the weather, did you say, or did I ask you, sir? Fa brutto, fa bello? Che colore il cielo? Piove o sole? Would you be so kind as to return outside to give me a definitive report? If my master finds me engaged in conversation, I am certain he would not consider it a wise use of time, not productive in the more apparent manner of making gesso, laying ground on pictures, working in relief, smoothing the surface of the plane, gilding, coloring, adorning with mordants — which I must attend to and upon which I must pee, or have I done already? Ah sì, mi ricordo, our introduction: as you perhaps observed and thought peculiar (I have lost perspective). We paint cloths of gold, we paint also on walls, we draw, all this and a great deal more we do, and will continue to, for the next five years and nine months: insomma, duecento settantacinque giorni to arrive at a total of six years.
"Once a week I ask my master, on the eve of what I would, were I directress here, allow as day of rest, what even Dio observed, if when these six years' time is spent, we might be something more

243

akin to man and wife, or man and mistress—I in truth care not which; my humble upbringing did not emphasize distinctions of this kind. My master is devoted to his work, he is assiduous as any man the Lord created, and I in my assisting him mean fully to enhance his capability as well as to address what he neglects, his manly, cioè human needs."

Transfer your attention to the large piece of fabric draped in the corner. Guarda. Senta. Two figures in white: "una domanda," says one to the other, mouths sensuous numbers: "uno, due, tre, quatro, cinque, sei; on the seventh day, master, may we make . . . love? quando lavoro finito, Lorenzo, amore?" and the second figure, perplexed, and far from playful, earnestly replies,

"Dimmi, Giovanna, what service could I be, to mistress or to wife, when my daily duties occupy me thoroughly as these?"

Then she, naively, "But could you not perform, Lorenzo, drawing and your coloring, gessoing and varnishing, gilding and your tempera, according to a pace you yourself set? Must you learn simultaneously every skill in such detail?"

"Which then would you have me eliminate? I must know how to work with glue and fasten cloth on panel. And if I have the wherewithal to prime with chalk, but lack the skill to smooth the surface of the picture ground, how then can I go on to polish it? If I favor using bole to making gesso, I am surely incomplete, and any worthy artisan will tell you burnishing and gilding in themselves could take the practice of a lifetime."

"Perhaps then, that should be your task, to choose one expertise among these crafts and concentrate your energies, be known throughout the world!"

"O lady Giovanna, it is simply not conducted thus among the artisans; my master would not have it, for all these labors are related by their nature, and to understand the whole necessitates the study of each part."

"Lorenzo, may I ask, are you then but a mirror for your master?"

"Giovanna, are you but a hindrance to your own? Have I not told you every interruption, every conversation, is attention thieved from art, and energy that would be better spent producing? There is, as you yourself observed, a great deal to accomplish on our agenda. Have I yet mentioned tempering colors and laying on flat ones? Powdering a drawing, scraping and engraving, to rule lines, to adorn and varnish pictures . . ."

*Mary Caponegro*

"O Lorenzo, I am enervated even as I listen. If only we could lie together in repose." The figures draped in white arrange themselves accordingly. The sun will rouse them soon enough. Suspend the counting sheep — and pigs, and chicken, minivers, for that matter, porringers — until tomorrow. ("Al meno fino albero, Lorenzo, stai tranquillo.")

Aren't you bold to pull back the curtain: a cloth of gold? Shame on you, what do you expect to find? An artist's workshop is no place for titillation! Would you seek to watch their breathing as they sleep? Your consolation prize: a sand-colored cloud: an entire flock of moths in flight! (just as well to interrupt their gnawing of the now nearly denuded fur of the miniver pencil someone remembered to bake but neglected to protect with clay) There is so very much to look after.

And suddenly she's there again, before you, as if to scold you for your curiosity, as if she'd put a decoy in your path, and now resumes, at dawn, the day, without a pause. "May I suggest to you, O goodly stranger, that what you see before you is deceptive; you or I don't see as artists do" (she is presumptuous — if she only knew — but she links you, proving, you assume, she holds no grudge) "as my master does; for example, you see farm animals, and assume I am a dairy maid; you see a fig tree in our yard and think I tend a garden for its beauty or its bounty; when in truth the milky juice of that most sensual fruit is here gratuitous, irrelevant to its tender shoots required for tempera, and mere appendage to the woody trunk, from which we cut our panels and to one of which I one time lent my spit. You see fur pelts hanging from the doorway and assume them to be for my adornment and my warmth. But sir, I am no woman of luxury, for my father was a man of modest means. I play none of these aforementioned roles. Rather I am apprentice to my master, who sees, when you and I see white or black, a range we cannot fathom, distinguishes a black made from the tendrils of young shoots of the vine, from a black of the skins of almonds, from black of the kernels of peaches, and the most distinctive black of all, that which lies under gold, my master has schooled me to know, is the brightest of blacks and begets the most brilliant of golds."

And even she, Giovanna, unschooled until this time, in art and craft, can recognize the most singular black of her most grotesque

245

imaginings, that her teeth will turn if she adorns herself against his master's rules; in tandem with her withered face; it seems absurd, it is extreme, it must be gross exaggeration, but such a poignant, captivating face, if not conventionally attractive, does Giovanna have; her father called it pretty, and she prefers her teeth remain akin if not to pearls to chalk, to plaster, but not, O Dio, to part her lips for smiling, laughing, tasting, asking something of her master, only to reveal two rows of almond skins, or peach kernels; no, the teeth must remain closer to biaca, to sangiovanni, and her face whether rouged or no, be smooth and fine, like gesso sottile's silk. She has learned much since she began this post, but all the time is haste and fretting, labor and exhaustion until at last there is, albeit briefly, the black that night offers, when there is brief respite, and in which she places her impassioned fantasy of white — whose complement in day occurs each time she makes a formula with egg yolk, and separates the viscous white surround, she cannot help but think on it: that first task she performed for him, his strange request: her spittle smeared on hardest wood.

To Cennino Cennini of Colle on this day ottavo Dicembre, mille-quattrocento trenta-sette

I beg you, honored master, to consider my request to take on an assistant, in this expanded separate territory. I am embarrassed to admit that without your eyes nearby I am less prone to blunder, as my wish to please you is immense. I do realize I make unorthodox request; please remember this would be a temporary arrangement only. I am aware that as apprentice, I am meant to do all duties, be industrious, improve my skills, increase my productivity, complete all tasks you set, but I feel my frustrations impede my progress, and perhaps with assistance, temporary assistance, I could learn by the example of one who stands in relation to myself as I to you. I could approach your standards, that is to say. Thank you, master, for your consideration.

P.S. If you like, we could make a date in the future for you to visit, and determine whether I have by that time made sufficient progress to merit an apprentice, if ~~you~~ ~~deem~~ me ~~worthy~~ ~~of~~ ~~assistance~~. Granting my request requires no effort on your part, ~~as~~ ~~I~~ ~~have~~ ~~in~~ ~~mind~~ a ~~suitable~~ ~~apprentice~~. ~~If~~ ~~you~~ ~~prefer~~ ~~you~~ ~~could~~ ~~propose~~ ~~who~~ ~~would~~ ~~become~~ ~~my~~ ~~apprentice~~.

Determined to instruct you now, she carries on: "My point,

O pensive stranger, is only this: Thus what we see as nourishment or sustenance, moreover succulence, what we take between our lips to put against our tongue and such or crack between our teeth to rend from tough exterior an oily savory essence meant to please the palate, is, in these quarters, something meant to serve the eye, which focuses all other senses, toward a far greater glory. Insomma, my master sacrifices life to make all manner of work to please the eye, for others' eyes to gaze upon, and obtain a love through indirection. My master consequently has no time to gaze on me; and thus I would be interested to see if he would notice were I, in consequence of indulging in cosmetics, as forbidden by the dictates of his master, to wither as his master warns a woman would, that is my visage, or were I to open up my mouth to answer him one day and spit, from toothless gums, a shower of blackened pits in lieu of words."

"Giovanna, do you monitor the sun for me? Can gilding be conducted yet?"

"Alora" — sotto voce — "had I asked of the weather, kind sir, a gray day, a fair? These mutations occur frequently; each inquiry might legitimately receive a different answer.

"But if our gilding is postponed, it is instead the most perfect of all colors, upon which we embark: oltre marino to clothe Maria Virginie, not to be confused with azurro della magna, a color of great merit itself, but lesser in comparison. The color of Our Lady's mantle is always blue, as clear a sum as one plus one is always unambiguous; the room for variation lies within the blue itself; how rich, how luminous, how splendorous," and this responsibility, if she can meet the challenge, is in the hands of Giovanna on this day: ottavo Dicembre, millequattrocento trenta-sette. But why, she cannot help but think, could it not be red, as the Virgin waits to bear the child, her whole life since girlhood for the sake of an offering of monthly blood to ready her to bear in secret the flesh that housed His sacred saving blood.

Her existence for the sake of one extraordinary child, begotten in a manger. "I suppose I can console myself to think of that humility, and have a hope for my own possibilities, as distant as they seem; but children here, can you imagine, stranger? I've too much to attend to, and during these six years when all other women's wombs bear fruit I will elect to be engaged in other creativity.

"These animals, per esempio, are like children, i miei bambini" —

247

she coos at those within arm's reach and actually nestles them against her breast—"always needing minding, always trying to drink our formulae, eat from the precious porringers' contents? If only they would leave alone the porringers, the recipes can so easily be ruined, and they made ill, and they have not sense to make their mess outside (as you have noticed, amusing how your fingers make a clothespin for your nose, sir). The sheep so used to grazing chew whatever comes to hand, to mouth, their jaw in motion morn and evening; sir, you surely see a woman occupied in this peculiar fashion has too much to bear to bear a child.

"And yet I need to entertain myself, for it is a dry speech, you see, this following of instructions, this sharing of ingredients and formulae, not a normal discourse, no play in it, no heart in it, no feeling, and so perhaps I chat too readily, too hungrily, with you, who happened here quite by accident, and whose ordinary hunger, I poor hostess, have not means to satisfy, as bread is here reserved for erasure of the pencil's errors. For what would rub away mistake if our bellies housed the bread? If I indulge your appetite it will in effect perpetuate imperfection.

"Forgive me, per piacere, I began to speak of color and I strayed. My master has no doubt decided to postpone our gilding until later, absorbed in what he writes; thus I can start my principal activity. Today is the Virgin's feast day, for whom we make blue, because she will be painted by my master in her mantle. We who have as our objective perfection must focus our attention on this noblest of colors, according to the master of my master (though in my own attempts to make it I've begun to find it less entrancing, truth be told). Our Lord who made the sky, which is, I assume, our template, would be, secondo me, disturbed at such a clumsy, cioè labored synthesis. Nonetheless it is the companion of gold in its glory; we gild day after day in honor of the moon and stars which occupy the midnight sky, whereas if we were truly God: one stroke and we exist; if there need be a thousand steps to perfection then what is beauty worth? But it is not my place to question, and even doubt cannot hinder my devotion or my application. What greater proof of this than the fact that I myself have quarried this lapis lazuli in the mountains to the west—the mountains my master makes a picture of with those rocks behind the chickens as his model—with the least ashes available, as instructed; I was very careful to distinguish between this (oltre marino) and azurro della

248

magna. And now I pound in this bronze mortar, then grind it on the porphyry slab not allowing myself to be distracted and hence delayed by noting the beauty of quartz against lapis, like a kind of star, and then I sift it through this special covered strainer — such as one might use for spices, in the course of normal cooking, such as did my mother for my father: another procedure, sir, entirely — and then pound again. I must not make it too fine, or the intensity of color will diminish. Now for each pound of lapis, I must add six ounces of pine resin, three ounces glue, three ounces new wax — which if my master had extracted from his own ears might facilitate our communication, as calling back and forth above the din of this peculiar domicile is ill-served by additional impediments — all of which I have measured in advance.

"And now? They must all be melted together in a new pipkin. Then they must be strained through a piece of linen which according to my master I am fortunate to find, as he implied I was profligate with it when I bled in menses. ('We have so little linen, Giovanna,' he complains, 'to serve our art. You must replenish all supplies.') He thinks perhaps I should arrest the flow that makes me woman, to fashion me disguise from inside out in case his master comes to call and finds his unlicensed apprentice is missexed. Alora, where was I: through linen, si, into this glazed basin, to which I'll add a pound of the lapis powder, mixing it well to make a paste, keeping my hands moist with the linseed oil. I must stir it every day for three days and nights, and keep it fifteen days or thirty days. After which time, the azure can be extracted. Then I shall take the two sticks, a foot long, round at the end and polished, with handle neither too thick nor thin as written by the master of my master. Then I will add from the original glazed porringer the paste to a porringer full of lye, which I will have prepared, and heated to be moderately warm, and then with the two sticks, I will mix it with one stick in each hand, emulating the manner of kneading bread, such as I once did with my mother in the house of my father, such as occurs in normal households that are not consigned to making art — bread such as we rarely eat in this house. When it appears to be perfectly blue, I will pour it from the glazed basin, into another, adding more lye. When this in turn is intensely blue, I will pour it in yet another basin, continuing on until the hue is tinged with color. And then, can you guess? I must dispose of it. Good for nothing, says my master.

"Pero, non e finito! Then I must place in order the basins on a

249

table, and beginning at the first I must stir up the azure with my hand, which will have sunk down by its weight to the basin's bottom. The first drawn extracts are best, the first porringer always better than the second. And then it shall be for me to decide how many shades of azure I would have: three or six or what? If for instance, there are eighteen basins of extract, and I'd wish to make three of azure, the contents of the six basins are mixed together, to make one shade. The azure from the first two extracts is worth eight ducats an ounce. But the last two extracts are worse than ashes, despite the fact that the lapis I procured had hardly any ash. Daily it shall be necessary to remove the lye, that the azure be dry. When it is dry, I'll put it into purses made of skins, bladders, of animals I myself slaughtered, I who was thought by my father to be a squeamish girl, turning my head from blood.

"All this then, for what precedes the painting of a picture, sir. Is it not wondrous? Or perhaps ludicrous, I can't decide? I pray I have not revealed too much, but you can hardly be competitor to us, for if you were yourself apprentice to a master elsewhere, you would not have had the leisure to linger here. I must memorize through song and rhyme and recitation, so as to make less dry his master's intricate recipes, so intricate that no one could commit to memory from one hearing: my master needn't fear. Devoid of narrative the tedium does haunt me."

"Giovanna, to whom do you now speak?"
"A beggar, sir, who when he sees what we provide prefers perhaps to go without, and begs no more."

"But you, sir, never utter, you gaze intently at me and all of my surround, just barely blinking, your pupils marching back and forth from left to right as if to find a linear way to catalogue this chaos; your nose offended, your ears assaulted; it is vertiginous, I grant you, you should seat yourself, collect yourself, and I will show you that which we collect, as I've no other hospitality to offer. You too might wish for stasis, not this process all exploded but a dainty single image with quadrangled boundaries politely offering itself for focus. But when you watched me make the oltre marino, I hope you felt a certain soothing meditative quality, methodical, sequential; it may in retrospect collect you, as I always pray, it will do me. How you happened upon this house I have no notion, but I imagine it is not what you expected. And this unites us, stranger, for I too had no inkling of the life I took upon myself.

"In point of fact, sir, as I labor, measuring and mixing, I find my- self wishing my master could imbibe the blue of evening's sky, the gold of the sun, even the gold of which my hair would seem to be spun; so said my mother, as she braided it for me before bedtime when I was young. 'You will make the girl conceited,' scolded father always: 'she will expect a spouse more grand than we can manage to provide with our modest dowry, lacking jewels; a bit of fabric, some preserves in crystal jars, at most one pig, two chickens'— it may not be apparent to you now, sir, as I need to pin it up and twist it round lest gesso coat it, soil it, or lest a carefully crafted angel's nimbus appear to unravel before the viewer's eye because my strands' inadvertent contribution rested where it ought not. For in this workshop we use strokes as delicate as hair; and the brushes that we use are made of finest animal hair to make the whirl cascading down a painted woman's back, but if some part of me infected this, it would be tainted. Illusion of strictest imita- tion must not collide with the ungainliness of flesh and blood.

"And yet flesh is something more than word; flesh is other, is it not so, stranger? Master, for example, has no manual for my menses, and thus cannot accommodate, cannot adjust our schedule. He shades vermilion with fine lake to make with paint the drops that mark a dead man. And the holy blood of Jesu Christo is revered. But dragon's blood and lake to me suggest an imagery definitively womanly. If you'll excuse my frankness, sir, the pip- kins I could fill with what spills from inside of me, one quarter of each moon, as if eggs were also breaking there, within my womb, an egg with color even darker than those cultivated here, so gold inside as to be red, as these tarruci oranges we in Toscana and Lazio and Sicilia so prize, those rubied fruits would stain a linen more than I, and no one turns from them. In my humble opinion I think dragon's blood no more exotic for a color than a woman's blood yet no color is attributed to her, sir, in our quite extensive palette. Niente, non importa, I would have no energy to do so, fill- ing pipkins far too frequently already, sir, including on those days each month that hinder my efficiency, and thus don't please my master, though his reticence about the matter inhibits true dis- cussion, just as once when we were fashioning a painted cloth of gold to make a woman's petticoat, I thought his stammering and awkwardness preceded some most unsavory admission, such as my dismissal, or some complaint about my person or my manner, untidiness or such; in truth I thought he was about to say my menses interfered too much with my abilities as apprentice. I will never know what master sought to tell me then, something related to a letter he had finally finished, I felt the weight of it, but if I prod him now he is steadfast in his refusal, says he 'will say no more on the subject' although the subject is as yet undeclared. In any case, I can tell he thinks on numerous occasions he has made a great mistake in endorsing my apprenticeship. His discipline exceeds mine by mille braccia. Not even Sundays does he rest, not even feast days of our Lord which were, in my upbringing, never questioned.

"But perhaps after his six years, all the accumulated Sundays and feast days and week days can be ours, because I, Giovanna, do think I could easily lie with my master for six consecutive years, in strictest sequenced symmetry to these of toil, thus to have reward and work in equal measure, while he would study with my good assistance techniques his master did not encourage him to learn; and we too would think it appropriate on Domenica, Lunedi, Martedi, etc.; tutti festivi et tutti feriali to pursue a craft whose manual we might together write, in an ink almost transparent, in an ink resembling that more liquid part of the chicken's egg not favored for our working formulae and we would likewise be occupied constantly by our leisure, pursuing that postponed art with alacrity and diligence, crafting day by day and night by night.

"Alora, all very well for me to weave my fantasy, for drudgery invites revery: Giovanna's cardinal rule, and it is human nature, I believe. But were the master, I mean master's master, to appear, here, in our midst, as close to me as you now stand, there would be nothing short of mayhem because a female would not likely be appointed to my post, and a mistress is I fear forbidden; thus what disguise could I possibly acquire? Neither helper nor whore — and do not think I haven't schemed, sir — to protect my master's dignity and allow me to remain here in this household, this workshop, as his assistant in this curious amorphous space. There is no place for me, a woman.

"Unless I be but form, unless I do not move, and be content to find reflection in a mirror master makes in paint or plaster, unless I cease to breathe, sir, like that man there behind the furthest pipkin about whom I would beg you not to draw conclusions.

"You, understandably, see all manner of sharp tools nearby this wounded man, and assume them weapons. Those tools, however, did not make those wounds, but recreate them elsewhere on a surface that could serve as mirror. Insomma, that man serves as still life; the world and all of God's creation one vast still life, awaiting its depiction; and all that grows wild or cultivated, all that is concocted and assimilated upon this property: each is merely one ingredient toward achievement of perfection, for which the soul is instrument of measure, but the eye is ever mediator."

"Giovanna, a chi parli?"

"Nessuno, Lorenzo, a me stessa."

"Non domenticare Giovanna, I am the safeguard of my master's secrets, his formulae, his intricate techniques; I pray you be conservative in your speech. You must be circumspect. Ti prego."

Now whispering not to you, but to the first reluctant, then aggressive miniver, who does not shun its mistress's lap, as she strokes her cheek against its fur, "Miniver, would my master care what else besides his master's precious secrets I might give away?"

She begins, the animal still in her lap, to pile all items in her immediate purview into groups more uniform than any you have thus far witnessed, forgetting entirely for the first time your presence? Eventually you realize each thing between you now occurs in groups of six.

### INVENTORY

from chickens, eggs which in turn make gesso, their bones to grind and fire for priming

from calf and lamb, parchment

from rabbits, their skin for glue

from minivers, their fur for brushes

from birds (geese and vultures), their quills in which to insert the fur bristles of the miniver; feathers to smooth away error (or stroke lightly her pleasure when master is not watching her discreet dilatory gestures).

"Stai tranquillo, creature, do not protest, it is only a single bristle plucked, you should by now be well accustomed, you will disturb my master; come now, goose, your honking is excessive, a single feather does not diminish you, O do lie still."

from olives and linseed, their oil.

253

from fish, their innards for glue, their bones to grind for priming, and their form entire for casting.

from hogs, the white better than the black, their bristles for brushes.

from poplar, willow, linden, fig tree, wood panels upon which to draw.

also from the willow, sticks to make charcoal.

Containers and vessels for all that is created: bottles and pipkins and porringers; casseroles, bowls and jars and tubs and dishes.

Scissors, penknife, hammer, chisel, wire, axe. . . .

Etcettera

Pull back the curtain. But do not be seen. A woman and man, both clad in white. He's weary from lack of sleep, and she whispers as they stir, his hand on hers, perhaps the fifteenth porringer this evening, "Master, will you promise me one thing, please promise me that when the last of these . . . tasks is done, you'll put your hand, with equal ardor, on this form which you have often cast, I should say tried to cast." She looks out into the area behind this small enclosure with her enormous fawn-colored eyes, likewise glazed with fatigue, which has the effect of making them appear to protrude even more than usual, as she makes ready to retire: "Lorenzo, anch'io, sono stanca."

"We are not here in the habit of enumerating sheep to aid our path to sleep but for our weekly inventory, no matter how sleepy we might in counting find ourselves to be; we don't indulge our weariness as we take record of our raw materials: we catalogue our flora and our fauna; our subjects and our objects; our models; our both animate and still lives in this vast warehouse where life is seldom still on its tumultuous trajectory to utter peace and harmony; paradoxically there's precious little poetry on the way to art, and our exhaustion serves as antidote to the insomnia that might lead those in normal beds in normal households such as I imagined as a child — to use this child's device, a formula so innocent, to move from day to dream: uno due tre, quatro cinque sei, poi presto dormire. Shorn or no it matters not; they only need appear, and before long a child hears bleating that lulls him, that pulls him into sleep. O would that I could pull the wool over my master's eyes, for when he is weary I sense he becomes susceptible to my suggestions, surrenders all defenses, all his fortresses of color to dream in richest black and white.

"You, stranger, with no model for the singlemindedness and devotion you perceive in me might find inside your mind some box to put me in called category: a clinging or a doting or a nagging wife, perhaps demented in degree of my resolve. But I am none of these as much as volunteer apprentice, though I could not say precisely, yet, what I expect to learn. Nor should you assume I carry out my master's bidding uncritically, unquestioning, for we do argue, at least discuss, as he does never, to my knowledge, with his master. Perhaps you think that latter model more worthy: unexamined emulation. But how could I, in female form as my soul finds itself to be, be mirror of the space between my master and his master? I would do better to adapt the tasks I find as I cannot adapt what Dio has made as me. This is not a woman's role, then, your raised eyebrow denotes, but I would ask you why a woman unencumbered by a husband or a child could not devote some portion of her time to a most worthy cause. I wield an axe as well as any man, with practice: these varnished panels against the far wall prove me true. As to immodesty of modeling, I am certain that has crossed your mind; may I be frank: if this is meant to glorify our Lady, I suppose I'd just as soon disrobe my person as to take the veil. You must remember that an artist sees with more refinement than do you or I, sir; quindi, you'd serve me well to lower your eyes, sir, if you intend to stay throughout this coming session—when the figure casting starts; it is a most complex endeavor, in some ways harder still than gilding, for again, we never finish as my master lacks apprentice while I am model, and chi sa? Perhaps my master so loathes the imperfection of the disproportionate female body that he cannot bear to complete the task, for he invariably runs before the greasing is completed, to 'relieve himself,' he says, and does not heed me when I urge him to do just as you saw me when you first arrived, to contribute to the making of our mordants. On the contrary, he flees, declaring, 'I'll say no more upon the subject.'

"Once when we had run low on oil, for I had yet to milk the olives of their liquid, I said, 'Master, could you not, in emergency, grease me with another substance?' 'But there is not alternative, for we have run out of linseed oil as well, Giovanna.' 'Can we not then be resourceful, master,' I had asked, 'carry on beyond the book and be, in truest sense, creative?' Perhaps I had allowed the two

255

*Mary Caponegro*

supplies to diminish simultaneously; perhaps I put both bottles in an unfamiliar place. Was that so great a sin? I had not meant to thwart but rather to enrich routine. There is alas no danger my disrobing will distract my master. In general no sooner have I done so than he seems perplexed, becomes intent instead on gilding, and must be reminded that the weather is a factor in our ability to carry out that task."

OF GILDING

To Cennini of Colle on this day, ottavo Dicembre, 1437

Master, believe that I've become a better craftsman since my last attempts. But gilding continues to elude me. I concur it is the highest challenge, as you have indicated. I beg you to forgive me the wrinkle in the gold leaf, the less than perfectly smooth surface. I confess I sought, only in wish and not in deed, the company of woman, but one woman, and in my mind's eye only, master, on the night before the gilding. And how my trembling hand betrayed me, just as you had predicted; but master, understand, this was result of mere imagining (perhaps because I, Lorenzo, maker of images, know the power of picture, sometimes greater than what is represented). The very image of her shuddering under me creates my yearned-for, heaving pleasure, and leads me to declare that no artisan in Italy, indeed in all the world, could ever craft a surface smooth or lovely as her infinitely tender flesh, that I confess when I have touched within the needs of my profession only, I also longed to linger in for other purpose. O master, when in my dreaming (during the meagre sleep my labors offer) she was spent in my arms, I was blinded to the brilliance of this metal and its quest for immortality. At these times six years seems indeed eternity, until apprenticeship is through, and then, I would assume, I shall be encouraged to use my own judgment; I can dictate what serves well or ill my art.

"Scusa, stranger, the weather? Note for me, if you would, its demeanor, for if it is windy but not sunny I can set the glue to dry, and if it remains cloudy we can resume our ever-interrupted gilding, alternate activity to our ever-interrupted figure casting, which is not contingent on the shift of cloud and sun as much as the mysterious mercurial constitution of my master.

"Do you not find it fitting, sir, that gilding be conducted under canopy of cloud? For if the sun graced the sky, would it not mock the gold which we produce in emulation? I do not wonder it retreats (to our advantage, technically). Nonetheless, we remain apprehensive lest it reemerge, and carry on with caution. Sometimes I feel I do no more than go through the motions of our gilding, since we seldom advance further than the preparations, and pecatto, you are unlikely to witness my master in the actual act, but I can visualize all the steps from the few times we have executed them to completion, and as I practice enumerating them you may through your imagination see the esoteric process.

"Thus for my master, I lay the panel flat on two trussels, which I have taken pains to secure away from the chickens and the white pigs, whose motion and whose racket might disrupt this most important process. I shoo them inside if they come near, to do Lord knows what mischief to all our other dormant preparations. And I pass my feather which I do not allow myself to be distracted by, over the panel, then the raffietto after, to discern any roughness, any knot. If there are no knots to be removed, I burnish with coarse linen the bole, and at this point, he, Lorenzo my master, brings the tooth which I myself cannot claim to have extracted from the lion. Better that it be in his possession than mine, as I might idly stroke with it my skin and even without asking I know my master would consider this highly inappropriate, for it is even more important for the burnishing of gold than bole, this tooth, and necessary to us, as we are not of sufficient means to use, in lieu of such, a ruby, sapphire, emerald or topaz; for a man devoted to his craft has no time to make profit in this life, and a girl of modest dowry such as I cannot offer jewels: a country girl from Arezzo, as I mentioned, not Firenze, where the lips and cheeks of women are as much akin to rubies as the jewels I imagine to comprise their ample dowries.

"Once cleaned and burnished, I put for him into a nearly full glass the egg white tempera and mix it thoroughly with water (and its frothing causes me to reflect upon another image which I promptly, dutifully banish), and then with the pencil of the miniver's tail, those fine hairs, which I myself preserved in clay to keep away moths, I wet the bole, holding the pencil in my right hand, while he in his right hand takes with the pincers the fine gold to lay on the square card, somewhat larger and turned up at each corner.

"He wets the bole equally, so that no part has more water on it than another, and then taking great care not to wet the card, he releases the gold, and as soon as it has touched the wet part, he snatches back the card, because now it has become part of the panel itself. When my master sees, however, that some of the gold has not adhered to the panel, I offer him a piece of the clean cotton with which I stand ready, so that he can gently press it down, but I can see that he is anxious lest the precious substance go to waste and he need to start again all over. In this manner he is to gild the other parts of the panel, and before he lays the second piece of this finest thinnest golden stuff, he wets the panel, trying not to wet the first piece he has just laid down, but he is clumsy with the fur-tipped pencil of the miniver, and wets what he should not and we must begin anew, and how I wish I could soothe him in a way my instincts tell me, but instead I must give him only the brick-sized cushion covered in fine soft leather, such as might comprise the boots of a gentleman of Florence, and on this he rests the remaining strips of gold, which will adhere to the handle of the miniver pencil once it has been wet with his lips and which if he would ask me I would myself wet, as I did the cuttle bones for priming on that first day and which I am tempted to take, after he has done so, discreetly, into my own mouth.

"It is always my task to supply the giornata, for there would be no point in laying more gold on the surface than can be burnished in a day, although we are so often interrupted by the sun or other intruders (not you, sir, of course, I mean not people but circumstances, creatures, exigencies of our particular ambiguous household) that excess is rarely a problem. It pains me to see my master err, for I have seen him succeed as well, and he is admirable in dexterity and concentration. When having begun again from step the first, he does succeed in joining the two gold strips or pieces by breathing from his mouth upon it. And when I witness this, I feel covetous of that substance for reasons far more esoteric than its preciousness or permanence. And then the sun, which we are often pleased to see and in my childhood I would always welcome, interrupts again our labors, we cover all with a clean handkerchief (again it seems to me in our humility for or penance for our hubris) and choose among the hundreds of lesser activities on our agenda."

"Perche non e mai finito, questa cosa, Giovanna?"
"Non e mia culpa, ma il sole, guisto?"
"Non so, ma vorresti auitarmi?"

"Si, per sei, ma non per sette, dieci o settanta anni."

It is inevitable that there be occasional irritability between master and apprentice. It is as clear a sum as one plus one, or orpiment plus ultramarine makes green, that disappointment following anticipation yields frustration which in turn creates a wish to blame, which soon enough evaporates, under sun or under cloud; for there is far too much to do to indulge pettiness or bickering.

"But when we burnish gold laid not on panel but on even surfaces, we do so with a piece of lapis amatisto, warmed and felt to make sure no powder lies under it, as one feels powder between one's teeth, (those who have not lost their teeth to vanity) and if so it is swept (the gold) with miniver tail. The gold is burnished gradually, first one side then the other, and its surface should be smooth as a looking glass, such as might be used by the haughty heathen women of Firenze who love their beauty more than God, who think their own reflection good as gold. I wonder, stranger, might the mirror crack if they smiled in satisfaction, showing two dainty rows of blackened pits? Might it break, to make a jagged outline such as that which you peered through initially to see this circus of a workshop, and be less easily mended than the gold, which is repaired with another piece of itself lain over it and breathed upon, and then burnished immediately? When properly burnished the gold will appear brown, from its own brightness."

To Cennini of Colle, on this day, ottavo Dicembre, 1437
Master, yesterday I took the bird that screeches at me night and day; the one that you've bid me ignore and I confronted it; wrestled with my own hand til that screeching ceased. O cock that crows at dawn and dusk and sometimes through the night, I had to write my own instructions for attending you. I sang her name in order to drown out the fowl's fury as he took flight. I revere my honored master, but he would make my song in flight into a dead fish. You warned me that my hand would shake were I to keep the company of women. On the contrary, from but thinking her, its rhythm is more certain; its motion is deliberate and vibrant. Note well, dear master, this flapping fish that surfaces at every inconvenience will be no longer humble, nor be vulnerable to hook or net. The wish to glide, the wish to fly, now vies with my desire for perfection. I bid you note this detour.

"Persistent, patient, silent stranger, how uncomfortable to find yourself confronting what is already in progress, with no conclusion imminent. A species of explanation as to how this arrangement came about would be the minimum of hospitality. Perhaps you'd like to know how this began. (I suspect you may possess a nature curious as mine.) I knew Lorenzo from my father's trade, and came to him as messenger when papa was ill. During that visit, I observed a greater disarray than what you now behold. Could I offer help, I asked him, for my mother raised me to be generous and industrious, and I shan't make you guess the nature of my master's first request to me. (Compassion was my impetus at first — then I realized I simply liked my master's company; he amuses me so serious and earnest.) On that day he brought me bones, not of the chicken, but the cuttle fish: ground into fine dust, such as you and I, sir, shall become, rotting away to that which you see before you — a thought by which perhaps you are made squeamish, though be consoled, the soul of course shall go to God, inviolate, while we, the we you see, shall wither worse than the women of Firenze damned to perish by means of mirrors as they foolishly favor the coloring of flesh instead of represented flesh."

DEAD MEN AND BONES, PISS AND SHIT, FIRE AND CHAOS, FRUIT AND FEATHERS, ROTTING MATTER EVERYWHERE, all on the path to putrescence, the path to milk from matter lasting beauty.

"Excuse my digression, sir, the bones, I had begun . . . that he had very finely ground and asked me, he asked me, pardon my giggling, my sighing; you must never tell him — this is deeply secret, sir — he asked if I would be so good as to take a half bean of the bone's ground dust and mix it with saliva. (I didn't know then the purpose: to prime the panel he would draw on.) 'Whose saliva shall I utilize,' I asked him, as I knew he had many folia of instructions. 'I don't believe the source is specified,' said he, 'but I am certain, as I think upon it, that this is a less than refined act to ask a lady gracious as yourself.'

"'No, no,' I protested, 'nothing that assists you is beneath me,' surprised by my own conviction, and pleased by his concern, 'it would please me to contribute to the honor of our Lady, and your drawing' (for I knew even then he consecrated all his works to our

Lord and the Virgin). So I surrendered modesty and made the little bubble form from my pursed lips, to mingle with the dry dust of cuttle bones, this tiniest of alchemies; and he gently took his forefinger and rubbed with it the dampened spot my mouth had made, to spread the mixture all over the surface of the wooden panel which he held in his left hand. 'Please guide my finger too,' I requested of him, 'hold and move it in the appropriate motion.' Then emboldened in a fashion I would not disclose to everyone, to anyone, in fact, but you whom I will never see again, who has no consequence to master or myself, who seems in silence not to judge, 'what else,' I asked, 'might I prime for my master?' and found my finger at his lips or his at mine, I can't recall; it seemed the same, until he fled reciting every shade from blue to yellow, green to red. I feared my imminent dismissal, having only just been hired, and have numerous times since then regretted gestures of the sort, which I, alas, am past controlling. As clear as day they are improper here. Yet, even reason seems to buttress my assumptions. The animals, for instance, who share our house, think nothing strange in bathing with their own secretions.

"And in the manual I, Giovanna, aim, if ever time permits, to write, I will include what master's manual omits. Per esempio, if the body is creative, should not the artist who inhabits it be in equal measure, exploiting all resources, nothing wasted, nothing overlooked? I feel that I can say to you, a stranger, more straightforwardly than I can say to my retiring master: why piss and spit be privileged over other liquids? And why saliva in one's palm but not skin's other surfaces? And if man's body be the model of all beauty, and thus each man inherently correct in form, why not make that truth available to all concerned, at least to Giovanna, earnest, eager, diligent apprentice, who seeks to learn all that she can in as expedient a manner as possible.

"'Do you think it evenly distributed, good lady?' was the last question my master asked before I made transgression (I speak still of our introduction). 'My less than expert eyes would judge it so,' said I, and that was the inception of this professional collaboration. Many curious acts I have performed in even three months' time but none gratuitous, and I learn much. Oh do excuse the hog who butts his snout against your leg; don't mind his grunting; he too is hungry; I must pluck more bristles from him for my master's pencils and it aggravates him; you can understand. He too prefers to be fed. I have only plucked the miniver this week,

whose tail I shall bake once the casserole of coals is removed from
the stove. When did I place them there? He, the silly hog, seeks
mischief, since I fenced the geese away from him. Their honking
never ceases; they are worth less than their feathers. O to be a hen
with a simple task of warming with her body what she lays, how
singular, how sedentary, how salutary."

HONKING,    SNORTING,    GRUNTING,    CACKLING,
BLEATING,    COOING,    SCRATCHING.    How can a man
think? How can anybody concentrate? Where can you take refuge?
Why can't you remove yourself, as if instead of egg, your feet were
lodged in glue?

Peer through the curtain. This golden cloth: a perfunctory gesture of modesty; like a veil of gossamer golden thread, revealing
something between silhouette and flesh, a fresco come to life,
between shadow and painting, fra chiaro et scuro: veiled figures
who erect a wooden case, tall enough to embrace the one but not
the other, figures from whom voices emanate:
    "It surprises me your master bids you make a cast of female
form, as he claims none are perfectly proportioned."
    "It is so, Giovanna," replies the male apprentice; "only man in
all his parts is measured justly. In woman there is greater variation,
and thus no true standard. This is as the master lectures on the
subject."
    "But is it not strange, Lorenzo," the female challenges, "that in
all the world there be not one, not even one breadth of shoulder,
width of hip, one curve of breast or calf or span of hand that
might be, by pure accident or indeed divine design, formed in just relation?"
    Giovanna is admittedly not proportionate in strictest symmetry,
the breasts grander than the hips, the left of the former not precisely the equal of the right, nor aureole either, once one looks
more closely, as precision of depiction can demand, and suddenly
this slight asymmetry intrigues Lorenzo and you who watch
him watching. As if he'd finally found perspective (paradoxically
through your hidden eyes) or seen it for the first time truly, as
she, his model and apprentice, enters the tall wooden case built to
the height of a man's chin, with the templet of copper adhering
but not pressing against her skin. In a way, her nose conjures the
beak of a bird, while the lovely nearly bulbous eyes a fish; it's all

askew, one out of scale with the other but somehow pleasing, yes, intriguing, against the plaited golden hair, itself like ripe wheat in sunlight, like gold foil under moonlight; Lorenzo is not poet, he is painter, draftsman, craftsman. He needs time to fashion words, requires quill and parchment. Patience.

"My master"—he must struggle to keep his composure—"would refute the very possibility, signorina, but I imagine even he, were he to see, for instance, evidence, set as it were, in stone, in plaster . . ."

"Or in flesh?" she interrupts him. "What if proof in very flesh?"— she holds his hand against her.

"He, my master, would never be, as artist, so stubborn, as to disbelieve the truth before his eyes."

The apprentice continues her interrogation: "And how would truth in such an instance find him?"

"Alora, if such proof somewhere on God's earth existed, I would consider it my duty to display it."

"Less simple a matter than to display to God, whose eye sees all, whereas your master only sees what would be put in front of him?"

He makes ready to pour the plaster front and back, but how can he without the help of his assistant pour both simultaneously?

"But master, do display for me the evidence that would support your master's bias. What better opportunity shall there be? Moreover, how can I learn without such tools as would persuade me intellectually, through reason and through demonstration. Otherwise this theory remains for me abstraction."

"This theory, Giovanna, is merely a matter of measure. Master teaches that the body of man can be measured in faces: one from navel to thigh; two from thigh to knee . . ."

"In that case I could take my face against these measures that your master dictates, as you hardly could contort yourself in such a manner, to illuminate me."

"Shall I grease you, woman, lest this plaster harden long before we begin to cast? Have you placed the olive oil within my reach this time?"

She turns clandestinely to you, who thought yourself well hidden. "His eyes, it seems, do scan my parts with admiration. Could you afford me objectivity, O stranger?" (You are embarrassed to be discovered.) "Do I deceive myself, do you suppose? Do I read as his desire my own? Of course you could not see his eyes as I had bid you cast down yours." Discouraged for a moment only, she carries on with he who tries to cast her.

"Is it then erroneous, Lorenzo, that all the creatures fashioned by our Lord, in his own image, are innately perfect?"

"In essence it is so, that we inherit the Lord's perfection in what resembles him, but the ideal beauty of the artist has as his vocation this: to craft a beauty visible as aid to beauty spiritual. But we must interrupt our discourse to begin the casting; speaking will be difficult as I begin to cast the face."

"But of the figure casting, master? Yet again postponed?"

"Invece il viso oggi. Your face so near me causes . . ."

"Master, causes?"

". . . so near inspires in me the necessary . . . to do the far more difficult casting . . . of the face. Il corpo a domani."

"Master . . ."

"Basta."

"Master, would you make of six years seven, ten or seventy?"

"Madonna, Giovanna, do you help or hinder?"

There is only occasional irritability between apprentice and master; who are not, after all, engaged in competition, altercation, but benign cooperation, yet when under pressure of long hours and unrelenting labor, anticipation preceding disappointment is as guaranteed a recipe as any color in their repertory.

"Va bene, master, as I will be henceforth indisposed, I cannot serve you in the usual manner, so you must work independently."

"Esatto, Giovanna. The first step, I know without regarding my instructions, is to shave the beard with the razor in my right hand."

"When casting MAN, master, not a woman; feel how smooth a woman's face is." Through the gold veil, she places his hand against her cheek. "I think it better to practice such steps as can be practiced on a woman, while a woman lies before you. Therein lies reason."

"Hai ragione, Giovanna. If I can find my miniver pencil, I will then proceed to anoint the face with oil of roses."

"O dear master, how the fur-tipped pencil pleases my cheek and nose and chin as you stroke."

"Giovanna, it will be better when the plaster stills your tongue, for you distract your master. These techniques are not designed to be . . . responded to, capito? If you are ready, then, the capo on your head, and the band sewn around it. And then I insert into each ear this piece of cotton; tell me if I go too deep."

"O hardly, master, you can press more forcefully (if you like)."

"Sewing is not my greatest skill, so this capuccio to your collar is askew. Without your assistance, it will be particularly difficult to place securely this hoop of iron, two fingers wide; do not be frightened of the sawlike teeth inside."

"On the contrary, master, I find it fascinating every time."

"It may be unwieldy for me, but I shall take great care, don't fear, that it not touch your face."

"But you, if it would help you know the subject whom you cast, should feel at liberty to touch her face."

"We must not delay the placing of the two small silver tubes, light and like fingers, to fill perfectly each nostril."

"Then do insert them, master, where you would. Sono pronta."

Her master does so. His subject ceases speaking, and presently her skin begins to turn a blue that has little resemblance to azurro della magna or oltre marino, a blue her master has not seen and has no reference for. A blue that comes from inside, and cannot be synthesized. But you, more worldly, watching, you have traveled, observed with objectivity the world in its variety. You can immediately identify the problem, and feel compelled — you cannot help yourself — to solve it. He (or someone) failed to pierce them like a trumpet, to allow for respiration. The subject simply cannot breathe. Thus the golden-tressed apprentice faints away, but fortunately lands on piles of fur and feathers, instead of fire. Six chickens squawk in unison; six eggs release six liquid suns, six pipkins tumble. . . .

"Per mia vita, put your mouth on mine." You hear a phrase that no one said, yet in a timber rich as cream or yolk of egg, lodged, intractably in your head, as if instructions from a place beyond your own volition. In this emergency you have an obligation to draw back the cloth and enter; the circumstance demands your interference. You have witnessed, silent, long enough.

To my valued apprentice, Lorenzo ———— on this day, tredicesimo Dicembre, il millequattrocento trenta-sette

I will henceforth have a new apprentice in my studio; thus there is no need for you to return there. You may continue to work in your separate structure, if it please you, or you may apprentice yourself to a new master, but if you elect to do the former, and wish assistance, you must interview for a new "apprentice's apprentice." I realize we

*Mary Caponegro*

were only in the infancy of your own apprenticeship, but I have found not a more worthy, Lorenzo, but a more suitable apprentice, quite by chance. For just as new chemical ˜ecipes for color come to us when we are otherwise engaged, precisely when we do not seek that thing which we discover, I have now found that openness to change is a necessary ingredient in the development of the artisan. It need not be widely disseminated at this time; I inform you only because you are directly affected. Complete revised instructions shall be forthcoming. Yes, the taking of action and a willingness to adapt, to change, even a certain impetuousness in certain instances: these shall be prized qualities, which may surprise you. Your disobedience, incidentally, need not be punished. There is no more to say on the subject. Nor need you send whatever correspondence may have accumulated in my absence, as it would very likely be irrelevant. Buona fortuna, Lorenzo. Ti ringrazio.

Cennino Cennini

LIBRO DELL'ARTE (TREATISE ON PAINTING)

HERE again begins the book of the art, made and composed by Giouanna —————————, in the reuerence of God, and the Virgin Mary, and of St. Eustachius, and of St. Francis, and of St. John the Baptist, and St. Anthony of Padua, and generally of all the saints of God, and in the reuerence of Giotto, of Taddeo and of Agnolo the master of Cennino, and of Cennino the master of myself Giouanna, and for the utility and good and aduantage of those who would aspire to attain perfection in the Arts, that they might know what lies before them, and not be rash or unconsidered in their aspirations . . .

# Four Days in Vermont
## Robert Creeley

Window's tree trunk's predominant face
a single eye-leveled hole where limb's torn off
another larger contorts to swell growing in around
imploding wound beside a clutch of thin twigs
hold to one two three four five six dry twisted
yellowish brown leaves flat against the other
gray trees in back stick upright then the glimpse
of lighter still grayish sky behind the close
welted solid large trunk with clumps of gray-green
lichen seen in boxed glass squared window back
of two shaded lamps on brown chiffonier between
two beds echo in mirror on far wall of small room.

.

*(for Maggie)*

Most, death left a hole
a place where she'd been
An emptiness stays
no matter what or who
No law of account not
*There but for the*
*grace of God go I*
Pain simply of want
last empty goodbye
Put hand on her head
*good dog, good dog*
feel her gone.

.

267

*Robert Creeley*

Tree adamant looks in
its own skin mottled with growths
its stubborn limbs
stick upright parallel
wanting to begin again
looking for sun in the sky
for a warmer wind
to walk off pull up
roots and move
to Boston be a table
a chair a house
a use a final fire.

.

What is truth "firm (as a tree)"
Your faith your trust your loyalty
Agrees with the facts makes
world consistent plights a troth
is friendly sits in the common term
All down the years all seasons all sounds
all persons saying things conforms confirms
Contrasts with "war" equals "confusion" (*worse*)
But *Dichtung und Wahrheit*? "Wahr-" is
*very* ("Verily I say unto you") A compact now
Tree lights with the morning though *truth* be an oak
This is a maple, is a *tree*, as a very truth firm.

.

Do I rootless shift
call on the phone
daughter's warm voice
her mother's clear place
Is there wonder here
has it all gone inside
myself become subject
weather surrounds
Do I dare go out
be myself specific
be as the tree
seems to look in.

.

Breeze at the window
lifts the light curtains
Through the dark a light
across the faint space
Warmth out of season
fresh wash of ground
out there beyond
sits here waiting
For whatever time comes
herein welcome
Wants still
truth of the matter.

.

*Robert Creeley*

Neighbor's light's still on
outside above stoop
Sky's patchy breaks
of cloud and light
Around is a valley
over the hill
to the wide flat river
the low mountains secure
Who comes here with you
sits down in the room
What have you left
what's now to do.

                •


Soon going day wanders on
and still tree's out there waiting
patient in time like a river and
truth a simple apple reddened
by frost and sun is found
where one had left it in time's company
No one's absent in mind   None gone
Tell me the *truth* I want to say
Tell me all you know   Will we live
or die   As if the world were apart
and whatever tree seen were only here apparent
Answers, live and die. Believe.

# The Four Year Old Girl

*Mei-mei Berssenbrugge*

## 1

The *genotype* is her genetic constitution.

The *phenotype* is the observable expression of the genotype as structural and biochemical traits.

Genetic disease is just extreme genetic change, against a background of normal variability.

Within the conventional unit we call subjectivity due to individual particulars, what is happening?

She believes she is herself, which isn't complete madness, it's belief.

The problem is not to turn the subject, the effect of signifiers or genes, into an entity.

Between her and the displaced gene is another relation, the effect of meaning.

The meaning she's conscious of is contingent, a surface of water in an uninhabited world, existing as eyes and ears.

You wouldn't think of her form by thinking about water.

You can go in, if you don't encounter anything.

Though we call heavy sense impressions stress, in fact, all impression creates limitation.

I believe opaque inheritance accounts for the limits of her memory.

The mental impulse is a thought and a molecule tied together like sides of a coin.

A girl says sweetly, it's time you begin to look after me, so I may seem lovable to myself.

She's inspired to change the genotype, because the cell's memory outlives the cell.

It's a memory that builds some matter around itself, like time.

2

Feelings of helplessness drove me to fantastic and ridiculous extremes.

Nevertheless, the axis of her helplessness is not the axis I grasp when I consider it a function of inheritance.

Chromatin fails to condense during mitosis.

A fragile site recombines misaligned genes of the repeated sequence.

She seems a little unformed, gauze stretches across her face, eyelids droop.

When excited, she cries like a cat and fully exhibits the "happy puppet" syndrome.

Note short fingers and hypoplastic painted nails.

Your entire axis speaks other than the axis you grasp, when you consider her the function of an individual.

The break on maternal chromosome 15 demonstrates that parental origin determines expression of the
   defect.

Feeling manifests in experience enactment of inheritance, insofar as its reality is a life force.

Insofar as fate is of a real order here, signifying embodiment, the perceived is present in the womb.

A gap or cause presents to any apprehension of attachment.

In her case, there's purity untainted by any force or cause, like the life force.

Where, generically, function creates the mother, in this case it won't even explain this area.

She screams at her.

A species survives in the form of a girl asking sweetly.

Nevertheless, survival of the species as a whole has meaning.

Each girl is transitory.

3

Her focus extends from in front of her into distance, so she's not involved in what she looks at.

Rhodopsin encoded by the unaffected gene could sufficiently convert photons to retinal impulse, so she sees normally for years.

The image, the effects of energy starting from a real point, is reflected at some point on a surface, a lake or area of the occipital lobe.

You don't need the whole surface to be aware of a figure, just for some points of real space to correspond to effect at other points.

There's an image and a struggle to recognize reception of it.

She sees waves and the horizon as if she were water in the water.

The mother's not looking at her daughter from the place from which the daughter sees her.

She doesn't recognize abnormal attributes.

The daughter resolves this image as a fire below in the woods, red silk.

There's a speck in her eye from light reflecting off the tumor.

The subject sums up effects of genes at the level at which she constitutes herself out of effects of words.

In the waiting room, she hopes a large dog will walk up to her, be kind and fulfill her wishes.

Between what occurs as if by chance and, "Mother, can you see I'm dying?" is the same relation we deal with in recurrence.

Is not what emerges from the anxiety of this speech the most intimate aspect of their relation, beyond death, which is their chance?

Obedience to one's child is anxious, heartfelt, but not continuous, like a white mote in her eye.

Within the range of deteriorating sight, in which sight will be her memory, disobedience moves toward unconsciousness.

273

4

Her skull is large and soft to touch.

The thoracic cavity small, limbs short, deformed and vertebrae flattened.

All the bones are undermineralized.

Bluish light surrounds her.

This theme concerns her status, since she doesn't place her inheritance in a position of subjectivity, but of an object.

Her X ray teems with energy, but locked outside material.

By transferring functional copies of the gene to her, he can correct the mutant phenotype.

One creates a mouse model of human disease by disrupting a normal mouse gene in vitro, then injecting cells containing the mutated gene into host embryos.

DNA integrated into the mouse genome is expressed and transmitted to the progeny.

Like touch, one ancestral cell initiates therapy.

The phenotype, whose main task is to transform everything into secondary, kinetic energy, pleasure, innocence, won't define every subject.

The mother is not simply a record, but exhibits in the present.

Her genotype makes a parallel reality to her reality of now.

She stands over her and screams.

That the exchange is unreal, not imaginary, doesn't prevent the organ from embodying itself.

By transferring functional copies of the gene to her, he might correct reversible features of the mutant phenotype, lightly touching the bad mother, before.

5

On her fourth birthday, a rash on the elbow indicated enzyme deficiency.
Her view folded inward.
Ideas about life from experience are of no use in the unfolding of potential, empty and light, though there's
    still potential for phenomena to be experienced.
A moment of seeing can intervene like a suture between the image and its word.
An act is no longer structured by concerning a real that is not caught up in it.
Instead of denying material, I could symbolize it with this mucus and its trailings.
The moment the imaginary exists, it creates a setting, but not the same way as form at the intuitive level
    of her mother's comprehension.
In all comprehension, there's an error, forgetting the creative function of material in its nascent form.
So you see in her eyes her form of compassion for beings who perceive suffering as a real substrate.

275

6

An image creates its past, but not like form at the intuitive level.

The mother must have done something terrible in past life, to be so bereaved.

Ambiguity of the form derives from its representing the girl, full of capability, saturated with love.

If the opposite of possible is real, she defines real as impossible, her real inability to repeat the child's game over and over.

Parallel woven lines of the blanket extend to water.

Just a hint of childish ferocity gives them weight.

At night, inspiration fell on her like rain, penetrating the subject at the germline, like a navel.

Joy at birth, a compaction of potential and no potential, is an abstraction that was fully realized.

Reducing a parent to the universality of signifier produces serene detachment from her desire, abstract as an electron micrograph of protein-deplete human metaphase DNA.

Its materiality is a teletransport of signified protoplasm across lineage or time, avid, muscular and compact, as if pervasive, attached to her, in a particular matriarchy of natural disaster, in which the luminosity of a fetal sonogram becomes clairvoyant.

The love has no quantity or value, but only lasts a length of time, different time, across which unfolds her singularity without compromising life as a whole.

# Calamity Jane
## *Martine Bellen*

Here, the season of manifest destiny
And breaded trees

Land-hungry time
Backstairs time

In each of us
An eye witness

Marthy Cannary
By herself

An eye witness

\*

Born 1852, Missouri
oldest of six brats

rider until I became an expert rider,
able to ride the not rideable
horses, which I spent
my early and later life riding

overland to Virginia City, 5 month
journey, hunting the plains
or adventuring, shooting
and riding way beyond

many times crossed
the Rockies
to Montana, our wagons
lowered over ledges,

boggy places, no use
to be careful

lost all, horses and all,
then there were dangers,
streams swollen; mounted
a pony to swim through currents and save

lives or to amuse ourselves.
Narrow escapes. Simple escapades,
reached for obstacles and overcame
as God is witness.

At Black Foot mother died,
I buried her under the spring.
She taught me weather,
strength and to cuss. Then

To Salt Lake. Where my father dies.
Joined General and his campaign.
Between Deadwood and Custer
Molested very little.

Ordered out to the Muscle Shell
Or Nursey Pursey Battle; in saddle
Swirled to catch and cradle
Egan in my arms. Christened
Me Calamity, heroine.

*

To rely on what
One had once
Lost faith

Perseverance keeping
The quiet outer
Fact

Synchronicity and spirit

\*

Doris Day is Calamity sipping sarsaparilli

Bill can't see her beauty till she drops
her coat, can't see her
face or coif. Or hear her
sing, "My gun got so hot had to sit
with a muzzle between my legs."
Her magic: pink chiffon.

made into a woman

"no changeless essence . . . no eternal verities"

    *Custer, Custer, elle était plus qu'une prostituée*
a true star of gold
      *ornée d'une étoile*
*la défroque* of all *théâtre*
      *tout le monde*

Jane Russell and Jean Arthur,
John Wayne and Bogie too.
The frontier's Florence Nightingale.

Custer, she is more than a prostitute,
an *assassine-squaw*

First met up with her long about '75. Business was off so rooming
cottages built and ladies called for to occupy them. They was of the
sporting variety, would have to be wanna come to Fort Laramie.
Common like Jane. Her and some few others followed Gen. Crook
and when Gen. Merritt sent wagons back home the women rode
with the wounded.

Tongue River

\*

The Gold Rush was a period in American
history when men were digging and mining.

*Oremos, oremos*
*angelitos semos,*
*del cielo venemos*
*a pidir oremos*

of riches and respect, out of gulches
came jealousy, destruction of the unseen.

. . . we little angels
from heaven come
to ask for treats

selves, hearts and emptiness

\*

Spectral
War vets sit
Armless

Incrusted black
Marble
Ploughshare

Hero infatuations
And Methodist
Prohibitions

Painted sex
Front tier stage
Ghosting tips

Chartreuse plumes chanteuse.
Cheyenne. *Le chuk wagon.*
Young muscled whackers,
Triple-barreled and stallion-tailed

*Martine Bellen*

Deadwood, New Dakota
Derring-do boom
Gold Black Hills

From Kingdom Come
Calam & Wild Bill
Parade down Main

\*

Donned in buckskin, in beaver,
hammered silver, the sun
children, five men

And Jane joins the pageantry
on horse, not prospector
but sentimentalist scout

The Queen with rosemary
potpourri and cowhands
never bedded sober
or pennies in her pocket

                to awaken on a familiar cot and recall
a fairy tale

"you're a wonderful little woman to have around in times of
calamity," says Captain Egan when I save his life.

                to awaken in an unfamiliar fairy tale

\*

Letters to your
self, inflammation of bowels
weaver and vowel lover

sense of restriction like touch

281

part of her
life nutrient

confessions encoded
in the photo album
diary of a surface
wound

Your rest in her sleep

\*

Master says, "With your eyes, what have you
Seen? With ears, what have you heard?
What have you said with your mouth?"

As none of these was ever practiced

From where come such colors, sounds and scents?

*Be not afeard. The isle is full of noises*

\*

Hat Creek
Calamity Peak
Drunk at Jack's Bar
Fell in a lake

Relationship with memory,
the dark star

"Deadwood Dick,
Rider of the Lugubrious Hills"
Disaster

(Now, isn't that rich)

Beautiful white devil of the Yellow
Stone, Heroine of Whoop-up,

In the melodramatic role
Calamity Jane she expounds

(Tight as a three-leg goat)

Billings, Montana, *Gazette*.
Daughter of Janie & Wild Will
Exclusive. Mother's secret diary.
her confessions. her letters.

The real Calamity Jane for one dime only

Her deeds and miscredits

*

Student asks, "Are clouds
running from or chasing the moon?"

"With your mind, what have you fathomed?" replies Master.

Basic fears never materialize
Wherever the body travels
Hometown strangers send it back

of characters she once was

As in the Noh play, when the lover
Arrives at noon to find no reflection
Alive, she collects change of dreams

after the lust is gone

They can meet in different parts

previous world

Shadows lengthen
in anticipation of shades

*Martine Bellen*

*

Replace the word *power* with . . .
The costume of one's sex.
Passion for male clothes
and companionship
a paradox-mask.

"Pard we will meet again
in the Happy Hunting Ground
to part no more," the stone signature,
written, not in letters, but in her
where signatures of all things
can never be erased, ceased
the afterglow

gun

Imaginary

*

Hog ranch on the outskirts
Institute for Ladies and Gayeties


to accept her
sleep as his access to her pleasure


exhibit her
exclusively
cow-craft


Bill she thinks she is.
And discovers the cruelty
of identities, difference

\*

Forces of air into peaceful
movements; sound
(gentle and
directional)
reveals
the deep
vertebral column

They weave sashes and blankets
Swap stories

migrations over imaginations

orchestrated

held in irons for that which they depend upon

one custodian must bear
the water jar

must gather
clay, shape and fire

beside the power
behind the prayer of ocean

will draw water from the distant
moon without end

until the sky is dry
her eyes

witness
herself

\*

A door above
your head left ajar
for the emergence

of far-off planets
echoing eloquence
toward bottom.

They switch the date of death
to coincide with Bill's
and bury her by his side

Which animals befriend her?
the cat, the kite, the mule:
stubborn, hunter, stray

Le Diable Blanc
at the Number 10 Saloon
Mount Moriah

broken light and grasses
chilled in winter glass
a double sunset

*That you choose to destroy, but save
instead, is the purest act of Love.*

# Inside and Outside: Pages From the Atlas

## William T. Vollmann

### BERKELEY, CALIFORNIA U.S.A. (1992)

OUTSIDE THE VAST SQUARES of yellow bookstore-light, the panhandlers, longhaired and greasy, held out their palms, asking for their dinners, and two started fighting, while inside people turned the pages of picture-books whose flowers smelled like meadows of fresh ink.

I don't want her around me! a panhandler shouted. I don't need that fucking bitch! I hate that monster.

Inside, everyone pretended that the shouting was silence. A man looked at a book and wanted to buy it, knowing how wonderful it would be to sit in his own house with a drink in his hand looking at this thirty-eight-color picture-book printed on paper as smooth as a virgin's thigh while the sun kept coming in through the leaves —

Outside, somebody screamed.

The man bought the book and went out. He saw a man smashing a woman's head against a window of the bookstore. The glass shattered, and as the woman's livid and half-dead face shot into the yellow light he saw it become beautiful like the planet Saturn ringed by arrowheads of whirling glass that rainbowed her in their cruel prisms and clung to wholeness in that spinning second also ringed by her hair and spattering blood.

The man ran back inside where the woman's mouth lay peaceful. He opened his book and invited her in. Gently he raised her head and pillowed the book beneath. Spangles of blood struck the pages like a misty rain, becoming words which had never existed before.

She began to bleed faster and faster. Her hair grew down between the words like grass, underscoring and embellishing them with fragrant flourishes. Her eyes and teeth became punctuation marks. Her skin became pages of bloodless purity. Her flesh kept company with the threads and glue; the plates of her skull broke neatly into cover-armor. Then there was nothing left of her above the raw red throat.

He picked up the book, which spoke to him, saying: Now you have loved me, and I will love you forever. But where are my hands? Where are my feet and my breasts?

I'm sorry, the man said. They're outside.

Bring them in, the book told him. Bring them through the window.

Holding the book tight, the man ran out to obey her, but police had already coagulated from the night. When he tried to smash the corpse's shoulders through the window, they led him into the squad car. He knew that they would take him inside.

Where are my hands? the book wept.

They took you away, the man whispered.

The book began to bleed despondently.


PHNOM PENH, CAMBODIA (1991)

Once when the thiodorazine wore off he found himself with a Bible because they'd taken away the other book to be kept forever in a long manila envelope labeled EVIDENCE. But the woman he'd helped and loved had finally found him. She whispered to him from the Bible telling him to ask them for an atlas, and when the psychiatrists agreed because that was a sign of healthy involvement with the world, he opened the atlas at random, and the wide heavy covers flipped down to anchor him in the new country which he would soon find; and he looked and read **KAMPUCHEA**. So he entered a dark-staired hallway without electricity in Phnom Penh, kids hopping barefoot everywhere, silhouettes in hallways, black crowds watching in the hallway, smells of sweat and body odor and death, fat girls peering out of a dark doorway, giggling. Three girls leaned out. Warily they smiled. The door opened on a sunny place where more fat girls peered out carefully. He stepped into the new part of the hall that the open door had made, the bright part, and they beckoned him in. People were watching. He stood there in the place between outside and inside, entering a nested memory of an openwalled restaurant not far away where he had sat, feeling neither inside nor outside, a Chinese movie shouting along on the TV, while boys rode past one and two to a bike; awnings swirled in the breeze. Then he came out of that memory and entered the open door. All the pretty girls sat on the floor or the rumpled bed, watching TV. The madam closed the door behind him and then he knew that he had truly been admitted to the inside. But he also knew that he could not stay. Sooner or later he'd have to rent one of the girls, or else they'd make him leave. And even if he did rent somebody, so that he could come inside her, eventually he'd finish or his money would be finished and then he'd have to go back into the black hall again, which was outside like the far side of Pluto.

He closed the atlas. They gave him two more pills and checked beneath his tongue to make sure that he had swallowed. Soon he could feel himself going inside again.

## HONG KONG, TERRITORY OF UNITED KINGDOM, SOUTHEAST ASIA (1993)

The woman whispered, so he opened the atlas; and the harbor burned with bluish-gray fog, cool winds ruffling nothing on the blocky buildings across the water which were backdropped by camel'sback hills the same color as the fog. He went among the tea-colored faces in round glasses, became present on the ferry across the gray-green sea. The happiness of going without map or guidebook, having no idea what he'd find, prevented him from recognizing the danger of the tall white buildings like punchcards on the horizon.

Not only this outsider, whose education in boundaries had been so abundant, but also the other inhabitants of Hong Kong, that abstraction as readily graspable as a parallelogram, often a strange woman's voice calling to them from across the water, the voice of a woman neither inside nor outside, who therefore called from loneliness, wanting to be loved so that her hands at least could live with her brain and skull; but to most others her pathetic aspect, which did require something of them, made them prefer not to recognize her: of course it was also that they were completely inside, so that they had little use for somebody who was neither one nor the other. Better not to acknowledge *any* ghost. Of course he was compelled to, because he already had. It is not as easy to get rid of consequences as first principles. He heard her desperate whisperings as he got off the ferry and approached the bank walled with sparkling transparent cubicles in which people paced or pressed or sat downgazing at computer mysteries; in the lower levels, where the public was permitted to come, embankments of metal and marble gleamed like sunlight, while the uniformed ones swarmed safely behind. Below this was a glass floor of many rectangular panes, joined by silvery rods; beneath this the gloomy silhouettes of the lowest walkers passed at obscure diagonals, all at the same pace.

He descended the slow escalator that brought the red uniforms and red displays into broader angles like an airplane approaching the runway, falling from the ceiling, which was a Ptolemaic crystalline sphere.

To cross the street you took an escalator above the statued men at the bank, crossed a marble bridge of potted plants whose leaves gleamed almost as coldly as the black shoes of the officials who marched so soundlessly, followed the V's of darker marble like caramelized sugar on a pudding dessert, turned left at the stained glass window, and then you could look down at the red and silver taxis, the blue and tan double-decker buses, the gray cars and white cars — all very clean, of course — sliding below you along the immaculate street. Then you came to a glass door which let you outside. You followed a walled path, which traversed a steep hill bulging with ferns, lilies, gingko trees and tall palms whose tea-colored darknesses strained toward the glowing fog and were undone by the weight of their own success, their umbrellalike spreadings and droopings from the resolute stalk were a falling back of darkness into darkness. This was the Battery path: a pavement of roots, like the muscles in athletes' shoulders. This was a city of clean paths telling him which way to go.

Waitresses paced inside the glass house with the waterfall outside, and it was just the same as the birds in the aviary. The waterfall, the skyscrapers, the marble tables of the restaurant, were all so incongruous. On the ledge above the waterfall a statue of a boy stood with his arm upraised, and then the camera finished flashing and the statue moved once more.

In the twilight, the swarms in suits and uniforms hurried along the edges of black buildings whose tiles were as slick and shiny as new cakes of soap, each building with a different brand name glowing from it like a pulsing wound. So many crowds! The city's metonym was this tank of shrimp thrashing white legs at each other, bulging their eyes out and straining to fly in the water like beta-test helicopters. He was the soft red carp breathing with difficulty between two reddish companions, its eye bulging and rotating with almost the same intensity as the white spots on the shrimp's scratching legs. But who were these other fishes like slabs of ring fungus swishing their fins lethargically in the murky water, straining and crowding? So many! He'd never know them . . . Behind the counter of the next window, uniformed men weighed out so many different barks and leaves and colored roots and dried sea creatures on white paper. People sat at stools before them, as if by a soda fountain. The men weighed out abalone shell for livercures and dyes, terrapin shells for lung complaints and renal bleeding, sea horses for impotence, hawksbill turtle shells for epilepsy, oyster shells for acid stomach, geckos to quench thirst and increase virility, centipedes to stop hemorrhages, tiger shins for arthritis, stag penises for a cold uterus, fossil bones for insomnia and amnesia, sulphur for virility, cinnamon for diarrhea, eucommia bark for hypertension, castor beans for cutaneous ulcer, red beans for headache. A jewelry window said: 61% OFF. He saw gold chains and crosses on squares of white paper. The next window was crammed with twenty-three-carat gold sunglasses round and oval and square, even a pair that folded down the nose, and a pair not much bigger than a fountain pen; it would barely cover one's pupils. He passed another long narrow jewelry shop at whose red velvet tables the clerks sat punching calculators, drinking Cokes and wearing golden spectacles as fierce as new-cut diamonds. The flow of red characters on yellow awnings bored into his eyes with the same brightness as the golden objects for sale in the windows. A crowd of dark-uniformed policemen stood straight, their black walkie-talkies and holsters and nightsticks hanging correctly down; they walked with their hands behind their backs.

Eastward, where the streets became grayer and narrower, there was a stand of aquariums in the street, the goldfish and the other deep blue ones he didn't know slowly fanning their tails within glass worlds like the spirits in the bottles in the liquor store whose walls formed part of the thoroughfare, or the banana-clusters which hung over the apples in the fruit stand, beset by swaying red lights. The signs were carved and painted now, not lighted. Sometimes they halfway or entirely spanned the narrow alleyways like stilt roots and flying buttresses. Windows and gratings and balconies clutched each other across spaces of narrow darkness.

A girl in pink, with scarlet lips, was leaning against the ice cream freezer in the liquor store talking with her friend, and when her mouth shaped itself into O's the crimson seemed to rise like smoke-rings to join the red signs and suddenly the man was lighting a cigarette, and the fire at its end seemed to have come from her mouth. She touched his hand. Across the street, a man was searching through a pile of apples, and when he found one that seemed redder than the rest and held it up, the watcher looked at the girl and saw that her mouth had just made an O again. Enchanted, he came closer, until he could hear her speak waterfalls that peacock-tailed so brightly down the wall of the Stock Exchange, losing themselves in the hill of potted yellow flowers which bordered the long, long escalator. (Underneath were the hundreds of white gambling booths.) Her ruby syllables rolled him away, so that floundering past a marble lobby (evidently of a seafood restaurant in whose immaculate tanks swam crowds of giant silver carp), he could peer but briefly into a small store to see the round table and the two girls slowly slicing a mound of ginseng. He fell through a red bubble of her delicious spit, tumbled into the market of dried fish whose broad gray mummies lashed together resembled palm fronds, was carried through the restaurant whose two men in black tuxedos were just lighting the final torch around the golden border of a red sign that contained something incomprehensible to him; and like the men in suits and ties on holiday riding escalators up the hills of Ocean Park he swam volitionlessly past the two ladies whose store contained nothing but dried white shark fins, each behind its own pane of glass like some strange sea-trophy; that was when he realized that he was in the sea.

A man unhooked a bundle of dried fish from the awning pole of his shining store, covered the boxes of nuts with burlap, returned to unhook the bale of dried eels, then the hanging light bulb, then stepped outside and pulled down a rusty wall of darkness over everything.

Next door a stern man was still sitting behind his desk, emperor of rolls and scrolls of marbled cloth, and the man stared out the window, he gaped his gristly jaws and gulped, which proved him to be a fish.

The people whose *ahs* and *ows* twisted in the guts of the night now drowned the scarlet-lipped girl's speech entirely, so in hopes of finding other luminescence he ascended a steep hill of meat and lighted produce stands whose pears and potatoes shone like lanterns (their bok choy greener than darkness, their cats mewing like tweaked piano wire). Strings of lights transected the heavens to encourage the ones struggling up that coagulation of night, carrying those purchased brilliancies away darkened in plastic bags.

The Sinew Co. was now being closed, but inside the shopping malls, people were still peering and pointing, the women especially wistfully touching the glass of Rainbow Leatherware Co. and Rolie Collection.

The ferry buildings were like space stations, with their lights and roundness and dockings; but they did not whirl, only rose and fell, and a reflection of the sea rose and fell in their televisionlike windows. Beyond the Star terminal rose a golden bowtie of neon, tall and absurd, crowned by a white trapezoid and a blue spire. Forgetting the scarlet-lipped girl, he let himself be caught by the blue neon-light on black water.

*William T. Vollmann*

The thin old man with the white star on his chest stood holding the gangplank railing in a gloved hand, watching something too proud for others, who came running, the blackhaired girls with arms folded over their breasts, the skinny boys jutting out their chins, the ladies in glasses happy not to have missed the ferry, the married couples (wives on their husbands' arms). Then the whistle blew, the ferryman braced his foot against the bulkhead and strained at the rope, winching the gangplank up against the door. He stood watching Kowloon come closer (another ferry passing the black water, a vast illuminated casket). He remembered the Japanese restaurant where the indigo-pigtailed waitresses stood in corners with their hands behind their backs, white bows tied behind their short black skirts, and they wished him happy New Year and grew into the New Year like those tropical trees tasseled as if by strings of lime-colored beads. But he himself was coming outside his life again as steadily as the Kowloon ferry bearing through the cold and fishy night. The ferryman stood still, squinting at a newspaper, his pinkish-orange face worn down almost to a skull by rain and fog and wind. He stood without support, swaying easily with the lurching deck. The horn sounded three times; the water began to burn evilly with the red and blue neon reflections of Tsim Sha Tsui, and he locked his newspaper away to again pull on his plastic gloves. He stood by the gangplank, patiently watching the greenish-gray window-lights and orange-gray wall-lights come closer. Then he gripped the rope, unhooked the chain and let the pulley go. The crowd went out calmly, lighted faces going steadily into darkness.

# Guignol's Band
## *Louis-Ferdinand Céline*

*— Translated from French by Dominic Di Bernardi*

THE DOOR'S ALREADY MOBBED. . . Even though we'd raced over. . . so's the gate. . . so's the sidewalk. . . and every copy of the *Times* opened wide. . . Every last one of them had to be here about the want ad. . . A great-looking house. . . real posh. . . surrounded by a big garden. . . flower beds, roses, out of this world. . . some flunkey held the people back. . . urging patience.

"The Colonel is not ready!. . ." He shouted from the steps to keep them at bay.

Ah, hell! we didn't come here for this! Ah! waiting around wasn't our style!. . .

Suddenly Sosthène explodes in a squeal over everybody's heads. . . "The Colonel! The Colonel! Quick! Quick! We're from the War Office. . . Emergency! Emergency!. . ."

He brandished his big roll, unfurling it above the mob. . . like a banner!

"China! China!" he declared. . .

Naturally everybody cracks up. . . his chance to slip to the front. . .

"The fool! The fool!"

They think he's nuts.

I hurry after him, we're through the door, standing on the carpet, this is one magnificent vestibule! We give our shoes a good wipe. . . Huge paintings, antique tapestries. . . I'm an expert. . . It's a fantastic joint. . .

More servants pop up out of the woodwork. . . I bet they're here to give us the boot!. . . Sosthène jumps down their throats. . . "War Office! Gas masks! Gas masks!"

He scowls, throws a scare into them, they keep looking, a little leery. They block the Chinaman's path. They all circle around his gown for a look-see at his embroideries, especially the one covering his rear. . . He shows off his dragon. . . a beautiful blue and

295

yellow fire-breathing beast! He's an instant smash!
"Speak English!" he goes to me, "speak English!"
His plan is for me to start shooting my mouth off.
But no need. . . a very young girl. . . just a kid. . . but so
pretty, a sweetheart!. . . fair-haired, a real charmer. . . Right off
the bat I'm all admiration. . . ah! ravishing!. . . ah! I'm knocked
off my feet!. . . Ah! Love at first sight!. . . Ah! Those beautiful
blue eyes!. . . That smile!. . . baby doll, I adore her!. . .
I shut my ears to the bullshitter beside me!. . . I've shut out
everything, dead in my tracks, I'm speechless. . .
If only it wasn't for these crummy rags!. . . I'm so ashamed. . .
If only I'd had a quick shave. . . wasn't in such deep shit. . . I'd
come right out and tell her what she's doing to me. . . how wonderful it is. . . No! I wouldn't. . . I'd keep it all to myself just the
way I am now. . . head-over-heels. . . drooling. . . miserable. . .
Ah! I feel such joy!. . . I'm afraid to breathe!. . . Ah! she's so
beautiful!. . .
The servants are puzzled. . . They were supposed to wait for
their boss. . . They go off, leave us there. . . both standing in
front of the little girl. . . we don't know which way to turn. . .
How old is she? twelve. . . maybe thirteen, I'd say. . . anyway,
that's my guess. . . and those calves!. . . short skirt. . . what
grace. . . what superb legs. . . tanned, muscular, you name it!. . .
she must be athletic. . . athletic girls always drive me crazy. . .
That's just the way I picture fairies, in the same kind of short
skirt!. . . And she's a fairy!. . . That creep Sosthène leering know-
ingly. . . stealing winks at me. . . His sort shouldn't be allowed
to look at her unless he's on his knees! stretched prostrate, begging
her forgiveness!
"Uncle! Uncle!". . . she even talks too!. . . she's calling her
uncle! What a voice! Pure crystal!. . . Ah! I'm hooked!
Sosthène gives me another wink, she catches him!. . . He'll ruin
everything!
"It's OK! It's OK!. . ." he whispers back.
The lousy bum!
"The Colonel's coming!"
He's announced.
And here he comes.
"Virginia!. . . Virginia!. . ."
He walks up to us. He talks to his niece.
Ah! her name's Virginia. . . Such a pretty name, Virginia!

The Colonel's a porker, big and bloated, bursting at the seams, nothing like Colonel des Entrayes from my war days! With that big butt and tiny head, he looks like a cannonball in his dressing gown, with sharp beady eyes, plus a scowl, actually a facial twitch constantly running back and forth across his nose from cheek to cheek, a rabbit wrinkle, he's always nibbling. . . He's bald. . . a chrome dome. . . He's got an eye that tears. . . just one. . . He keeps wiping it with a finger. He studies Sosthène. He looks at Virginia sternly.

"Why are they here?" he asks her. I can understand his English.

I jump right in.

"The War Office!" I declare very firmly.

Spunky move!. . . I'll run the whole show!

I add: "The engineer only speaks French!. . ."

I point to Sosthène de Rodiencourt.

"Oh! Oh! But he's a Chinaman," he says with surprise.

Now that tickles his funny bone! He takes in the odd bird from head to toe. Sosthène unfolds his maps all around. . . his rolls of paper. . . he yanks out a steady stream of papers from his beautiful yellow gown. . . Ah! the Colonel's a tough customer, but this is starting to distract him. . . He lets Sosthène jabber away, eggs him on with his gestures. He shows us into the living room like real guests. He leads the way. . . I'm afraid to take a seat. . . but then I dare. . . Such so-oothing armchairs! I slump down! Luscious monstrosities! Colossal sponges! Sopping up every drop of my exhaustion!. . .

Sosthène's still rattling away, dithering in the middle of the room, he didn't sit down take a break nothing. . . gesticulating, haranguing, spluttering. . . Now he's brandishing his copy of the *Times*, the want ads. . .

"Do you understand me, Colonel! I tell you I'm just the man you're looking for! So you agree, OK? You can count on me one hundred percent! Me! Me!"

He's talking just about himself. Thumping his chest real hard. He's afraid he's not getting through! Then he goes over for a look out the window, shows the Colonel the crowd! all those people milling around down there. . . mobbing the sidewalk. . . He won't have any more of that! no sir-ree, won't hear another word! He won't put up with any competition!

"Ah! my Colonel, it's too bad! I'm telling you to your face! All those people have got to go! This situation's got to end!"

Ah, really he'd rather just leave!. . .

"I work alone or I walk, old boy! Come on, let's go!. . ."

He leads me away. . . A question of dignity!

Everybody's laughing, including the servants. . . holding him back by his basque. . .

"No! No! Sit down, sir!"

He's won. . . The guy's a riot!. . .

The Colonel wants to keep laughing, he makes him run away and back. . . pop his hat on and off. . . All this right in the living room. . . A real sideshow! Darling little Virginia is having as much fun as anyone, but she doesn't want Sosthène to work himself sick playing the buffoon!

"Sit down, sir! Sit down!"

Ah! But that's not what the Colonel wanted! he wanted the whole show with dressing gown, dragon, the works. Sosthène didn't catch on. . . he reeled off his life story while bopping along, bolting back and forth like some loony. . . his death-defying exploits in India, his unburied treasures. . . which slipped through his fingers. . . his raw deals with the Gem Company. . . and loads of other stuff. . . just like that while strutting around. . . his technical innovations, the veritable revolution in electromagnetic circuitry. . . the great debt science owed him. . . his special poison-gas detector calibrated to the millionth particle. . . all the patents he'd taken out since Berlin in 1902! everything he'd been chiseled out of. . .

"Drinks!" the Colonel orders.

A flunkey bustles off, comes back with an armload. . . an entire cellar of bottles, flasks, whiskey, cognac, champagne, sherry. . .

The Colonel pours himself a glass, then another, then another. . . He's drinking all by himself. . . And then another!. . .

"Baah!" he goes after each swig. . . The stuff packs a wallop.

He nestles back in his deep armchair, groans "Oooh!. . . Oooh!" over and over again. . . his belly's shaking. . . he's having a ball. . . he loves Sosthène. . . thinks he's one funny guy. Meanwhile I've been dying a thousand deaths, especially in front of the girl! Sosthène's still darting me those glances. I wish the guy would shape up. . . No fucking way! He's on a roll!

"My dear Colonel, let me congratulate myself on being the perfect man to fit your bill!. . . I'm not afraid of coming right out with it! Lead us to the laboratory!. . . Just you wait and see!. . ."

Ah! ah! now the fun's really starting, and I mean the grand old rip-roaring variety! The Colonel's tickled pink. Slapping his thighs, crowing in delight. Out in the middle of the room Sosthène's still raring to go. . . running through his little act all over again. . . the flunkeys must be in a complete fog. . . he's just some loony, that's all! Every word out of his mouth is drowned in laughter. . . he's happy he's a hit. . . Great technique!. . . The Colonel offers him a drink. . . he doesn't want anything alcoholic. . . Soda water for him! plain soda water!

I go over for a glance into the street. . . the applicants are still milling around. . . Quite a mob. . . it keeps multiplying. . . more people constantly arriving. . . the ad hit its mark. . . they've all got the *Times* over their heads!. . . It's raining now, a real downpour. . . Somebody's got to send them away, take charge. . . but the Colonel's not charging anywhere. . . He's still checking out Sosthène. . . I wonder if he understands French. He knocks back another glass of whiskey! Oooh!. . . His gasp echoes through the room. Each swig must scorch his mouth. . . But anyway he still hasn't kicked us out yet! That's the main thing! I'm sort of just twiddling my thumbs. . . Too bad Sosthène won't shut his trap. . . keeps raising such hell. . . I wish I were a tiny mouse. . . and could hide here forever!. . .

And now the rain's coming down even harder!. . . Genuine torrents lashing the windows. . . The job-hunters are soaked to the bone!. . . A rumble's mounting from the mob outside. . . gets to be disturbing. . . The Colonel's not bothered. . . He claps his hands. . . The lackeys bustle off, come back with more trays, set out a whole tableload of food. . . packed with eats, hors d'oeuvres!. . . what a terrific spread!. . . what mouthwatering goodies!. . . I'm drooling. Foaming at the mouth, that's a fact! My head's spinning. . . meat pies, anchovies! slices of ham! beef! Gorgonzolas! whole heaps! Grub galore!. . . Ah! a wonderland of great pickings!. . . you can't imagine how it looked to my starving eyes! Mountains of butter!. . . Foothills, and soaring peaks! Ah! Everything's a blur! Ah! I'm seeing double! Triple! Before my eyes Sosthène starts swaying, shoots to the ceiling, stretched full height, for one second poises on tiptoe between heaven and earth. . . then whoosh! he swoops on the tray!. . . On all fours! Flat on his belly! Wolfing down, inhaling everything in sight!. . . a mastiff! growling like mad. . . Such a horrendous spectacle!. . . Got to find somewhere to hide!. . . The Colonel keeps his trap shut. . . tickled pink!. . . Anything but sore! He must have taken a shine to us!

Fact is, the guy's elated!. . . Ah! he's never laughed so hard!. . . He leans down to help Sosthène stuff his face!. . . Shovels in whole platefuls of hors d'oeuvres! dumps them right into his mouth. . . And Sosthène just can't get enough. . . he asks for more. . . Ah! what a pretty sight this is in front of the girl!. . . My Chinaman's turned into a mad dog! greedy, lapping chow right from the rug! What an exhibition!. . .

Colonel O'Collogham invites me to some chicken, but I'm not getting down on all fours!. . . on second thought, I'm famished. . . dizzy from hunger! About to collapse! But I hang tough! Won't touch a crumb! Not on my belly, on my butt or on my feet! I don't want to eat ever again in front of my walking miracle, my fantasy! my soul! my dream!. . . I'm palpitating, quivering!. . . Nailed to the spot!. . . On fire!. . . Dizzy with joy!. . . it was love at first sight. No, I'll never put food in my mouth again! I love her! I love her too much! How could I chew in front of her? Stuff my face like that other guy? The nerve of that pig!. . . So what, I'll die, tough luck!. . . I'd give my life for her!. . . die of hunger! but my goddess, my soul! she's inviting me to have a sandwich. . . or two. . . or three. . . how can I say no? she insists. . . smiles at me. . . I give in. . . helplessly. . . I give in!. . . Ah! she's got me beat!. . . I swallow it down!. . . bolt my food in turn!. . . The Colonel congratulates us. . . I'm excited, I've been beaten. . . We're devouring his four trays!. . . digging in with great gusto all around.

"Bravo, boys! Bravo!"

He's glad we've picked it clean. . . Ah! yes, now he's a real buddy! Let's do justice to his sandwiches! his leg of lamb! his caviar! his sweets, his bombe glacée! Magnificent tutti-frutti ice cream!. . . we inhale it!. . . But there's no contest, Sosthène's making the biggest pig of himself!. . . He's putting away at least a month's supply!. . . And whenever his jaws stop chomping he's right back to blabbing! Talking big! Dishing out his crazy stories!. . . he piles them on between mouthfuls. . . what a champ! what crapola!. . . nothing keeps him from yakking about how terrific he is! he lays it on thick. . . he's worked umpteen wonders!. . . Here comes another feat!. . . This invention, that invention!. . . his big spectroscopic mirror able to detect gaseous emissions. . . patented in Liverpool!

I think Sosthène's putting the Colonel to sleep. . . he's nodding back in his armchair. . . yawns quietly behind his hand. . . Ah! now I sneak a peek at the little girl over there, that radiant

mystery. . . Good God, she's beautiful!. . . What an angel!. . .
What gentle grace!. . . And what darling mischievousness too!. . .
I motion her on the sly that I think Sosthène's talking too much!. . .
I'm taking a risk. . . She answers back on the sly. . . she's really
very nice. . . "Let him go on!. . . Uncle's falling asleep!. . ." In
fact her uncle was dozing off. . . Me too in the end, my eyes start
blinking shut. . . I'm really done in!. . . Sosthène is still talking. . . I'd like to stay awake. . . Look at Virginia again. . . Never
take my eyes off her!. . . adore her. . . but my lids won't stay
open. . . my eyes heavy, burning. . . Ah! I mustn't seem very
nice. . . nor fun to be around. . . nor even funny. . . I can't make
her laugh like the other goof. . . I can't feel a thing except on the
inside. . . The way my heart's pounding. . . I'm heavy. . . made
of lead. . . lead over my eyes, filling my head. . . I'm pumped
full of lead. . . Ah, I give up. . . I'm lead through and through. . .
down to my bones. . . only my heart is light. . . pounding every
which way. . . and that's just how I fall asleep, head in hands,
elbows on knees. . . because I'm just too weak. . . I'd rather not
drop off in front of the girl. . . but I give up. . . give up. . . Oh!
please let me do anything but snore!. . . Virginia's standing right
there in front of us!. . . How comfortable this living room is!. . .
I'm only half dozing!. . . nodding off and on. . . I wish she wouldn't
see me sleeping. . . I can still hear the other guy's bullshitting. . .
"Colonel sir. . . Colonel sir. . ."
He won't give it a rest!. . . his lousy voice lulls me. . . lulls
me. . . I can't catch what he's saying.

We woke up the following morning around six. . . slumped back
in the armchairs. . . everybody else had gone up to bed. . . They'd
left us sleeping.
As soon as he heard the house stirring Sosthène started sniffing
all around. He went down to the kitchen to boil some water. But
he couldn't find any fixings for the coffee he wanted. . . he came
back up to the living room, we polished off the eye of lamb and
the meat pies. . . the leftovers. . .
Sosthène was raring to go. . . He went to wash up. . . another
trip downstairs to the kitchen. . . This time he came back with
an iron. . . He started pressing his dressing gown on the large
dinner table. . . fussing over the pleats. . . at last be finds a
flunkey. . . just passing through on his rounds. . .
"I'd like to see your Colonel again, Mr. Collogham! And make it

snappy!. . . I'd like to have a word with him!. . ."
I had to act as translator. Nobody showed up.

We ran over to see whether any applicants were still waiting outside. . . They hadn't even gone home to bed! Or else they'd come
back at the crack of dawn. . . Either way, they were pale as
ghosts. . . we could see them a long way off, their sorry figures,
heads still plastered with the *Times*. . . the rain hadn't let up. . .
the footman was motioning to them that they were just wasting
their time. . . They didn't give a damn, they weren't budging. . .
We were motioning to them too. . . telling them to clear the hell
out! They didn't understand. . . Meanwhile the Colonel is announced. . . He's on his way down to breakfast. . . In a bubbly
mood. . . happy. . .

"Let me shake your hands!"

In a leaf-print dressing gown. . . well rested. . . he's in excel-
lent spirits. . .

"Boys!. . . Boys!. . ." he claps his arms around us. . . cordial as
could be. . . whisks us away. . . Ah! this can't wait!. . . we
chug along. . . wind up back in the garden. . . between two
groves. . . a small hidden shed, camouflaged with ivy. . . plus
grass, weeds, rubbish and twigs scattered all over the roof. . .

"Shh! Shh!" he goes. . . starts clearing his throat, but breaks
into a coughing fit. . . he pops in a big candy drop. . . doesn't do
any good, he keeps sucking, sucking. . .

"Did you sleep well?" he asks. . .

At last he's done hacking, we step inside the shed. He shuts the
door carefully. . .

"Do you know about gases?" Another question.

"Oh! Yes! Yes!. . ."

We didn't want to miff him. . . All at once he stoops over.

"Right there!. . . There!. . . he shouts. . .

He opens a forceful tap. . . and how it spews! spews!. . .
psssst!. . . violently. Took us by total surprise, whew. . . Full
blast right in our faces. . . Couldn't dash to the door fast enough. . .
Quicker than when we got here!. . . What a fruitcake!. . . Racing
off, we can hear him behind us. . . roaring with laughter, busting
his gut! We zip around the lawn three times from sheer momentum!. . . coughing hacking. . . Ah! he really let us have it!. . .
We flop down on the grass. Pooped. . . I had such an acrid taste in
my throat I was afraid to take another breath. . . Small wonder
that jerk had such a cough. . . The pair of us was coughing too!

Sosthène even worse than me!... I puke up a gob of blood...
I'm choking... All this hacking tearing me to pieces!... Ah!
I've got my own bag of tricks! Look at that fresh gob! Hey, this
is no joke!... Ah! I'm getting out of here... I shout over to
Sosthène...

"You deal with this wiseguy's crap yourself! I'm fed up with his
gas taps! Be seeing you! Love and kisses to blondie!..."

"Ah, don't do this to me!" he grabs me, absolutely beside himself... flings himself around my neck... kisses me...

"You'll kill me if you do that!"

He begs me... beseeches... with excuses, sweet talk... the
Colonel was just kidding us, horsing around... a typical English
prank, an eccentric's whim... The problem was I just didn't understand England... this was no big deal at all...

So in the end I let myself be bamboozled again. The Colonel
comes looking for us, his estate is one big amusement park... he
leads us farther off to another hut, another shanty, entirely camouflaged with ivy like the first... Ah! This time I'm watching
my step, God damn it!... The next trick he pulls will be his
last!... I won't come back!... I peer in from outside... A real
junk heap in there, motor belts, small dynamos, spilling all over
the tables, a worse clutter on the floor... heaps of hammers, bit-
braces, one big load of machine rubbish...

"Here's where I work, gentlemen!..." he announces, proud as a
peacock... "Work! Work! me and my engineers!..."

Whatever, but today it stands empty... Engineers my foot...
the place is deserted...

Again he stoops... Pssst! A yellow stream... he found another tap! Pssst! Blowing into our legs! Didn't have time to spot
it... Ah! this moron's a genius when it comes to acting dumb...
he goes into ecstasies, starts dancing around! hacking the whole
time! hacking away!... Bouncing around, batty over his gag...
He's got a special knack for this kind of crap! And he's running his
legs off! Smug silly son of a bitch! I'd like to cram his gas taps down
his throat!... I always run into these prize pranksters...

"Shut up,you dumb idiot!... That's our first experiment!..."

Sosthène latches onto me... he moans, he can see I'm about
to clear the hell out, he puts on a sad face so I won't leave him high
and dry.

"Ah! Our first?... that's a hot one, you fairy... Skip to the
last, why don't you?... I'm going to drop dead coughing!..."

No kidding, I can't take any more. I'm oozing blood, some yellow gunk, from all the holes in my head. . . from my nose, my ears. . . See ya!. . . What a big joke!

The Colonel's getting a big kick anyway, he doesn't give us a break, he's coughing, coughing like crazy, but having a blast. . . He leads us even farther off. . . Sniff! Sniff! Sniff!. . . He shows how to clear our systems out like it's still part of the joke. . . The trick is to blow out backwards!. . . such a reek and rasp in your throat. . . way down inside. . . a burning sensation. . . scorching you, worse and worse. . . I'm going to puke up my lungs!. . . Smmmuuff! Smmuuufff! No good! damn!. . . He's still sucking on his big licorice drop. . . I should have just left! the hell with Sosthène! They'd have worked out something between them!. . . But then there was the kid. . . If I blow this place. . . then I blow all my chances!. . . I'd never be able to set foot here again!. . . My rotten attitude makes her uncle sore. . . Ah! I forced myself to stay on. . . I kept coughing. . . coughing. . . sniffing. . . trying out his little trick, sniff! sniff! tagging along after him, I was a coward at heart. . . Now we're climbing stairs. . . one floor. . . two. . . this is the place. . . he plants us in front of the door.

"Wait!" he goes.

_ I'm sure he's going to pull the same thing again! ah! I'm positive! I let the jerk know what's on my mind. "Wait and see! This time he'll kill us!"

Ah! I feel jumpy, I want to get out of there.

"So, bye-bye, Sosthène, I'm beating it!. . ."

I can hear the crackpot through the door rummaging around his gear.

"Wait! Wait!" he shouts from way back inside.

He's scared we'll get away.

"Hear that?. . . He's getting the pipes ready!. . ."

I was sure, really sure. . .

"No! No! Wait a second!"

Fine! I wait, I let him talk me into it again. . . since I'm totally whacked, I take a little breather. Now the wall starts shaking. . . this hanging tapestry starts rising. . . higher and higher. . . up like a theater curtain. . . and who do I see before my eyes. . . center stage?. . . Our very own funny man!. . . in person, and all tarted up! hilarious! in dress uniform! epaulets! sabretache, the works!. . . A quick costume change. He wants to blow us away with his wealth. . . He's putting on the ritz now. . . A Colonel!

shako! big sabre! just magnificent!... A gala performance!...
frogs! boots! spurs!... tight-fitting khaki, red inner lining!... Ah!
His head's out of this world!... A feathered shako no less!... A
walking costume drama!... Could that be an English uniform?
where did he dig up all that gold?... Ah! Sosthène in his yellow
dressing gown looks pretty shabby compared to this! his little
asshole dragon!... his mimosa trimmings! Man oh man! It really
cracks me up!... He holds his pose an instant for our admiration... turns on his heels walks off struts back onto the small
platform! The Colonel in fancy drag! What a knockout!...

He gives us no time to think... Bam! he pounces back on top
of us!... He leads us off somewhere else again... not allowed
to catch our breath!... down a short corridor... up one floor...
a flight of stairs... up another... Whew! here we are!... in
front of the attic. He shows us around... the "Hall of Experiments" as he dubs it... right under the rafters, it's enormous...
a kind of misshapen hangar... I spot the experiments... another incredible pigsty!... everything you want, scrap metal,
glassware... heaps of junk like over at Claben's... I keep running into messes, junk collectors, pack-rat setups... I'm sure
he'll lock us in... That's his one big obsession! What's he going
to come up with now?... where'd he stick the taps?... ah! I'm
certain, I hunt for them along the walls... in the air... everywhere... along the floor...

"Shhh! Shhh!" He comes back acting real mysterious... everything's a big secret!... Anybody follow us?... he asks, grows
worried... Then he leans over... calls... shouts down the
stairs.

"Virginia!... Virginia!..."
Twice more... Nobody answers...
He turns back to us.
"She's shrewd!..."
So now we know.
He gobbles down his cough drop. He could tell a tale or two
about Virginia... Oh, man! And how!... He listens... No!
No! not a sound... He shuts the door very gently... creeps
back to whisper his secret... practically right against our
ears...

"Me! Collogham! Colonel! Royal Engineer!"
He gives a military salute.
"That's right! Thirty-two years of active duty! India! Here!...

the Empire is in danger! Grave danger! Gas! Gas! Did you smell it, gentlemen?"

You better believe we smelled the gas.

"The devil! Gentlemen! Look, gentlemen! Sin! Lucifer! Sulphur! Did you smell? You understand me? So you've got to pray to God! And right now!. . ."

That's an order.

"Pray to God! And right now!. . ."

"Pray to God?. . ."

I just stand there like some ass.

He grabs my hands, pushes them together, he's going to make me say my prayers. . . He's dead serious. . .

"Right! Now, down on our knees!. . ."

He too kneels down, in dress uniform. . . All three of us on our knees. . . It's got to warm his cockles.

"Pray to God!" he yells. . . "Pray to God!. . ."

No choice but to obey.

All I know is the "Our Father!". . . I recite it. . . Suddenly he sticks his face into mine. . . wants to double-check my devotion. . . gives me a hug. . . a kiss on the forehead. . . he stands up, genuinely delighted!. . .

"Oh! You understand!. . . Oh, you understand!. . . my dear, invincible! in. . . vin. . . cibelle!. . . allies! magnificent allies!. . . China! Frah-hance!. . . Stay on your knees!. . . I'll consecrate you!. . ."

This is a big-time event. Got to keep a straight face. . . he unsheathes his sword. . . hits me. . . with a tap on the shoulder. . . Presto!. . . We're consecrated!. . .

"England Rules the World!. . ." he squeals. He waits for us to take up the chorus.

"Hip! Hip! Hurray!. . ."

Gotcha!. . . we belt it out, and throw in a "Vive la France!" We're in the spirit! He's rejoicing!. . .

"Gentlemen!" he gives us a hug. . . "You've understood! The Boaches are kaput! Gas! kaput!. . . Finished!. . ." He guffaws!. . .

Exuberant outbursts make me suspicious.

"Heads up!. . ." I shout over to Sosthène. . . this time I caught him in the act!. . . he dove under the workbench!. . . He's going to open another tap! No!. . . that's not it! A new trick! Oh, I got scared! He's lugging out two huge contraptions, masks sort of, wild gizmos with monster goggles. . . plus tubes, coils winding around every which way. . . little ones and big ones. . . a diving mask kind of thing. . . but even more freaky-looking. . . really incredible gear. . . got to weigh a ton. . . we lend him a hand, he couldn't manage on his own. . .

"Gentlemen! Safety first!"

You can see how proud he is. . . showing off his treasures. "William the Conqueror 1917! Off to Berlin! To Berlin! Modern!. . . Modern!. . ." That's his grand announcement. He whisks off his shako. . . He's going to put on his device. . . His goal must be to head out for Berlin with it on. . . I won't stop him. . .

Ah! Just our luck, we came up with a real prizewinner! he gives us the rundown on his doodads. . . they're all different. . . mustn't mix them up. . . these here're valves!. . . Those over there too!. . . But those other ones aren't!. . . That one's a carboy!. . . the heaviest of the lot!. . . with a big lead tube. . . that other thinga-majig with the so-called valves opens at the top. . . see that copper connecting panel that pulls down and seals off your eyes, plus the red and blue goggles. . . Now Sosthène's got to give it a go!. . . Come on, let him sniff in the valves!. . . He'll get a kick out of it!. . . We'll each get our turn, of course!. . . They start discussing technique. . . I watch them, they're getting on my nerves. . . Sosthène in his Chinese drag. . . the other guy in his operetta getup. . . They're firing each other up. . . I just stand back and think. . . I'm not involved. . . But they'd like to fill me in on the sniffing hookup anyway! Ah! I positively refuse to listen to a word! They want to suck me in. . . Aw! I'd like to tell them to take a flying fuck! The whole deal stinks, and that's that. . . The only thing that holds me back is Virginia. . . So my mind keeps working. . . working hard. . .

The Colonel's geared up, totally gung ho. He's got another idea. . . "All three of us! All three of us off to the war! War! Ouarr! Ouarr!. . ." With him in that mask, don't forget. . .

Is this what he was getting at the whole time?. . . He wanted to roll back the Germans with his valve-equipped snout. . . Oh! he could be my guest. . . Damn! he's outdone himself this time! Just as I suspected!. . . I motion to Sosthène for us to scram. . . this time it's settled! End of the line! But forget it, they're bosom buddies! absolutely nuts about each other. . . they want to stay together forever. . . the instruments turn them on. . . Sosthène's not even looking at me anymore. They're going to throw a scare into the Germans!. . . They promise each other, swear up and down. . . They gobbledygook nonstop back and forth in broken French and English. They must be getting everything ass-backwards. . . In short, they adore each other. But there's no way you'll see me marching off. . . in some gas mask or shit mask. . . Ta-ta, lame brainchild! The pair might as well go and get hitched. . . I'll forever hold my peace. . . Why don't they lug along his ancestor, Achille de Rodiencourt?. . . Sosthène went on enough about him. . . First of all, I knew about helmets. . . I'd worn my share in battle. . . with thick plumes, brush, the works. . . I was thinking back. . . Those helmets in the 14th Cuirassiers were a lot lighter than these. . . and they were the real thing too. . . Oh! Yowee! My head's still hard from wearing them. . . But now rigged out in those supposedly anti-gas toad eyes of theirs. . . what kind of crazy shit would they cook up next?. . . oh! life throws so much crap your way! And there was more to come. . . Plus with my fruitcake Colonel into the bargain. . . they were hitting it off fantastically!. . . They didn't give another second's thought. . . They were pouncing onto the equipment. . . Pulling apart, breaking everything up. . . Both on the same wavelength. . . smashing every single hookup to pieces. . . busting away with hammers!. . . screwdrivers!. . . they were popping pins. . . going full blast. . . ripping fragile membranes!. . . raging rummaging it's horrendous. . . like they're in the grip of a fever. . . But booming with laughter, and happy. . . as though the gadgetry had gone right to their heads! If I open my mouth they'll gang up on me. . . a frenzy of destruction! they don't give me another thought. . . they've got a vendetta against their junk. . . They lunge on top of it. . . Savages. . . one on each side!. . . Let 'er rip!. . . they grab the gorgeous masks. . . dash them against the wall! and then dive on top of the debris!. . . all I can see is a pair of butts! the embroidered Chink, and the scarlet-lined Colonel. . . flinging around all their doodads. . . chucking them up in the air!. . . Fistfuls at a time!. . . they come raining down. . . falling back. . . the nails. . . the Muscovy glass!. . . They must be high on gas. . . having one hell of a time!. . . crazy bastards!. . . Ah! they were turning my stomach. . . So long! I could have slipped out without any fanfare. . . They wouldn't even have noticed. . . All right then! Do it!. . . I start moving!. . . And then plop! I chicken out again! Can't get the girl out of my mind! I hesitate, all mixed up, unhappy. . . How am I going to tell her good-bye?. . . It'd sure bring me bad luck to slip off like some bum. . . after the way she was so nice. . . so generous, especially toward both of us. . . and we acted like such slugs, especially the other guy over there, the weirdo from China. . . Ah! I wanted to see her once more all the same. . . let her know before I left that I wasn't a zero. . . just have a word or two. . . and not just slink off like some slob, some yahoo, some brainless pig. . . True, she was just a girl, but she had the poise of a woman. . . You could see that in the way she gave orders. . . and made her presence felt. . . she was a mistress of the house made in heaven. . . Ah! I'd just wait for her, that's that!. . . my two whacked-out roughnecks would run out of steam soon enough, then conk out on top of their rubble. . . Even now they weren't whaling away quite as hard. Crazy fits don't last forever.

The situation dragged on for a while. . . they were having way too much fun together. . . they kept it up for another three hours at least, putting/pulling things together/apart, and then playing tricks on each other. . . they'd hide utensils. . . then make them reappear smack on each other's heads. . . openly thumbing their noses at each other. . . an absolute free-for-all! Monkeys cutting loose!

Sosthène had tucked up his shirt with diaper pins.

"The membrane from one calf embryo, gentlemen!"

The Colonel was demonstrating everything. . . his great invention, the one he'd clicked onto his belly, a stroke of genius! how he "houmiidified" the gases, the air and the nitrogen! dissolved them together through a slow dripping process! with the poisons! you really should have seen his setup! Sosthène stood there jaw to the floor. . . drank up every single word. . . mimicked every move. . .

All at once the Colonel shoots upright with a start. . . frozen motionless finger in the air. . .

"Piss! Piss!" he shouts. . . "My prostate!. . ."

With his eyes locked in a stare as though he were hearing voices!. . . Here we go again, another song and dance! Then he pokes around his underpants, sticks his finger in his butt. . . and dashes off, he's gone!. . .

Afterwards we got used to this, it came on him every now and then, especially after having worked himself up. . . and whenever it did, clear the way, for Christ's sake! But this time around I was all too glad. . . I had to give Sosthène a piece of my mind. I was going to set him straight.

"Sosthène! Sosthène!" I grabbed him. . . "Sosthène! How much longer is this going to go on? Could you please tell me, huh? Do you have any idea, dear sir? Because you can count me out!. . . No way I'm going back to the war!. . . Just forget it!. . ."

Ah! I've gone and left him speechless. . . He looks at me, knocked for a loop.

"What? You were the one who used to talk about dying! About suicide! Despair! Now you're shaking in your boots?"

Ah! I've taken him aback.

"I thought you'd be happy!. . ." he throws in, "that you'd jump at the chance!. . ."

Ah! his nasty dig rubs me the wrong way! I can't believe it, the guy's making fun of me!

"And what about you, Mister Smooth Operator!" I snap back. . . "Magic, my balls! Still enchanted by your journey to India? Are you leaving or aren't you?. . . Maybe you'd better stick to one spot?. . . You old swindler con artist cuckold!. . ."

I let him have it. . .

"You old phony!. . . You old bullshitter!. . ." I throw in.

I was out for blood.

"Oh, my, oh, my, oh, my!" he goes. . . "Oh! where are your manners!" He scowls. . . I've put him through the wringer.

"Where'd you learn to treat people that way?. . ." he asks me, very high and mighty.

"And what about you, you old con man!"

The situation was turning ugly. . . I repeated loud and clear: "I'm not going to go and get myself killed to save your ass!"

"How's that supposed to happen? You silly fool, can you just tell me how? This is our lucky day! A break beyond our wildest dreams! Our one chance in a thousand! Don't you understand what we're dealing with?. . . We're about to rake in 1,500 pounds!"

He's acting infuriated!

"Where'd you see 1,500 pounds, huh?"

"But that's what the Colonel's offering us!"

"Ah! That's what he's offering us! So where is it? All right, fine, I'll take you at your word, I want some clothes right away! A suit, a brand-new one! Those are my terms. . . quite reasonable. . . not a luxury. . . you've let me know often enough. . . 'Clothes make the man, my son, clothes make the man!'"

The truth is he'd rubbed my nose in it. . .

"Very well then! So's twelve pounds enough?"

I set my price, I wanted a peek at this supposed pile of dough, at least some hint it existed. . . Look I'm not asking for 1,500! just twelve!. . . merely a small down payment!

"I'm off! For some duds! So I won't embarrass you!. . . I don't have a Chinese gown, milord!"

"Oh! you're in such a big hurry, so rude. . ."

That's just his style, the slob!

"You're going to blow the whole deal! The Colonel's very favorably disposed toward us. . . But we can't be blunt! That'll scare him off! Simple as that! Plain as day!"

"Come on, let's go! A small advance! I can't stay in these stinking rags. . . Just look at me! I make a lousy impression! It's even awful inside the house!. . . Do you have any idea? You yourself spelled it out for me! You kept saying, 'Appearances, Ferdinand, appearances!' Just take a look at the young lady! What can be going through her mind?. . . Appearances! Two bums, that's who's landed on her doorstep! You in Chinese drag, me in rags! Ah! Not exactly charming!. . . I've been sleeping God knows where, you know it too! I'm not presentable anymore!"

"Ah! So you're interested in the young lady? I see! I see!"

"Butt out, shithead!"

"Ah! the little rascal's horny!"

"I'm horny!. . . Horny!. . . We'll see about that."

As if that's any of his business. . .

"But what about the Ouarr Minister! War! Didn't you hear?"

He's back feeding me his line.

"He's put in his order! I swear to it!"

That was a lie! He was off on the same old bullshit! What I needed was my twelve pounds so I could deck myself out!. . . I didn't want to hear about anything except my demand, and right now! And no substitutes!. . .

"The Colonel's got ideas!". . .

"Everybody's got ideas! Nobody gives a shit, you fucked-up old fart!. . ."

He was pissing me off!

"The world's lousy with ideas. . . I'm in this for my shoes, period! Plus my tweed suit!"

I kept hammering away! Twelve pounds! Twelve pounds!. . . An advance! A small advance!

I was a broken record.

"So the love bug bit you? You're hooked, Romeo?"

He was striking back, real proud of himself.

"Love, shit! My shoes matter more! I've got holes over my ass! Can't you get that through your head, you idiot?. . ."

"What're you going to do with this money?"

"Put some clothes on my back, milord. . . A real fine-looking outfit! And do you proud! Dazzle you!"

"It's your fever talking, of course!. . . Your fever!"

He had an explanation for everything.

"I've had it with walking around in rags!"

"Well, I'll tell you what then, stop by my place, ask Pépé for a beautiful gown!. . . One of my very own!. . . Something real beautiful with flowers! I'll lend it to you!"

"One Chinaman's enough!. . ."

"Your big hurry is going to ruin it for us! It's real simple, I'm warning you. . . This is a bad move! absolutely reckless! You go and do this and you wreck all our chances in one swoop! Hold off until Monday. . . I'll have time. . . next week. . . I know! I'll talk to him tonight!. . . That's the best I can do. . . It's such a delicate matter in French! You want me to come out and hit him up just like that? Oh, no, no, no!"

He was sick.

"No way! No way! I'm not waiting. Go screw yourself! I'm clearing the hell out of here!"

Ah! I'm incorrigible!

He looks at me hard, rolling his eyes. . . my decision just floors him.

"Oh, yes! You'd better believe it! I'm pigheaded! Six pounds!. . . Six pounds I say, and right now!. . ."

I dropped my price. Six in cash.

"You can't cough up six pounds?"

Back to dickering, dragging his feet. . .

"Let's say tomorrow! Tomorrow morning!. . ."

"No way! No way! Right now or forget it!. . ."

He could see this was going all wrong. He turns his pockets inside out. . . his whole dressing gown. . . not one red cent!. . . his linings. . . zip. . .

I did some arithmetic! A decent suit?. . . That would come to at least three pounds. . . four pounds. . . a nice raincoat: twelve shillings!. . . and I wasn't going for an elegant look! Just something to see me through, something presentable. . . As for the footwear, we'd get back to that later. . .

"Yesterday you were so happy!. . ." He was surprised. . . "You had no complaints about anything whatsoever!"

"Yes, but today I've changed!. . ."

"Ah! My, oh, my! the youth of today, will you just look how capricious they are. . . how moody. . ."

He huffs, puffs, grumbles, gropes around his body. . . smacks his forehead. . . He's thinking. . . darts a glance at the ceiling. . . the shelf. . . the odds and ends. . . the long line of flasks. . . motions me. . .

"Hand me that one over there!. . . There, the big shiny one!. . ." I hand it to him. It's heavy.

"OK, scram! Get the hell out!"

He jams it down deep into my pocket.

"Well, what are you waiting for? Clear off, quick! You're set!. . ." I look at him.

"Stop by Petticoat Lane. You know where the market is, right?" I did.

"It's mercury for thermometers!. . . it'll bring you seven or eight pounds at least!. . . but now watch you don't get ripped off!. . . It's pure stuff!. . . Top quality!. . . be careful!"

Ah! he whispers in my ear. . . and he sends me off! I hadn't thought of this!. . .

"Come on, stop dreaming!. . ." he shoves me along. . . "You want to deck yourself or don't you? You'll be a knockout in your raglan!"

And he shoves me out the door! Ah, pretty gutsy move all the same!

"A cheviot wool suit for Monsieur! Lady-killer!"

I pat the flask, can't make up my mind.

"Ah! You got to decide what you want. . ."

He hit the nail on the head! he's right. Now I'm the one hemming and hawing.

"Off you go! Damn! He's going to come back up!"

Ah! he's making up my mind for me, for Christ's sake!

"Bye!" I go. . . "So long! I'm out of here, got that? I won't be long!. . . Back in a flash!. . ." I had a suit picked out in my mind. . . one I'd seen in the shop windows. . . at the corner of Tottenham-Euston. . . a real beaut. . . beige check, the latest style back then. . . I had spotted it. . . I can see the thing. . . I was afraid it'd be gone. . .

313

I snapped up what I was after. . . I got back before six, absolutely dressed to kill. . . a real bargain. . . not where I thought in Tottenham. . . but at Süss's in the Strand, practically brand-new. . . Did a good job fencing the mercury. . . Three pounds fifty exactly. . . it was worth the trouble. . . didn't run into any of the wrong people. . . handled the matter quickly. . . galloped from one tailor to another. . . couldn't rest easy out on the street, far from my friends this way. . . while I was gone they could be up to anything!. . . I bought the *Mirror* on the run. . . nothing more about Greenwich. . . Looked like they'd forgotten about us. . . Even so it didn't calm me any. . . Ah! pins and needles!. . . I didn't dawdle around the street corners. . . I was a handsome devil, true enough. . . One pound fifty, every last stitch included!. . . genuine homespun cheviot wool!. . . Just take a look at this clubman! Whoosh!. . . I race along!. . . Willesden!. . . There's the house, I spot it!. . . the gate. . . Not a single competitor at the door. . . not a soul. . . they got it through their skulls all the same. . . I enter through the small entrance to the garden. . . here I am in the main vestibule. . . I clear the stairs. . . a lackey stops me. . . steers me toward the salon. . .

My first thought: "Disaster!. . ."

I barely sit myself down when another door opens. . . the Colonel and the little girl. . . No need for chitchat. . . I was sure!. . .

"Oh, there you are!. . ."

How happy they were to see me again. . . the pair was quite amiable! He's sucking on his candy. . . a piece of nougat. . . he looks me up and down. . . He's taken off his gorgeous gold, back to everyday clothes.

"Oh, isn't he smart? Such elegance! What a young man!"

That was all.

But he ends with a point-blank question: "What about the mercury?"

So that's it!. . . I was sure!. . . He's attacking me! And at the same time, laughing. . . busting out. . . Man, oh man, they're having a great time!. . . Ah! what a terrific trick! The girl, too. . . They're delighted, the pair of them. . . Easy to please! Ah! right off, I'm sure as hell. . . Sosthène. . . Ah! the sly bastard! Let me lay eyes on him!. . .

Not hide nor hair of him, naturally. . .

I turn red. . . green. . . start humming. . . what are they going to do with me?. . . Am I going to ask their forgiveness, or what?. . . Throw myself at their feet!. . . beg!. . . the hell with this! Enough already! That's just too bad!

"Can I go?" I just come out and ask. . .

"Sit down! Sit down!"

Couldn't be kinder, more cordial. . . They won't hear of me leaving. . . They're getting too big a kick out of watching me. . . They don't look a bit mad. . . But that doesn't mean anything. . . the English are two-faced, every last one of them!. . . They'll put on a simpering show for you. . . But this was all a setup, I'd bet my life on it!. . . A trap, end of story!. . . And I'd walked right into it, dumb ass!. . . The police were going to turn up. . . Nabbed, Madame, caught red-handed! we could have a little fun with him. . . "Come clean, young man! Where'd you get that suit? Come on, out with it!. . . In the can, kid! Six months for this! Three months for that!" Not to mention my IOUs! Man, oh man, it wasn't hard to imagine! They were playing me for a sucker, and how!. . . Ah! their little plan went off without a hitch! I'd gotten screwed over. . . A lamb to the slaughter! An eleven-. . . twelve-month stretch!. . . Where could that other crook have got to? A sure bet he was up in the attic. . . What if I went on up to tell him a thing or two?. . . Or if I filled in this pair?. . . Now he's in civvies, the senile old fart!. . . Was he ever really a Colonel? Maybe he was just a stoolie for the cops?. . . Ah, shit! I was hurting all over. . . Ah! more blabbing!. . . badgering!. . . gesturing!. . . smooth talking!. . . Ah! they were making my head spin, and that was that! Enough already! Enough was too much!. . . Let them go ahead and think anything they wanted!. . . "Give up! Give up! Stay in your seat". . . That was the voice of reason. . . I was going to let them have their way with me, but then damn, I had second thoughts all the same. . . I'm not any dumber than they are!. . .

"So Matthew's on his way?"

I just come straight out and ask them. I know the score.

"Inspector Matthew?. . . Huh? The cop from the Yard?"

"Matthew? Matthew?" they don't understand me. . . don't have a clue!. . . That beats everything!. . .

"Tea? Tea?" they offer me instead.

"Come on, have some tea! For God's sake!. . ."

They really are lousy hypocrites. . . getting a kick out of seeing me squirm. . . a bungler, trapped and bound. . . Entertainment.

That's just like these people. . . They're rich, they're English, and they're rotten swine. . . one and all, regardless of age or sex. . .
  "OK, let's have some tea!. . . I'd love some. . ."
  Since we're waiting for the police. . . I'll keep my cool too. . . don't want to be more jittery than they are!. . . When all's said and done what the fuck does it matter to me!. . . Let's go ahead then!. . . And keep going!. . . I don't really have anything much to lose!. . . Let's start the fun! The girl's babbling away. . . fluttering about. . . all around me! indescribably titillating. . . constantly hopping. . . what lovely muscles!. . . She conducts the conversation! And such a chatterbox! Bold for her age. . . talks to us about the movies. . . cricket. . . sports. . . contests!. . . all the while capering about. . . Nobody brings up my mercury anymore. . . The Colonel wipes his mouth. . . about to get up. . . His prostate again? No. He informs us it's something else. . . he's going to work. . . He leaves me and the darling to our private chat. . . Ah! such weird behavior. . . He goes off sucking on his candy. . . Ah! he's got a few surprises in him all the same. . . He excuses himself with great politeness. . . He is going upstairs to his Experiments. . . To rejoin Sosthène with his masks. . . Good!. . . Very good!. . . Couldn't ask for better!
  I'm calming down after all. . . since that's the thing to do around here!. . . Any way you look at it I'm not risking a thing. . . Why should I knock myself out? They're not worried. . . I stay in my seat. . . have some more tea. . . it helps me keep my composure. . . the girl pours me a cup. . . Ah, how beautiful she is!. . . how wonderful! I just can't get over it. . . what a smile!. . . All this for me!. . . both of us here together!. . . Her uncle's one funny bird. . . I do some thinking. . . Ah! what a mischievous little imp. . . a tease, she must know what's going on. . . I want to bring up the mercury with her again. . . it's nagging me. . . bugging me. . . No way! She won't stay still. . . It's in her nature to keep moving. . . she even makes me dizzy, I have to admit. . . bouncing around, pirouetting like a pixie. . . all around me through the room. . . What lovely hair!. . . what gold!. . . what a doll!. . . Whenever I say something she looks at me. . . she's pretending like my situation is no big tragedy. . . but I'd like a big tragedy. . . I spot a twinkle of malice in her eyes!. . . I wish she'd keep on smiling forever. . . even at my stupidity. . . idiot that I am in this suit of mine! To think that was my only reason for going out!. . . I've made myself look ridiculous. . .

plus the mercury into the bargain! really, what a rotten impression! A thief! I'm so ashamed. . . on tenterhooks. . . I blush. . . can't get out a word. . . I listen to her. . . her twittering. . . English bird-talk. . . I don't catch everything. . . She speaks a bit quickly. . . English from the lips of little girls is whimsical, playful, mischievous. . . it bounces around too. . . tinkles. . . laughs over trifles. . . capers. . . flutters. . . What cheerfulness!. . . What bright reflections, first blue, then mauve. . . her eyes completely captivate me. . . Happens in a flash! I forget. . . can't see a thing anymore. . . she's just too nice to be around, a blossom! yes, a blossom. . . I breathe in. . . Bachelor buttons!. . . a bird I said. . . I prefer bird. . . never mind! I'm bewitched. . . Her eyes, bachelor buttons. . . a little girl. . . and that short skirt. . . Ah! she's just too attractive, damn it all! her blond hair fanning out. . . when she hops, brightening the air. . . Ah! just too beautiful!. . . I'm going to faint. . . She's adorable!. . . Ah! I calm down!. . . The hell with this, tough!. . . I shouldn't. . . He's left us alone, the old crank!. . . And here the two of us are together!. . . Ah! I'm too comfortable in this armchair. . . I feel awfully damn good. . . I'm quivering! quivering. . . Ah! this little kid's so beautiful!. . . ah! how I adore her!. . . She makes my mouth water. . . How old is she? I'll ask her, just watch me!. . . On second thought, no, I'm too afraid!. . . I have some more tea. . . don't eat much. . . still careful not to go overboard. . . I remember the last time. It's horrible to be chewing with her looking on. . . to sit there chomping away, gulping down, under her beautiful, adorable eyes. . . I could never. . . I'd die first, ah!. . . a pang of politeness eating away at me. . . I lost my appetite, even if I were skinny as a rail, I still wouldn't have touched a crumb. . . I'd've gone to my grave with my pangs, so there!. . . all out of burning love for Virginia!. . . Did I get her name right— Virginia?. . . I've got to ask her, but do I dare?. . .

"Virginia?. . . It's Virginia?"

"Yes! Yes!. . ."

Ah! Too beautiful. . . everything is too beautiful! Her eyes! her smile! her thighs! I can see them when she jumps, those thighs of hers. . . she doesn't care. . . muscular down there, pink and tanned. . . her dress too short. . . Ah! she's keeping me great company. . . or else just keeping an eye on me. . . Really got to keep that in mind. . . pack of hypocrites. . . but I don't feel like going. . . I'm caught!. . . And she's the one who caught me!. . .

Ah! I'm afraid to move a muscle. . . Maybe she would have called for help if I did?. . . Some private little chat this is! I mind my p's and q's. . . I let myself be charmed, listen as she makes her very funny remarks, her wonderful little comments about everything. . . and nothing. . . I turn down the cookies. . . she's not happy. . . she scolds me. . . I'd gobble down the lot for just one of her smiles. . . every last cookie, the tray, the table. . . I'm already her prisoner. . . in the most beautiful prison in the world!. . . Ah, I'd stay right where I am and not ever move. . . I go: "Yes!. . . Yes!. . ."

I really do want everything she wants. She wants me to have more tea. . . I fill up, stuff myself. . . but she's the one who makes me stand up. . . walk over to the shutter. . . she wants to show me something. . . right there in the shutter. . . in the ivy. . . Ah! yes! I can see through the glimmer. . . the tiny eye of the sparrow. . . Ah! even he was on the lookout. . . tweet!. . . twee. . . you bet he sees her! now this is something really extraordinary! a big bold sparrow with ruffled feathers! just like her!. . . waiting. . . peering. . . gazing at us with his tiny round eye through the slit. . . itsy-bitsy eye in a pinhead. . . all black and glossy with his tweet! tweet! tweet!. . .

"He's waiting too. . ."

She lets me know. . . Just so I'd understand. . . so I'd be as patient as the sparrow. She laughs.

Curious how looking back after ages and ages, from practically the next century, I still think about that sparrow. . . She was the one who showed it to me. . . Whenever I see a shutter, a thatch of ivy, I always think about its tiny eye. . . Ah! when you come down to it you don't bring back much to remember from a whole lifetime made up of petty hassles, wild brawls and promises — I mean not much pleasant. . . well, just a few measly scraps. . . life's not exactly crawling with such occasions. . . Everybody knows what I'm talking about. . . For me that little sparrow is something I'm always happy to remember. . . I want it to stay right where it is. . . it'll fly away once I'm dead and gone. . .

The kid was one clever cutie. . . chatting me up skillfully. . . psyched me out as sensitive, hooked. . . because I was all ears for her prattle. . . so then, she talks about her big dog, her spaniel. . . and here he comes. . . big paunch. . . coughing, trotting like the Colonel. . . like her uncle. . . The animal's hopelessly clumsy, pretty old already, wheezing, drooling, she does his thinking for

him, it's wonderful how she thinks and speaks in her dog's place. . .
for him. . . and he's as glad as could be about it. . . wagging
his tail. . . it's goofy but magical. . . I'd like to understand the
spaniel, the bird, plus her just like that. . . ah! plus every animal. . . horses too, for Christ's sake. . . I'd like to carry her off
with me. . . a fairy. . . What joyful power. It's joy. I'm bowled
over. . . so happy there right next to her. . . I fawn all over
her!. . . It puts knots in my chest when she stares at me. . .
makes me go all tickly inside. . . to hear her English, so lively,
so whimsical, a twittering garland in the air. . . full of secrets,
rascally. . . Ah I had no idea. . . that dog's a mischief-maker!. . .
Ah! I ask to hear more!. . . for her to keep telling me stories
about Slam, that clumsy creature. . . ah! give me more!. . . it's
absolutely delightful! absolutely divine!. . . No kidding, she's a
real live fairy! much more than a child!. . . the dog understands
her too. . . they're both talking about me, about my suit, my behavior. . . he answers with his tail, he beats, raps the carpet. . .
It's true. . . You can see they're in tune about everything. . . She
must understand me too. . . Ah! all of a sudden it's another
world!. . . Now she wants to take a stroll. . . we stroll around
the table. . . it's the Garden of Earthly Delights. . . with the old
spaniel. . . a nice threesome all in tune. . . I'm walking in a
dream. . . she guides me by the hand. . . she leads our way into
wonderland. . . from one little word to the next. . . about a lump
of sugar. . . the pâté on her plate. . . the swallow due to arrive. . .
Ah! such magical theatrics. . . Ah! how I love this stuff!. . . Ah!
how I love her!. . . we're taking a stroll to fairyland!. . . And
open your eyes, we're here!. . . the whole salon all around is an
enchanted fairy world!. . . I didn't know. . . she teaches me. . .
Ah! how I adore her!. . . everything's about to come alive. . .
start talking. . . laughing. . . the big fat cushion and the old
fleabag. . . plus the armchair!. . . the teapot with its long neck!. . .
the entire household going all out!. . . every body and thing in on
the act. . . dancing in its own way. . . miracle theatrics. . . the
big, three-legged pedestal table. . . crosses the room with its pot-
bellied swagger. . . almost like Boro. . . all this from one little
word to the next, one little word from my fairy. . . and I understand everything! no more need for chat. . . One smile makes me
understand!. . . And the enormous chandelier in the air. . . the
immense candle-studded crinoline petticoat!. . . Dripping crystal tears. . . trickling all over!. . . An enormous scale. . . real

fancy-shmancy!... Ah! this is all just so weird! My eyes are playing tricks!... I see all the candles! the wicks! I'm drenched in tears!... chandelier tears! A big tomcat leaps on me... up from the cellar madly meowing... all velvety soft and warm... Meow! Meow!... he ni-nibbles... ni-nibbles... he's got his own chamber music... and then in my ear, because he's a confidant too!... We understand each other right off... Ah! I'm not myself anymore... Ah! I can see into my heart!... into my own heart... solid red... Ah! I purr along with my meow cat... Ni-nibble!... Ni-ni-nibble!... absorbed just like him! He sharpens his claws on my shoulders... Ah! how pleased Virginia is! Such a wonderful way to act!... Pretty Virginia!... I'm blissed out! simple as that!... it sort of just snuck up on me all by itself... just with one of her smiles!... she's really behaving like a darling... outdoing herself... I ni-nibble... ni-nibble! I am her heart!... my heart... her heart!... Ah! I'm talking gibberish... I adore her like mad!... A peak of delight just the way things are... I just need to shut my eyes now... drop off... very gently... Nibb-bble! nibb-bble!... nibb-bble!... drooling... defenseless in ecstasy under her spell... about time too! I've been all aches and pains for months... in my head... my hip... now I don't feel a thing anymore... just a gentle warmth... I let go... let them go ahead and execute me!... If they dare! If they dare! In a word I'm lulled, lulled... I forget... But somebody throws a rock at me!... it hits me right in the side... I jump with a start... shoot to my feet!... What a rude awakening!... The bad guys are here! I sit back down... If they're keen on it, who cares! I'll give myself up to the hangman... Her eyes!... her hair!... A little girl! before anything else! Ah I'd kiss her in full knowledge of what I was doing before I go to the gallows... before the final end!... Ah! the wonderful enchantress! With open eyes... but careful! watch out, for Christ's sake!... all of a sudden I'm choking... just been stabbed... by jealousy! Maybe she's the Colonel's daughter? And not his niece, by some chance?... maybe his mistress?... his baby doll?... Ah! the question nags at me... Still more lies?... his mistress?... who knows what else?... A dirty old man?... I see red! I'm burning up with jealousy! A raging inferno! I ask her savagely...

"Is he your father? The Colonel?..."

Ah! Learn the whole story! Pronto!

"Oh! No! Not my father! My uncle!"
What a beast I am! Such questions!
"My father's no more!. . ."
Her fragile so graceful face. . . her small pointed chin starts quivering, quivering, in tears. . . Oh! I've distressed her!. . . Clod! moron! Ah! the spell is broken. . . Ah! I've hurt her!. . . ah! what sorrow!. . . I ask her to forgive me!. . . I'm sorry!. . . I collapse!. . . I'm going to die if she cries. . . I come right out and tell her!. . . make threats. . . Ah! she's got to forgive me!. . . she gives a little shrug. . . I want her to pity me. . . dog that I am, me too!. . . a dog! That's all I am! A filthy dog!. . .
"I'm a dog! A dog!"
I bark!. . . bark!. . . I'm showing her that I love her. . . that I adore her!. . . she thinks I'm full of horseplay, even so. . . I gesture. . . bark, behave like a beaten beast. . . run around under the furniture on all fours until my head hurts like hell. . . It's all a little too physical for the likes of me. . . I've got this buzzing, and I mean through my whole head. . . plus the whistling. . . my head's throbbing. . . all my chimes are ringing. . . my cauldron's bubbling. . . I'm thundering. . . boiling over. . . rolling around on my belly!. . . moaning. . . writhing on the cushions!. . . I want her to forgive me, I'm unworthy, unworthy. . . I'm simmering over with love. . . that's a fact!. . . Ah! I'm in raptures!. . . true raptures!. . . I want her to understand me!. . . Maybe she's still too young?. . . Maybe I'll wind up scaring her?. . . by flailing around this way?. . . And I bang my miserable arm. . . it sends such a pain shooting through me I let out a howl, and I wasn't fooling!. . . I mess up my suit, my handsome brand-new suit. What a big waste!
"Virginia!. . . Virginia!. . ." I plead. . . "This happiness is too. . . too great!. . ."
I ask her to forgive me once more. . . ten times more. . . a hundred. . . I climb up into her lap. . . I'm going to let her hear my most tender prayer. . . I want to adore her until I die. . . That's what's in my heart!. . . and even more!. . . Death's nothing. . . just a sigh!. . . But I'm sighing up a storm. . . I'm talking worship here, a hundred times more intense!. . . That's just the way I am!. . . She laughs over seeing me so hot and bothered. . . wrinkling crumpling my whole suit jacket. . . She scolds me. . . Ah! I'm such a kick even so, despite everything. . . A one-man circus. . . She's sitting there in front of my face. . . nestled back

321

in the armchair. . . laughing. . . legs crossed. . . those lovely thighs of hers. . . ah! I'm so ashamed!. . . ah! I adore her!. . . she's wearing short blue socks. . . Ah! she's really just a little girl. . . ah! yet another danger! ah! but I adore her!. . . Why have we been left alone together?. . . Why didn't her uncle come back?. . . Maybe this is another trap?. . . My suspicions are back. . . A stab of doubt. . . of sharp fear!

"Matthew! Matthew!"

I'm sure!. . . Ah I don't find them funny anymore. . . I get to my feet. . . quivering! Ah! I'm shaking in my boots again. . . obsessed by that cop!. . .

"Sorry! Sorry, Mademoiselle! You're too beautiful! Too wonderful. . . I'm going to die with my heart on fire!. . . Fire here!. . . Fire!. . . Right here!. . ."

I show her my heart. . . She touches my chest!. . . Ah! the way I make this child laugh. . . She still doesn't know me!. . . In the end she makes me sore!. . . I'm going to sink my teeth into her!. . . Ah! I can't think straight anymore!. . . I look at her legs, those firm, muscular, wonderful pink legs down there. . . long. . . tan. . . I'm going to kiss those thighs!. . . I'm afraid! What if she sends me packing?. . . If she called to her uncle for help?. . . What a dirty pig I am!. . . Ah! I could gobble her down whole. . . ah! I adore her!. . . All or nothing!. . .

She's unfazed, doesn't take me seriously. . . she just wants to talk about the movies. . . on and on about the movies now. . . she goes to see them on Regent Street!. . . Haven't I seen *The Mysteries*?. . . Mysteries. . . Ah! mysteries? Ah! She's grating on my nerves. . . teasing me with perverse glee. . . Mysteries! Mysteries! I could tell her about a few mysteries that don't turn up in movies no way no how. . . the dirty little brat's so frivolous with these mysteries of hers!. . . *The Mysteries of New York* seems to be the title. . . Oh, brother, *The Mysteries of New York!* I could tell her about a few mysteries all right that are just around the corner! horrible and tragic mysteries beyond any stretch of her imagination. . . cruel little girl!. . . and how real unhappy I am. . . Me, unhappy?. . . I surprise her. Ah! she's poking fun!. . . with a beatific smile. . . she's too young! she disgusts me!. . . I give her such a laugh. . . So I strike back!. . . in a flash! Enough!. . . Of these flirty games. . . I bawl her out, the dirty little snotnose! She makes me run through my list of insults. . . That's how unhappy I am!. . . it's all her fault, it's not my arm... I own up, I'm war-torn... Maybe she caught a glimpse of my arm? Of the state I'm suffering in? I peel away my clothes on purpose, show her... She touches... gives a little "Ah! Ah!"... and that's the end of that!... she's not exactly surprised... And what about my head, she get a look at that?... my ear?... Doesn't scare her!... Maybe she doesn't believe me?... these scars are the genuine article... maybe she thinks it's all a scam? Like with her uncle? And Sosthène? That this was all one big costume party... She's got eyes all the same... what's she think, it's some magic trick?... Ah! hell, she's pissing me off all over again! Ah! so she wants to see atrocities?... The movies are doing a real number on her... Blood's what they need to have in them, Mademoiselle... Now she's looking at somebody who can tell a story or two about battle atrocities!... how the blood oozes all over the place! So, listen up, darling!... Me, live and in person, the one and only!... Plus the hail of bullets, such fun and games... the hell of combat! bellies splitting open! slapping shut! heads blowing apart! guts everywhere!... gurgling!... Ah! those slap-bang massacres! That'll give her something to shudder about!... So listen up, honey!... Slaughter fests so red, so thick, they coat every square inch of the ground with a sludge, flooding the furrows with mashed flesh and bone, hillocks and hills! and overlooking ravines full of cadavers that still have a spark of life in them, still sighing! and the cannons rolling over them! Caught up in a charge! oh yes, no exaggeration!... whirlwinds, you heard me!... And then the transport vehicles! and then the whole cavalry trampling over them!... over and over again! banners unfurled and whipping in the wind... and such an incredible din... a roar filling heaven and earth! Ten! Twenty! One hundred thunderclaps! I imitate the screams from the carnage for her... the groans, the cheers!... doesn't make any impression... leaves her cold, doesn't even look like she's entertained... Doesn't she think I'm the world's greatest hero?... Ah! damn it now, this takes the wind out of me! The most fantastic combat-scarred soldier ever?... And here I am shouting myself hoarse!... Spitting, foaming... I charged too, Christ Almighty!... Badada... dee... I show her! at the head of the toughest squadrons!... the fiercest!... the most ferocious!... I outdo myself!... It's got nothing to do with the crap in the movies, got to admit after all!... all these wacky goings-on give her the jitters! Ah! how about this one!... An earthquake when

the division rushes into battle! This is the big time! At the Bat-
teries! Come on, you old nag!. . . Breaches!. . . Bullets flying
like crazy!. . . the whirlwind of the cavalries!. . . Bats out of
hell!. . .

The whole thing gives her a big laugh!. . . Ah! little dummy!. . .
she just doesn't get it! I collapsed, that's a fact!. . . plopped back
into my armchair!. . . really shook up. . . wiped out. . . A waste
of breath!. . . such nastiness!. . . the spell was broken!. . . I
should have spared myself the trouble. . .

Later on in life you come to terms. . . deal with everything. . .
make do, stop your singing. . . you ramble on. . . then drop to
a whisper. . . then fall silent. . . But when you're young that's
damn tough! You need bigger than life! Blow-outs! marching bands!
and whoops, look out! Ka-boom! Thunder and lightning!. . . you've
got high standards!. . . Truth is death!. . . I gave Truth a good
run for her money as long as I had it in me. . . flirted with her,
feasted her, flung her around in a little jig, put fresh life into her
time and time again!. . . Decked her out in bows, made her juices
flow in farandoles that went on and on. . . Alas! how well I know
that a moment comes when it all falls apart, gives way, gives
out. . . how well I know a day comes when your hand drops,
drops back alongside your body. . . A gesture I've seen thousands
and thousands of times. . . the shadow. . . the last strangled
breath. . . And all the lies have been spoken! all the announce-
ments sent out, the three knocks are going to ring out somewhere
else!. . . to signal the start of other comedies!. . . Get me, you
slobbering brat? Look at me!. . . Now it's my turn to entertain
you, sing you a ditty, "This little piggy!". . . No, better yet, give me
three fingers!. . . now we'll hear the adventures of the fourth!. . .
the wiliest. . . the smallest. . . the most famous. . . your little
pinky. . . the one that goes wee-wee-wee all the way home!. . .
Back then I had big ideas about myself. . . I aimed to create terrific fireworks when the mood hit me!. . . sometimes I fizzled!. . .
got to come clean, admit it. . . with Virginia, zero. . . she didn't
want anything to do with mysteries, she thought listening to me
was a kick, kind of funny, nothing more. . . she didn't take me
seriously. . . I was just some Frenchman after all, no doubt. . .
she was English. . . Romantic is how I wanted her to see me, not
as some phony clown, some sideshow comic like Sosthène. . . I
tried showing her everything, my arm, the hole in my head, my
scars, the long ones, the short ones, even made her feel my skull,

but I didn't scare her, not one bit!. . . Ah! callous! and in a way I found surprising in such a young girl!. . . A cynic deep down!. . . Ah! slowly it dawned on me!. . . I was the one under her spell, swooning! in raptures, her victim!. . . Ah! I stroke her hair! Never mind!. . . I run my hand through her curls, so thick, so deep!. . . Ah! the electricity of her soul! I tell her about it! I fall into a swoon! Feel her full charge in my fingers! Ready to put my hand between her legs!. . . Down there I'd have hold of her soul! I tell her as much, beg her!. . . Can't get her soul off my mind. . . A cute, spiffy pixie, standing right there in front of me, so bright and so bitchy!. . . Ah! I'm ready to explode!. . . Can't take any more!. . . I admired her magic. . . let myself be bewitched. . . want her to admire me. . . to love me truly madly deeply!. . . I launch back into my adventure saga!. . . Ah! I'm not through by a long shot!. . . There's the one about how I rescued the captain! I want her to know everything! my extraordinary valor!. . . dragging him by his hair across the entire battlefield. . . and he wasn't some Goldilocks like her! no! no! jet black! short and spiky stuff, like on a horse! between thick swarms of hot lead, literal clouds of smoke and bullets! the bombs falling so fast and thick the sky went dark. . . over both of us, the captain and me. . . I mimicked the gunfire for her, did my rendition of the whistles and blasts. . . Even after this she didn't give a hoot! I was ludicrous! Wasting my breath!. . . And I was really going at it too!. . . flailing my arms around so much it hurt!. . . But I just stayed put! Didn't touch her! A flop!. . . Didn't make her tremble, shudder, beg for mercy, apologize a thousand times over! Cry for help! Throw herself in my arms! Ah! my beautiful girl! Ah! have pity! Rotten slut!. . . True, she was a teaser. . . maybe worked for the cops into the bargain, a stoolie, simple as that!. . . Which would explain her sly come-hithers. . . her thighs. . . this way she was behaving. . . in short, just what kind of joint had I stumbled into?. . . cutest little darling in the world!. . . so I amuse her, do I! What an act! she's putting one over on me! Turning on the charm for the cops!. . . Ah! You're a pretty one, Mademoiselle! A real charmer, my balls! Ah! the little birdies! I'll keep you lingering! She's just waiting for the cops, end of story! The kid was in on it! Of course! Little Miss Innocent playing me for a sucker! she must be having fun!. . . And big jerk that I am, jumping around. . . it's really true, a life of vice starts right in the cradle! Ah! a sudden thought! Those cops are taking their time getting here! If you ask me. . . they must be dawdling over at Matthew's. . . He's going to show up with them. . . I'm sure as hell. . . Even so I ask her: "Matthew?. . . Matthew?. . ." I'm dead serious.

She doesn't get it. . .

"Don't get it?. . . Don't get it?. . . What a smooth operator!. . ."

Ah! it's damn awful how treacherous this is. . . bottomless pits of dirty tricks. . . Come on, got to give her a kiss still and all before I leave. . . it's been eating at me for an hour. . . got to take the chance. . . it'll be over. . . she was no better than Finette. . . when you really came down to it, all said and done. . . Two-of-a-kind no-good two-timing sluts!. . . but this one here, is she ever precocious! Geez, what a nasty business all the same! I felt like letting out a howl. . . I wanted to be certain despite everything. . . one more go-around. . . I wanted to ask a question. . . to put my mind at rest. . . But she's the one who launches into me.

"You're just like the movies!" That's what she's come up with! "You're sad! and then you're happy!. . ."

That's the impression my pantomime made. . . pretty unflattering. . . at present she was sure. . . I was like the movies! Like the movies or nothing!. . .

Ah! I had no comeback for that! I could leave!. . . But how could I go back to being all alone?. . . No can do now. . . Right away I was frightened. . . I couldn't live without her anymore. . . ah! what a scary thought! cripes! Never mind! I'll stay right where I am, won't budge. . . sorrow nails me to the spot. . . stand here glued down dumbfounded. . . without a clue. . . ridiculous!. . . all I could see now were her eyes!. . . How would I manage out in the world? I'd bang into everything. . . And what about the others? The two goofballs?. . . The thought set me off again! what the hell could they be doing? were they ever coming down?. . . What catastrophe were they concocting up there under the rafters?. . . What a pair of first-class nitwits!. . . I had time to think about them even so in my helpless confusion. . . Ah! there was a surprise in store!. . . Some big deal in the works! Rats! I shake a leg! I force myself. . . Hey! I'll bawl her out! She's been rubbing me the wrong way long enough! I'm going to terrify her, for Christ's sake!

"You don't have a care in the world!. . ." I go to her, "not a care in the world, little birdbrain! Don't you know? I'm going to kill myself tonight!. . ."

Now that was a stroke of genius.

"You?. . . You?. . . You?. . ."

She refuses to believe me. . . I can see the merry twinkle in her eyes. . . What I wouldn't do to blow away Little Lambykins! I rack my brain again. . . give up. . . nothing I do works with her. . . How I'd love to make her moan, writhe, roll around, wail through her tears, the little bitch! Ah! so you're waiting for the cops!. . . The thought's back on my mind. . . I'll give those cops a show! Me! I'll knock off Sosthène! Do you hear me? Rotten clown! Crook! Stoolie! Smash him! Wouldn't that outdo anything in the movies? Plus her uncle at the same time. . . hell, yes!. . . while we're at it! Dirty little bungling Colonel! A wholesale slaughter! Buckets of blood! So much for the young miss! A massacre right in the salon. . . I'll fill the room. . . with puddles!. . . pools!. . . streams!. . . she wants a real-life movie! I promise her my own death, she giggles. . . well then, she's going to see something else! she's going to see a threesome die! A tensome! A dozen! the servants along with us. A mass murder! Like at Prosper's. . . like at Claben's!. . . and then I'll torch the place!. . . She'll see real good whether I dreamed it or not!. . . they'll all see real good whether I'm kidding! Ah! I'm going to kiss her. . . before things get cooking!. . . she doesn't want to, forget it, she ducks away, plays Hide-and-Seek!. . . I can't do anything right. . . Heaven in her eyes!. . . little spinning top!. . . Ah! she's so beautiful a miracle!. . . I forget everything just looking at her!. . . Ah! I'm losing my mind! my memory! Ah! I drop to my knees!. . . Gladly she takes my head on her lap!. . . Ah! dear wonderful creature!. . . Ah! the mushy words that come back to mind!. . . I'm melting under her touch! Melting. . . I ask her to forgive me! again! The day'll come when I cut out my tongue!. . . I roll around at her feet. . . The others'll see me. . . She's laughing again. . . Ah! how cruel she is!. . . Here come those confounded servants! you're never left in peace for long. . . they're bringing the table settings, it's almost dinnertime. . . scurrying back and forth, opening doors. . . I catch the aroma from the kitchen. . . my nose knows! It's leg of lamb. . . definitely. . . I sniff. . . can't control myself. . . Shame!. . . How hungry I am!. . . Still hungry!. . . yes!. . . Before dying, before suicide! the wholesale slaughters! Yes! Yes! Ah! the horror! Dirty little pig! I admit it! I'm rumbling with hunger. . . ravenous with pangs.

"Will you stay with us?"

She's inviting me. She's poking fun. . . I should leave. . . And so what about the mercury?... Forgotten... I forget about everything!... I'm going to see her uncle again! Sosthène! the whole family round the table! As though nothing were wrong!... Zero self-esteem left!... My pride flares up! The hussy's laughing!... She can see I'm suffering... from shame and hunger!... And here I never wanted to eat again!... Had absolutely sworn not to!... from the kitchen more whiffs of lamb reach our noses... definitely leg of lamb... I'd vowed to die! or at least run away!... But I'm already so tired... my head's buzzing... from hunger!... I'm staying put, never mind... so I can croak? fill my tummy?... I'm pulled both ways! so I can tarnish my oh so very tragic love?... She'll never understand me!... She's callow!... A darling... a fairy... but frivolous, a babe in the woods, flighty... she has me all wrong!... So should I bump her off then? Christ! she should make herself scarce!... love her unto death?... I'm raving... I crack myself up!... I'll kill her some other time!... So, chow down then! Come on, dig in! My appetite makes my head spin! the aroma reaching us... through the door... permeating... penetrating... I breathe in!... start drooling... Star-crossed love!... It's really tough!... Having a hard time holding back!... the leg of lamb!... I don't look at anything anymore... waiting for the roast... don't give a damn about the others... Let them show up!... the knives are moving around... the settings... the crystalware... goblets next... the champagne!... all stands ready!... the hors d'oeuvres... and sprays of roses!... Say, this is a real celebration!... All this expense for little old us?... Ah! wait now, what's that flask? Smack in the middle? the mercury!... my mercury! They're throwing it a party! They're throwing me a party! A flask like the other! a spitting image!... I recognize it!... as a centerpiece!... smack in the middle, sitting among the roses... they're going to throw a party for my mercury!... all in the family a chummy get-together! Ah! what a zinger! a real inspiration!... Ah! the perfect touch!... Ah! right on target! I understand I'm being invited!... that they're counting on me!... oh God! they're about to walk in... the whole crew... A spark of self-respect! Scram, Ferdinand!... I look at the lovely child!... She sort of smiles at me... Am I leaving? staying? I blush... stammer... show the girl the flask!... right there on top of the flowers smack in the center.

"Oh! how funny it is!..."

I don't find it one bit funny. . . you can see it's not her doing. . .
Funny ways of having fun around here. . .

"Don't pay any mind!. . . Don't pay any mind!. . ."

That's all she can come up with. . . for me to take it as some
sort of childish prank. . . I'm a despicable coward!. . . I'm all for
surrendering. . . I'm going to hang around here a little while. . .
I blush, but don't budge. . . doddering. . . spineless. . . until the
cops come!. . . and then they can haul me off!. . . the plot's been
hatched of course!. . . planned out!. . . they're all in cahoots!. . .
I'm convinced deep down. . . this business with the mercury is
the dot on the i, the crowning touch!. . . the mercury on the table!
the flask! the movies!. . . Come and get it, Monsieur!. . . You bet
I won't forget Sosthène!. . . That stinking carcass!. . . The pimp
was in on the con!. . . And I keep my eyes on the little darling
standing in front of me! She's a royal pain in my ass. . . I feel a
burst of energy. . . So what about it, you little cockteaser!. . .
Cutie pie! what's the name of the game you're playing with us?. . .
with the cats? the birds?. . . all the funny faces. . . the whole
song and dance?. . . What're you after?. . . with our play-acting. . .
smoke screen. . . ruses. . . What if I pulled your panties down?. . .
And spanked the hell out of you?. . . shameless hussy. . . what
would you say about a little number like that?. . . we're not talking little birdies! You're uncle's got it right! Punishment on the
spot! Ah! I'm feeling down in the dumps! So many things to decide!
Can't make up my mind!. . . about any damn thing!. . . threats!. . .
threats at every turn!. . . wherever I'm drawn?. . . the proof?. . .
that leg of lamb's just about here!. . . I can smell it!. . . the full
rich aroma coming in!. . . tantalizing!. . . coming up from the
kitchen. . . the butlers bustling around. . . all this bustling
makes my head spin. . . I sink back down in my armchair! Close
my eyes. . .

"Well, well, so here you are!. . ."

Sosthène walks onto the scene, very jovial. . .

"Ah! so it's you, you son of a bitch!. . . you just wait!"

Ah! he shakes me out of my stupor. . . ah! that bastard, I'll wipe
the floor with him!

"You dare show your face, slimeball?"

I collar him.

"Come, come now! what a temper!. . ."

He shoves me away with one hand.

"Mademoiselle, excuse him!. . ."

He's ashamed for me! He's apologizing for me!... The rules of behavior!

"You dirty bastard! You hear me, scumbag?..."

I don't want to drop it! I'm spiteful!

"I'll show you what I got in store for you!..."

"Come, come now! Let's calm down!... in front of this child!..."

He begs me to respect her ears... extends his arm... leads me away... Ah! it's the same old crap like with Boro!... They're all one big pack of hypocrites!...

Dinner's on the table! Here comes the Colonel! And the twit! They've both changed clothes... in overalls, high rubber boots... the Chinese and operetta drag over and done with... both down to business... experiments all the way! Scientists on the job! Next to that I don't exist anymore... even with my three pounds six! Right off I lash out... grab his attention!

"You're a pretty sight, Sosthène! Have you been stealing, too?"

Pow, take that!

"Not as much as you, you snappy dresser!"

He was expecting my dig. We whisper friendly cracks to each other... don't let each other be... the girl can't hear anything... the Colonel neither... he doesn't say a word... I watch him between his mouthfuls... he just keeps smiling straight ahead... his mind's not on us... He's a man wrapped up in his thoughts!... Every now and then he grumbles, "Hum! Hum!" then he helps himself to another big slice... ham, lamb... everything!... He's got a hearty appetite... And there's plenty to go around... you should see this spread!... I whisper to Sosthène again: "I'll make you pig out, you dirty bastard!... I'll give you a taste of the upper crust, you hear me, milord?... I'll make you eat shit!..."

He was really making me mad.

And the mercury flask sitting there right in front of our faces smack among the flowers, it was there for a reason!... The joke was on me!... to see the sort of face I'd pull... Ah, they were wasting their time!... I didn't give an inch, God damn it, not an inch!

"So tell me," I go and whisper up against his ear again, "so tell me, you lousy creep, whether the others are coming... your buddies... your cop pals, you know who I mean?... You sack of shit!... oh well, I won't be leaving by myself! cop! I'm warning you in advance, cop!..."

"Shhh! Shhh! Now stop it, you scoundrel!

330

He's offended. . . he finds me impossible!. . .
"What a way to act!"
He's complaining. . . Ah! I'm pushing him over the edge! My behavior's way out of line!. . .
"Be careful! Come on now! Shape up! You're not back in the barracks! You're making noise with your mouth! Not everything at the same time! Cut up your meat!"
I was behaving poorly, that's a fact, I was really worked up. . . it was his fault. . . the girl watched us whispering. . . fortunately the uncle wasn't watching anything. . . he just kept staring into space. . . eating in a trance. . . swallowing everything without looking. . . as in a dream. . . the celery. . . a big sardine. . . then a humongous hunk of Roquefort. . . And then some candy. . . a handful. . . he started the meal over again, backwards. . . beginning with the fruit. . . and the racket he was making, oh man! chomping like a dog!. . . ten times worse than me!. . .
"Well, well! You're not laughing, Sosthène?"
Nope! Not one bit!. . . Right there right across from him. . . Wasn't that funny? Wasn't it? Well? Wasn't it? Now there's an ass-licker for you!
Ah! I wasn't going to start up again bitching, bickering, pissing myself off! For what? It was pointless. . . It turns my stomach, but I just let it go, never mind, the hell with it! I'm all bickered out already. . . here we go then, a smile for all around!. . . that's it, I'm a dumb jerk just like them, and calm, I act polite and proper, of course, I'm everything you want!. . . Are those cops coming? They can show up anytime!. . . I'll be waiting for them here, they'll find me polite and proper! at my nice little family dinner, with the mercury in the center of the table. . . the flowers. . . the smiles. . .

---

Louis-Ferdinand Céline's third and last novel, Guignol's Band, *followed a more torturous road to publication in the original French than any of the author's other work. Although its first installment appeared in 1944, over four decades passed before a definitive edition became available. This first installment appeared in a 1954 translation. By odd coincidence, English-language readers have also had to wait forty years to find out what became of Ferdinand and Sosthène de Rodiencourt after they hopped a bus for Colonel O'Collogham's mansion in the hope of landing jobs as "Gas Mask Engineers." This disrupted publication history can be explained by the greater disruptions caused by history in Céline's life.*

## Louis-Ferdinand Céline

Guignol's Band (I & II) completes the author's first two autobiographical novels, and represents his often promised, and always delayed "London segment." Céline spent a little less than a year in the British capital between 1915 and 1916. Yet this segment took on a life of its own, and actually filled more pages than either of the preceding novels. What's more, Céline had projected several additional volumes in his notes! He began to elaborate on Guignol's Band in the early forties under the Occupation, and in 1944 consented only grudgingly to allow his novel to be published in part. He continued to think of his narrative as a whole, and as a work still in progress. On publication, Guignol's Band did not create much of a stir, disappointing his fascist supporters who had expected something more from the author of the right-wing, anti-Semitic polemics Bagatelles pour un massacre (1937), L'Ecole des cadavres (1938) and Beaux Draps (1941).

Céline provided his secretary with a typescript of an initial "complete" version of Guignol's Band, but continued to both revise and elaborate on his text throughout his flight from France at the end of the war and his eventual imprisonment in Denmark. Eventually he abandoned Guignol's Band in the late forties in order to dedicate himself to the more urgent task of composing the great prose chronicles of his later years: From Castle to Castle, North, Rigadoon. Within a few years of Céline's death in 1961, Gallimard published Le Pont de Londres (London Bridge), based on the above-mentioned typescript that Céline left behind in France, containing none of the author's subsequent revisions or corrections. It was only in 1988 that the definitive text appeared in the third volume of the Pléiade edition of Céline's work, representing a meticulous labor of collation among several manuscripts.

The restored Guignol's Band will surely take its rightful place alongside Journey to the End of the Night and Death on the Installment Plan, completing Céline's great fictional trilogy. His third novel shows itself to have been the crucial workshop in which he forged his "late" style: an elliptical, lyrical, free-wheeling new language whose lifeblood was popular French. And it is most especially in London Bridge: Guignol's Band II that the unbridled fertility and ferocity of Céline's imagination breaks free, anticipating the picaresque excess of Grass, Pynchon and company as well as the taboo-shattering drive of Nabokov in Lolita. His London is populated with outrageous, exuberant grotesques who would be right at home with the Joker, the Penguin, Catwoman and the rest of the warped underworld of the Batman series as redefined by Tim Burton. It should not surprise us that the rage and intensity of Céline's vision spans both high and low, literary and popular culture. Indeed, whether we like it or not (and how delighted Céline would be if we didn't), future generations may well view our intense, raging century as the Age of Céline.

As for the translation, I have done my best to obey the command of Céline's grandfather, as recorded in the stylistic manifesto prefacing Guignol's Band I. A voice booms down from heaven, instructing the author: "No fancy stuff, kid!" In other words, drop the literary flourishes and go for excitement, emotion and the music of speech.

— Dominic Di Bernardi

332

# NOTES ON CONTRIBUTORS

MARTINE BELLEN's "Calamity Jane" is part of a new collection of poems, *Wild Women*.

MEI-MEI BERSSENBRUGGE's most recent book is *Sphericity*, published by Kelsey St. Press. Her collaboration with the artist Kiki Smith will be published in two editions by U.L.A.E. and Kelsey St.

MARY CAPONEGRO is finishing a collection of Italian-inspired fictions begun during her fellowship year at the American Academy in Rome.

LOUIS-FERDINAND CÉLINE wrote three novels, *Journey to the End of the Night*, *Death on the Installment Plan* and *Guignol's Band I and II*. *London Bridge (Guignol's Band II)* is just out in English translation from the Dalkey Archive Press.

ROBERT CREELEY's *Histoire de Florida* is forthcoming from Ferriss Editions (Berkeley). *Echoes* (1994) was given an America Award in Poetry together with Jackson Mac Low's *42 Merzgedichte*.

GUY DAVENPORT's most recent books are *A Table of Green Fields* (New Directions) and *Charles Burchfield's Seasons* (Pomegranate). The excerpts from *The Cardiff Team* in this issue are about a fourth of the text as it will appear in his eighth collection of stories.

LYDIA DAVIS is the author of *Break It Down*, a collection of stories, and numerous translations from the French. Her novel, *The End of the Story*, has just been published by Farrar, Straus & Giroux.

DOMINIC DI BERNARDI's translation of Céline's *London Bridge (Guignol's Band II)* was just published by the Dalkey Archive Press. Among the French authors he has translated are Jacques Roubaud, Claude Ollier and Emmanuel Bove.

THALIA FIELD has recently completed an NEA-commissioned libretto: *The Pompeii Exhibit*, composed by Toshiro Saruya. The excerpt of *Ululu* that appears in this issue is from the first movement of a work in progress.

KATHLEEN FRASER's recent book, *When New Time Folds Up*, was published by Chax Press. The National Poetry Foundation will bring out her *Collected Poems (1964–1994)* in 1995. A book of essays, *Things That Do Not Exist Without Words*, is forthcoming.

PETER GIZZI is the author of *Periplum* (1992). The poems "Fear of Music" and "From a Field Glass" are from a work in progress entitled *A Textbook of Chivalry*. He recently received the Lavan Younger Poets Award from the Academy of American Poets.

NILI R. SCHARF GOLD's *Not Like a Cypress: Transformation of Images and Structures in Y. Amichai's Poetry* was published by Schocken Publishing and won the Ministry of Culture's Prize in Israel.

The *Selected Poems* of BARBARA GUEST was published this spring by Sun & Moon Press. Guest's collaboration with artist Anne Dunn, *Stripped Tales*, parts of which first appeared in *Conjunctions*, is now available from Kelsey St. Press.

GITHA HARIHARAN is the author of the novel *The Thousand Faces of Night*, which won the 1993 Commonwealth Writers Prize for Best First Book, and a collection of short stories, *The Art of Dying* (Penguin India, 1993). Her newest novel, *The Ghosts of Vasu Master*, was published by Viking (Penguin India) in 1994. She lives in New Delhi.

BERNARD HŒPFFNER has translated Jacques Roubaud, Guy Davenport, Coleman Dowell, H.D., Elizabeth Bishop and many others. He is currently working on the first French translation of Robert Burton's *The Anatomy of Melancholy* and finishing the writing of a novel.

YOEL HOFFMANN teaches Eastern philosophy at the University of Haifa, Israel. He has published several studies on Zen and Japanese poetry. He is the author of four works of fiction: *The Book of Joseph* (a novella and three short stories), *Bernhardt, The Christ of Fish* and *Gutapersha* (Keter Publishing House, Jerusalem; Rowohlt, Hamburg; and Feltrinelli, Milan). This is his first appearance in print in this country.

MYUNG MI KIM's books of poems are *The Bounty* (forthcoming from Chax Press) and *Under Flag* (Kelsey St. Press). The poems that appear in this issue are from the fifth section of *Dura*, a book-length poem.

EDDIE LEVENSTON's *The Stuff of Literature: Physical Aspects of Texts and Their Relation to Literary Meaning* was published by SUNY Press in 1992. He lives in Jerusalem.

MARK McMORRIS's long poems *Figures for a Hypothesis* (Leave Books) and *Peninsula, Sea Brush* (Burning Deck) are scheduled for publication this year. His writing will also appear in the anthology *The African Diaspora in Short Fiction* (Westview Press).

DOUGLAS MESSERLI is the author of *The Structure of Destruction* (the first volume of which appeared recently as *Along Without: A Fiction in Film for Poetry* from Littoral Books). He is currently completing *After: Poems and Translations Alternating*.

JUDY PFAFF's work has been shown recently at the St. Louis Museum of Art and in a one-person show at the Rose Art Museum at Brandeis. Her work was included in the 1987 Whitney Biennial and is part of the museum collections of the Detroit Institute of Art, the Philadelphia Museum of Art, Atlanta's High Museum of Art, the Museum of Modern Art and the Albright-Knox Gallery. Pfaff lives in New York City and is represented by the André Emmerich Gallery.

DONALD REVELL's fifth collection, *Beautiful Shirt*, was published earlier this year by Wesleyan. His translation of *Alcools* will appear in the autumn, also from Wesleyan.

MERIDEL RUBENSTEIN is an artist using photography and video. Her work is exhibited regularly in museums and galleries in the United States and abroad and is part of numerous public collections, including those of the National Museum of American Art and the San Francisco Museum of Modern Art. She is presently building a glass house/photo/video installation, *Oppenheimer's Chair*, commissioned for Site Santa Fe (July 1995).

LESLIE SCALAPINO's recent books include *Defoe* (Sun & Moon Press, 1995), *Goya's L.A., a play* (Potes & Poets Press, 1994) and *Objects in the Terrifying Tense/ Longing From Taking Place* (Roof Books, 1994).

JASON SCHWARTZ's first book, *A German Picturesque*, is forthcoming from Knopf.

D. E. STEWARD is the author of *Contact Inhibition*, a novel, and *To a Writer Down the Line*. "Agost" is a month from *Chroma*, the same unpublished work from which other months appeared in *Conjunctions* 11 and 14.

COLE SWENSEN's translations of *Art Poetique* by Olivier Cadiot and *Natural Gaits* by Pierre Alferi will be published this year (Sun & Moon Press) as will her book *Numen* (Burning Deck). She is also the author of *Park* (Floating Island Press, 1991) and *New Math* (Morrow, 1988).

JOHN TAGGART's most recent book is *Songs of Degrees* (University of Alabama Press, 1994), a collection of essays on contemporary poetry/poetics (some of which originally appeared in *Conjunctions*). His work appears in two recent poetry anthologies: *The Art of Practice* and *From the Other Side of the Century*.

WILLIAM T. VOLLMANN's next book, *Atlas*, will be published by Viking in early 1996.

MARJORIE WELISH's most recent book of poems is *Casting Sequences* (University of Georgia Press, 1993).

PAUL WEST won the 1993 Lannan Prize for Fiction with *Love's Mansion*. His most recent books are *Sheer Fiction* (McPherson) and *A Stroke of Genius* (Viking), a memoir of illness. His next novel, due this year from Scribner, will be *The Tent of Orange Mist*, about the rape of Nanking in 1937.

ELLEN ZWEIG is a video/installation artist and a writer. Her most recent installation was *Hubert's Lure*, a part of Creative Time's 42nd Street Project, New York City, 1994. *Critical Mass*, the collaborative installation by Meridel Rubenstein and Ellen Zweig, opened at the New Mexico Museum of Fine Arts in Santa Fe November 6, 1993, through February 13, 1994. Since then it has been shown at MIT's List Visual Arts Center in Cambridge, Massachusetts, and the Southeast Museum of Photography in Daytona Beach, Florida. Forthcoming are engagements at the University Art Museum in Laramie, Wyoming; the Bridge Center of Contemporary Art in El Paso, Texas; and the Scottsdale Center for the Arts in Scottsdale, Arizona.

# Conjunctions

## *Issues that Matter*

Issue 23: *New World Writing* – contributions from around the world, including: Coral Bracho, Paola Capriolo, Jean Echenoz, Faiz Ahmed Faiz, Juan Goytisolo, Claudio Magris, Friederike Mayröcker, Botho Strauss, J. Rodolfo Wilcock, Can Xue, and others.

Issue 22: *The Novellas Issue* – novellas from Allan Gurganus, Robert Antoni, Lynne Tillman, Arno Schmidt, and Paul West. Other contributors include: Robert Olen Butler, Barbara Guest, Wendy Walker, Harry Mathews, Ann Lauterbach, Nathaniel Tarn, and others.

Issue 21: *The Credos Issue* – credos from Simon Ortiz, Robert Creeley, Kathy Acker, Ishmael Reed, Anne Waldman, Victor Hernandez Cruz, David Antin, William T. Vollmann, Walter Mosley, and others. New work from Carole Maso, Janice Galloway, John Ashbery and others.

Issue 18: *Fables, Yarns, Fairy Tales* – contributions from around the world, including: Norman Manea, Jacques Roubaud, Kurt Schwitters, Scott Bradfield, Jerome Rothenberg, Romanus Egudu, A.K. Ramanujan, Grozdana Olujic, Liudmila Petrushevskaya, and others.

Send your order to:
Conjunctions, Bard College, Annandale-on-Hudson, NY 12504
$12 each for back issues

DISTRIBUTED TO THE TRADE BY CONSORTIUM BOOK SALES

DAVID MILLER: **Stromata**
Poems that "sift and resift the lessons of perception, in order to define just what it means to be alive and think." —Norman Jope. David Miller was born in Australia and lives in London where Stride Press recently published his *Pictures of Mercy* (1991) and *Tesserae* (1993). Poems, 64 pages, offset, smyth-sewn, original paperback, $8

COLE SWENSEN: **Numen**
New poems by the author of *Park* and *New Math*, that explore the space between science/mathematics on the one hand and transcendence on the other, between number and numen. "A calculus of light" —Michael Palmer Poems, 80 pages, offset, smyth-sewn, original paperback $8

DALLAS WIEBE: **Skyblue's Essays**
"One of our best writers of innovative fictions... And what do we find in this feast of short fiction? Well, energy, passion, parody, satire, a rich and often superb style, and somewhere in all this the credible, delicate confrontation of a lunatic culture and a struggling self." —Doug Bolling, *American Book Review*.
Fictions, 160 pages, offset, smyth-sewn, original paperback, $8.95

FRIEDERIKE MAYRÖCKER: **Heiligenanstalt**
[**Dichten** = : No. 1; trans. Rosmarie Waldrop]
Four fictions around Chopin and other Romantic composers by one of the most original and prominent Austrian writers, famous for the "hallucinatory" quality of her poetry and prose.
Fiction, 96 pages, offset, smyth-sewn, original paperback, $8

PAOL KEINEG: **Boudica**
[**Série d'écriture:** No. 8; trans. Keith Waldrop]
Tacitus records how the Romans were defeated by "a simple woman," the Breton Queen Boudica. Keineg's poems raise a monument to her courage and, by bold anachronisms, to Breton resistance of forced assimilation. Poems, 64 pages, offset, smyth-sewn paperback $6

Burning Deck has received grants from the National Endowment for the Arts, the Fund for Poetry, the Charles Phelps Taft Memorial Fund, and the Services Culturels of the French Embassy.
**Order from: Small Press Distribution,** 1814 San Pablo Ave., Berkeley, CA 94702 (800-869-7553)

# Flaubert compared losing oneself in literature to perpetual orgy.

*Here's your invitation to the party.*

*The Paris Review. It's the kind of writing that gives you goosebumps. That sends a shiver down your spine. That makes your hair stand on end. It's the kind of writing that's the result of a longstanding commitment to literature. A commitment The Paris Review has made for more than 40 years.*

*Whether you want short stories, poetry, photography, art or our renowned interviews, call (718) 539-7085 to subscribe and you'll get a better understanding of the place where Flaubert found his passion.*

**THE PARIS REVIEW** *The International Literary Quarterly.*

# THE AMERICA AWARDS FOR LITERATURE: 1994

(The "Ferns")                    Presented in memory of Anna Fahrni

INTERNATIONAL
*awarded to a living writer of international stature for a body of literary writing*
## Aimé Fernand Césaire
[Poet and Playwright, Martinique]

FICTION
*awarded to the most outstanding book of fiction published in 1994*
*by a living American writer*
## The Journalist, by Harry Mathews
[David Godine]
JUDGES: Jaimy Gordon, Steve Katz, Toby Olson

POETRY
*awarded to the most outstanding book of poetry published in 1994*
*by a living American writer*
## Echoes, by Robert Creeley
[New Directions]
## 42 Merzgedichte in Memoriam
## Kurt Schwitters, by Jackson Mac Low
[Station Hill]
JUDGES: Mei-mei Berssenbrugge, Kenneth Irby, Aaron Shurin

DRAMA
*awarded to the most outstanding new play of 1994 by a living American writer*
## The Hyacinth Macaw, by Mac Wellman
[Primary Stages, New York]
JUDGES: Constance Congdon, Len Jenkin, John Steppling

BELLES-LETTRES AND OTHER
*awarded to the most outstanding work of belles-lettres or collected or selected work*
*of fiction or poetry published in 1994 by an American writer*
## The Green Lake Is Awake:
## Selected Poems, by Joseph Ceravolo
[Coffee House Press]
JUDGES: Kathleen Fraser, Geoffrey O'Brien, Anne Waldman

THE AMERICA AWARDS
P.O. Box 57172
Washington, DC 20036